ITCHIWAN

J.J. Cunis

Publisher's Information

EBookBakery Books

ISBN: 978-1-938517-83-9

Author contact: jjcunis@gmail
& @jjcunis on Facebook and Instagram
Web: www.jjcunis.com

Cover art by Peter Cunis
Artist contact: @PeterCunisArt on Instagram

2nd PRV

DISCLAIMER BY THE AUTHOR
Anyone familiar with the cities, towns and the neighborhoods mentioned in this story, will know that I have taken considerable poetic license in my fictional portrayal. I've changed a great deal relating to the towns, their inhabitants, local establishments, and the like. This is intentional as this is of course a work of pure fiction subject to the demands of the story and my imagination. Further, any similarities between the characters, and events in this narrative and real persons living or dead is entirely coincidental.

PRAISE FOR ITCHIWAN

"I've never been a big fan of gore or horror but these Pukwudgees are somehow lovable in their horrific mayhem! Pomarat could become one of the most evil characters of all time!"
- *Tom Anderson, Author of the musical "The Dismal Life of Conrad Crum"*

———

"This isn't *The Scarlet Letter*. It's a roller coaster!"
Michael Varkas

———

"I felt like I was right in the middle of the story! What a wild and fun ride from start to finish – you won't want to put the book down! I had a blast getting to know every single character…even the Pukwudgees!"
Kaylyn Cunis

———

"Absolutely awesome! … every time I go back to the Cape I am going to keep an eye out!"
Kerry Corbett

———

"I read myself to sleep at night and wake up wanting more!"
Charles L. Cunis, LTC (Ret.) CTARNG

Dedication

For Charlie & Isabelle Cunis

&

Dorothy & Andy Stupka

Their example and lifetime of hard work made this possible.

"For every action, there is an equal and opposite reaction."
Newton's Third Law

"Fuck!"
Word of unknown origin suspected to be emitted in response to the opposite reaction which results from an action.

"The Orb"
"I don't know, Vern. I can't find anything to explain it! I did research it. It's one of those things like Stonehenge, Mayan pyramids ... they're just here. No one knows why or how, they just are. *Brett Simmons, Late August 1972.*

"Shit, so we got nothing. It just is? A fuckin' time machine in the ground?" *Vernon Otis, Late August 1972.*
"Yeah basically." *Brett Simmons, Late August 1972.*

"Pukwudgees"
"I know what you are!" Hysko, smiling, looked at her not knowing what she said but liking the soft tone of her sentence. "You're Pukwudgees!" *Abby Williams, 3 years old, Late August one possible 1992.*

1992 NEW SEABURY

1

BRETT SIMMONS NOTICED IT driving his BMW to the tennis courts, 'Crap!'

He'd better call Vern. Where the hell was Vern anyway? Vern might be dead for all he knew. They hadn't talked for twenty years to the day … four years after Timmy and Vern's brother, Amos disappeared. Those early years after the disappearance, Timmy's brother, Colin continually sent his cronies from Southie to the Cape trying to get a line on Vern. Knowing Colin, the snooping wouldn't end until he found Timmy. Timmy and Amos could be anywhere thanks to that damn hole in the ground. Brett saw that road being cleared into the woods would eventually pass right over it. It was bound to be discovered! Just what they did not want to happen. Shit!

Then he wondered about … the other four. 'Wasn't this the day it happened back then?'

Vernon Otis heard about the proposed development at Witch Pond from a friend at the D.P.W. Since then he'd been spending more nights at Poor Henry's Pub wondering if he should call Brett Simmons after twenty years. He didn't know what to do. Amos always knew what to do. But Amos hadn't been here for a long time. 'Fucking Amos! You were supposed to be back for supper after closing that Pandora's Box we opened!'

To David Bateman the road signified the development of fifty virgin acres and that meant work. He worked for Arsenault Tree Service which had been awarded the contract to clear and grub some three acres to the northeast of the pond – the soon to be Witch Pond Condominiums.

Being the first to arrive at the site on this late August morn, everything was peaceful. No heavy machinery running. Cool morning air filled his lungs. He hoped it would compensate for sucking unfiltered camels and diesel exhaust all day. Fuck it! He was only twenty-six and there was plenty of time to give up the cigs and start his own landscaping concern. Nothing big at first, 'Just pick up a couple of used mowers, snag a few contracts with some blue heads in Osterville and away I go.'

Sipping his coffee, he listened to the birds greeting morning's arrival.

He popped out a Camel and was about to light it when he was distracted by rustling in the bushes about fifty yards to the south. He rose slowly. The sound was too great for a squirrel or other small mammal. One time he had spotted a deer off Red Brook Road not far from here. There were still many in the area and if he was lucky he'd see one. He approached the sound cautiously and peered into the pucker brush. Stopping he cocked his head trying to pick up another rustle. But none was forthcoming. He felt something out there but after a few stationary moments he decided it had sensed him also.

David figured if he cranked the wood chipper up it would cause the deer to bolt. When the it roared to life, he scanned the brush for movement. But there was none. "Fuck it, if you're not going to show yourself."

He finished his coffee and tossed the Styrofoam cup into the gyrating blades. An instant later, it came out minced and unidentifiable. Although it was against company policy to operate the machine alone, David thought what the hell, he'd just process some of the shit lying around until the rest of the guys showed up. After all, he was sort of fascinated by the way things went in whole and in less than a blink of an eye were reduced to flying chips.

He put on his goggles and began tossing in loose branches.

WHIRR … GRIND … CRUNCHH … PHUMP … TAT… TAT… TAT.

Sometimes, when he got into the rhythm he imagined the branch was the uppity prick at the bank, "Sorry, you don't have your account number? How can we be expected to cash your check, sirrr?"

"In the poop chute with you, asshole!"

What a machine! At the end of the day, you're the calmest fella in town. 'I'm gonna miss this when I get my own biz', he thought grabbing another branch. As he rose, he caught the strangest sight out of the corner of his eye.

Standing not more than ten feet away were four small Indians in full Indian garb, they had crude bows and tomahawks and were grinning like all get out.

"What the fuck," whispered David as he slowly rose to an upright position taking in the full scope of this oddity. The Indians were grouped in a diamond formation clad in buckskin cod pieces, moccasins and had painted stripes on their chests and faces. Three had long hair pulled back and braided. The point man had a Mohawk and was bedecked in ornate beads leading David to assume he was the leader.

David sized up the quartet, which didn't take long since the tallest was maybe four feet. Yet, they were well built, leading him to believe they had to be dwarfs and not children. Their maniacal grins made them look unlike any dwarfs he'd ever seen in the movies or at the county fair.

"Ehhhh … boys, the pow-wow ended about two months ago."

"Pow-wow?" mimicked the one in the back, still smiling like a jack-ass.

"Don't you guys speak English?" asked David feeling a bit apprehensive about being alone with these fruit cakes.

"You guuuysss!" hooted the leader while craning his neck towards the brave on the left. They seemed to get a chuckle out of this for some reason.

The leader turned back and looked David in the eyes. David arched his brow. The leader returned the gesture without losing his maniacal grin. Then he deftly raised his bow with arrow nocked, and in a split second shot it into David's scrotum. All in one motion, the leader fell to his knee and the Indians in the rear fired three more arrows at his groin.

There was an intense ripping pain far surpassing the line shot he caught in the snuds in Little League. This immediately gave way to numbness as David's mind slipped into shock. Three more rips, another to the balls, one through his hand reaching for the first arrow and the last in his ass as he spun to the ground. He couldn't believe what was happening! He could hear their howling over the din of the chipper. The throbbing agony in his head was trapped in his throat.

Two of them picked up his legs, sending thunderbolts of pain shooting up his spine and finally, out his throat in a shrill wail. The others hoisted him under the arms jabbering some incomprehensible language.

"Oh God help me!" screamed David as a shaft of an arrow caught on the ground and ripped outward. Between flashes of terror and anguish the thought "What are they doing?" zipped through his brain. When he felt the heels of his boots rise and drop on a metal surface, he knew but his mind would not accept.

As they stuffed him in, the last thing David Bateman saw out of the corner of his eye was pieces of something carried in a red stream up into the sky.

"Oo gog! Hep meh!" chuckled the leader.

2

'BOGGER' RAYBURN DROVE UP Cross Road. His windows were rolled up and his assertiveness training tape was blaring "I WILL NOT be intimidated!". Thus he missed David Bateman's shrill screams as they meshed with the whine of the chipper. Mrs. Finch, however, never missed a thing. Her house overlooked the woods surrounding Witch Pond and she intently noted the time on her kitchen clock when the chipper blasted to life. Seven forty, a full twenty minutes before allowed by the town's by-laws! She pulled open the slider and waddled onto the deck in her terry-cloth robe and slip-in puff slippers. It was like if she went outside and got ten feet closer, she would have all the confirmatory evidence she'd need to get the cops' asses out here. 'They ought to shut those bastards down and hit them with a good stiff fine to boot!'

The police stopped coming after Mrs. Finch called three times in a week. First it was fifteen minutes to eight, then ten to eight two days later and finally three minutes to the hour. The police decided that coming out only encouraged the woman to be totally unreasonable and thereafter told her they would call the contractor and reprimand them severely, which they never did.

It had been weeks since the cops actually came out but Mrs. Finch's calls hadn't stopped. She reached the deck rail and by God she was right! That machine was running! She was about to go straight to the phone when Tabby, her cat, slipped out the slider.

"Oh shit on those bastards! They're causing me to lose my mind!" she blustered as she ambled down the stairs after Tabby. "I always remember to close the damn door behind me. Tabby …"

The eighty year old woman was no match for a cooped up cat with a shot at freedom. She gave up the chase at the edge of the underbrush. She was returning to the deck when she distinctly heard the wild screams that Bogger had missed along with momentary hitches in the monotonous whine of the chipper.

"Someone's been hurt. Serves him right," she mumbled but quickly admonished herself. "My God! What am I saying? I shouldn't be wishing that on anybody." She bustled inside and phoned the police.

"Mashpee Police," a male voice answered in a disinterested tone.

"Yes, this is Mrs. Finch at New Seabury ..."

"Hello, Mrs. Finch. The boys starting early again? I'll give a call to ..."

"No, no! It's not only that. I think someone may have been hurt! I heard a horrible scream and I ..."

"We'll send a cruiser right away. Now don't worry."

3

OFFICER FREDRICKS HUNG UP the phone and turned to Sgt. Sikes.

"That was our wakeup call from Mrs. Finch. She may be taking a new tack. She says she heard a scream and someone may be injured at the site."

The Sergeant looked at his watch, "Christ, it is kind of early for them to be starting."

"She sounded concerned, not irate."

"Send out Dimitri to be safe."

4

AFTER WATCHING DAVID BATEMAN processed like raw meat through a Cuisinart, the four diminutive braves proceeded to kick and hammer the chipper with their tomahawks, trying to shut the damn thing up. They didn't like not being able to hear the forest. They gave up when it was apparent that this thing's armor was immune to their blows. They backed down the cleared road making sure the thing did not follow. They hadn't gotten far when they came across David's black pick-up truck parked on the side. At first, they tensed and bolted for the brush lining the road. The chief, Pomarat, cursed the chipper, believing its loud clamor had prevented them from hearing this large beast of similar composition as the whining beast that simultaneously devoured and shit out the pale giant. They crouched silently and waited, but evidently the beast hadn't noticed them despite its large crystal eyes. Since the eyes had no pupils, Pomarat surmised that it was blind and thus its hearing and sense of smell would be great. However, with the roaring of its brethren just down the road and the fact that they were downwind, it could be assumed that those senses were blind also.

Pomarat signaled two of his men to flank the beast through the woods. They sped off in a crouch tracing a large arc to the left and right. They were no more than fifteen feet from the monster when Hysko, jumped into the road, drew his bow and launched an arrow right between the eyes of the abomination.

Pomarat and Hysko paused waiting for the creature to react. The forward party moved in closer with bows at ready should the wounded beast charge. But the leviathan did not even quiver. The four braves slowly approached the front angling in from their positions … still no movement. The chief lowered his bow keeping the arrow taunt with his left hand and withdrew his tomahawk. He launched the weapon at its head shattering the windshield and causing everyone to jump … still no movement.

The chief signaled Hysko to retrieve his arrow while his compatriots covered him. The beast must have been dead to begin with as one arrow certainly could not have fallen such a large monster without as much as a spasm. Hysko gingerly grasped the shaft and yanked it from the radiator. A stream of green fluid spewed across Hysko's arm. At first, he was startled but then he realized it was just the blood of this creature, strange color that it was, but everything had been strange since they chased those oddly dressed boys into the magical hole in the ground.

He must have hit the heart for the blood to spew with such force.

Pomarat complimented Hysko on his marksmanship and proclaimed they should carve out the heart for Hysko. Hysko sampled a taste of the fluid covering his arm. If this was how the blood tasted he wanted no part of devouring the heart. The chief had Sarkem boost Massot up on the beast. He peered into the cab looking for the chief's tomahawk. There on the seat was the weapon. Massot did not like the feel of the beast's armor. He crawled through the windshield on to the dash and grabbed for what was the steering wheel. With his free smallish arm he made a desperate swipe for the tomahawk but instead hooked a satchel, which he tossed out the open windshield with one motion. Still holding the wheel, he moved his body further over the dash.

As Massot drew his arm up for another swipe, Pomarat screeched an excited warning, "CRIDET! YA MACKI TA WAK" … "Run! Here comes its mate!"

Massot lost his balance as he was in his downswing. He fell into the cab, his body tumbling off the dash. His free hand reached for the wheel and hit the horn scarring the shit out of him and the braves. Sarkem dove for the brush as did Pomarat and Hysko. Massot let go of the horn as if it had come alive and fell to the floor. He was doomed! He had fallen into the belly of the beast that had screamed and now its mate approached!

5

TIMMY AND AMOS WERE amazed, as thirteen year-olds boys would be after their previous experiences with this mysterious hole in the ground … apprehensive when they went in and amazed when they got out. This time the woods were much like those that were present when they had found the hole. This caused the boy's hearts to sink thinking that they had pursued their prey back to exactly where they did not want them to go. However, things were different.

First, there was machinery running somewhere nearby. Second, the area around the hole was not scorched and the hole was not blocked.

The trap door they had crafted was gone. Scanning the area immediately around the hole, Amos as always, was the first to notice.

"Look! There are the two by fours we banged into the ground."

Forming a wide square around the hole were the ends of the four two-by's just visible above the years of accumulated decaying leaves. Amos brushed back the leaves revealing the studs that served as cross braces joining the four corner posts.

"Damn it!" cursed Timmy, "They didn't do what we told them!"

"I think they did," answered Amos running his fingers over the cross brace. "There's nail holes in this board and gouges as if someone pried off the trap door cover. The wood's really weathered too. It's been a while since we built this."

"Maybe only a couple of years," reassured Timmy.

"Naw, the wood's rotting."

"Shit! We should have figured this would have happened."

"It doesn't matter now," sighed Amos. "Somebody removed the trapdoor and the Pukwudgees are out."

Amos spotted an empty bottle of booze by the crumbled remains of what many years ago was a makeshift stone hearth. Sarah's pile of stone had been there when they went in the hole but the bottle had not. "Should we cover up the hole?" asked Timmy.

"No," said Amos, "they are some sort of Indians. They'll know exactly where it is if they decide to come back. Besides, who's to say this isn't as good a time as any to have them wreaking havoc on the world. We don't even know when it is yet."

6

BOGGER RAYBURN DIDN'T KNOW he had seen Pukwudgees darting into the underbrush. He caught a glimpse of them as his eyes returned from the cassette deck to the road ahead. His foot went to brake but didn't as whatever it was, was clear. He briefly pondered what he had seen and glanced in the mirror. A kid? Probably. Weird though. He was half dressed. Or was he? Bogger wasn't sure. His tape kicked in and his mind immediately focused on the message to the exclusion of all other thought. "Be Aware of Your Surroundings, Chapter Four!"

Bogger, the town's Conservation Agent, was making his rounds ensuring work performed over the past day did not infringe on the neighboring wetlands. Bogger was a rotund fellow, short on stature with stringy brown hair. He was easily intimidated by burly construction types thus he invested in a set of self-assertiveness tapes. He didn't dare buy them through his office, not wanting anyone to think that he may in any way doubt his own abilities. Most people who knew him doubted his abilities but never gave a second thought as to whether he did.

Nevertheless, his job was to protect the wetlands without regard to common sense or point of view. This he did with vigor and vindictiveness invoking the supreme power of the 'Inquisition' like Conservation Commission. Although the Commissioners signed the letters pointing out violations and action to be taken, such letters usually arrived shortly after Bogger had been seen at or around the site in question. He would have avoided talking to anyone if possible, preferring to scribble in his notebook and snap pictures with his Polaroid.

Bogger pulled up to the running chipper just as Timmy and Amos had entered the clearing on the far side of the machine. Bogger set the emergency brake, put the vehicle in park and turned off the engine without noticing the boys. The boys however noticed him and stopped in their tracks. Timmy was an expert on the vehicles of his day. This wasn't one of them.

The S-15 Jimmy, though not futuristic by any means, was smaller and possessed a grill different than any similar vehicles Timmy knew of. What did that mean? Would there be people still around that they knew? Is that good or bad with the Pukwudgees about? Shit! Too many thoughts too fast! More importantly, what about this guy in the truck? What's he like? And what's that machine for?

Amos had many of the same thoughts as well as a few of his own. He grabbed Timmy by the arm, ready to bolt if the man in the midget truck turned out to be hostile. Bogger hopped out and pushed his glasses up the bridge of his nose with his index finger. He noticed the two boys. He did not notice anyone else such as the contractor or his crew. "Be aware of your surroundings!" came into his head. Wasn't a truck parked down the road? Why was the chipper running unattended? Surely a violation. Which department? Building? Board of Health? Selectmen? Didn't he think he saw other kids up the road darting into the bushes? Maybe the guy who came in the truck was chasing them? Bogger hitched up his drooping draws and frowned his brow.

He summoned up all fifty-three minutes of his assertiveness training and in a quavering voice demanded, "Have you kids been monkeying around with this machine? You come over here right now!"

Mr. Fulbright, Amos's dippy English teacher, immediately sprang to mind! He spent all his free time roaming the halls, boy's rooms and locker rooms searching for boys skipping class or better yet, smoking cigarettes and reading dirty magazines. When he found one, he'd drag him by the ear to the principal's office, making a big deal of extracting and crushing any additional cigarettes the boy may have. Dirty magazines quickly disappeared into his rear pants pocket under his coat and were never mentioned.

Instinctively, Amos decided to bolt. This was not the person to discuss their dilemma. Timmy reacted to the tug on his arm and was right behind him. As they broke through the brush at the edge of the clearing, they felt a light breeze on their back from the chute of the chipper. They did not, however, notice the blood and bits of flesh and clothing clinging to the bushes. They kept running.

Bogger was relieved when the boys ran, thus managing to forestall direct confrontation even though his tapes advised to relish such confrontation as a means to exercise his newly acquired skills. He made a half-hearted attempt at pursuit, but stopped at the edge of the brush not wishing to needlessly risk picking up any ticks.

"I better not catch you around here again!" yelled Bogger as he hitched up his pants with more bravado now. He looked around to see if anyone had witnessed his act of ballsiness. But no one had. By chance he glanced down at the bush in front of him … force of habit … checking for wetland species. The ground around the bush was wet all right, but not with water. It appeared to be blood! He bent down to stick his finger in it and noticed the blood on the leaves as well as what appeared to be small chunks of raw meat, some with cloth stuck to it. Scattered about were white chips, resembling crushed shells. He also felt the breeze from the chipper chute on the back of his neck.

"Christ, those kids have been sticking animals in the chipper!" It didn't register that it was cloth not fur stuck to the flesh. Bogger rose and approached the machine, now noticing a stream of red spots on the ground, tapering off as the line got closer to the machine. He fumbled with the controls and managed to turn the damn thing off. He looked into the chute and saw similar material on the inside as that on the brush. Again, Bogger probed with his finger seeking confirmation of his visual analysis. He heard a car approaching. Dimitri arrived.

7

DIMITRI PULLED UP BEHIND the Jimmy and hopped out. "What's happenin', Phil?" Where is everyone?"

Bogger was Bogger when discussed in the third person among others and out of earshot. Bogger was Phil when spoken to or within earshot by people of compassion. If Amos had heard this individual referred to as "Bogger", he may have recognized him as a former classmate in 1968 who was noted for picking his nose and brown-nosing Mr. Fulbright, who in return, taught Bogger the finer points of being a man.

"I don't know, Steve," replied Bogger slowly shaking his head. "When I drove up I notice weirdly dressed kids back there on the road. They ran into the bushes. When I got here the chipper was running and two more kids showed up. I tried to grab them and find out what the hell they were up to, but they took off. I think they may have been putting animals in the chipper or something. There's blood all over the bushes and inside the chute."

"Where's the guy who owns the truck down the road?" asked Dimitri walking to the area Bogger had indicated he'd seen the blood.

Bogger didn't like being on the answering side of questions. That's why he had become conservation agent. He knew he didn't have a snowball's chance in hell of being accepted as a cop. Answering questions made him nervous, even if there was nothing to be nervous about. When he was young, the other kids would corner him with loaded questions like 'Did your mother ever catch you beating off in the closet?' He of course would instantly respond 'No!' And they'd snap back 'Good place, wasn't it? Ha, Ha, Ha!' Instinctively, he had a nagging feeling Dimitri was asking him a loaded question. Nervousness was evident in the timbre of his response.

"I wondered the same thing. I figured he might be off chasing those boys. Maybe he drove up, heard the boys screwing around with the chipper and scattered them."

Dimitri was squatting over the bushes not touching a thing but visually analyzing the matter clinging to it. He wasn't a homicide detective, but he easily recognized the bone chips and muscle tissue mingled in the blood splatters. He also noticed another thing that made him realize it was no animal … pieces of blood soaked cloth, denim and leather. "Bogge … a Phil" … he caught himself too late, "who turned off the machine?"

Bogger didn't miss the slip and stiffened, replying abruptly, "I did. Why?" There! He slipped in a question of his own.

"Because that means your prints are on the machine."

"So what?"

Dimitri rose and faced Bogger. All of a sudden, he didn't think it was wise to have his back to him. A grotesque murder had taken place and he hadn't seen any evidence of kids. He now noticed blood on Bogger's fingers, sleeve and jeans where he'd apparently wiped off his palms. He really didn't feel Bogger was capable of such an act, but who knew? Bogger was indeed one weird fucker and the contractor's people were always riding him. Dimitri decided since he was alone he was not going to take any chances. "Phil, please step over to the cruiser and put your hands on the hood."

"WHAT?!"

"DO IT! NOW!" snapped Dimitri with hitherto unevidenced fury. Bogger jumped, startled by the force of the command and reluctantly did it. "Alright, spread your legs and put your right hand behind your head."

Dimitri cuffed and searched him while reading him his rights. Bogger was dumbfounded. "Steve, what the hell are you doing this for? I told you some kids were monkeying with the machine!"

"I don't see any kids! That ain't an animal spread all over the bushes and someone's apparently missing." Dimitri called for backup after ushering Bogger into the back of the cruiser. Bogger was too shocked to respond. He still could not comprehend what Dimitri was talking about even though Dimitri had reported " ... an apparent homicide, suspect in custody ..." His assertiveness training was out to lunch. Dimitri would wait for back-up to ensure the site was not disturbed.

8

MASSOT HEARD THE BEAST pass. He could now hear his heart beating loudly in ears. After a short time, Hysko was on the hood of the truck peering in at him over the dash.

"Mack wa, suckten fa ya." (Let's get out of here.)

Massot was astonished. The beast had screamed but he was still intact. He decided not to waste any more of his luck. Luck was a finite commodity one was born with. Some more ... some very little ... just enough to get them born in some cases. He scrambled up on the seat, grabbed the chief's tomahawk and decided to forget the heart. Nothing in here resembled a heart anyway. He scampered up the steering wheel and went out the way he'd come in.

Pomarat listened in the direction the second beast had traveled. He could no longer hear the monster. Its sound had died abruptly. Now, he could only hear the chipper. Strange world, all these creatures make such loud noise. How can they hear their prey or their predators? He guessed with such armor, they did not fear predators. Yet, Hysko's arrow had killed this beast. Maybe, they only eat trees like the creature back up the road. Although, even it did not refuse the human we offered it. What a sorry human he was. He had no weapons to speak of, not much of a challenge. Those boys they had chased were greater warriors than that one. Where were those boys?

He was sure that he and his braves would flank them when they chose an alternate tunnel and came out of another hole. Those boys were probably miles away by now. Maybe they weren't. Maybe, they were watching them now preparing an attack! What happened to this place? It is not the same. Yet, it is the same ... but different. Pomarat had been in this area many times but he didn't know of the hole they had chased the boys into. And how did all these creatures come into the world so suddenly? The boys must definitely posses strong magic, maybe even stronger than his own. Why then had they block them from coming out of the hole with fire? If their magic was strong, they could have slaughtered us as we came out. Maybe, they were like us and wished to have some fun prior to making the kill. Or, maybe they needed time to create this magic. He scanned the surroundings summonsing his braves.

The chipper fell silent. The Pukwudgees froze. Pomarat signaled and pushed them off the road just in the nick of time! Another beast was coming up the road. This one was lower to the ground and bore strange colored antlers. The diminutive Indians watched crouched in the underbrush. This time they noticed a human inside the monster as it passed! Shortly thereafter, its noise abruptly ceased and they heard a thud followed by voices speaking a dialect similar to the boys.

Pomarat was torn between heading toward the voices or continuing to where he thought he had last seen the boys. He based this on the direction they traveled within the tunnel, though he was unsure things were as they seemed in the bewitched orb in the ground. His three braves stared at him now, anxiously awaiting orders. The boys had defeated him in a battle by prohibiting their initial exit from the hole with fire. He was determined not to lose the war!

However, the voices back down the road were getting angrier. There might be some mischief to be had if they returned to the site. No! The boys must pay first! After all, HIS magic was the greatest in the Algonquin nation! He had pledged his soul to Maktahdou, the devil himself, and no boys could be allowed to best him! He ordered his braves to follow him deeper into the woods. They would find those boys and they would devour their hearts!

9

"WHERE DO WE GO now?" asked Timmy as they sat catching their breath under a tall oak about a quarter mile from where they encountered Bogger.

"Great Oak Road must still be up that hill. I can hear cars." replied

Amos. "Hey, did you cut your leg? You got blood on your pants and sneakers."

"What? Damn!" Timmy rolled up his pants but no cuts were visible to his thorough inspection. "Hey, you got blood on you too!"

Amos repeated the inspection on his legs. "Well, it ain't from us. We must have run through something when we took off from that guy."

"I'll bet the Pukwudgees had something to do with it … the blood I mean." Timmy rubbed his finger across the stain and put it to his nose to smell. "How we gonna find them and what do we do when we do?"

Timmy looked at Amos awaiting a response. After all, Amos lived in Mashpee year round. Amos was also a Wampanoag Indian and recognized the Pukwudgees for what they were … mischievous, evil-doing, mythical people of Wampanoag legends. Timmy, a red-headed Irish kid from South Boston who summered with his family in Popponesset, mistook them for a comical group of midgets separated from the circus. If it wasn't for Amos's instant recognition of the mythical creatures and his cat-like reactions, Timmy would have been lying dead in some mythical era with an arrow between his eyes. That seemed like so long ago, yet it had only been yesterday in real time. Such was the magic of the orb down in the hole.

Amos absently lifted his football jersey and extracted the .22 caliber revolver wedged in his jeans. He had lifted it from his father's closet after they had prevented the Pukwudgees from exiting the hole in their time by setting a bonfire over it. Since the Pukwudgees were in the hole, Amos knew they'd have to be hunted down or risk them popping up at some future or past date and doing God knows what. Rather than worrying when that would be and what effect that could have on the world they knew or were to know, he decided to pursue them and avoid the ulcers. Timmy joined him simply because he couldn't resist an adventure.

"Well?" repeated Timmy after a respectable period of silence.

"I'm thinkin'! I'm thinkin! … Hold on!" snapped Amos. He had been thinking, wondering what his father would do. Now he realized he didn't know what his father would do. It was his mother who had told him of the Indian legends … the Pukwudgees, Maushop, Squant, and the Screecham sisters. His thoughts returned briefly to their encounter with Sarah Screecham and what he had told her and how he himself had ignored his own words. The only method mentioned of Pukwudgee extermination was when Maushop, the benevolent giant, squashed a few stragglers with his fists after a band of them had killed his sons. This was of no use to them since he and Timmy weren't much bigger than the Pukwudgees and were outnumbered four to two. "Look, we can do one of two things. We can try and track the midgets. But I don't consider myself a great tracker. I know I figured out how to follow them to this time period through that rotating orb in the hole. That was easy, they scratched up the hole they went into, but this isn't the orb and we're some distance from the spot where we ran into that guy who reminded me of Mr. Fulbright. In order to have any chance at picking up their trail, we'd have to go back where that machine was and I don't want to run into that guy. Besides, I don't know how much of a head start the Pukwudgees got on us. We were about a half-a-day behind them by the time we got the trap door built and followed them into the hole, though I'm not sure that matters down in that place. We may have been right behind them."

"Ya, it's still morning judging from the sun," injected Timmy "and if they slaughtered something on the path we just cut through that would mean it couldn't be more than a few hours ago."

"Even so, I still don't want to go back there. The other thing I figured we could do is find out what time period this is and go from there. Maybe we're not that far in the future. Maybe there's still someone around we know who can help us."

"Oh yeah! If this is more than a week in the future, which is a good possibility judging by that midget truck that guy was driving, anybody we knew probably thinks we're dead! And if they see us now at the same age and in the same clothes as when we disappeared, they'll think they're seeing ghosts."

"There's always Vernon and Brett," countered Amos solemnly.

"Fuckin' Vernon and Brett?" exclaimed Timmy now semi-delirious. "Some fucking good they were. The goddamn trap door is gone! They were supposed to make sure that damn thing was kept shut! They probably blabbed everything that happened to the cops and were put in the loony bin as suspects causing our disappearance."

"If they did that the cops would have went down in the hole looking for us. Then there'd be people from our time popping up all over time.

And there'd be more than that one fat shit standing around guarding the hole."

"Yeah, well what happened then?"

"I don't know! I can't think straight when it comes to thinking about that hole!"

The two boys stared at each other in frustration. Timmy broke the silence.

"Maybe you're right. Let's go see if we can find a car. Maybe they still stamp the date on the tail lights or have expiration stickers on the license plates."

10

MRS. FINCH STOOD ON her deck high above her neatly landscaped back yard. It sloped gently to the underbrush, which was the beginning of the vast woods surrounding Witch Pond. The deck offered a distant panoramic view of the small pond and the canopy of oak and pine around it that stretched for miles unbroken, hiding any activity which might be occurring under their boughs. Due to the distance and the trees, there was no way she could see anything that was happening where the chipper was running. She stared nevertheless, intently hoping to piece together what had happened from the sounds. Despite her age her hearing was still acute. Sometimes she could hear the pinging of balls and the cacophony of voices emanating from the tennis complex about a mile away by the edge of the woods.

She picked up a car arriving, and another car arriving after the chipper shut off. Then she heard some muted conversation which got louder at the end followed by a car door shutting and yet another car arriving. "Good. I'm glad I got some action this time," she thought.

One of the cars then left. Nothing more was heard. After about ten minutes, Mrs. Finch decided to go down to the backyard to find her cat. She pondered the sounds she had heard. Conspicuously absent was that of an ambulance. That meant no one had been seriously hurt, thank goodness. The shouting probably meant that the police had finally done their job and given the contractor a proper reprimand. She focused her mind on Tabby now. "Tabby! Tabby! You naughty cat, come back here!"

She scanned the woods for Tabby, but saw no signs nor heard indications of her pending return. "Now that you got a taste of freedom, you probably won't be back till suppertime."

While she was down in the yard, she decided to tend to some light landscaping chores, pulling up weeds and picking up twigs and small branches that had fallen on the lawn. She was at this for some time forgetting she was still in her housecoat and slippers. Suddenly, she heard a rustling back in the woods. She waddled back to the edge of the underbrush and called Tabby again.

There was no further movement or sound. "Tabby? Tabby you come out here now or there will be no treats for you today."

Out of the corner of her eye, too late for reaction, she picked out a gray furry object the size of a football hurling at her head. She heard the "Whoosh" just prior to the thing enveloping her face. Falling back on what luckily was a lush lawn, she clutched horrified at the thing that had smothered any screams or yips of surprise that had been making their way up her esophagus. Fur was what she last saw but that was not what she felt on her face. It was moist and meaty and had the odor of fresh raw hamburger though none of this really registered in her mind. Instead only the instinct to quickly remove it was at the forefront of her thinking.

Her otherwise arthritic fingers easily pried the flying fur thing from her face and held it at arm's length while lying on her back on the cold ground. Her eyes were momentarily obscured by a fluidly substance that covered them. She blinked several times to clear them, daring not to take a chance rubbing her face on the shoulder of her robe expecting another attack from the thing she held at bay. Once her eyelids had accomplished the task of restoring her vision, her heart sank into the cold earth as she recognized the fur ball blankly staring back at her with one eye closed and the other agape … "TABBY!!!"

She noticed the lightness of her pet and that his underside was not the soft gray fur with a white stripe, but instead it was a dark red fleshy mess which was dripping meaty fluid on her housecoat.

Tabby had been hastily skinned and gutted and somehow propelled on her face. The shock and terror squelched her attempt to scream. She dropped the carcass and propped herself on her elbows to survey the area from which the cat had come. Standing at the edge of brush were four dwarfish … what … Indians howling and laughing at the spectacle they had set in motion.

Mrs. Finch wiped the sleeve of her white patterned housecoat across her eyes not believing what she was seeing and noticed the sleeve came away red. Survival instinct kicked in and she rolled over and scrambled to her feet running or as close to as could be considered running. Hysko tossed his tomahawk, but due to his uncontrollable laughter it missed its mark and bounced harmlessly off the latticework enclosing the underside of the deck. Massot was the first to compose himself and give chase to the terrified woman.

In what was a Herculean effort for a woman her age who had just taken a nasty spill, Mrs. Finch sped up the stairs and managed to knock off a plastic flower box sitting of the deck rail with a swipe of her arm. The box tumbled down the stairs undercutting Massot's legs out from under him and sending him tumbling back down. His rolling body then took out Sarkem who was following. Pomarat cursed the misfits from down on the lawn and urged Hysko in pursuit.

Hysko leapt over his fallen comrades, one in pain the other still laughing hysterically, and ran up onto the deck. By this time, Mrs. Finch had gotten inside the house slamming shut and locking the slider. In times of panic and fear, instinct takes over. Most times it's right, sometimes it's wrong. Mrs. Finch should have continued running through the house and out the front door. She had no way to realize she was being pursued by imbeciles in the environment of the twentieth century (or any century after the seventeenth for that matter) and a four bedroom contemporary cape with modern appliances would have been a virtual maze to them. Instead she grabbed what instinct told her was her lifeline to the world.

Hysko could see her fumbling with a device she held to her ear. Without hesitation, having no experience with double pane super-insulated glass, Hysko sprang at the woman and was instantly knocked on his ass. The thud fouled up Mrs. Finch's dialing. She flicked the hook set until she received another dial tone. In her sheer terror, her fingers felt the size of hams and had difficulty punching up the numbers she had so easily dialed so many times before.

Pomarat had followed behind and witnessed his encounter with the invisible wall. He quickly stepped over Hysko and forcibly swung his tomahawk at the barrier. This was followed by a crash and a tinkling sound similar to when he flung his weapon into the monster they had encountered earlier. Sharp edges of the barrier were now visible and Pomarat savagely demolished them with several more swipes of his stone tomahawk. Mrs. Finch had swung around to face him with her mouth open just as the line began ringing. Pomarat brazenly strode up to her and lightly tapped her on the forehead with his blunt instrument that he now believed to be truly magical.

Mrs. Finch collapsed on the floor from the blow. The receiver fell from her hand as a tiny voice emanated from it saying "Mashpee Police". The chief startled by the sound, smashed the receiver and the small box to which it was attached with his now sacred tomahawk.

11

HYSKO STOOD JUST OUTSIDE the demolished slider, his hands stretched out apprehensively to ensure the barrier was truly gone. Massot was rubbing his elbow and Sarkem was still giggling. Pomarat, fed up with the performance of his braves in handling the old woman, reached out and viciously yanked Hysko in by his quiver strap. He berated his men for their shameful display. How did they expect to best the young warriors if they couldn't efficiently dispatch one old woman?

Hysko was especially hurt with his ego riding high after slaying the armored beast up the road. The chief ordered the men to search the strange hovel. He wanted time alone to think things out. Sarkem grabbed Massot by the arm. Mindful of efficiency, he went first to the old woman and put his ear to her chest to determine if she was alive. She was. This was good. The blood would not spoil the meat. He ordered Massot to prepare her.

Pomarat went out on the deck to survey the area. He liked the high vantage point it provided. There were so many things to ponder.

Thoughts had been running through his head at light speed. When this happened, Pomarat was unable to piece together a rational plan. Where were the young boys? How could the landscape change so? There had been no hovels of any kind, never mind the monstrosity he now occupied on the ridge. From the low vantage point at the edge of the forest he didn't see that there were similar such hovels on either side of the cul-de-sac that culminated at the Finch residence. They had been unable to pick up the tracks of four young boys … many others but not theirs. Strange tracks they were and none of them fresh except around the armored creatures. Had the boys' magic caused the change in the landscape and thus erased any trace of them as well? Pomarat and his braves had completed a wide 90 degree arc around the hole. This quadrant should have intersected the path that led from the marsh by the bay … the path down which they had chased the boys only yesterday. Yet the path and the tracks no longer seemed to exist. Nothing was right!

No magic was powerful enough to change the face of the earth! The boys would have to be in league with a spirit greater than he and there was no spirit greater than the devil himself, Maktahdou! Yet, had not Maushop, the giant wiped out two of his braves? Yes, but that was with brute strength not magic. Besides, those braves had not followed his instructions! They were supposed to burn Maushop's hut and catch up with the rest of the band. He had seen no flames but heard their screams from a mile away.

A vision had come to Pomarat the other night. Maktahdou had shown him that the two braves were pillaging the hut for souvenirs instead of burning it. Maushop returned to discover not only the two intruders but also the bodies of his five slain sons. Enraged he snatched the two little Indians with his enormous fists and squashed them like grapes.

This is what comes of not following instructions! Now their group was four. It was unlucky for Itchiwan to hunt in a band of less or more than six, the sacred number of Maktahdou. He should have never given chase to the four boys in the funny outfits. He should have continued north to the great marsh where the Itchiwan were encamped. He should have recognized the signs when his arrows missed its mark on the boy with the hair the color of fire.

Pomarat's thoughts were jumping all over the place again. He was also momentarily distracted by a clamor inside the hovel. Returning to his thoughts he was determined to settle down and figure this out. The best way to do this was to begin at the beginning of the events leading up to this situation.

Maktahdou had come to Pomarat in his dreams. He commanded him to assemble five of his best braves. They were to follow the river from the Great Pond to the south where it met the mighty waters. There they would find the hut of Maushop. Maushop was a thorn in the side of Maktahdou. Not only was he loved and revered by the Wampanoag nation, but he massacred Maktahdou's beloved pet, Talcamut. Talcamut was a giant crow the size of a pterodactyl. Talcamut lived on the island now known as Martha's Vineyard near the cliffs of Gay Head. It would fly over from the island and snatch small children and carry them back to the island where it would devour them.

The Wampanoag people went to Maushop, the giant and asked for his help. Maushop lived in isolation with his family because of his size. He loved children and agreed to do what he could to help. He waded across the sound and soon found the evil bird's roost as evidenced by a pile of small bones at the foot of the cliff. The site tore at the giant's heart and he vowed not to return until this monster had been destroyed.

Talcamut came at sunset. Maushop set upon the scavenger and a vicious battle ensued lasting till dawn. Maushop held a death grip on the crow's foot. The bird flapped, pecked and clawed with its free talon. Maushop deflected most attacks with his free hand. Some found their mark on his arms, shoulders and head. Maushop possessed great strength that was made even greater by his determination to avenge the deaths of all those small souls. As he knew they eventually would, the bird's wings tired and Maushop was able to yank the bird into his full grasp. With a leg now in each hand, he wrenched them from their sockets and snapped them. Talcamut screeched in agony but Maushop was not finished. He grabbed its neck, which he could easily break and end it. But he didn't. Instead he slowly gouged its eyes one at a time. Then grabbing it again by its broken dislocated legs, he smacked the crow against the cliff hard enough to hurt but not kill, yet. The demon's pet's suffering could be heard on the mainland. Maushop snapped its wings and gently left it in a heap at the base of the cliffs to die a slow miserable death while the gulls and crabs fed on its carcass.

Maushop again surveyed the bones of all the missing children and began to weep. When his weeping subsided he pulled out his pipe, sat on the cliff and smoked, mourning the loss of so many young lives. Then he rested there for several days.

Pomarat's mission was to pay Maushop back at the behest of Maktahdou. He and his band set out to slay Maushop's five sons. It took the band two days to reach the marsh by the bay where Maushop lived. Although the great marsh where the Itchiwan lived was some distance to the north where the great waters again met the land, the trip was lengthen by their insatiable urge to commit mischief along the way. When they did reach Maushop's home, it was near dawn. Maushop's sons were asleep and his wife was miles away camped on the beach awaiting his return from the Vineyard.

Maktahdou had shown Pomarat how to concoct magic dust which when blown into the eyes of a victim would blind, paralyze and kill them. They would need this advantage. Although Maushop's sons ranged from ages eight to fifteen, the eldest was twice the size of a normal human thus, four times the size of a Pukwudgee. Sneaking into the hut, the five members of Pomarat's band each selected a son. Pomarat covered their approach from inside. On cue from their chief, they each shook a shoulder and blew the dust in the boy's eyes when they opened. The boys screamed and clutched their eyes. The braves wasted no time in planting tomahawks in their skull … several times.

Pomarat inspected their work insuring the sons were indeed dead. Maktahdou was not one for shoddy work. Not wishing to risk running into Maushop himself, Pomarat ordered all but two to leave. They were to burn the hut and follow. Maushop was not one to screw around with. Anyone who could slay a beloved pet of Maktahdou deserved a wide berth. The fire would destroy the evidence, and the two braves were to make sure they covered the band's tracks.

As a result of their failure, their number was now four and Maushop now had a new purpose in life … hunting down Pomarat! If that wasn't enough, they had come across those boys on their return to their encampment. They had lured them into a tunnel and changed the face of the earth by the time they got out! Were these boys servants of Maushop's god sent to do his will as they had done Maktahdou's? Was this god greater than Maktahdou? He hoped Maktahdou had not heard that last thought.

Pomarat wished he had more sacred weed so he could communicate with Maktahdou for guidance. He'd have to return to the great marsh for more of that. Until then he'd have to wait for sleep and hope that Maktahdou would see fit to come. But he knew there would be no sleep for awhile. He could not risk it among all this strangeness. Would Maushop be part of this hallucination?

For now they would continue their arc around the hole. If they found no trace of the boys, they would set out for the great marsh. If they did find the trail, they would track down the boys, slay and eat them. This would remove all traces of their magic from the world.

He now had a plan! He now felt more at ease. However, he was again distracted, if not somewhat startled, by an explosion from inside the bowels of the hovel.

12

MASSOT SAT BESIDE THE body of the old woman. He searched his satchel for his cutting stone. Finding it, he glanced out at Pomarat who was sitting cross-legged on the deck with his back to him. Hysko and Sarkem had ventured into the kitchen. Awe overcame the embarrassment of being bested by an old woman. They found themselves in a wonderland of … THINGS! Never mind things … the material the things were made of were a marvel! They glistened and shone unlike the natural tones of rock, wood and fiber that made up their world.

Sarkem's attention was immediately drawn to the objects hanging on the wall in a neat row. They were pointed like his arrow but they glistened like the water when the sun sat at that particular angle. He hopped up on the square white box like object with the window in the front and sat on what unbeknownst to him was an electric burner. Hysko seeing what attracted Sarkem's attention hopped up on the counter. Sarkem grabbed one of the utensils by the handle. Hysko grabbed another by the blade. Sarkem admired his. Hysko instantly withdrew his hand from his with a yelp. A light bead of blood trickled from his finger. Noticing this, Sarkem lightly ran his thumb down the blade of his, appreciating the honed sharpness. What a wonderful implement! He tossed it in the direction of Massot in the dining room.

"I think you'll find this easier than that cutting stone, Massot. Be careful. One side is very sharp."

Massot had already opened Mrs. Finch's robe but was stymied by the garments he now encountered. He picked up the carving knife and eyed it admiringly. Rising to one knee, he deftly placed one hand over the old woman's mouth so Pomarat would not be disturbed. With his new tool in the other, he made an incision from the nape of the neck to the front of the throat in the process severing the jugular. As expected, Mrs. Finch's eyes shot open, her head jerked and blood shot across the room. Massot immediately rammed the knife up under the rib cage not wishing to take a chance of the woman turning and spewing blood in his face. There was one more convulsion and the lights went out forever for Mrs. Finch.

Massot was ecstatic over the efficiency of his new tool. He was amazed at the depth of the incision and the ease with which it was made. Normally he'd be hacking away with his cutting stone, which he would temporarily drop in order to grab his tomahawk to cease any convulsions. He also saw he could cut right through the garments rather than trying to rip them apart or find out how they came undone.

The fountain of blood had subsided to a slow drain. Massot got up, knocked over a dining room chair and lifted Mrs. Finch's legs over it in order to allow more blood to find its way out. While waiting for the blood to drain, he went to search for something to carry the meat and selected organs he would remove.

Sarkem was still on the stove examining all the knives. Hysko, having learned the proper way to grip these items the hard way, was immediately drawn to the large butcher knife. Sarkem pushed his hand aside explaining that one would be Pomarat's. Hysko then opted for the long slender slicing knife and a small paring knife. Sliding back down to the floor, Hysko slipped his knives into the thong of his cod piece. Sarkem placed the remaining three knives on the counter and surveyed the area for other items of value. He briefly fumbled with the knobs on the stove then reached over and shook the toaster oven.

Massot was busy pounding the cabinets at ground level. Hysko went on to check the rest of the hovel. To Massot's surprise, his pounding resulted in one of the cabinet doors opening. Massot swung open the door and exclaimed to Sarkem that he had found a passage. Sarkem was about to hop down when both he and Massot froze in their tracks. The cooling unit in the refrigerator had just cycled on. Sarkem grabbed the butcher knife and Massot his tomahawk and stood at ready to confront yet another strange armored beast. Sarkem looked to Massot. At the same time he picked up the smell of the hides burning and immediately following he felt his seat getting warm. Sarkem leaned over to look at his butt and in so doing placed his hand down on another burner. Immediately the heat registered causing him to snatch up his hand drop the butcher knife, and then jerk his head back banging it on the fan hood, scorching his butt further and falling off the stove onto the kitchen floor. Massot moved to put himself between the humming refrigerator and his fallen comrade. Pomarat glanced around from out on the deck, shook his head and returned to his thoughts.

Hysko returned, heard the refrigerator, belted it with his tomahawk and it cycled off. His pride now returning as he again defeated yet another armored beast of this world, he broke into laughter pointing to the blacken circles on Sarkem's rear. Sarkem got up slowly and gingerly rubbed his burnt hand. Massot gathered up the knives on the counter. Embarrassed by his mishap, Sarkem took the knives and told Massot to finish the woman.

Hysko announced he had found a pool of blue water in the hovel and wanted Sarkem to see. Massot went back to his passage in the cabinets and opened the door further. White and red satchels fell to the floor. Also inside the door were steel pots and pans. He placed one of the smaller pots on his head and decided it was too cumbersome and heavy to serve as a hat or a weapon. He rummaged through the satchels emblazoned with strange letters. He decided that these slick surfaced bags would be ideal for carting around the old woman's selected parts. He went back to the corpse and carried out his duties.

Hysko and Sarkem made their way down a short hall to a glistening small room. Inside, Hysko showed Sarkem the small pool with the blue water. Sarkem cupped his hand and tasted it. Grimacing, he promptly spat it out. Hysko's attention was drawn to the silver handle above the bowl. He twisted it this way and that. Suddenly the bowl roared to life.

Hysko jumped back falling into the tub, bringing down the shower curtain. Sarkem's face was close to the bowl. His eyes widened as the water was sucked away only to slowly return from under the rim.

He told Hysko it had to be an indoor stream of tainted water. Hysko scrambled out of the tub and smashed the damn thing with his tomahawk. The porcelain shattered and water ran all over the room. This revealed the source of the stream … a vertical tube. At its mouth the water was clear. Sarkem tasted it and found it to be ok. He placed his water sac alongside the tube allowing the water to trickle in. He advised Hysko to do the same. But Hysko waved his hand in disgust and went off to explore the rest of the house.

He wandered into what was the living room and froze when he was confronted by a two dimensional image of a human being on the far wall, a man … the late Mr. Finch. Unlike the other artwork he had seen in the hovel, this was life-like. He moved to the left … the eyes seemed to follow though the man did not move. It was obviously an image like a reflection in water, but Hysko did not like it. He pulled his bow over his head and shot the image between the eyes for good measure. The eyes still stared. He looked around the room and noticed other such images, though much smaller, adorning the walls and perched on furniture. There was some of the man on the wall with what appeared to be a younger version of the old woman in the other room. There were others of younger humans all with big grins on their faces. Hysko was spooked! He did not like this one bit. He began swinging his tomahawk wildly around the room smashing the images. He tripped over the hassock and his hand hit a button a large box like object. He fell to the floor and immediately was back on his feet looking for more images to shatter. The man with the arrow in his head was now to his right but his eyes were still upon him.

Sarkem and Massot came to the archway through which Hysko had entered the room. Hysko looked at them but they were transfixed by something behind him. Their mouths were agape and their fingers were pointing. Hysko slowly turned just as the volume kicked in on the big 35" screen. There in full color smiling at him was the head of a mammoth two-dimensional bobbing and grinning black man screeching "JELLOOO PUUUDDINGGG!"

Hysko collapsed and wet his cod piece. Sarkem hurled his tomahawk at the black devil. His aim was good. The screen exploded showering the room in glass.

13

POMARAT WAS NOT THE only one to notice the explosion. Mike Treflin was jogging in front of the Finch house when he heard it. Knowing Mrs. Finch was an elderly widow, he decided to check it out.

Pomarat came into the living room. Sarkem and Hysko were jabbering away trying to recount what had happened with their limited vocabulary. Pomarat vehemently commanded them to shut up as he picked up the sound of footsteps outside. Once again everyone froze.

Pounding on the hovel was accompanied by a muted, "Mrs. Finch, are you ok?" The braves readied various weapons in the direction of the pounding, only to be startled by a chime sound inside the hovel that apparently came from behind them in the hall. They whipped around but found nothing to attack. Again the chime sounded ... over and over followed by pounding. The braves didn't know which way to turn. Finally, they heard footsteps leaving the hovel.

Out of the corner of his eye, Pomarat caught a dark human shadow through the shear muslin curtains drawn over the picture window. The shadow came closer and raised its hands to its brow. Pomarat approached the shape raising his sacred tomahawk. He let loose a vicious blow throwing all his weight behind it. The tomahawk blasted through the glass, the multiple panes minutely diminishing some of its velocity but making up for it with chards of splintered glass which found Mike Treflin's face and hands. The actual blow from the tomahawk turned out to be a glancing one like a bat coming down off center on a basketball.

Treflin staggered backward falling through a rhododendron. He screamed in agony, confused as to whether to run or remove the pieces of glass perilously close to his eyes. Pomarat hacked at the remaining glass, clearing a passage to give chase. He hopped on the sill and was halfway out when he discovered there was a series of hovels similar to the one they occupied lining the way, which culminated here. He stopped! They were right in the midst of a village with many armored beasts!

"HEY! WHAT THE FUCK IS GOING ON OVER THERE?!"

Treflin scrambled in the direction of the voice. Pomarat saw it came from a hovel to the right of theirs. Treflin stumbled and tried to regain his balance only to drive the glass in his hands deeper. He let out a howl and yelled, "Help! Help! There are burglars in the Finch house!"

Norm Johnson, Deputy County Sheriff, Retired, was coming out of his garage with his three golfing buddies ready to drive down and tee it up on the ocean links course when he heard the window break and saw Mr. Treflin stumbling around.

"HEY YOU LITTLE SHIT! YOUR ASS IS GRASS WHEN I GET A HOLD OF YOU!" he bellowed at the emerging Pomarat. Pomarat realized this blubbery old man was directing his anger straight at him.

Norm's playing partners ran to their golf bags which lay next to the trunk of the Ford Crown Victoria parked in the drive. Two yanked out their Ping putters, the other selected a Taylor-Made sand wedge. Norm went to the glove compartment and selected a .45 automatic. They all stormed the Finch house, weapons in hand.

Pomarat did not like the odds. He did not like the look of their weapons, and he was in no position to get a shot off with his bow. He decided retreat was in order. They would fall back into the woods and attack if they followed. He popped back into the living room and ordered his men to leave … quickly.

They darted through the house and out the backslider. Massot paused to snatch the CVS bag full of Mrs. Finch's select parts.

One of the Ping putters stopped to help Treflin. The other ran to the front door first trying the knob then slamming the door with his club. Norm and the sand wedge ran around to the back of the house anticipating the escape route of the intruders. They cleared the side just in time to see four midgets scampering into the underbrush at the edge of the backyard. Norm ordered the sand wedge to check out the house and call the cops. Norm rambled to the edge of the brush and let off four of his seven rounds while issuing the perfunctory "Halt! Or I'll shoot!"

The midgets were too fast for him. He was debating whether to follow when the sand wedge re-emerged on the deck. "Norm! Get up here! It's horrible!"

The Ping putter from the front door had just reached the backyard. He and Norm climbed the deck stairs. The other Ping had gotten Treflin back to Norm's house and was calling the police. The Pukwudgees stunned by the report of the .45, established an ambush formation should Norm chose to follow.

14

VERNON OTIS SHOWED UP at the Police/Fire complex after checking in at the D.P.W. As was the case for the past week, he was to work on a culvert to re-route water run-off so as not to undermine the drive leading to the complex. And as was the case for the past week, he arrived hungover and sore. Usually he was just hungover, but since he heard of the development at Witch Pond, he'd been spending the hours after last call keeping vigil out at the hole, wrestling his conscience over what to do.

He hadn't called Brett. It would be too weird after all these years. Brett was rich and successful and he was a drunken local native. Figuring out how to approach Brett gave him a headache. It was easier just to forget about it. He probably wouldn't recognize him. Christ that was lame. After what they went through as kids, how the hell could he have forgotten him? Yet, like himself, maybe he was trying to forget and Vern didn't want to be the one to destroy that effort. No, he'd figure this out by himself. If Brett was still coming down to the Cape, he'd know about the development. And, if he gave a damn, he'd find him.

For a few years after Timmy and Amos disappeared … NO, went in the hole after those fucking demon dwarfs … Brett would call on Vern when he came down for the summer. But as they grew older, class difference and peer pressure made these encounters awkward. By the time they were seniors in high school … Brett in Concord, Vern in Falmouth … there was nothing left to discuss which hadn't been gone over a million times before.

"When do you think they'll come back?"

"You haven't told anybody what happened have you?"
"Is the hole still sealed?"
"Anything new on time travel?"

During the first few years they'd camp out at the hole the last week of August waiting for the secret knock. In their senior year, Brett the preppie and Vern the townie agreed there was nothing left to discuss. Vern promised to keep the annual vigil. Brett promised to learn whatever he could about the concept of time travel. Each promised to call if anything happened. That was the end of it.

Something was happening. Land near the hole was being cleared. Both knew but neither called. Time, once again had screwed things up.

15

VERN SPENT THE NIGHT in the woods keeping his vigil with a fifth of hooch. While there, he'd think - and he'd drink and think - and drink. The survey stakes indicated the development would come real close to the hole. It was amazing the engineers doing the resource mapping had not stumbled across it already.

Vern had decided to at least disassemble the crude blockage they had constructed so many years ago. It would be too easy for someone to trip over even though it protruded no more than a few inches above the ground. If the hole was found in this day and age, God knows what the result would be. Was it worse to take the chance of unleashing four vile runts on the modern world with bows and arrows, and having everyone scratching their heads for a week or so wondering where the fuck they came from? Or should he risk giving the bureaucrats of the federal government access to the fine tuning knob of the world's past and future?

The latter was frightening beyond anything he could ever conceive. The Cabinet kooks of whatever President was elected would have perpetual hard-ons trying to determine what to tinker with first. Vern began prying off the trap door. He threw the wood into his pickup and covered the hole with branches and leaves. To attack the buried studs and the cross braces was too much in one night for a man in his condition. He sat himself down to do some more thinking and maintain the vigil.

"Alright," he took a slug of the cheap imitation of Jack Daniel's as he got comfortable against a tree, "The hole's unblocked. What can happen? Not much probably. What are the chances of them popping up now, in this year? Slim and none. Same as me winnin' Megabucks. Shit, how am I going to keep this hole from being discovered once they start this project full blast? Got to nuke the fucker, that's how! Ya, but what about Amos and Timmy then? They can still come out in some previous time. What if the blast destroys the time thing throughout all time and they get stuck in some God forsaken era? Well how the fuck are they going to function in this era? Tell me that, Mr. Philosopher! How the hell will we explain them, two thirteen year olds with no history? Why the fuck am I thinking about this anyway? I'd be lucky to get my hands on a cherry bomb!" He took another slug and rolled over. All this thinking was too much and he wasn't getting anywhere. Slowly he faded off under the stars, maintaining his vigil in his stupor.

16

VERNON'S EYES SLID OPEN as his mind recognized the chirping of birds. The sun had not yet broken the horizon but its light began filtering through the trees. He got up and went home to shower and get ready for work. Every movement of his head, vertical or horizontal, caused the swivel mounted hammer to strike home with a resounding soft thud sending a tremor of pain across his eyebrows and out his pupils. He picked up a bottle of Advil at Andy's Market and wolfed down three with his coffee. Ibuprofen was a wonderful drug, more sure-fire and quicker than aspirin. Like all good things, scientists would probably soon discover that it encouraged brain hemorrhaging. Not that it mattered to Vern, the way he treated his body.

He'd been working on the culvert a good half-hour when he decided to go up to the station house and take a leak. As he approached the front door, Dimitri pulled up with Bogger in the back of his cruiser. Dimitri helped Bogger out. Vern noticed Bogger was handcuffed. He wondered what that two-faced slime ball had done now. Probably was caught exposing himself to spotted turtles.

"Shee-it! What's goin' on Steve? What did Phil do?" exclaimed Vern as he held the front door.

"None of your business, Vern." remarked Steve ushering Bogger past.

"I didn't do anything Vern! It was some damn weirdly dressed kids!" pleaded Bogger.

"What're you talkin' bout Phil?" pressed Vern, his curiosity sparked.

"Bug off Vern!" snapped Dimitri over his shoulder, "Don't you have work to do?"

"Yeah, yeah I do. I was just coming in to get a drink and take a squirt."

Vern casually broke off for the water cooler and lingered as long as possible without being obvious. It was long enough to pick up "… suspicion of homicide … any idea who the victim was … I.D. the truck … road to Witch Pond." Bogger was taken to a back room for prints and photographs. Vern's curiosity was peaked. He crushed the paper cup, dropped it in the bucket and sauntered over to the desk.

"Hey Billy? What's goin' down?" ventured Vern conspiratorially.

Sergeant Sikes was finishing off a few things wanting to get back with Dimitri himself. He glanced up and with that patriarchal manner stated simply, "Nothing Vern. Don't you have work to do?"

"Come on Billy! I was just curious. I heard Steve say homicide! It ain't everyday there's a murder in Mashpee. Shit, you guys don't really believe Bogger kilt someone do you? Maybe he'd flick a few snorts or somethin' but …"

"Vernon, it's none of your goddamn business! Read about it in the papers! Now get the fuck out of my face! You look like shit."

"I gotta take a shit as a matter-a-fact, if ya don't mind," said Vern in a manufactured mildly miffed tone. He decided he'd camp out in the can as long as he could hoping to pick up some more tidbits of information. He shuffled down the hall to the men's room where he selected the stall closest to the wall.

Sikes shook his head and returned to his work. He thought briefly about Vern. What a promising athlete he had been coming out of middle school. The Falmouth High football coach was licking his chops waiting for what he was sure would be a premier tailback/safety. Mashpee had no high school and there was little chance of the parents affording private school. The kid ran like the wind and had the lateral moves of Gale Sayers. Yup, Vern had promise and would probably have been in line for a college scholarship if he kept his nose clean.

But that all changed when his brother and the Irish kid from Popponesset disappeared. Ever since then Vern had been going downhill. Sikes had just joined the force. Vern knew something but wasn't talking. Whatever it was it was definitely tearing away at his insides. By his sophomore year he started hitting the bottle big time. Although he made varsity, he turned out to be another mediocre starter. In his junior or senior year, he was suspended from the team for smoking marijuana. Yup, he'd probably carry what he knew to the grave and if he kept up the way he was going, that wasn't that far off.

One thing Sikes had to give Vern credit for was having the sense to rent an apartment over a bar. They had picked up Vern a number of times for D.U.I. back in the seventies before the laws became strict. It was customary to hold drunks known to the force in the tank overnight and let them go in the morning with a fine. Times changed and Vern adapted.

Sikes finished his entries into the logbook, tossed it into the desk tray and went back to join Dimitri. Vern, to enhance his cover, did take a shit. It also gave him time to think. He pondered broken tidbits of the conversations he overheard … "weirdly dressed kids" … "homicide" … "Witch Pond."

The last was the clincher. He had spent the night there. Weirdly dressed kids combined with homicide spelled Pukwudgees. But that didn't really fit either. As he recalled what seemed like ages ago, the Pukwudgees were shrimps, but there was no way those grim hard faces and muscular bodies could be deemed kid-like. Maybe he felt that way because he was a kid when he last ran into them. Maybe, however, it was actually Timmy and Amos that Bogger had seen. What the hell were they wearing that day? Vern didn't exactly remember but as he recalled nothing they wore back then would be considered exceptionally weird now especially in Mashpee where a lot of the locals were so poor it was not uncommon for clothes to be handed down through three or more siblings. Besides, Amos and Timmy wouldn't kill anyone.

Vern wondered if he was seeing ghosts where there weren't any. After all, he spent the night by the hole. If anyone had popped up they surely would have awakened him with either a tap on the shoulder or a tomahawk to the head ... a thought which caused him to promise not to get so stewed if he went out there again. Should he go out there again with a homicide hanging over that area? What about the hole? If Bogger was the killer there was nothing to fear, right? Ya, except the cops would be all over the place looking for clues.

He needed to know more. The inside of the station house wasn't new to him. The cells were in the back left-hand side of the building. There were two ways to get there. One was through the door by Sikes' desk. That took you through a bullpen where the officers had their desks. The other was to continue down the hall past the restrooms through a double set of metal doors. Once through the doors, you went left down another hall past a couple of interrogation rooms to a locked door behind which were the holding cells. On previous visits to the tanks, he usually entered the former and left the next morning the latter way.

The way by Sikes' desk was definitely out unless he wanted to get himself arrested for something first. Getting arrested while he was supposed to be working wouldn't go over too well with his boss who'd love an excuse to can his butt. He'd try the other way. Maybe they hadn't had anyone in holding for awhile and had gotten lax about locking the door.

Vern wiped his ass and pulled up his jeans. He heard the distant but familiar thud of a cell door closing indicating that Bogger had probably finished being processed and booked. He'd have to be quick! Bogger had no doubt been given his one phone call and some lawyer would soon be following the route he intended to take to the interrogation rooms. Knowing what Bogger pulled down for a salary, it would probably be Dick Strumawitz who charged next to nothing and delivered less.

Vern stepped into the hall and glanced down at the desk. Sikes had not returned. He slipped through the metal doors and slinked into the hall that went left. The hall that went right led to the locker and assembly rooms. He listened intently to see if any other cops were down there. Odds were there weren't ... it was a small town. But you never knew. The beating emanating from the veins behind his inner ear kept him from discerning any conclusions on this matter so he continued on down the hall. He arrived at the usually locked door and peered at the slit between the jamb and the door. The bolt wasn't thrown! He'd fully expected the door to be locked and he'd have to turn around and go back to work. But it wasn't! Now what? How could he have expected to hold a meaningful conversation with Bogger within earshot of the bullpen? Maybe Sikes and Dimitri had gone out front. Ya! So what? The minute that gerbil saw him, he'd start ranting out a litany of "I didn't do it Vern!" and alert everyone in the place. Best to go back to work. 'No! Fuck it! I'm this far. I'll take my chances no one's out there and hopefully Bogger has the presence of mind to keep quiet. Maybe the stupid fuck will think I'm trying to bust him out or something and freeze trying to decide whether to participate.'

The veins accelerated their madding beat. He placed his hand on the knob and inched his face to the small glass window in the door. Looking inside he could see Bogger sitting on his bunk with his head in his hands, the epitome of the cliché "I've been framed." Vern glanced sidelong and could see no one. Ever so gently he began turning the knob, feeling, sensing, and trying to anticipate with his eyes any impending sound it would make. Then it came! The sound of a key slicing into the cylinder and then slamming the bolt home!

Dimitri's face passed into view. His eyes passed Vernon's face and didn't notice … but did. The eyes came back with alarm. The bolt hammered back and Vern felt the knob twist violently in his hand and the door slam into his chest.

"For christsakes Vern! What the hell are you trying to pull now!" yelled Dimitri grabbing Vern by the back of the collar and the belt in his pants. Dimitri was strong. Vern's toes were barely skimming the ground as he was hustled back up the hall and out the double doors.

"Come on man, I just wanted to talk to Bogger! I wasn't up to nothin'! I swear!" protested Vern in the best voice he could muster considering the massive wedgee he was receiving.

"Your nose is gonna get you in big trouble!" huffed Dimitri pushing him off onto the desk.

Sikes was returning to the desk looking anxious. "What the hell are you doing Steve?"

"Showing this nosy asshole the door! I caught him trying to sneak into the holding area!"

"I didn't mean anything Billy. I was just curious, that's all" pleaded Vern.

"Forget him, Steve. Vern get the fuck back to work before you get your ass canned" commanded Sikes in a stern yet fatherly tone. "Now move!"

"But … "

"I SAID MOVE!"

Vern began a slow dejected shuffle to the door. Sikes didn't wait for him to get out of earshot. "Steve, Fredricks says there's a serious problem at the Finch residence. Matthews and Cabrel are probably there by now. You get over there and send Cabrel back to the homicide site. I got a feeling the problem at the Finches is related and I want you to get a look at what happened. Fredricks is calling the Staties again. Matthews can fill you in."

Dimitri passed Vern on the way out and gave him a light shove. "God you're slow! I hope you're not letting that nose get the best of you again!"

Vern gave him a half-hearted smile. Something big was up at the Finch place and he was going to find out what. He kept a respectable distance behind Dimitri.

17

BY THE TIME VERN got to his truck, Dimitri was long gone … lights flashing and sirens wailing. Vern knew Finch lived somewhere in the Fells Pond section of New Seabury. He had heard tell of her morning wake up calls from a guy at the D.P.W. who hung out with a guy from the fire department, who hung out with Officer Fredricks.

It took him about ten minutes to get to New Seabury. Driving past the second cul-de-sac in Fells Pond, he caught a glimpse of a blue strobe off the face of one of the houses. He jumped on the brakes and put it in reverse. As he coasted down the road, three cruisers and an ambulance were parked by the house at the end. One was State Police, the others were Mashpee. Vern parked a good distance away, making sure he wouldn't be accused of being in the way. He could still be accused of being nosy. Hopefully he wouldn't be noticed at all. He wandered up to a small group of neighbors who had assembled in front of the Finch house. He overheard the traditional on-looker's banter of "What happened … I don't know … Did you hear the shots … Yeah, that's when I came out."

One man commented that the paramedics had gone over to Johnson's with a stretcher. Another said that was weird because most of the cops had been running in and out of the Finch house.

At that moment, Mr. Johnson, Officer Matthews, a State Trooper and two guys with golf clubs emerged from the Finch house. The trooper broke off from the group and headed to his cruiser. The rest headed for the Johnson place. Matthews asked everyone to go home on his way by. Johnson echoed his request "Come on folks! These guys got a lot of work to do. I'll tell you all about it later."

Everyone moved up the street a little, almost shuffling in the same manner Vern had back at the police station. Nobody really intended to go home. Something major had obviously happened and enquiring minds wanted to know. Vern tried to stay close to the State cruiser. He focused all his concentration on what the Trooper was about to say into the radio shutting out the discussions of the neighbors.

"Dispatch, we got another homicide, possibly related to the first. An ex-County Deputy claims he saw four suspects and got off several shots at them but doesn't think he hit them. I'll need dogs and a search team. See if you can shake free a chopper. They took off on foot into the woods. Put an A.P.B. out for four Native Americans, all approximately three and a half feet tall …"

"What? Come back … " crackled the radio.

"You heard me right. Four midget Indians with muscular builds, probably dwarfs or something. One has a Mohawk haircut, the others have long hair in a braid. They're wearing … ehhhh … cod pieces with no shirts. One apparently has a target like design on his butt and another was carrying a CVS bag. They're all armed with primitive weapons … bows, arrows, knives … approach with extreme caution! They are extremely dangerous and unstable! I'll call on a land line with more info. Over."

"What the fuck is a cod piece?"

Matthews smirked "It's like a woman's string bikini or those bathing suits the Canadians wear to show off their junk, only buckskin."

"You been to the other location, yet? Over."

"Negative, the local officer who investigated is here. Another officer is back at the site. I suggest we get another car over there right away. Over."

"On the way. Out."

Vern heard enough. The Pukwudgees were out! Not only were they out, now there were gonna be cops and dogs sniffing all over the place. There'd be a good chance they'd sniff their way right back to the hole. He didn't know where the first homicide had taken place but it had to be closer to the hole since it happened earlier. Removing the barrier from the hole had been a bad idea. The Staties would find it and turn it over to the Feds. "Shit! I fucked up again!" he hissed to no one in particular.

He had to find Brett! He would like to find out exactly what happened to Mrs. Finch but that would have to wait. Then another thought struck him like a slap in the face. Amos and Timmy! Were they out too? Was one of them the first homicide? Shit, come to think of it they'd still be around thirteen years old! The neighbors began to notice Vern, an Indian with his hair pulled back in a pony tail, dirty work clothes and mumbling to himself to boot. He definitely wasn't from the neighborhood. Vern was suddenly snapped out of his thoughts by the conspicuous silence. He glanced up at the small group who had now focused on him.

"Oh, hi. How ya doin'? I was just driving by when I caught sight of the … " Vern stopped himself. Why was he explaining his presence to these people? Because they caught him talking to himself that's why. No, that wasn't it. It's because he was a townie minority in an upscale section of town. He decided he didn't owe them anything.

"Well, I guess I better get back to work and earn those hard tax dollars you pay for my services. I'll be back for lunch though to catch up on what happened." With that he left for his truck. The neighbors stared at him as if he was speaking Japanese. One asked, "What the hell is he talking about?" The others shrugged and returned their attention to the crime scene, which was rather uneventful, since everyone was inside a house.

18

TIMMY AND AMOS CAME to a clearing. Laid out before them was a massive tennis facility. The pinging of balls had drawn them here.

"We ought to be able to find out 'when' it is now," beamed Timmy marveling at the several modernistic vehicles parked in the lot.

"Wait! Let's sit here a second and figure out what we say if anyone asks us anything."

"No one's going to say anything except 'Get the hell away from my car!'"

"How do we know if our clothes are right for the times?"

"That guy's clothes back in the woods didn't look all that different from the kind of stuff we wear. It wasn't like he was dressed like Buck Rogers or somethin'. And his car was just like a shrunken Suburban." answered Timmy itching to get down and to get a preview of what the automotive future held in store.

"Alright. Let's go. But be subtle! Make like we're taking a shortcut through the parking lot or something."

"Hey I'll be subtle as a fart in church!" giggled Timmy punching Amos in the arm. "My older brother Colin always says that. It cracks me up."

Amos cast him a sidelong glance. They pushed their way out of the underbrush and trotted down the incline to the parking lot. Luckily, no one was in the lot but there were plenty of people on the courts judging from the number of pings. Timmy recognized the Mercedes logo on the first car they came to. Next to it was what appeared to be a brand new 1966 Mustang convertible. The Mercedes, although different, was not all that much different from its sixties version. Timmy's spirit rose thinking they weren't all that far removed from their time. But then he noticed the Chevy Lumina. That was nowhere near their time. That was a spacecraft! He bent down and checked the license plate on the Mustang. In the upper right hand corner was a green sticker with the number '92'.

"Holy shit Amos! It's 1992!"

"Quiet! Christ, you want someone to think were lunatics. Keep going!"

"Ya but it's twenty-four years later!" exclaimed Timmy in a more subdued tone following Amos as he picked up the pace.

"So what? After where we've been that's nothing."

"Well that means Vern and Brett are in their thirties," whispered Timmy grabbing Amos by the arm to slow him down, "and probably totally unrecognizable."

Amos stopped and with a sly smirk said, "I'll find them."

"How the hell can you be so all fired sure?"

"Because, I sense their presence!"

"You what ..."

"Look over there!" smiled Amos pointing down the line of cars to a black BMW with 'BRETT' on the license plate.

"Holy shit! You think that's our Brett? "

"Don't know for sure, but I'll bet it is. He put his name on everything ... his shirts, his sweaters ... he even had his initials on his snot rags! It was like he wasn't happy unless everyone knew who he was." Timmy climbed a small knoll to get a view of the courts and the many players occupying them. They were too far away to be recognizable especially when you weren't sure what you were trying to recognize.

"Come on," said Amos. "We'll wait for him to finish and come back to his car."

19

VERN WANTED TO DRIVE over to the hole but knew he couldn't. Instead he headed for the Marketplace. The nearest pay phone would be there. He hoped Brett was around. He'd be around somewhere. That rich fuck never had to work a day in his life if he didn't want to. He's probably down here all the time when the weather's nice, 'networking'. 'Networking' was the rich man's term for chargeable fucking off. Come winter he'd be off networking in Florida or somewhere else that was warm. Shit, if only Vern had money he'd be an excellent 'networker'. God knows he had spent years practicing at Poor Henry's Pub.

Vern pulled up to the phones in back of the marketplace. He had Brett's number memorized from the years of checking the new phone book to see if he was still listed. The phone rang several times before a woman answered.

"Hello?"

Vernon didn't expect a woman though it was logical to assume Brett may have met someone and got married. He was momentarily off balance. Quickly he summoned his best grammar and responded. "Hi, this is Vernon Otis. I'm looking for Brett Simmons. Is this Mrs. Simmons?" He regretted this question as soon as he asked it. What a dope! It slipped out as innocently as 'How's the weather'. What business was it of his who she was?

"No …" a pause followed by a chuckle that wasn't the 'ha ha that's funny chuckle', more like a 'who's this asshole chuckle'. "I'm a friend. Brett's not available. Can I take a message?"

"Yes! No! Look I'm sorry. It's none of my business who you are. I'm just nervous. I grew up with Brett here in New Seabury and haven't seen him in awhile. I'm only in town for the day and hoped to see him before I had to take off," lied Vern knowing he had to say something to get back on the good side of this woman.

"Well you may be able to catch him up at the Tennis Club if he's still there. If not try back here later."

"Thank you very much, I'll do that."

"Bye."

'I'd sure like to see the face and body that goes with that voice,' thought Vern as he hung up the phone. 'No time for snaking. I got to get my ass up to the courts.'

However, as he drove, his mind wondered about the voice. So, a friend? Brett wasn't married? Or maybe wifey was back up in Concord or wherever getting the kids ready to start school. No, that didn't figure. That girl would be letting the answering machine pick up if there was a Mrs. Simmons. No, Brett hadn't considered marriage for the same reason he hadn't. It'd be tough to hide the stuff they'd seen and been through from someone that close. It would come out in a moment of weakness, drunkenness or self-pity.

"Yep, lost my brother and one of our best friends in a hole in the ground with a time machine in it! They'll be coming back though. That's why I go off into the woods every August, so I can open the trapdoor if they give the secret knock. Been in the hole myself! Yep, brought back some mythical creatures from hell too! That's why they went back in. To save the world that is. Now you can't tell anyone! Don't want the government getting their hands on this thing. They're crazy you know! Probably try and change history!"

No, it was easier and safer to go through life alone, less chance of being committed because of committing.

Driving to the club, Vern passed the road leading to the construction site by the hole. A cruiser now blocked access removing any second thoughts Vern may have had of checking things out. He slowed instinctively at the sight of police and continued on. He pulled into the handicapped space by the tennis pro shop entrance. He briefly wondered how many times someone handicapped had legitimately used the space. After all it was tennis, not bowling or darts. Hopping out of the cab, he bound up the steps to the pro shop without noticing the young boy rising to his feet across the parking lot.

Despite the twenty plus years separating them, Amos immediately recognized his twin brother. One of those weird phenomenon thoroughly documented on Oprah and Geraldo that inexorably links twins. Twins have been known to sense the other's pain or danger no matter what the distance that separates them. In this case, the twins were separated by decades not miles.

"We're all here, Timmy", mumbled Amos in a trance like state.

"What? Was that who I think you think it is?"

"Ya, man that was Vernon."

"You sure?"

"YES!"

20

THE GIRL IN THE tennis shop eyed Vernon suspiciously. Vern took no notice and approached the counter focusing on the court time sheet on top.

"Hi, I'm looking for Brett Simmons. I was told he'd be here."

"We don't allow our club members to be disturbed," responded the girl politely but firmly. "If you give me your name, I'll ask one of the attendants to see if he's still here and let him know you wish to see him."

"That won't be necessary. I see his name right here on court four and I'm in a big hurry." replied Vern as he tapped the sheet and made for the courts.

"Sir! Wait! You can't go out there!"

"I won't be a minute," he said over his shoulder as he ran down the stairs.

The girl was about to give chase to at least alert Mr. Simmons. She only got to the exit when two raggedy looking boys came in the other door from the parking lot. She was caught between watching the register and warning Mr. Simmons. The register came first. Mr. Simmons was a big boy and there were plenty of people around.

"What do you boys want?"

"My father just went out there," said Amos pointing at the courts.

"Yeah, and he's looking for my dad, Brett Simmons," piped in Timmy enjoying the ad-lib.

"Oh? …"

"We just got selected to the all-stars and Amos's dad brought us down to tell my dad!" beamed Timmy showing Amos how proficient he was at making things up on the fly.

More at ease now with this plausible scenario, the girl told Timmy and Amos they could wait on the observation deck and were not to go down on the courts. Then she added, "You better have your fathers check out your legs. You've bled right through your jeans."

Timmy and Amos looked down and Amos replied, "It ain't nothin'. It doesn't hurt none."

"Have them look at it anyway! It may get infected!" she scolded them as they ran out on the deck.

Vern had reached Brett's court. Brett was surprised to see him even though he more or less was expecting him to pop back into his life with the development being built by Witch Pond. Brett also knew this was more or less the time of year that they had kept their vigils. He wondered if Vern still did. Brett excused himself to his playing partner and extended his hand to Vern.

"Long time no see. How goes the battle?"

"Brett the battle's begun and all hell has broken loose!" said Vern returning the handshake. "Man, we gotta talk and pronto! Can you get away so we can go somewhere and have a beer or something?"

Brett knew from the look on Vern's face that the time had come, the time was now, 'ole Brett Simmons you must face your past now'. Brett told his playing partner. "Something's come up! I gotta take off, Karl!"

"Anything serious? You need anything?"

"No, no. I'll give you call to set up a time to resume this ass whipping."

"You're lucky he showed up when he did. I was about turn things around." said Karl good-naturedly.

"Ya right!" chuckled Brett as he packed up his gear. He wrapped a towel around his neck and wiped his brow. "The day you … fuck me!"

Vern turned and looked in the direction of Brett's rapt expression. "Oh … my … God!"

"Did you bring them with you Vern?"

"No man, I … "

"Come on let's go. See ya, Karl." said Brett absently.

1968 POPPONESSET

21

RACISM HAS BEEN AROUND forever. It provides an outlet for a segment of the population that has an inherent need to criticize, belittle and vilify. In the absence of race, this segment of the population would seek out other differences, a much more difficult task, but essential to their mental well being. They would morph into differentists.

Popponesset Beach in the sixties provided an illustration of this. Comprising the eastern half of Mashpee's shoreline, Popponesset Beach was a summer haven for well-to-do whites from the greater Boston, Providence and Worcester areas. Predominantly Irish, Italian and WASP with a smattering of Jews, Slovaks, and Germans, the beach was devoid of segregationist tendencies. Occasionally, a 'whop', 'mick' or 'kyke' slur could be heard but only among parties who had become close over the summers. People came here for the natural beauty and recreational opportunities. Many came from city neighborhoods where ethnic similarity thus security was the norm. Security necessitated due to years of racism fostered by systems that pitted races against each other for purposes of obtaining the cheapest labor. Although ethnic competition for jobs had started dissipating in the sixties, the homogeneity of the neighborhoods remained. The traditions of racial distrust handed down from father to son would take more generations to weaken.

Having a summer home on the Cape was being well to do. In Popponesset, the lots were seven to eight thousand square feet. There was no geographical division of ethnic backgrounds in this grid-like area abutting the ocean. The fathers were here two to three weeks a year and weekends. The mothers and children were here for most of two months. Some families stayed two weeks and rented their place the remainder of the time. The population was a dynamic organism of constant change unlike where they came from.

However, in the early sixties something happened which unleashed the differentism some people needed to exhibit. The company that developed Popponesset took the undeveloped land to the west and north of it and began developing a themed residential/resort community with its own private golf courses and beach club. Although the area of beach designated as the beach club was small in comparison to Popponesset Beach, it had two shacks that served food and had rest rooms, showers and lockers. To be a member you had to own property in the new development and pay annual dues. Since the company had also developed Popponesset, they allowed Popponesset residents to join the clubs as non-residents with slightly higher dues. Although this seemed fair and somewhat chivalrous to the developer and purchasers in the new development, it was considered demeaning by some of the residents of Popponesset.

They had been content for years to pack snacks and drinks if they did not live right on the beach. They never thought twice about wading waist deep in the mild ocean to take a leak. All of a sudden some Popponesset residents felt inferior to their neighbors a quarter of a mile up the beach who could piss in toilets and obtain food, drinks, chairs and umbrellas from lifeguard attendants. So what if they were offered the use of the amenities … they had to pay more. They didn't want to hear that was because New Seabury residents paid more for their lots. They had been snubbed! Those that snubbed them were snobs! Never mind that many of the snobs had previously lived in Popponesset with them.

Admittedly, those who perceived themselves as snubbed were few. But they were an overbearing outspoken few who tended to dominate the many who came down to Popponesset to relax not argue. So the many would just nod their head and excuse themselves to wade into the ocean to piss when the first break in those one-sided conversations occurred.

Mrs. Mary O'Rielly was one of the few. Mr. Colin O'Rielly Sr. was one of the many who would wade when she started her diatribe on the uppity snobs over at New Seabury. As a matter of fact, Mr. O'Rielly could be considered an associate snob since he had immediately hopped on the opportunity to become a non-resident member of the beautiful new golf course that opened. He would have gladly forked out the dough to join the beach club if it would shut Mary up, but Mary wouldn't hear of it. All their summer friends were in Popponesset and why should they have to pay extra to use 'THAT' section of beach. Colin Sr. thought the dues were reasonable considering the facilities, but he wasn't about to argue with her. He only wanted peace during his weekends and three weeks a year. Mary and the kids spent the whole summer and she evidently needed something to bitch about.

Mary had her counterparts in New Seabury as well as 'similars' in Popponesset, male and female alike. Colin Sr. had his counterparts and similars also but they were the silent wading majority. More obvious in difference but less visible to the chronic differentist were the year round Wampanoag population. Being less well off, they did not frequent New Seabury or Popponesset except to fish. Since the best fishing was at dusk and dawn, their presence rarely coincided with the differentist. The only other place they all had in common was the grocery store in the center of Mashpee.

Nevertheless, the Wampanoags tended to be invisible to the differentist, especially when the differentist would push right through them to reach a particularly attractive green bell pepper or loaf of bread. That's not to say the Wampanoags did not have their own versions of Mary and Colin Sr. They did. The Mary's held a lasting grudge that their lands were taken from them. The fact was that unlike Indians elsewhere, the local Wampanoags had been given the town now known as Mashpee in exchange for not participating in King Philip's War in the 1700's. They took it and divided it amongst themselves individually, similar to the ways of the white men. They chose not to maintain tribal ownership (what became known as a reservation in the late 1800's). Exercising their freedom of ownership, many of their descendants sold their parcels over the next three centuries. Usually those that sold held the choice parcels. As a result, there followed at some point, an influx of development and ultimately white tourists, a classic case of history repeating itself … another place … another time.

Thus it was ironic that Timmy, Southie Irish, Brett, suburbia WASP, and Amos and Vernon, two townie Indians, became such close friends in the summer of 1968. The Mary's of Popponesset, New Seabury and the Wampanoags were always the most vocal and unrelenting thus exuding the most exposure to the young. Since the boys were all more or less around thirteen years old, maybe they had not been exposed long enough to prevent them from striking up a friendship. Maybe at that age, there are still so many things in the world which are the cause of wonder and fascination that they haven't the time to pay attention to the bafflegab of these individuals for whom the wonders of nature … environmental and human, have lost their luster.

22

TIMMY O'RIELLY WAS AN early riser at his summer home. He loved to be the first up, slipping on his bathing suit and heading to the beach to see what wonders the ocean had washed up on the sand that night. Maybe if he was lucky, he'd find a sand shark or horseshoe crab. He'd seen a picture of his brother Colin with his foot perched atop a pilot whale but his father told him that was on the north side of the Cape. He said it was unlikely that he'd come across one of those on the south side. Still, he had heard the ocean was largely unexplored and there was no telling what strange creatures he may come across. North side, south side, it didn't matter. It was all connected as far as he could tell, so he was liable to come across anything.

It was on one of these morning jaunts that he first met the Otis brothers fishing in the surf off the spit. He approached the boys picking up the pace noticing they both were reeling frantically between slow pulls on their monstrous rods causing the tips to bow like sickles. Vernon was the first to land his prize dragging a giant bluefish out of the surf up on the shore. Quickly, without giving any notice to Timmy, he slipped his rod in a length of pipe in the sand. He took a pair of pliers out of his cut-off shorts, stepped on the flapping fish with his bare foot and adeptly yanked out his homemade plug. He grabbed the fish by the tail and tossed him back up the beach by a pile of what had to be ten or more blues flapping about. He was back to his rod preparing to cast when Amos was landing his fish.

Timmy was amazed! Fish were flailing wildly on the beach. Fish were churning wildly in the water. Gulls were circling and swooping snagging bits of fish from the froth. These two boys who appeared identical were moving about hurriedly paying no attention to Timmy. "WOW!" said Timmy.

Vern glanced at Timmy now as his plug sailed through the sky and expertly landed in the center of the savage school of fish. Amos also cast a glance his way as he slipped his rod in the pipe. Almost the instant Vern's plug hit the water a large blue struck it leaping high in the air.

"WOW!" exclaimed Timmy again. He'd never seen anything like this spectacle. Vern yanked and reeled setting the hook.

"Hey! You guys need any help?" offered Timmy wishing to be part of the excitement. Vern pulled and reeled slack. Amos by now was ready for another cast.

"Yeah," said Vern between grunts, "go guard our pile of fish."

Timmy was thrilled to be of assistance and ran over to the flapping mass of blues and assumed watch. Then he realized he didn't know what he was guarding against. The two brothers were busy pulling in another pair and Timmy didn't feel he should bother them now with what probably was a stupid question. So he kept his mouth shut and stood guard against what he did not know. There was no one else on the beach and if there were they could have spotted them a mile away. Besides how could anyone sneak off with a pile of flapping fish?

One of the last fish caught began flapping wildly in spurts in a last ditch effort to escape back to the sea. Maybe this was what Timmy was to guard against. Dutifully, Timmy went to retrieve the escapee the way his father had showed him to handle largemouth bass at the Quabbin Reservoir when they fished. He was about to slip his fingers under the gills and thumb in the crook of the mouth when Vernon violently tossed the monster he just landed hitting Timmy square in the butt with enough force to knock him face first into the sand.

"Hey!" whined Timmy quickly scampering up and brushing himself off.

"You don't wanna go getting those fingers of yours anywhere near that suckers mouth if you want to keep 'em, Red. He'll chomp them clean to the bone. Grab him by the tail."

Timmy looked down at the gaping mouth and noticed tiny lines of teeth. It was hard to believe they could inflict much damage.

"They don't look like much," said Vern reading his thoughts, "but they chomp, grind and rip and don't let go till they get a tasty morsel for their efforts."

"What am I supposed to be guarding against anyway?" asked Timmy not wishing to dwell on his near loss of a digit.

"Nothing really," responded Amos dragging up another bluefish, "except with you being there we can concentrate on fishin' and not worry about the gulls putting peck holes in our fillets."

Vernon had cast out his line but there was no strike this time as he worked the lure back to shore. "Things are slowin' down Amos. I'll try another cast but I think we'll be going to bait pretty quick."

"What's he mean?" asked Timmy to Amos who chucked his fish on the pile.

"When you stop getting hits on the surface, you switch to bottom fishing and go after the big fat fucks that trail the school sucking up the scraps cause they're too big and fat to catch anything that's swimming."

Amos pulled a fillet knife out of the scabbard looped around his belt and handed it to Timmy. "Pick out one of the smaller fish in the pile and cut a couple of sections about an inch wide each a few inches up from the tail. They should look like a miniature version of those swordfish steaks you see in the market. I'm gonna try a few more casts with the plug."

Timmy was thrilled to have something more useful to do than be a scarecrow, or in this case a scaregull. He looked about for something hard to cut on. He found an old concrete mooring anchor partially buried in the sand. He had no reservations about hacking up the fish. He only hoped he sliced it correctly.

He visited his uncle's farm in Northampton last year and had embarrassed himself, earning the nickname Timmy 'the Tomahawk' O'Rielly. He, Colin and his two cousins had accompanied his Uncle Pat to prep a few chickens for the evening meal. Uncle Pat had his oldest boy, about Colin's age, grab a live hen and bring it to a stump by the pigpen. There, Uncle Pat took the hen's two legs in one hand and laid her on the block. In the blink of an eye, he brought a hatchet down with his other hand and dispatched its head. He then shoved the body in one of the dozen tin funnels attached to the fence surrounding the pigpen. These allowed the blood to drain out the neck cavity into the slop trough where the pigs jostled for position to suck it up. Timmy's cousins begged their father to let them do the next one, wishing to show off their skills to their city cousins.

Uncle Pat gave the oldest the hatchet and tossed the severed head into the trough where it was immediately devoured by a lucky pig that happen to be in the right place at the right time. Each of the cousins performed the exercise skillfully. The youngest cousin then innocently passed the hatchet to Timmy. Timmy was grossed out by the whole scene, especially with the ravenous pigs. But his pride was at stake. Anything they could do, he could do. Still he wished his cousin had given the ax to Colin.

"Now Timmy, you don't have to do this," said Uncle Pat sensing his hesitancy. "You're our guest and we don't ask guests to make us supper."

"No. I can do it," boasted Timmy half heartily.

"Alright then, ya gotta hold those legs together real tight and keep holding them till you get it in the chute. Give it a nice hard quick chop."

Uncle Pat picked up a chicken and brought the legs together so Timmy could grab them with one hand.

"No, use your left hand if you're right handed," instructed Uncle Pat. "Tight now! It won't hurt them for long."

Timmy obeyed feeling squeamish knowing that the living thing in his hand would soon meet its end by his hand. Summoning an image of himself as a muscle-bound hooded executioner from the Middle Ages, he worked himself into the state of mind necessary to accomplish his task. His older cousin leaned into Colin's ear and whispered "I bet he misses." Timmy was now in his own world. Only he and the chicken were real. Everything else was soundless and in the background. Laying the hen on the stump, he swung the hatchet with a roar of fury which alone should have given the chicken a heart attack. Timmy's eyes closed for a second in the descent. The power of the swing caused him to relax his grip upon impact. The results were disastrous to his ego and the hen.

The blow had not completely severed the head and its legs escaped Timmy's grasp. The chicken kicked frantically and landed on the ground running. To Timmy's horror and everyone else's amusement, there scampering around the barnyard was the proverbial chicken with its head cut-off ... only in this case, not completely. Its head was hanging to the side, flapping about, held on by strand of skin. Blood was gushing up and out of the neck, and its eye was blinking as if to try and fathom what just happened to it. Otherwise, it ran like a perfectly normal chicken escaping from a dog. Everyone except Uncle Pat had a good laugh at Timmy's expense. Uncle Pat told Timmy not to bother chasing it, it would keel over in awhile.

Mindful of that experience Timmy had selected a small bluefish from the bottom of the pile ensuring it would be dead, or near so. He performed the surgery producing two mini-steaks for the boys without incident. They changed their tackle, baited up and cast out where the school had been.

"Now we wait," said Vernon. "Hopefully not for long ... so who are you?"

"I'm Timmy O'Rielly."

"Where you from?" asked Amos.

"Popponesset."

"Summer people, eh?" inquired Vern. "How long you down for?"

"All summer."

"Ouwee! Your folks must be rich!" smiled Vern.

"Who are you guys?" answered Timmy changing the subject from him to them.

"I'm Amos and that's Vern. We're brothers if you couldn't tell. We live here year round back outside of New Seabury."

Amos's rod tip quivered then jerked. "That one's yours, Timmy. Go get him!"

Timmy looked at Amos in disbelief. "You mean it?"

"Yeah, I mean it! Now hurry the fuck up before he yanks my pole in the water!"

Timmy rushed to the pole pulling it carefully out of the pipe. He felt a whopper of a tug just in time to yank back and set the hook. Vern reeled in so the lines wouldn't cross. Timmy reeled slack and pulled. It was like pulling on an immovable object. This was like nothing he had caught from the lake. It required all his strength to pull back the rod yielding only a few rotations of the reel. Pull ... reel, pull ... reel, step by step, inch by inch and then that moment every fisherman always remembers ... the monstrous fat blue broke the surface and flipped in the air!

"Holy sheet, Timmy! That's some big fish. You better not lose it!" chided Vern slipping his rod in the pipe.

Timmy's arms were getting tired. There was still a long way to go. His adrenaline and determination to land this fish gave him the strength to continue. 'This is so fucking exciting,' he thought as the fish jumped again. Excitement slowly gave way to terror as he pulled back on the rod with no resistance. He reeled and reeled with his tip up. No resistance! Reeled, reeled ...

"Drop the rod!!!" screamed Amos.

"What?!" yelled Tim thinking he meant him to drop the rod entirely as if lightening was going to shoot up the line.

"Lower the tip! He's swimming at ya!" Amos barked reaching in to loosen the drag wheel on the old Penn reel.

Timmy dropped the tip just in time. All the slack had been reeled out of the line. The blue burst out of the water closer than Timmy had ever expected almost causing him to actually drop the rod. When it jumped it torpedoed back the way it had come snapping its head viciously. The drag loose, the line whirred, giving without snapping.

"Alright! Slowly bring the rod back up." instructed Vern. "Tire the fucker out! If he didn't spit the hook on that one, you got him good. Won't be pulling no more stunts like that! That was his grand finale! Bring him in Tim."

It took a minute or two but Timmy landed the granddaddy blue. Amos rushed down to the water and grabbed him by the tail. Holding it vertically it was half the height of Amos.

"Shit man, we won't fillet that baby! You'll be wanting to take that sucker back home to your Daddy and see if you can get him to lay out the money to have it stuffed and mounted," said Vernon.

"Jesus! Ya mean I can have it?" exclaimed Timmy bursting with exuberance.

"Sure, you caught it," replied Amos as if it was only common sense.

"Ya but it's your stuff and all."

"Don't worry about it. We got plenty for supper," said Vern pointing to the pile of blues up on the sand.

Timmy put the rod in the standpipe and beamed over his catch that Amos made sure to bring far enough back from the surf. He pulled a pair of pliers out of his pocket and handed them to Timmy. "Since it's your fish, you can have the honors of getting the hook out. Looks like he swallowed it good. Watch your fingers and don't mangle his mouth in case your Dad does stuff him. Nothin' worse than a mounted fish with a mangled mouth."

"Don't worry about the guts, they're gonna have to come out anyway."

23

VERNON SAID TO AMOS it was time to begin filleting since there was no way they were going to top Timmy's catch out of that school. Timmy was hovering over his fish with pliers like a new dad hovering over a half-opened diaper brimming with baby shit. He didn't know how to approach it.

"You guys want to come over my house and play football or something on the beach?" asked Timmy finally pressing down the fish's side with his palm and grabbing the metal leader with the pliers.

"Naw, we gotta get these fillets back so our dad can start smoking them," said Vern. "Just jiggle the line easy like so you can get the hook out far enough to grab it with the pliers."

Timmy puzzled at the thought of their old man lighting up and taking a drag on raw fish. "Don't you eat them?"

"Eat what? The fish?" asked Amos.

"Yeah, the fish."

"Of course we eat them," Amos stated frowning at Timmy.

"After your dad smokes them?"

"Yeah."

"How can you? What's left?'

"They shrink a bit but there's still plenty to eat," responded Amos still confused.

"Oh," uttered Timmy turning his attention to the hook which was now within reach. "How about coming down to Popponesset Beach after you give the fish to your dad?"

Vern glanced at Amos with a smirk, "I don't think it would be a good idea for a couple of rag tag Indians to show up there alone. If you hadn't noticed we gotta much deeper tan than you."

"Oh yeah," said Timmy focusing for the first time on the color of their skin. "Well why don't we meet somewhere like Callahan's market and figure out something to do."

"What ya say Vern? We ain't got any chores or nothing and dad will be happy with this stash we're bringing him," responded Amos adeptly dispatching another fillet and stuffing it in the bag they brought.

"Yeah," said Vern "we'll meet you down there in about two hours."

Red seemed alright, and he and Amos needed to expand their horizons.

They finished up filleting and tossed the carcasses back into the surf for the dogfish and the crabs. Timmy successfully extracted the hook and picked up his trophy by the tail.

"I'll see you in a couple of hours then."

"Yep," said Vern.

"Hey, I know you're Indians and all, but why doesn't your dad just smoke a pipe or something?"

The twins looked at each other perplexed while mounting their bikes. "He does! See you later, Timmy." responded Amos not getting the point but answering the inquiry.

24

MARY O'RIELLY WAS FLABBERGASTED. "Mother of God! Don't go bringing that thing in my nice clean kitchen!"

"Oh Ma, don't you want to see it?" asked Timmy holding it up with both hands. "I gotta show Dad and Colin!"

"You can show them outside! Now get it out of here right now!"

Colin Sr. emerged from the hall bathroom zipping up his trousers. "What've ya got there, Timmy? You find it on the beach?"

"No! I caught it!"

"Colin, don't you go calling him in there! Where's your sense? Both of you, OUT!"

Colin Sr. went out with his son, "Come on, Tim. No sense arguing with your mother. You'll only get old before your time. You say you caught it? Now how the hell did you do that?"

"Don't you be swearing in front of the boy!" scolded Mary after them as they went out on the back steps.

"I ran into a couple of boys fishing up by the Spit. They let me try it and I caught this! Isn't it a monster?"

"That he is. That he is!" stated Colin Sr. hefting the fish in his hands. "What do you plan on doing with it?"

"Well, the boys said maybe you'd want to get it stuffed and mounted. You should have seen the fight it gave me! It jumped! It charged! And it snapped!" blurted Timmy doing body contortions, snapping his neck while jumping off the steps in a re-enactment of the struggle.

Colin Sr. regarded his son with admiration and amusement. "These boys didn't happen to say where you can find a taxidermist down here did they?"

"No. But there's got to be one in the phone book or something. I can ask them. I'm gonna meet them at Callahan's later. Maybe Callahan knows somebody. Where's Colin? I gotta show him!" Timmy was hopping around all excited that his father was actually considering getting his fish stuffed.

"Colin's off somewhere." Colin Sr. could see that Timmy would be heartbroken if he suggested anything other than stuffing. Burying in the back yard was definitely out of the question.

"I'll see who we can find. In the meantime, we'll have to figure out what to do with this baby so it doesn't spoil."

25

BRETT SIMMONS WAS A fat boy. Not a kid who couldn't reach his ass to wipe it, but a kid termed chubby by considerate adults and tubbo by his inconsiderate peers. Brett's family was rich. They had a house at New Seabury. Mommy was a fetching blond bitch who took up residence there from the third week in June to Labor Day. Daddy was a high powered Boston attorney, who rarely made it to the summer house except in the fall and the spring when mommy and Brett were back in Concord.

Brett was a mistake that made this mismatch perfect. Daddy could stay in Boston and fuck every hot thing in a skirt. And mommy had her selection of cabana boys, assistant golf pros, pool cleaners, contractors and whatever wandered up the beach.

What Brett had was a bundle of cash to get lost. So he'd ride his bike down to Callahan's and stuff his face with whatever suited his fancy. Little did he know as he sat on bench outside of Callahan's, devouring a chocolate chip mint double scoop ice cream cone, that this would be the day that eventually morphed him into a flat stomached blond haired young captain of industry following in his Dad's footsteps. But Brett, a smart boy learned from his parent's example. He would never slip a ring on his finger, only many latex ones on his dick. An inconvenient chip off the old block, so to speak.

26

TIMMY RODE HIS BIKE to Callahan's. Dropped it outside and went in without a notice of Brett. He stepped up to the register and said to Willie, a friend of Colin's from back home, "Give me a Coke".

"Read the sign squirt!"

"What fuckin sign, Willie?"

"The one that says, 'No shoes, no shirt, no service!'"

"Come on Willie, I got my sandals on! Give me a break will ya"

"No shirt, squirt!"

"You're just being an asshole!"

"Rules are rules, squirt," Willie shrugged with a smirk.

Timmy stormed outside mumbling "fucking shithead motherfucker"

Brett glanced up briefly and went back to his cone. Timmy caught the movement out of the corner of his eye and noticed Brett … and his shirt, which had "Brett" embroidered on the breast. Timmy stopped.

"Hey, Brett!"

Brett stopped licking and looked up at him.

"Hey, Brett, can I borrow your shirt for a minute?"

"What?"

"Can I borrow your shirt for a minute?"

"Why? How do you know my name?"

"It's on your shirt! Fuckin Willie won't give me a Coke unless I have a shirt on"

"Who's Willie?"

"The kid at the counter."

"You know him?"

"Yeah, he's a friend of my older brother."

"Then why won't he give you a Coke?"

"Because I don't have a fuckin shirt, and it's a chance for him to legitimately bust my balls!"

"Oh"

"Come on just give me your shirt to go inside and get a Coke. I'll give it right back when I come out."

Brett licked his ice cream and pondered the request. "How about you give me the money and I go in and get you a Coke?"

"Why? You think I got Cooties or something?"

"No, it just would be easier."

"Okay, here's a dollar. I'll be out here waiting for the change."

"Okay, I'll be back." Brett took the dollar and went inside and bought the Coke. He came back and gave it to Timmy with his sixty cents in change. Then he sat down on the bench next to Timmy and resumed his attack on the cone.

"Thanks, the name's Timmy O'Rielly, Brett. Where do you live?"

"In my house, you?"

Timmy chuckled at this, took a swig of his Coke and sat back and said, "You know Brett, you're alright."

Brett smiled and muttered "At least someone thinks so."

27

IT WASN'T LONG BEFORE Amos and Vernon rode up to Callahan's on their bikes. "Hey! You came!" said Timmy rising off the bench.

"Yeah, we came," said Vernon. "It's not often we can traipse around New Seabury in the middle of the day after the rich folks get up. Who's the 'Brett'?"

"He's alright, just met him," responded Timmy.

"You must've had itchy palms this morning, seems like you're meeting everyone. You running for selectman or something? Where you from Brett?" asked Amos.

"Around," replied Brett in his cautious manner.

"Like … New Seabury around … or Popponesset around?" pressed

Vernon.

"New Seabury" answered Brett too quickly.

"Yeah, I figured," said Amos, "the micks don't wear their names on their shirts less they work at a gas station and the Jews and the Wasps would hate to be mistaken for micks in Popponesset."

"Cut the shit, Amos!" interjected Timmy. "I get enough of that shit at the beach with my brother and mother and the fucking neighbors. What do you guys wanna do anyway?"

"I dunno," said Vern, "we can't go to your beach and play ball and I'm sure you don't want to venture outside the gates and see how the other half lives, cause I'll tell you right now, nothing's going on there either."

"Do you guys play tennis?" asked Brett.

"TENNIS?" exclaimed the three boys in unison, none of them having a clue as to the rules.

"I didn't think so," said Brett, "how about giving a hot foot to the pool boy who's fucking my mom?"

The three boy's jaws dropped and looked at Brett, the wind out of their sails.

"What," asked Timmy?

Brett proceeded to explain to them his family situation and how he was daily, given a wad of cash to allow mom to get her jollies while dad did the same back home. At this point, Brett had to confide in some-one or else go nuts. And this was the closest he had come to anyone (sad to say) since he started summering down here.

"So, you're down here sucking ice cream, because your mom's fuck-ing the pool boy! Fuck! Why don't you…"

Timmy was cut off by Vern, "Wait, wait, wait… how much she give you to get lost?"

"I got $19 dollars left" said Brett.

"A buck for the ice cream … so she gives you $20 a day?" calculated Amos.

"Yeah."

Amos looked at Vern then at Brett, "Everyday?"

"Yeah, except when dad's down which isn't much."

"What you been doing with the change?"

"Eating some of it and pocketing the rest, and … buying stuff."

"Fuck, you sure you want to jeopardize this meal ticket?" asked Vern.

"Look," began Brett, "I've been thinking about this a long time. I've planned everything out … after all I've had a lot of free time. The meal ticket won't end. It will be suspended for a few days, long enough for her to find a replacement and I will not be connected to this in anyway."

"WAIT A MINUTE! YOU EXPECT US TO DO THIS?" demanded Amos, always quick on the uptake.

"Not if you don't want to. It will be funny though!"

"How do you see this happening? And what do we get?" asked Vernon.

Brett outlined his plan concluding, "… and each of you gets $20 and the show of your life."

"I'm in!" stated Timmy.

"Us too," added Vernon.

"What's this 'us' shit, Vern? You got a mouse in your pocket?" remarked Amos, shaking his head.

"What? Come on, Amos. This will be a gas!"

"Come on yourself. We shouldn't even be down here never mind creating mischief."

"Yeah but it's twenty bucks … each!"

"Fuck" muttered Amos reluctantly against his better instincts. Forty bucks would go a long way back in town.

28

THEY SPENT THE REST of the day gathering supplies for tomorrow's mission. Brett purchased lighter fluid and a garden spade from Callahan's and asked Willie for two paper bags. Willie looked at him crosswise, but wasn't about to question the kid who was always in there spending money.

"Mom's cooking out tonight and we need the bags for trash," said Brett seeing the look on Willie's face.

'I suppose that's how they get so fucking rich. Won't spring for a box of Glad Bags,' thought Willie as he put the kid's change on the counter saying nothing.

"Come on," said Brett out on the porch, "I know where there's a lady with a Great Dane."

The boys pedaled out to the Fells Pond section of New Seabury and parked a distance from the lady's house. "She'll be walking him anytime now. She does it every day. You can set your watch by her," explained Brett. "If we're lucky he'll take a dump in the mulch area on the other side of the driveway. There should be plenty more there too. All we need! Then she'll walk it up to the tennis courts and back."

"How do you know all this shit?" whispered Timmy as they sat out of sight a few houses down.

"I told you, I've been planning this for a long time. Usually after Callahan's, I go to the tennis courts to play or practice and I see this woman walking the dog everyday!" explained Brett.

"Shhhhh! She's coming out!" hissed Amos pointing at the house.

Sure enough the great gray beast with white spots came enthusiastically out of the front door, dragging his master heading straight for the other side of the driveway. The master had a choke chain and was able to control the beast. When it got to the mulch, he sniffed around till he found a previous deposit, which gave him the inspiration to cock his haunches and produce a fresh creation. Satisfied, he proceeded to an oak tree at the end of the driveway and lifted his leg, signifying to all other dogs and animals … "MINE". Then he proceeded to lead his master on their regular daily journey.

"Who's collecting the shit?" asked Vern.

"Me and Timmy," said Brett. "One of you go up a few houses and make sure she doesn't come back and the other stays here and covers the other direction. If anyone comes, let out a bird call signal."

"What????? What makes you think we can do bird calls?" asked Amos.

"You're Indians! Mingo on Daniel Boone always used bird signals," replied Brett exasperated.

"Who the fuck is Mingo?" asked Vern.

"You know, on TV," said Brett.

"We ain't got a TV," responded Amos.

"Fuck it, just go 'Ahwho … ahwho'," said Timmy getting nervous.

"What kind of a fucking bird is that?" asked Vern smiling.

"I don't fucking know ... an owl ... a fucking owl," said Timmy wishing to get this over with.

"Owls sleep during the day," said Amos rubbing his chin and chuckling. "Just go, we'll let ya know if someone comes. We'll yell, "Someone's coming!"

Brett gave Timmy the spade and he took the spare bag. Amos went in the direction of the dog and lady. Vernon stayed where he was.

Timmy began scooping the feces into the bag Brett held open. "Watch it! Don't get it on my hands!" hissed Brett holding the bag. After collecting the sixth load, Brett said that should be enough.

The boys rode back to Callahan's and parked in the grove behind the store.

"Okay, we'll meet back here tomorrow about the same time," said Brett.

29

AT CALLAHAN'S THE NEXT day, Brett went over the plan again. Thursday was pool-cleaning day at the Simmons'. "I'll show you where my house is and how to get in the backyard to the pool and which slider leads to my parents' bedroom. A chain link fence surrounds the backyard. The yard's surrounded by woods in the back. I'll show you a place you can quickly get to so you can see what happens without them being able to see you."

"Where you going to be?" asked Amos with arched eyebrow.

"After I show you this stuff, I'm going to the tennis courts and hang out there being seen by the staff so I have an alibi. That's why you're getting the twenty."

"Each!" reminded Vern

"Yeah, each," confirmed Brett.

"Don't you want to see this?" asked Timmy with Southie common sense.

"Fuck no. This is my attempt to make it go away, which it won't for long."

After an awkward moment of silence and looking at feet Vern said,

"Okay, let's do it?"

Brett beamed as the plan he had been working on for so long was coming to life.

30

THEY BICYCLED TO BRETT'S home in the Highwood section of New Seabury. Brett showed them the gate to the backyard pool and then the place where they could watch the action. From that vantage point, he pointed out the slider to the bedroom. He reinforced his previous instructions, "Remember, the pool guy will be here soon. He'll go out back do the chemicals, test the water, and start skimming the pool. Soon my mom will come out with a drink and lead him back to the bedroom. Give them fifteen minutes ... then do it!" He stared at his three accomplices then noticed ... "Hey! None of you have a fucking watch!"

Amos looked at Vern and said, "We're Indians, we got the sun."

Brett pondered this and said, "What if it was cloudy?"

Timmy piped up, "I can count to 60 fifteen times."

"And I can count to 900," added Amos.

"I'll meet you at Callahan's later," said Brett.

Brett didn't figure 900 out till he was at the tennis courts.

After Brett left, Timmy looked at Amos and said, "I was thinking of using fingers and toes, which would be good for twenty minutes."

As they were laughing, "The Pool Man" van pulled in the driveway. A blond tanned twenty something with a muscular body jumped out anticipating one of the side benefits of his low paying summer job. Life was good! He was always up, so to speak, for the Simmons' on Thursday, the Marino's on Monday, the Goldman's on Tuesday, and the O'Connor's on Wednesday. He'd rush through the other jobs on those days, so he'd have extra time for these.

He quickly brought his equipment to the backyard clad only in cut-off jeans and sandals, and went about his business. Shortly after he began skimming the pool, Mrs. Simmons on cue, came strolling out carrying a Budweiser and a mixed drink of some kind in a short shear robe which hid nothing. She gave the Bud to the kid and kissed him deep on the lips.

"OH MY FUCKING GOD!" whispered Timmy, gazing at the statuesque blond with the beautiful tits and legs, while he felt a rising in his swim trunks.

"Holy Shit!" whispered Vern almost indiscernible.

"Shush!" said Amos in an even a lower cadence, also sporting a chubber.

Mrs. Simmons took "The Pool Man's" hand to lead him to the house. He had laid the skimmer by the pool when he accepted the Bud and kiss. As they entered the bedroom, Amos whispered, "Start counting off your toes and fingers" to Timmy.

"Fuck the counting! Did you see her?!"

"That's Brett's mom!" replied Vern.

"Yeah, she's better than Playboy, and she moves."

"Forget that, you can jerk off later. Who's going to do what?" asked Amos marking the sun.

"I'll dump his stuff in the pool," said Vern, "you and Timmy do the dog shit, fire and banging shit."

"All right, dump it quietly. Timmy, you spread the dog shit close to the slider where he's sure to step in it. When you finish spreading it, I'll dose the bag filled with sticks, grass and crumbled newspapers with lighter fluid and place it just far enough away so it will catch his eye. Once Vern is out of the backyard, I'll light the bag. When it starts flaming, you rap on the slider and scream 'FIRE'. Then both of us screw and all meet back here. Got it?"

"Why do I do the dog shit?" asked Timmy.

"Cause you're experienced! You collected it."

"How much more time?"

"Judging by the sun, I'd say it's time."

"You don't know, do you?"

"Fuck no, you believe that shit?"

"I just was wondering. Let's go."

31

TO TIMMY, HE WAS now Peter Graves … Mr. Phelps, and the 'dun dun dah dah dun dun' music was running through his head. Vern was pure stealth. They noticed the slider to the bedroom was not closed but the screen and a shear curtain was. They crouched close to the bedroom and listened. Herb Alpert was playing on the stereo and there were sound of passion and bed frames creaking filtering to the outside. Amos signaled Vern to begin. No sound was created as the skimmer and its hose were disconnected, gently placed in the pool and sank to the bottom. For good measure, Vern took the chemical basket, unscrewed the tops and placed it in the pool. All the chemicals escaped as the weight of the containers caused them to sink to the bottom. Vern signaled he was done. Amos signaled him to get out.

A noise came from the bedroom as Amos and Timmy were on either side of the slider. Mrs. Simmons was wailing "OHHH YES! OHHH YESS! OHHH YEEAH!" The Pool Man was going "UNHNNN, UHHNNNN, UHNNNNNN, EHHH." Amos pointed to the bag of shit in Timmy's hand and proceeded just off the small deck, soaking his bag with lighter fluid.

Timmy dumped his bag in the area where "The Pool Man" would be sure to step when he saw the fire. Then, using the outside of the bag, he spread it to cover a larger area. Timmy looked at Amos. Amos lit the bag. The flames rose slowly, then high. Amos screwed. Timmy banged on the glass screaming "FIRE! FIRE!"

The last thing he heard as he screwed was a curse in unison, "WHAT THE FUCK!"

32

THE BOYS WERE BACK at the hiding spot, panting and sweating when the chaos ensued. Unfortunately, things didn't go exactly as Brett had planned. Evidently, the concept of a woman liking to be on top never entered the mind of a thirteen-year-old. Missionary was the norm. As a result, mom was the first out the slider, hastily trying to gather her sheer robe in the process. Her bare foot caught a healthy pile of poop causing her to slide and fall awkwardly on her arm, which was trying to close her robe. "The Pool Man" was close behind with semi-erect tool losing its gusto.

"AHHH, SHIT!!!" screamed mom as a bolt of pain shot through her arm.

"FUCKING NO!!! NOOOO!!!" screamed "The Pool Man" completely naked, sidestepping fallen mom and the shit looking past the burning bag seeing all his stuff had been thrown in the pool.

"HELP ME! I THINK MY ARM'S BROKE!" Mom was lying in poop clutching her arm and writhing in pain. "THE FIRE! ASSHOLE!!'

'The Pool Man' ran past the burning bag to the pool pulling at his blond locks in all his nakedness seeing his equipment at the bottom screaming "FUCK, FUCK, OH FUCK!"

Mom screamed propping herself up with her good arm, hand sitting in another wad of dog-do, "WHAT ARE YOU DOING??? GET BACK HERE AND HELP MEEEE!!!"

Amos, Vern and Timmy had all they could do to control their urge for exclamation. All Brett's mom's privates were in clear view. Under other circumstances, this would be cause for a major boner. But the fact she was in pain and lying in shit negated them from getting chubbers. Things had gone wrong. 'The Pool Man' was the one supposed to step in shit and get a hot foot from putting out the fire. But he proved to be only interested in his stuff.

"*We gotta get out of here*" whispered Amos, "*this ain't gonna be good.*"

The boys left as 'The Pool Man' dove into the pool to retrieve his stuff while mom tried to get back on her feet. 'The Pool Man' managed to scramble his equipment out of the pool before he felt the burning sensation permeating all over. He also, noticed his amber skin had turned a glowing scarlet as a result of the chemical overload that had been released in the pool. Panicked, 'The Pool Man' ran back into the house bumping the bent over Mrs. Simmons sending her face first into the poop, resulting in another ear rattling shrieking scream.

This didn't stop 'The Pool Man', as he was intent on getting to the shower to ease the intense pain engulfing his entire body. His mind kept rattling "I'M FUCKED! I'M FUCKED! I'M SO FUCKED!" never giving a second thought to the plight of Mrs. Simmons.

33

BRETT SHOWED UP AT Callahan's a couple of hours later. Timmy, Vern and Amos ran up to him, "What happened? What happened?"

"What do you mean, 'what happened'? You tell me. I haven't been home yet. Can't, till suppertime. That's what she gives me the twenty for. Did you do it?"

The three boys looked at each other.

"What? What's a matter? Did you do it!?" pressed Brett.

"Yeah we did it," responded Amos slowly "but it didn't turn out exactly as planned."

"What ya mean?"

"Well … err … your mother was the first one out … and stepped in the dog shit … she … a … slipped … she said she thinks she broke her arm."

"Christ! What about the dickhead pool guy?"

"He avoided the shit, ignored the fire and jumped in the pool after his shit."

"What happened then?"

"Don't know we screwed."

"It's four-thirty, I'll head home and see what's up and we'll meet back here tomorrow at noon."

"NO!" said Vern. "We'll meet behind the church just outside of New Seabury at noon. Your mother screamed after she fell. No telling what happened after we left or who saw us leaving the neighborhood. We'd stand out like a sore thumb – two darkies and a carrot top."

"Okay, behind the church then. I know where it is." Brett left not knowing what waited for him at home.

34

THE BOY'S WAITED ANXIOUSLY behind the church, sitting on the pavement with their backs against the foundation. The temporary structure served as a place of worship for the Catholics of South Mashpee. They wondered what Brett had learned and whether he'd show.

Brett showed, out of breath on his bike. "My mom's arm is in a cast! The pool guy's fucked! Probably lost his job and in the hospital with chemical burns all over! I can't stay long, Dad's coming down today!"

"Wait wait wait! Slow down!" said Timmy. "What happened when you got home?"

"Nobody was home. There was a note on the table from Mrs. Marino. She said she took mom to the hospital, should be back soon. Told me to cook a TV dinner for supper. It also said to call Mrs. O'Connor if I need anything."

"What did you see in the backyard?" asked Amos.

"The shit was on the deck, the bag had burnt out leaving a black spot on the lawn and the pool smelled like chlorine from 20 feet away!"

"Sorry man, we screwed up," said Vern remembering as they all did the visage of Brett's mom's naked body writhing on the deck in poo.

"No you didn't! Mom's okay. She'll be out of action for the rest of the summer and you really fucked up the pool guy. I overheard mom talking to Mrs. O'Connor on the phone this morning from upstairs in my room. Told her all about what happened. Seems like her, Mrs. Marino and Mrs. O'Connor were all screwing this guy and trading stories! Dad's pissed because he has to come down and get the pool fixed. Mom told him the pool guy accidentally dropped his chemical basket in the pool and dove in to get it. They're both pissed because their summer sex life is put on hold till next summer. The pool guy's fucked because his company has to drain and refill the pool, free! IT IS FUCKING PERFECT! Here you go, twenty for each of you as promised!" Brett passed out the twenties.

"Wow!" said Amos.

"Are we gonna see you again?" asked Timmy.

"Anybody say anything about the dog shit and burnt lawn?" queried Vern.

"You're okay. Mom asked me what I was doing yesterday. I told her I was playing tennis with Joe O'Connor, which I was. Mrs. O'Connor confirmed it. So I'm in the clear. And she won't be asking anyone if they saw anything. She hosed off the deck this morning and called the landscaper and had him replace the burnt spot with sod cut from the way back."

"So, what now," pressed Timmy?

"Well, the gravy train is over, but I can still hook up with you guys, if it's okay … but not at Callahan's. I got to get going though. Dad should be here soon."

"Let's meet here tomorrow at 10," said Amos.

"10's good. See you then."

Brett took off leaving the boys to ponder. Vern broke the silence. "We're fucking rich! We should go to the movies!"

"We should be in the movies after what we did!" added Amos.

"What da ya mean?" asked Vern.

"Never mind, let's go get a soda or something. And don't go flashing your money around. People be wondering where we got it."

35

THUS CEMENTED THE BROTHERHOOD of the diverse quartet. A secret shared … the first but not the last. They shared a magical summer which would span three months for Timmy and Amos, and twenty-four years for Brett and Vern. They met at the church the next day as planned. Over the course of the summer they grew close. In latter days of August, running out of ideas as to how pass the days, Vern said, "Hey! Let's see if we can find Sarah Screecham's place!"

"Who the fuck is Sarah Screecham, your girlfriend?" asked Timmy, amused by the name.

"No, she's … was … a witch," answered Amos, remembering the tales his mom would tell Vernon and him when they were little. "She supposedly lived in the woods by Witch Pond, over by the tennis courts. The pond was named after her. "

"A fucking witch!? Neat!" exclaimed Brett.

"Yeah, a shape shifter too!" added Vern sensing the excitement of his audience. "You ever hear of Black Bellamy?"

"No, who the fuck was he, a slave or something?" asked Timmy.

"Black Bellamy was a pirate!" Amos continued. "Black Bellamy was messing around with Sarah's sister, Hannah who lived on Grand Island off Cotuit. Sarah left Grand Island before Bellamy came into the picture and set up shop at Witch Pond. Hannah became the custodian of Bellamy's treasure and kept it secret by burying the poor bastard who brought it there. Some say Hannah couldn't resist the temptation of admiring the treasure and dug it up only to have two blue long dead hands lunge out of the sand and strangle her! They say her screams can be heard to this day on the night air on Grand Island!" Amos waited for the effect to sink in.

"So why is Sarah the witch and not Hannah?" ventured Brett.

"Cause once Sarah moved to South Mashpee, the game dried up everywhere except around Witch Pond, where she lived. And when the Indian hunters would hunt there, they couldn't hit shit with their arrows or bullets." added Amos.

"She was really a hooker, and the hunter's arrows and bullets weren't shooting game. They concocted this story to explain why they came back with no meat!" Vern quickly chimed.

"Fuck you Vern, you don't know shit except your own fantasies!"

"Hey, it just makes sense. She must have been real good at witchcraft of a different nature! If I lived in that time, I'd be hunting there every day!"

"Come on let's see if we can find her hut!" Timmy interrupted desiring a new adventure.

For the rest of the day the boys traipsed through the woods to Witch Pond. Once there, Amos said they should circle the pond 30 feet from the shoreline looking for rocks or wood. One hundred and eighty degrees from their start point, Timmy saw rocks, many rocks.

"What's that!?"

"Looks like a collapsed chimney!" whispered Amos approaching the pile. "Very old."

"So that's it? A bunch of rocks that might be a chimney?" said Timmy after a big letdown.

"No, no, no" said Vern. "This might be the place. Let's each take a quadrant and check out the ground for more stuff and move outward."

"Like what?"

"I don't know, wood, metal, stuff poking out of the ground. We'll start back to back and move outward." The search was uneventful for about ten minutes, until the lower half of Brett's body disappeared. His whole body would have vanished if he hadn't managed to grab a tiny holly bush.

"FUUUCK! HELP! I'VE FALLEN IN A FUCK'IN HOLE! GET OVER HERE!" Brett felt the holly start to shift as if its roots were becoming dislodged. "HURRY!!!!!!!!!!"

They ran to Brett and found him with two or three of the holly roots still holding. Only his head, shoulders, and arms were still visible. "QUICK DO SOMETHING! IT'S SLIPPING!"

Amos and Vern grabbed his wrists. Timmy, trained by his aunt, a C.N.A., who had showed him how to get grandpa out of his lounger, lay prone on the ground and reached down in the hole for Brett's belt or the back of his pants. Between the three of them, they were able to extract the hefty Brett from the hole.

"Shit, that was close! No tellin' how deep that fucker is!" exclaimed Brett as he gingerly rubbed his aching arms. The other boys sat and lay on the ground looking at the hole. "What is this, a trap or some sort of den for an animal?"

Amos answered, "No animals that big live in the ground around here. This may be what we're looking for, some kind of tunnel that she used for disappearing. How big is this hole?"

Starting at the edge where Brett clung to the holly bush, Amos made his way with his hands along the circumference. He pushed aside the ages of leaves. Under the leaves were criss-cross patches of marsh reeds, holding the weight of the leaves. He completed the circumference revealing a hole of almost three feet in diameter. "Big enough to fit a person, and someone made that mesh of reed to hide it. Nearest marsh reeds are about a mile away.

"Let's go in!" urged Timmy.

"I don't think so," said Vern. "If Brett's feet were not touching bottom when we pulled him out, there's no tellin' how deep it is or what's at the bottom. Could be a trap with poison spikes."

"If it is a trap," said Amos "it was for small animal like a raccoon or two legged animals like Brett, because it's not big enough for a deer. But Vern, you're right. If we're gonna explore this, we better be prepared. Today we should find some more long sticks to replace the reeds Brett busted through and cover up the hole again. Then we should set a mark so we can find it tomorrow. We'll need flashlights, pocket knives, and a long rope ... and water."

"Why water?" asked Brett. "There's a whole fucking pond right over there. Carting water in here is heavy. We can just get it here."

"Alright, smart ass, canteens or bottles, something to carry the water in. Can you and Timmy come up with a pocket knife, flashlight and canteen for each of you?" asked Amos looking at them.

Brett nodded and Timmy added "Sure and we have a coiled up clothes line rope down in the basement!"

"Great bring that. We'll meet at the 'Tennis Facility' sign tomorrow at eleven. Cover up the hole." The boys gathered sticks and leaves and set up a marker in the vicinity of the spot.

36

"NOW WHAT?" ASKED BRETT as the group reached the hole the following day.

"First we fill up our canteens and jar in your case, Brett," smirked Vern.

"I've never been camping! It's all I could find!"

"Yea, yea, let's get water."

"Why do we need water?" asked Timmy innocently.

"Water? It's good for a number of reasons," answered Amos. "My dad says if you ever take a trip, bring water. You can drink it, wash wounds, put out fires, and soften earth. Who knows what we'll need it for."

"Let's not get crazy here. This may be a short trip, like ten feet." Brett intoned thinking this Indian shit was getting a little out of hand.

"I'm getting water, you do what you want."

"Okay, I'll fill up my jar."

"We'll tie this rope to the oak over there and drop it in the hole," directed Amos when they returned.

"Hey! Why don't we tie the other end of the rope round a log or rock and lower it in the hole till it hits bottom. Then we can figure out how deep the hole is before we go in," exclaimed Timmy.

"Why don't we just shine our flashlights down the hole first and see what we see," chuckled Vern.

"Yeah!" said Brett as he knelt down and began clearing the leaves and mesh support from the hole. The others joined and pulled out their flashlights and shined them into the hole. "It's only six or seven feet deep! And then it curves off!"

"We should use the rope anyway," said Amos.

"Okay, who goes first?" asked Vern surveying the faces.

"Me, Me!" exclaimed Timmy.

"I'll go first," said Amos.

"Why you," responded Timmy wanting to be first.

"You know what to do if a badger's down there?"

"A what?"

"A badger!"

"No, what do you do if a badger's down there?"

"You get the fuck out of there as fast as you can before he rips you to shreds!"

"So … what are you saying, you're faster than me?"

"No, I've seen your skills at handling a bluefish, and at least I have seen a badger and know how they move."

"What the fuck, do you think, you're Marlin Perkins or something?"

"Who the fuck is Marlin Perkins?"

"He's the guy with Jim on Mutual of Omaha, on TV. He wrestles alligators and all sorts of animals. Jim actually does all the shit, Marlin sits in the boat and talks about it."

"Timmy, I told you, we don't have a TV. But I've seen a badger in real life. They're viscous little shits. I know their sounds and actions."

"Okay, you go first, but I'm next."

"Yeah, but wait till I say come down, I don't want you in the way if there's a badger down there. This is the plan, I go down the rope first. When I get around that turn and can see what's ahead, I'll call Timmy. When Timmy gets there, Brett comes down."

"Why am I last," asked Vern upset.

"Cause if things go wrong, I need someone I can depend on to be on the outside."

"Oh … Okay," said Vern, realizing the compliment.

37

THE BOYS DESCENDED. FINALLY, even Vern went down. The tunnel ran almost flat but still descended after the bend. The four of them were bunched up on their hands and knees trying to see what lied beyond the reach of their flashlights.

"Turn off the lights for a second, I think I saw something," whispered Vern. They did but second thoughts were 'What are you crazy?' Yet Vern was right, they could all see a dim oscillating light at the end of the tunnel.

"Come on," said Amos. He crawled forward using the oscillations to light the way. They followed. After a short distance, the tunnel ended in a cavernous cave within which was a rotating translucent globe. It emitted a low continuous humming noise that they hadn't noticed earlier. There was a two-foot drop to the cave's floor from the tunnel. Amos hopped down, "Wait here. I'm gonna walk around this thing. There's about three feet between the thing and the wall of the cave."

"What is this thing?" asked Timmy.

"I don't know," said Amos.

"This is fucking weird!" said Brett.

"Yeah Amos, I don't know if we should be fucking around down here." added Vern.

"Let me go around it. You guys should be able to see me cause you can see through the globe. If you can't see me yell, so I know."

"Wait! I'll follow ten feet behind you," said Timmy, "you face the globe and I'll face the wall of the cave. Maybe there are some instructions or something on the wall."

"Okay, but stay close," said Amos, "and tell me if you see anything and I'll do the same. And you guys keep an eye on us and let us know if you can't see us."

"Okay," said Vern and Brett looking at each other and nodding.

Amos and Timmy made their way around the cave. Amos checked the ground ahead and what was within the globe. He could still see Vern and Brett, and assumed they could see them. Timmy scoured the cave wall from floor to ceiling but saw nothing odd, just dirt and rock. Their circumference around the globe was uneventful. Timmy and Amos found nothing. Vern and Brett could see them though blurred, the whole time until they came back from the left. Amos figured it was about 40 yards in diameter.

"So what is it?" asked Vern when they were all together again.

"A clear giant rotating testicle!" said Timmy, attempting to relieve the tension.

"Fuck you, this is weird!" said Vern.

While the others were arguing, Amos turned toward the globe and slowly stuck his hand in, and pulled it out. It was like slowly penetrating a bubble without it bursting. "We can go in this thing!" exclaimed Amos.

"What'd ya mean?" exclaimed Vern frustrated with his conversation with Timmy.

"Where's the rope?" asked Amos.

"I left it at the bend in the tunnel," said Vern.

"Go get it!"

"You go get it. Who made you the boss?"

"I'll get it," said Brett as he scampered up the tunnel before anyone could object.

"How much more rope we got Brett," asked Amos as Brett dropped back into the cave.

"I don't know, about 15 to 20 yards I guess."

"Perfect!" stated Amos. "I'm going to go in!"

"Are you fucking nuts?" screamed Vern.

"While you morons were arguing, I stuck my hand in and pulled it out. Nothing happened! Now I'm going all the way in, but I want a rope tied to me so you can pull me out if something goes wrong."

"Wait, you guys just went around the whole thing and didn't see anything. Why do you want to go in it?" asked Brett.

"Cause it has to be something! Somebody dug this hole and this thing is at the end," Amos reasoned.

"What if it turns you into a raccoon or something," answered Vern.

"Why would I turn into a raccoon?"

"Well, Amos, you know as well as I do that the hunter who killed Sarah Screecham said he shot a deer and then never found it. But the next day he went to Sarah's hut and found her dead from a bullet wound. So … maybe she came down here to go back and forth … or … shape shift. But that time she fucked up."

"Fuck Vern, the hunter probably shot her and concocted the story about the deer. You doubted the story yourself!"

"Yeah, until I saw that fucking thing! God knows what it does!"

"Well let's find out! If I turn into a raccoon, pull me out. That must have been how she did it, if the story's true. More than likely it isn't. It was just a plain old simple murder. And why the fuck would I shift into a raccoon when she was supposedly a deer."

"Cause you're smaller than her and you look like a raccoon. You still didn't answer what this thing is!"

"Well I want to find out!"

"I'll go with him!" intoned Timmy.

"Man, you'd run into a brick wall for the fun of it, wouldn't you?" answered Vern.

"Maybe, if there's a chance of coming out on the other side."

"You fucking Irish guys are crazy!"

"Not yet Timmy. If something happens there's a better chance of the three of you pulling me out than the two of them pulling the both of us at the same time. I'm going in."

Amos tied the rope to his belt and walked through the rotating translucent membrane. The boys watched him walk towards the center of the orb his head swiveling around and up and down. Then further he walked … something was happening … he was fading! "HEY!" screamed Brett. "COME BACK! SOMETHING'S WRONG!"

Amos couldn't hear them over the dull hum of the orb. He was also too mesmerized by what he saw!

"HE'S GONE!" yelled Vern. "PULL HIM OUT, NOW!"

Vern, Timmy and Brett yanked on the rope. There was resistance. Amos felt himself spun around and pulled to the ground. He could see the rope but could not see his friends on the other end, just wall and holes … many, many holes. He felt himself being dragged back. Was it the boys, or something else?

The boys yanked again causing Amos, who was attempting to get on his feet, to go face first into the dirt. "FUCK!" Amos yanked back.

"FUCK, SOMETHING YANKED BACK! KEEP PULLING!" commanded Vern.

Amos managed to get to his feet and dig his heals in so he controlled the speed at which he was being pulled back. He couldn't see them outside the membrane because there seemed to be just walls and holes pressed against the membrane wall. It seems as if the path Timmy and he had used to circumnavigate the perimeter of the orb was gone and the earth had compressed around the orb, creating thousands of new holes in the process. There was only one hole he and Timmy noticed while circling the cave, the one they came in. Now there were thousands and thousands! And the orb seemed ten times larger on the inside! The rope led to one of those holes … he could not see what lay in it. Common sense told him it was them, but irrational sense wondered if it was. What did they see to cause them to pull him out? None of this made sense at all.

"PULL!"

"HEY, HE'S STARTING TO FADE BACK IN! LOOK!" exclaimed Brett.

"Why is he resisting?" asked Timmy.

"I don't know, let's get him out!" ordered Vern.

They continued to pull. Amos continued to resist, not knowing for sure what was happening.

"Come on! There's three of us and one of him, FUCKING GET HIM OUT!" Vern started pulling harder as did the others. Amos's feet started moving faster still trying to dig in. He could still see nothing except the rope to the edge of the membrane and the blackness of the hole to which he was being pulled. Finally three outlasted one and Amos popped through the membrane seeing his friends were on the other end of the rope.

"What the fuck did you do that for!?" yelled Amos as he and they fell to the ground, chests heaving.

"Are you, you?" asked Brett.

"WHAT THE FUCK???"

"Yeah it's him. Aliens don't know the word 'Fuck'." answered Vern.

"Why did you guys do that?"

"You faded then disappeared! Why did you resist?" asked Timmy.

"Disappeared??? I couldn't see you guys … inside. Things are different in there." Amos laid back and rested contemplating what he saw. The others waited for him to speak.

38

"LET'S GET OUT OF here," said Amos, "Bring the rope." Amos got up and started to climb up the tunnel, then stopped and returned. He examined the path around the orb. He proceeded to circle the orb again feeling the earthen wall as high up as he could reach.

"What's he doin'?" asked Timmy.

"I don't know," said Vern.

"Come on let's go," said Amos as he returned from the other side.

"But …"

"I'll tell you when we get out," said Amos to Brett as he climbed up the hole taking the rope with him.

When they all got out, Vern asked, "Now what?"

"We get heavier branches and shit to cover up the hole. Nobody can find this. I don't know why, but I'll tell you what I saw after."

The boys did as they were told piling up branches that had fallen from nearby trees over countless winters and storms, undisturbed. Amos had untied the rope from the oak and laid it under gathered leaves. After a suitable pile had been assembled, Amos said "We'll spread out, each ten feet from each other and then walk in a circle around this hole. We'll …"

"What?! Amos? Why …"

"If you let me finish, VERNNNN … we're looking for other holes, I saw other tunnels in the orb, but not when you pulled me out. I want to make sure there are no other holes."

"How many other tunnels?" inquired Timmy.

"Thousands! Just do this. I'll tell you what I saw after we do this circle."

"Thousands?"

"Yeah, maybe more. Let's just do this so I can figure this out."

The boys did an uneventful circle covering a fifty-foot radius from the hole. They returned to the crumbled chimney and waited for Amos to speak.

"When I was inside, the orb was ten times or more bigger than when I was outside. The dirt walls seemed to be compressed against the wall of the orb. In other words, the path, Timmy and I took around it was gone. And there were tunnels ... holes ... like the one we went down ... everywhere! There were so many holes! And they all would change position ... like one of those puzzles you hold in your hand, with a bunch of tiles and one's missing and you slide the tiles around to solve the puzzle. Remember, the orb looked bigger from the inside. And when you guys pulled me, I couldn't see you till you pulled me through."

"Yeah! As you kept walking towards the middle, you faded and disappeared," added Brett. "That's why we pulled you out!"

"But I was still there. You couldn't see me and when you pulled, I realized I couldn't see you, I didn't know what was pulling me. The rope was still there though. That's the key! We can't go back in that thing without a rope. And if we're going to see where another hole goes, we need more rope cause the holes don't go back here ... and they move around."

"Go back in?" asked Brett incredulously.

"Yeah, go back in. We got to figure this thing out."

"Ehhhh, ... Amos, if we're going back in, why did we pile all that shit back over the hole?" Vern replied.

"Cause we're going back in tomorrow, early, like eight in the morning! Today we got to get more shit."

"Like what?" asked Timmy.

"Like more of that rope you brought. You got anymore?"

"No."

"Then we got to buy some. We also need lighters or matches for each of us, and some sort of weapons."

"Weapons?" Vern arched his eyes, "What the fuck you think is gonna happen?"

"I don't know, but whatever happens I don't want to be standing there with pocket knives. The lighters are to make fire or light if the batteries in the flashlights die."

"I can get a bunch of lighters and matches," said Brett, "my Mom and Dad smoke like chimneys, they're all over the house. You and Vern got to get the rope though, the nearest hardware store is in town by where you live. Here's five bucks to get some."

"Thanks!" said Amos, "Vern, we got to get there before the store closes."

"Wait! What kind of weapons?" asked Timmy.

"I don't know … something you can carry on you while your hands are free and crawling through tunnels." said Amos.

"Okay …" replied Timmy trying to figure out a suitable weapon.

They left and went back to their bicycles. After Timmy and Brett left, Vern turned to Amos and asked, "Why are we doing this again?"

"I don't know, but I know if I don't, I won't be able to stop thinking about it."

"Whatever, you say Amos. Curiosity killed the cat. I hope it don't get us kilt."

39

"WHAT DID YOU GUYS bring?" asked Amos as a new day had dawned on Witch Pond.

"I got four lighters and four books of matches," said Brett, "one each for each of us."

"What about a weapon?" asked Vern.

"Well, I got this sling-shot and some BB's. I made it to shoot birds and squirrels."

"Fantastic," exclaimed Amos as he examined the homemade weapon crafted from the V of a young tree with a strip of bicycle inter-tube rubber serving as the sling and a sneaker tongue serving as a pouch. "How far can it shoot?"

"I don't know, maybe 20 feet to do damage."

"Ever hit anything?" asked Vern skeptical.

"Yeah, Billy Goldberg, he stole my lunch money.

"And your parents didn't take it away from you?"

"No, nobody knew what happened. I was twenty yards away and

hidden. He thought a bee stung him. Nice welt on his ass! He couldn't sit right for days."

"Christ, you're a regular assassin, Brett. Remind me never to get on your bad side," chuckled Vern turning to Timmy.

"I brought a shillelagh!" beamed Timmy proudly displaying his weapon of choice.

"Shillelagh? What the fuck do you do with that? It looks like some sort of hammer or something."

"Exactly! It's blackthorn wood, an old Irish weapon. Mom and Dad brought it back from Ireland. It's been sitting in the basement. Some are walking sticks … others are short hammers like this one."

"What's that writing on the side?" inquired Brett.

"May you be in heaven before the devil knows you're dead."

"What does that mean?"

"I don't know, they say it at wakes. What did you and Amos bring?"

Amos produced a cork screwed stake with a large eyelet on the end, a coiled up clothesline rope just like Timmy's and they each produced long blade hunting knives.

"Wow! Nice knives! What do you use them for?" exclaimed Timmy.

"Gutting large game," said Vern matter-of-factly.

"What about the squiggly thing?" inquired Brett.

"This is our lifeline," explained Amos. "We screw it in the ground inside the orb and tie each of the ropes to it so we can get back."

"What do you think is going to happen?" asked Timmy.

"I don't know. But I saw the holes move and I want the ropes anchored. I don't want the ropes moving too. It's like the crumb trail in Hansel & Gretel."

"God, you think a lot, don't you?" commented Brett.

"And you don't, Mr. Pool Man Ambush Master Planner?"

"Good point."

They climbed down the hole hearing the drone of the orb as they got closer. Vern and Brett were apprehensive about what was to come. Timmy was excited, having his shillelagh's rawhide strap wrapped round his wrist. Amos was Stanley determined to find Dr. Livingstone. In this case, Livingstone was a story of a she named Sarah Screecham.

40

"COME ON," SAID AMOS as he walked through the membrane of the orb. Timmy followed without hesitation. Vern and Brett had the look of someone waiting for a dentist's drill to hit a nerve as their leg and outstretched hand entered the membrane. Relief flooded over them when nothing happened. They joined Timmy and Amos in the center of the orb. They were astonished at how the thing grew when you were on the inside. The whole perspective was different. The walls of the cave had compressed on the orb. And the holes! They were everywhere! Moving every few seconds like the letters on the arrivals and departure board which hung from the ceiling at major train stations. Timmy was looking all around turning slowly with mouth agape.

Amos was busy twisting the stake into the ground. When it was firmly planted past the coils, he tied the rope from the hole they had come in to the eyelet at the top. Then he did the same to the other rope, uncoiling it and laying it on the ground. He walked to the wall of the membrane.

Vern noticed and asked, "What are you doing?"

"Quiet, I'm thinking. I want to see something." Amos continued peering at the wall watching the rope which was visible up to the membrane. Then the holes shifted but the rope remained constant. Now it clearly ended in front of another hole. The rope had not moved but the holes had. Amos sat on the ground and contemplated this.

"What's the matter?" asked Brett.

Amos snapped out of his thought, "Two of us got to follow this rope back out, up the tunnel to the oak and make sure everything's the same."

"What d'ya mean … the same?" questioned Vern.

"The hole moved and the rope didn't. Before we do anything, I wanna make sure we can get back."

"So what if it isn't the same?" asked Brett.

"I'll go!" said Timmy.

"Wait, fucking Timmy! What are you thinking, Amos! What's going on?" pressed Vern.

"I … think … nothing's wrong! But I want to be sure."

"So, who's gonna go out! You an' Timmy here? What if it has changed? Changed like what??? WHAT'S GOING ON IN THAT SKULL OF YOURS!"

Amos exhaled exasperated that he had to explain the theories that had rolled around in his head prior to being able to confirm them. "All right we'll all go out, see if it's the same. If it is we'll come back in."

"IF IT'S NOT, THEN WHAT?"

Vern was beginning to irritate Amos. "THEN WE'LL FIGURE IT OUT! COME ON!" Amos turned and walked through the membrane. The others were left to look at each other in confusion, but quickly grabbed hold of the rope and followed Amos.

As before, the orb seemed small from the outside and the path around it was back and there was only one hole. The rope was vibrating as Amos was well up the tunnel. They followed. When they emerged from the tunnel, everything looked the same. Amos was examining the ground and brush. "IT'S THE SAME! Here are our tracks and the brush is here!"

"Yeah … and?" prodded Vern.

"The rope is constant, but the holes change! I knew it from the last time! Now it's confirmed!"

"Okay Mr. Science, so what does it mean?"

Amos looked at Vern with a smile and said, "This half is safe! I'm sure the other half is too, as long as we got the rope."

Vern, Brett and Timmy looked at Amos as if he was speaking Chinese. Brett muttered to Vern, "If the rope's so fucking important, maybe we should get some metal cable."

"Come on, let's go back in. We're wasting time," said Amos as he headed for the tunnel again.

41

AMOS WALKED AROUND THE edge of the membrane wall examining the holes.

"What are you looking for?" asked Timmy.

"Don't know yet, but I'll know it when I see it. Come over here Timmy, stand next to me. Now reach out that shit-stick or whatever you call it at the dirt around that hole. Try to mark the dirt." Amos pointed at a particular hole that seemed to be right in front of them.

"It's a shillelagh!" said Timmy as he took a whack at the dirt. "DID YOU SEE THAT!!!"

"Yeah," said Amos.

"WHAT? WHAT? What did you guys see?" asked Brett coming over with Vern.

Talking basically to Timmy and deep in thought, Amos said, "When the shit-stick went through the membrane, we couldn't see it anymore. I couldn't see your hand either till you pulled it back in. And there's no mark on the wall."

"Yeah that's what I saw," said Timmy, "but I didn't notice there was no mark. And it's a shillelagh not a shit-stick."

"That means there's a path around the orb by that hole just like our hole! I'll be right back!" Amos ran to the rope, followed it through the membrane and up the tunnel.

Vern was able to get out a trailing, "Wait …" before he was gone. "Where's he going?" asked Vern to the others.

"I donno, he's your brother. Should we go with him?" asked Brett getting anxious.

"I bet he's getting a longer shit-stick," volunteered Timmy, figuring out the puzzle. "He wants to mark the holes, but can't reach them without exiting the hole."

"Why doesn't he just jump out and mark them and jump back in?" questioned Brett.

"Cause I don't know how the holes move yet!" said Amos coming back through the membrane with a five-foot branch. "They might move anywhere. We could be here all day trying to find where it moved to, if it moved before I came back in."

"Yeah, but … couldn't that be true even if we're on the inside and it moves and we can't follow it?" inquired Timmy.

Amos pondered this, Timmy could be right. "Fuck it! Watch for the mark and try and follow it!" Amos waited for the holes to move again and when they did, he thrust his branch at a random hole and like Zorro, roughly traced a 'z' on the wall when the end struck solid. He pulled back the branch. Sure enough there was a hole with a crudely marked 'z' against the membrane wall. "KEEP YOUR EYES ON THAT HOLE WITH THE 'Z'! IT'S GONNA MOVE!" screamed Amos.

All the boys fixed their eyes on the 'z'. Then just as when a train departed at Grand Central Station and the big board would clack and change, all the holes moved. The 'z' moved horizontally one position to the right.

"It's right next to where it was!" exclaimed Brett.

"Keep watching!" yelled Amos, waiting for the next move. Again the holes move and again it moved horizontally next to where it had been. Amos took out his knife and marked an 'X' in the ground inside the membrane. And carved out 'Up 4' meaning the fourth row of holes up from the bottom. "No one step on this," said Amos indicating his marks on the ground.

"Why?" asked Vern getting impatient with being left out in the snow.

"Cause now we can figure out what hole we want to try," said Amos as he walked to another position at the membrane looking up and down then moved to the left.

"Shit! You got something in mind! Don't you?" said Vern knowing Amos.

"I do," answered Amos.

"What?" said Vern exasperated at having to drag it out of him.

"I'm looking for another hole with marks!"

"What kind of marks?" asked Timmy.

"Don't know. I do know that Sarah Screecham probably knew about this 'thing'. Because everybody thought she was a witch. She supposedly lived right next to it. And probably made regular use of this thing to avoid or 'disappear' from people."

"Yeah guys who stiffed her after she porked them" interjected Vern laughing.

Amos ignored him and continued, "She has to be the one who made the reed mesh cover from the marsh. She had to have used this thing in some way. And if she could find the tunnel she came in, I'm guessing she must have marked it in some way so she could get back. There's no other rope here or sticks like we brought."

"You ever thought she was really a witch and created this thing with the help of the Devil?" asked Timmy seriously.

"I don't believe in witches," said Amos. "All legends are exaggerated stories blown-up by each teller over the ages. Everybody spread out, and look for a hole with marks."

"Ya mean like that one with four 'SS's around it?" asked Brett pointing to a hole on the bottom row then moving one hole to the right as the holes changed.

42

AMOS RAN BACK TO the center of the hole, grabbed the second rope and the long branch. He waited for the 'SS' hole to shift again. "Come on, this is the one!"

"The one what?" screamed Vern.

"The hole we're…" The hole shifted one to the right. Amos thrust the branch in the center of the 'SS' hole, without finishing the thought. He turned to the others, "I'm going, come if you want to. If not, I'll come back after I tie this rope off wherever it goes."

"Wait…" yelled Vern, again too late as Amos was gone through the membrane.

"Fuck! He did it again!"

"I'm going too!" said Timmy as he grabbed the rope and exited the membrane.

"Shit…"

"I think we should go too Vern," said Brett.

"WHY?!"

"Cause I think we should stick together and not get separated."

"He said he'd come back and … never mind grab the rope and let's just go!" Vern and Brett grabbed the rope and followed. Sure enough, there was a path around the shrunken orb and only one hole with four 'SS's visible from their vantage point. The hole however, was the same proximity to the path as the hole they came in and not by their feet as it appeared from inside the orb.

Amos had taken his flashlight out of his back pocket and turned it on as he crawled up the tunnel. Sure enough as he expected, he came to a mesh reed screen, although these reeds were green and fresh as opposed to brown and old. No light passed through, meaning leaves were on top. He was lightly pressing the mesh looking for the 'give' point when he heard behind him, "Hey!"

"Timmy? You came?"

"Yeah."

"Hold the rope and the flashlight and shine it up here."

"Okay."

Amos resumed testing the mesh with both hands now. He found the give point.

"HEY! YOU GUY'S UP THERE?" bellowed Vern from the bottom of the tunnel.

"SHUT THE FUCK UP!" hissed Amos in as loud a whisper as he could manage.

"Did you hear something Brett?"

"Yeah, someone sort of whispering."

"What did they say?"

"I don't know, I couldn't make it out."

"WHATTTTT!" screamed Vern.

"Fuck! Timmy, get down there and keep them quiet. God knows what's outside this hole."

Timmy left the rope and flashlight and scampered backwards down the hole to where Brett and Vern were standing staring in the hole for another message from above.

When he appeared, he was whispering "Shhhhh! The hole is covered and we don't know what's outside!"

"You mean you ain't been outside yet?" asked Brett in a low tone.

"No. You know the mesh cover you fell through? Well its back, unbroken and the reeds are green."

"Shit, are you guys sure we wanna go up there?" asked Vern getting nervous, more nervous than usual.

"Come on, be quiet," said Timmy as he made his way back up the tunnel. Brett and Vern followed doubtful of their choice.

When Timmy got to Amos, he asked, "You find anything?"

"Yeah, which way the mesh opens. Is that Vern and Brett?"

"Yeah."

"You guys … can you hear me?" Amos whispered to the shadows past Timmy's butt.

"Yeah, this is nuts, Amos," whispered Vern.

"Just be quiet. I'm gonna lift the cover enough for me to get out. You guys stay here till I check it out."

"What if there's something there?" asked Brett.

"I'll either yell 'Help' or 'Run'. If I yell 'Help', everyone come out with your weapons. If I yell 'Run', get back to the orb, cut the rope to our hole and go back up our tunnel. Don't forget the rope! Bring it with you."

"How will you find your way back then?" asked Vern, concerned.

"If I yell 'Run'… it's really, really bad, and I ain't comin' back and I DON'T want whatever I see to come back either."

"Timmy, switch places with me. I'm not going back no matter what he says. You and Brett can cut the rope."

"Vern, if I say 'Run' there's nothing you can do! Go back with them!"

"Shut up Amos! I'm staying no matter what you say! How do you know if you're gonna make the right call! I'm covering you no matter what."

Amos looked at his brother and realized that he would do the same. "Timmy, change places. Vern if I yell 'Run', wait! Don't come out and be prepared for something to come in. If nothing comes in, wait and listen and use your senses, like when we hunt."

"Okay."

43

AMOS SHIMMIED OUT OF the tunnel with the rope, barely lifting the mesh covering. He quickly looked all around like a nervous chipmunk on the lookout for predators. The area was basically the same but not. It was wooded but the trees and undergrowth were different. Some of the same species but also others he had not seen before. He crawled into the underbrush. It seemed safe enough, but then the smell of smoke reached his nostrils. His first instinct was to head to where the pond would be. As he suspected – maybe hoped - it would be coming from a fully intact chimney, which was collapsed ruble by their hole. That would go a long way to validating the theories he had about what the orb … but first things first. He had to tie off the rope and get back to the boys before they got antsy and started jabbering about what was going on and what they should do.

He spotted a large birch, which could serve as a tie off point while keeping the rope reasonably well hidden from a casual passerby. There had been no birch trees anywhere near their hole, only oak and pine. He tied off the rope and crawled back to the mesh covering the hole. "Come out now, but stay low and follow me. The coast is clear," he whispered. Vern, Timmy and Brett made their way out of the hole following Amos's example and crawling to the underbrush. They huddled together, the others digesting the similarities and differences of this place and theirs. "This place ain't ours," said Brett in a low tone.

"We'll see," said Amos. "Let's head to where the pond should be. Vern, we go like we're stalking game. Timmy and Brett, that means like that Marlin Pecans guy and Jim when they're sneaking up on things."

"It's Perkins," said Timmy "and I know what you're saying."

"Is that smoke I smell?" said Vern.

"Yeah, I think it's from the crumbled chimney which I don't think is crumbled here," answered Amos.

"Here? What are you saying here is?" inquired Vern suspecting he knew the answer.

"I'll explain it if I'm right…" and started to move. But this time Vern had his hand on Amos's shoulder before he got up. He would not be left with a trailing "Wait…" again.

Vern turned him around, "No you'll tell us now! The rest of us ain't walking into this with our pants down and innocent!"

"What the fuck does that mean?" asked Timmy to Brett.

"It means Vern doesn't want to get fucked by whatever idea Amos has in his head, if it turns out to be true,"

"All right, I'll explain," said Amos plopping back down.

"How did you figure that out Brett?" whispered Timmy amazed.

"Shut up you two!" said Vern, "Let Amos tell us before he decides to bolt again."

Amos took a deep breath, "I think the orb thing is some sort of doorway through time. Like a time machine, but not a machine like we know machines. We can pass through it like a bubble. It rotates with nothing driving it. It changes what's on the outside when you're on the inside but when you're outside you can see the inside and nothing is changing."

"A fucking time machine! Neat! Who put it here?" said Timmy in a hushed tone.

"Don't know, aliens, God, humans in the future … I don't know" continued Amos. "But we went looking for the hut of Sarah Screecham and we found crumbled rocks, this hole and the orb thing. When I saw the thousands of holes and then we looked for other holes above ground and found none … I was confused. The legends say she was a witch. Which means she could do tricks, cause there ain't no witches…"

"How do you know there aren't any witches?" challenged Timmy.

"Okay, I don't believe in witchcraft, I've seen shamans doing their stuff, they use tricks."

"But…"

"Let me finish! I think she was using the orb to hide from the guys who came to see her and she didn't want to see them. She must of found the hole by accident and figured out she could cover her tracks from the hut to the hole as opposed to running away and having these guys track her to wherever she went. Remember, according to the stories these guys were hunters, but they were also trying to get something on the side. So I think she took care of the guys she liked and hid from those she didn't. And those were the ones who created the legend cause they wasted the day trying to find her and returned with no food."

"You think too much Amos," said Vern. "So you think 'SS' is the real Sarah Screecham and this is the hole in her time."

"Yeah, I do and I think she is the only person who may know how this thing works."

"So you plan on sitting down and having a chat with her?"

"I hope so."

"Her sister supposedly killed fucking pirates!"

"Are you coming with me? Cause I'm going."

"Jesus! When you get a bee in your bonnet there's no stopping you is there?"

"No. You sound like Mom."

"You sound like Dad, with all these fucking theories."

Timmy and Brett looked at each other realizing they were on the outside looking in as far as this conversation was going.

44

THEY FOLLOWED AMOS TOWARDS the pond crouching all the way and were greeted with the vision of the chimney in its infancy with cabin attached and smoke emanating from it. "What are we going to do?" whispered Timmy as the boys gathered at the edge of the underbrush before the clearing around the cottage.

"I think we should wait here and see who comes in or out," said Vern.

"I'm gonna go up and scout it out," said Amos.

"Me too!" said Timmy.

"Fuck, here we go again!" exclaimed Vern.

"Let's all go, it's better when we're together," interjected Brett, getting sick of the arguing. He got enough of it at home when his mom and dad were together.

Silently, they approached the cabin, keeping low. Amos reached the small window and looked in and saw only a crude bed, table, two stools, and a pot hung to simmer from the hearth of the chimney. He also saw a small window on the other side of the cabin. "Vern, I don't see anyone. Come here and watch while I go around to the other window and check out the blind spots."

"Okay, Timmy, you go with Amos and watch his back. Brett, you stay here and cover mine," hissed Vern.

"Ehhhh, how do we do that?" asked Brett.

"We're going to be looking inside, you guys watch the outside and warn us if someone's coming," said Amos.

"Okay, but what if someone comes?" continued Brett.

"We run like hell!" said Vern.

Brett didn't like the sound of that. He was the slowest of the bunch. But he kept his thoughts to himself.

Amos and Timmy made their way around the cabin passing a closed door on the way. Vern kept watching the inside for any signs of movement or a shadow indicating someone was inside. Brett scanned outward, nervous as hell.

Amos's head popped up in the window across the way. He looked around now being able to see the rest of the cabin and the other side of the one door they had passed. There was no one home. He whispered across to Vern, "I want to go in. There's no one here. I'm goin' in through this window. There's a door to your left, you Brett come in through there."

Vern nodded okay.

Amos turned to Timmy. "Listen, you stay outside. If anyone comes back, they'll come from the side with the door. That means you can see when they come in from this window. If that door opens, after the rest of us are in, you lay low and wait. You're our safety net. If they capture us, wait till they sleep or leave again and see if you can spring us."

"Okay," said Timmy, his heart beating and savoring the excitement of this adventure. This was even better than swiping candy from Connolly's on L Street back home.

Amos scrambled through the window. Vern and Brett came through the door. They all looked around the sparsely furnished cabin. Timmy watched the door intently from the window. Amos examined the contents of the cabin, a couple of buckets, ladle, plates, bowls, spoons, forks, knives, mugs, rags, a straw broom, basin and lanterns with urns of oil. Vern went to the pot over the hearth and dipped his finger in the broth and stuck it in his mouth, definitely, venison, onions and other spices which weren't readily apparent to him. It was good though, so much so he dipped his finger for a second taste and looked around the room for a spoon.

Amos found a chest. In it were women's clothes. This had to be 'her' place. Now he had to decide how he could stage their meeting. He sat on one of the stools. Brett had already occupied the other.

"Now what do we do?" asked Brett.

"This stew is pretty good," said Vern.

The door slammed open and a girl, no more than twenty five years of age, with pale skin discolored by dirt, flaming red hair, piercing blue eyes, and two flintlock pistols, cocked and pointed at the boys, burst into the room. "WHAT ARE YE RUNTS DOING IN ME HOUSE!"

Timmy slinked down from the window and listened and thought 'Oh shit! She has guns.'

45

THE THREE BOYS STOOD with their mouths agape from the combination of having guns pointed at them and having a stunning though soiled beauty on the other end of them. Amos was tongue-tied ... the objective of his quest was in front of him and overwhelming to his pubescent senses. He was expecting someone older, more ragged. She was ragged but beautiful! Vern who had no objectives said, "We're just looking for something to eat."

"LIAR!" she pointed one of the pistols at Vern's forehead. "SPEAK THE TRUTH FOR I KNOW WHAT IS TRUE! AND TELL YOUR CRIMSON HEADED FRIEND OUTSIDE TO COME IN OR I'LL BLOW YER HEAD OFF!"

"Timmy! You better get in here now!" said Amos snapping out of his stupor, realizing his brother's life was in danger.

Timmy came through the door and Sarah motioned with her other pistol for him to get over with his friends while keeping the other trained on Vern. "YE CAME OUT OF ME HOLE! I'VE HEARD ALL YER TALK! SO ... TELL ME ... WHAT ARE YE DOING IN ME HOUSE! AND DON'T LIE! OR I'LL KILL THIS LIAR!" staring directly at Vern. "YOU TWO INDIANS SHUT UP. I DON'T TRUST INDIANS! YOU, THE FAT QUIET ONE, TELL ME YER PURPOSE!" Her eyes set on Brett and he was scared to the point of wetting himself.

"I can explain," started Amos.

"QUIET, INDIAN! I WANT TO HEAR FROM HIM!" pointing the tip of a pistol at Brett.

Brett broke down like a two-dollar watch, which in hindsight probably saved Vern and Amos from a molten ball in their bodies, and Timmy and he from a life and death struggle with a wildcat with two pistols that would have been quickly converted into swinging hammers. "We found this hole when we went looking for your hut."

"HUT? HUT?! THIS AS FINE A HOUSE AS YE WILL FIND AROUND HERE!"

"No, that's not what I mean! We're from the future! You are a legend ... we heard stories of you when we were younger ... or Amos and Vern did and told us. We were looking in the woods to see if we could find where you had lived … your house. We found that chimney, pointing to the hearth, crumbled and in a pile. Then we found the hole thing."

"Yer clothes are odd like none I've ever seen," said Sarah bringing it down a notch. "All of ye, into that corner by the hearth. Fat One, ye stand in front of them. The rest of thee sit. I want to hear more." The boys did as they were told. "Tell me about the hole, Fat One."

"The name's Brett. That Indian is Amos and the one you have your other pistol on is Vern. You already know the crimson-headed one is Timmy. Are you Sarah Screecham?"

"I'LL BE ASKING THE QUESTIONS, FAT BOY BRETT! Ye just tell me about the hole."

"Well, we went down it and there was this rotating globe thing. And when you went inside, everything changed and there were thousands of holes and the dirt walls move in. But when you go out the walls go back to where they were, but only one hole remained ... the one you're connected to. We came out your hole and saw your house, fully intact and the chimney smoking. We had to investigate. We've never time traveled before! This is all new to us."

"WITH THOUSANDS OF HOLES TO CHOOSE FROM WHY DID YE PICK MINE?"

"Cause we were looking for your hut … I mean house. Then we found this hole within the orb and Amos decided that it is what we were looking for. He wanted to find a hole with marks and I saw the hole with the four 'ss's around it and he got excited and said that's the hole we want."

"Sit down Fat Boy Brett. Stand in his place Indian Amos. So ye seem to be the leader. Tell me leader and the knower of me story, why are ye looking for me?"

Amos looked directly into her beautiful eyes, "As Brett told you, we're from the future, 1968 to be exact. We were looking for something to do. In our time, you are history. You are a legend, whose story is told over and over again to young Wampanoag children by their mothers."

Sarah pondered this. If what they said was true, there were stories about her that lasted 250 years. What had she done that merited that? She was a hermit in the forest. She had serviced the locals to make ends meet. Where was the legend in that? It had to be her use of globe of

Satan. “What stories were ye told?!”

“I don’t think we should tell her,” said Timmy. “It could cause history to change!”

“Did I say ye could talk crimson headed ONE?” Sarah shifted the pistol that was on Vern to Timmy. Vern breathed normally again.

Timmy’s words were not lost on Amos, “If I tell you the stories, you have to tell us how you used the globe thing.”

Sarah let out an honest laugh. “Indian Amos, didn’t yer father ever tell ye, you’re in no position to bargain if the other party is pointing a pistol at ye.”

“He told me if you don’t ask you’ll never know.”

“That be true. Now what are the stories?”

“You sure you want to know?”

“I WANT TO KNOW! NOW TELL ME!”

“The stories say you were a witch.”

“A WITCH!?”

“Yes a witch. That pond outside your cabin is called Witch Pond, after you in our day.”

“Why was I thought to be a witch?”

“Ever since you moved to the pond, the Wampanoag hunters claimed the game dried up. They said you could disappear and were a shape shifter. They said when they found game you bewitched their arrows and bullets so they missed their mark.”

“So that’s how they explained their afternoon romps to their wives! And this is the home built by me father who has long since passed. I did not move here I was raised here,” said Sarah distantly.

“So you’re not a witch or a shape shifter?” asked Amos.

“I know not what a shape shifter is. As for a witch, I wasn’t, but believe me I’ll make them think I be from now on! I bewitched their ‘arrows’ all right … made them straight … and their bullets always fired, but no more. They’ll have a witch all right, not only at home but here!”

“That’s exactly what Vern said!” said Brett understanding completely the undertones of words. Timmy was lost, focusing on the pistol.

Vern slammed his elbow into Brett’s ribs.

“Oow!”

“So Indian Vern, ye did not think this story to be true! Thee are wiser beyond yer years. Is that the only story, Amos?"

"Yes."

"How do I die?"

"Don't know," lied Amos.

Sarah knew he was lying when his eyes dropped to the ground. But she let it go, not really wanting to know herself. "Ye can sit with the others Indian Amos."

46

"Do ye want some stew?" asked Sarah after contemplating what had been revealed.

"Yeah!" said Vern enthusiastically having already sampled it.

"I'm beginning to like ye more and more Indian Vern," said Sarah with a sly smile that melted Vern except in one place. "Take off yer clothes and put them in the corner."

"Take off our clothes?" asked Brett perplexed.

"Yes, I see ye came with weapons and if ye come from the future God knows what other magical instruments ye may be hiding. And Indian Amos, I will tell thee what I know about Satan's globe."

"Take off your clothes and do as she says," commanded Amos excited about the prospect of learning about the orb. The boys stripped to their skivvies carefully insuring their clothes and weapons were in separate piles in the corner.

"Now stand over there side by side, and make a slow circle."

The boys stood side by side naked except for their underpants, all were sporting chubbers due to the erotic nature of their situation, except for Vern who was sporting a full-fledged boner after her last compliment to him.

"Ye boys remind me of yer great, great grandfathers! Sit! Except Timmy the Red. Get four bowls and a ladle and serve the others." Sarah observed, looking for unnatural bulges. Timmy served a bowl for each and sat. "Good, what do ye want to know about Satan's orb?"

"Have you ever tried another hole?" pounced Amos.

"Yes, once and never again," answered Sarah pulling up a stool. "I just use the hole for hiding from cheap hunters I don't want to see now.

I cover the tracks to the hole and they think I disappear. Thus they call me a witch, to my thinking."

"What happened when you tried another hole?" pressed Amos.

"I came out in a time when trees and thickets were missing for miles and miles. I wandered about minding me way. The pond was gone but the oceans were closer, both north and south. I could see both from a nearby hill! The land was almost barren … just sand for as far as me eye could see. I saw tracks of beasts like nothing I'd seen, large enough where I could lie inside without touching the edges. I headed back to the hole. Then in the distance, I saw a huge bird-like thing with long pointed beaks coming out the front and back of his head! It was a hundred times the size of the biggest eagle! It be a beast of evil like no other! And it saw me and turned. I ran. I was like a squirrel in size to it! I got to the hole and crawled back in but not before seeing this bird had no feathers and had skin like a serpent! It could have been the devil himself! I decided the hole was a creation of Satan."

"Did you mark that hole?" asked Vern.

"No I was scared and hurried back to my hole."

"How did you know which one was yours?" Amos quickly asked.

"I had marked that one before I tried another hole."

"With an 'SS' on the four corners?"

"Yes, ye already know that!"

"The holes move, the one you tried must have been far, far away from yours. Where was it when you went in?"

"It was Indian Amos. It be on the opposite side at the bottom of the globe."

"How did you get in it if it was so low?"

"When I used the hole to hide from the hunters, I brought me bow. I would tie hemp to the arrow. To pass the time, I would shoot at the holes. Then I would retrieve the arrows by following the hemp through the globe to the hole it had lodged. No matter where the hole was inside the globe, it was always five hands above the path around the globe when I came out. Devil's work I say."

"We should leave," said Amos.

"LEAVE?" exclaimed Sarah rising from her stool. "WHERE DO YE PLAN ON GOING?"

"Back to where we came from," said Amos.

"Ye aren't going anywhere! I've told ye what I know about Satan's globe. Now ye will tell me what ye know! Start by telling me about 1968!"

"We don't know much about the globe. This is the first place we came to find out more about it. As far as 1968, I don't know where to begin. It's been over 250 years since your time!" said Amos.

"Tell me anything! Can ye take me back with thee?"

"NO!" said Amos, Timmy and Brett in unison.

"Sure!" said Vern simultaneously.

"Vern! We can't take her back anymore than we can stay here," explained Amos, "it can screw up the future … hers and ours."

"What's not to say this is not part of the future? I mean coming here and bringing her back."

"Because that means her future as we know it already will not be, which means our past to now might not be! Fuck, we may not even be!"

"So ye know me future," said Sarah softly.

Amos realized his slip, and looked at her as a boy who had been caught in a lie. "Sarah … that thing is 'Satan's globe' as you have named it. It brings us knowledge we should not know and the temptations it opens up can only be evil. We should go back to our time and bury this hole and seal it. As far as you, you should use it to hide only and not try other holes no matter how tempting. Take comfort in knowing the mesh cover you built was still intact in our time, meaning that in more than two hundred and fifty years no one has found the hole. And when we get back we'll make sure no one else will."

"So is knowing me future one of those temptations?"

"Yes."

"Then go!" said Sarah with resignation in her voice.

Amos, Timmy and Brett went to the corner to get in their clothes and weapons. Vern stood looking at Sarah. "If they're gonna seal the hole, I'll come back before they do. I swear."

"I think temptation is talking. But that is sweet of ye Vern," Sarah caressed her hand along his face and kissed his forehead. "Yer undergarments are stretching to their limits," casting a glance down below. "Go get dressed with the others," she said waving her pistol in the direction of the corner. "We'll both see what the future will bring."

47

SARAH'S WORDS WERE PROPHETIC. Curiosity killed the cat … or revived it! Nice saying, which has a basic foundation in truth. The boys would leave Sarah's time and go back to their own, taking their two ropes, weapons, and corkscrew stake with them. Brett remembered to grab his water jar which he had left on the path surrounding the orb. But what Amos had learned from Sarah about the hole and his thirst for knowledge would make him unable to resist temptation to venture back in and thus change all their lives.

Ironically, what Sarah learned from the look on Amos's face when she questioned him about her own future, caused her to avoid the hole altogether, believing her track covering skills to avoid cheap tricks were sufficient. They wouldn't have been. The legend would have come to pass had not Vern stalled joining the others and whispered still in his skivvies "Quick! Tell me something about Hannah no one else knows. I'm coming back to get you when I am older and bring you back. If I tell you the secret about your sister Hannah, you will know it's me."

Sarah stopped and starred at Vern considering his proposition. How did he know about Hannah? She looked at the other boys seeing they were hastily getting dressed and intent on gathering their things and getting out of there. She took a chance and bent and whispered to Vern, "Hannah is me brother, Henry. The bearded one likes him to dress as a woman, and will kill anyone who suspects he isn't one."

Vern looked her in the eye with confusion. Sarah hissed, "Remember that and I will know."

Then she raised her voice, "STOP YOUR NONSENSE YOUNG VERN! CONTROL THAT THING BETWEEN YER LEGS AND GET DRESSED WITH THE OTHERS AND GO!" She accompanied that with a wink.

The seemingly minor transgression of time by the boys had changed what may have been … a history written before the transgression. Each trip into the hole thereafter would do the same! And there were more. Which history would come to pass?

1992 NEW SEABURY AND BEYOND

48

POMARAT SIGNALED HIS BRAVES to break formation. The angry men who chased them were now pre-occupied with what they found in the Finch home, namely the gutted Mrs. Finch. Pomarat had his braves follow as he ran through the underbrush heading north. He was scanning the ground all the while trying to pick up a sign of the boys. By his reckoning they had completed a full circle around the hole.

What he didn't realize was that when the boys drove them back into the tunnel with fire, he had retreated and chose another hole which came up in a different time. Nor did he realize it had been a full day until two of the four boys followed them back down the hole that had been scorched and then to the hole he had taken. And thus the two boys had come out behind them. If Pomarat had backtracked and continued his circle round the hole, he would have crossed the boy's tracks when they re-emerged. But he didn't and decided to head north to his home turf, or where his home turf had always been.

"Crestid farstif arminkin arsted fen takar sinctoe femiss bot! Fedle trap da fhat de skefaram!" yelled Pomarat. They would go back to the river and follow it to the great lake and from there follow their trails to the great marsh ... to their tribe, a trip that would take less than a day on a straight run, but could last a week when confronted by a changed world. Massot, Sarkem, and Hysko were happy to be heading home.

The journey started uneventful, but Hysko signaled to stop as he tried to understand the strange sounds he was hearing. The band crouched and listened. There were the sounds of the armored beasts with the crystal eyes, which apparently could not see or smell but wandered aimlessly. They were getting accustomed to these. But there were voices in the distance ... voices saying phrases meaningless to Hysko, like "Thirty love!" and "Match point!" But the new mysterious sound was "Twunk-ping"! There were many of them and they were continuous and new to his keen sense of hearing. He looked to Pomarat. Pomarat signaled them to continue to the river. There were too many voices for their small band to deal with. The new sound puzzled him too, but now was not the time to investigate. It was time to make their way home and replenish their band to six.

They continued not realizing one of those voices was the fat boy that they had chased down the hole, now a man twenty-four years older and no longer fat. Nor did he realize that one of the armored beasts belonged to another of the boys, now a grown man also. The other two boys were still boys and were also approaching from the other side of the tennis facility, but made no sound.

The band kept going and encountered a hard surfaced path similar to the one they saw out the front window of the Finch residence, but wider. The road paralleled their intended path so they kept off it crouching down every time an armored beast went speeding by and there were several. "These beasts seem to be more plentiful than humans," thought Pomarat. "They are blind and can't hear! Why do we stop!" Pomarat ordered his men to ignore the passing beasts and keep up their pace to the river and stay well away from the hard surfaced path.

Things were going smoothly until they came to a hovel similar to Mrs. Finch's but more spread out and having over twenty armored beasts apparently at rest just outside. Pomarat signaled the band to gather round him at the edge of the woods. In their own language, Pomarat explained what they already surmised. "We must get past this hovel and the sleeping beasts and cross that hard surface to the woods on the other side to get to the river! From what I've seen, each beast usually carries a human rider and that would mean there are many inside that hovel. We are but four and there are at least twenty beasts here. We must carefully pick our battles in this strange world. We will stick to the tree line to the right and cross the hard surface to the river. If a beast awakes without its rider, run to the river! Do not try to kill the beast. They are lethargic and seem to bear no menace except when directed by their rider and their riders seem to be inside the hovel."

The wisdom of their leader and his powers of his observation amazed the braves. That's why he was the leader and they weren't. They started towards their goal of the river and were halfway there when a hard charging beast sped into the hard surfaced pasture where the other beasts were sleeping. This beast was different! It had no top! The rider was clearly visible and was female with fiery red hair and the beast was blaring a sound that was alien to the band.

49

COLLEEN HAD FORGOTTEN TO set her alarm after a night of partying. She happened to open her eyes and see the clock at 10:00. She rolled over to continue her lovely rest, but something in her subconscious roared to her frontal lobe. "FUCK! YOU'RE LATE AGAIN!"

She jumped out of bed as a jumble of thoughts tried to rearrange themselves into coherent stream. "Oh shit!" and the memories from her childhood converted it to song "I'm late! I'm late, for a very important date. No time to say Hello. Goodbye, I'm late! I'm late! I'm late!"

She jumped into the shower, popped back out and did her best to make herself presentable for work as the Resort Accounting Manager at the 5-star resort known as New Seabury. She was supposed to be there at nine but would probably not show up till eleven, not that it mattered, the Controller was her friend and the CFO was preoccupied with other shit. But there were the ancillary other departments that she was responsible for monitoring. They were always looking for ways to cut off her balls, which she didn't physically have. That didn't keep them from believing she did based on her demeanor.

"Fuck this is the third time this month!" she thought as she popped a cassette by the Rolling Stones and started up her Jeep Wrangler. 'Shit, I didn't put the top on last night. Thank God it didn't rain.'

She sped to New Seabury with *Sympathy for the Devil* blaring from the speakers, thinking I got to get my shit together. She whipped into a parking space at the reception center and grabbed her bag, rummaging through it for her office keys, hoping she could pass unnoticed when she went in. But deep down she knew that was futile. There were always snipers in the trees who were all too eager to try to pass news of her lateness up the ladder, surreptitiously of course. Today she would definitely not be able to slip in under the radar.

She happened to catch movement up on the knoll in front of her Jeep. She focused. She wasn't drunk or even hung over thanks to her extra hours of sleep. 'What the fuck!' There were four little Indians gathered on the knoll looking at her and the one with the Mohawk was pointing at her! One pulled out a long slicing knife and began running towards her Jeep. Fuck! She reached in her bag and found what she was looking for in the special sleeve designed for something like this. Massot was at the driver's side front bumper, still on the run with Mrs. Finch's slicing knife upraised and not slowing. As he reared back his arm for a thrust to the heart, he was confronted with a fine continuous spray into his eyes which immediately blinded him and caused intense pain. This was followed by a shod foot to the face which sent him reeling back into an adjacent beast and then to the ground.

Colleen wasted no time hopping out of the Jeep and slamming her heel in Massot's groin for good measure. She made a beeline for the Reception Center as Massot screamed out, "Katou! Katou! Crit fatou skamen siek! E fatum!

The three braves stood in momentary confusion by Massot's words "Witch! Witch! She has the magic! I'm blind!" Pomarat broke the confusion ordering Sarkem and Hysko to retrieve Massot. He simultaneously knocked an arrow and let it fly at the fleeing red head.

Colleen heard the 'whizz' of the passing arrow as it lodged in the column of the portico very near her head. She did not slow but burst into the Reception lobby. "CALL THE POLICE! SOME FUCKING DWARF TRIED TO KILL ME IN THE PARKING LOT!"

"Huh?" said the lone front desk clerk in the lobby who had been playing solitaire on the computer. Colleen looked around. Everybody must be in the back offices.

"CALL THE POLICE! NOWWWW! TELL THEM THERE'S AN ATTEMPTED MURDER AT THE RECEPTION CENTER AT NEW SEABURY! HURRY!" she ordered as she returned to the glass plate door and slammed the deadbolt. The young clerk was frazzled. She fumbled the phone and wondered what the number was, then saw it taped to the counter with the Fire Department, hospital, and local clergy. Colleen looked to the knoll and her eyes met with the little shit with the Mohawk. The other two were dragging the comrade up the knoll. He stared at her long and hard trying to find some clue as to why he could not hit redheaded people with his arrows. Colleen gave him the finger and went to the back office to assemble the masses, so much for sneaking under the radar.

50

WHAT DID THAT MEAN? The middle finger upraised in an antagonistic fashion, was it a curse or a spell? Pomarat did not know. He did not like this. But no time to dwell on it, that would come later when they got to the great marsh to the north. The braves had returned with a blind hurting Massot and Pomarat told them to move with great haste to the river. Sarkem asked if they should go after the witch. Pomarat said they should head to water to relieve Massot's blindness, they were outnumbered here.

With Hysko and Sarkem supporting Massot, they crossed the road to the Reception Center and were half way across when a Mercedes SE came screaming down the road. Saul Kaufmann was late for his tee time on the Ocean Course. He saw the kids dressed as Indians crossing the road just in time to swerve to the right, hit the curb, and launch into the stone wall fronting the Reception Center. Luckily he grazed it and came to a stop. He looked back for the kids and saw them as they ran into the woods on the other side of the road. Two of them were carrying another. "Oh my God! Did I clip one? Why are they running?" thought Kaufmann. "I better call my lawyer."

He got out of the car and started walking to the Reception Center. The kids were now well into the woods and out of sight. He tried the door at the Center and found it locked and began knocking … at the same time two State Police and one local cruiser whipped into the parking lot sirens blazing. 'Fuckin' A!' thought Saul, 'How the fuck could they get here so fast!' Not having known of any of the chaos that had just occurred, he assumed it had something to do with him.

Colleen and the back office staff had seen everything from a window. Upon seeing the cruisers, she ran to the lobby to tell the officers what was happening.

"I DIDN'T HIT HIM!" said Saul approaching the two Staties and the local cop.

"Calm down! Are you the one that called?" asked the lead Statie. The two State Police cruisers came in response to the fellow officer's call from Mrs. Finch's, one from the Bourne barracks, the other from the Yarmouth barracks. They had been flying, considering the distance.

The local was Officer Fredricks, who had been manning dispatch, till Sgt. Sikes ordered him to respond to the latest call from the Reception Center.

Sikes was out of cops, Cabrel was guarding the chipper site and Dimitri and Matthews were sent to the Finch residence. Sikes took over dispatch and had called the Captain who was meeting with Selectmen on budget issues and advised him of what was going on after the Finch homicide. He also got permission to call in five other off-duty officers, leaving just enough to man the next two shifts. The Captain played this to his advantage with the selectman before he left, "Gentlemen and ladies, I've been called back to the station. There were two homicides this morning and a botched third," he paused for effect as the part-time suits' jaws dropped with questions that had not yet formulated in their brains and only came out as, "What?"

"I'm out of officers, and have to call in off-duty officers for overtime. I have only one officer at headquarters manning dispatch, and monitoring a suspect in a holding cell. THIS IS UNACCEPTABLE! I WARNED YOU THIS COULD HAPPEN YEARS AGO!" with that he left the Town Hall, glowing inside that he had left those sanctimonious assholes in suspense. Jeffery Summers, a newly elected selectman in his late twenties, asked the others after he left, "You think he staged this?"

"Jesus Christ, Jeffery, we better figure out what's going on fast. It's big and we better be on top of it or the papers will be shitting all over us," said a much older Jim Masterson, a longtime selectman and friend of the Captain. "And don't get in the cops' way!"

51

"I'M THE ONE THAT called," said Colleen, coming out the door. "They're getting away! They ran into the woods across the street."

The Statie motioned to Fredricks to come over. "What was the call? We just heard on the radio you were responding to a call at the Reception Center. We were coming because of Trooper Black's call at a Finch

Residence. What's going on?"

"Why don't you ask me? I made the call and the things that tried to kill me are getting away! You two are sitting here asking who called who!" Colleen fumed.

"Colleen?" asked Fredricks.

"What! How do you know my name?"

"I went to school with you in Bourne." Fredricks had taken over the interrogation without the Statie realizing it.

"I'm Matt Fredricks."

"Oh yeah! I remember you, you ..."

"Never mind, we'll catch up later. The caller said someone tried to kill you. I need to hear how and what they looked like, and what happened. Based on what we know, I don't think they'll get far. So tell me."

"There were four midgets, no ... dwarf Indians. One came at me in my Jeep over there with a long knife. He was trying to stab me when I shot him in the face with mace. I ran to the reception center and one of them shot an arrow at me and missed. I got inside and had the clerk call you."

Fredricks now noticed the arrow lodged in the column of the portico. Saul had made his way to the second Statie who had arrived, hearing the entire conversation. "So this has nothing to do with me?"

"Should it?" asked the Trooper noticing him for the first time. "Is that your Mercedes against the wall?"

"Yeah, I almost hit those midgets she was talking about. I thought they were kids, and I saw two of them dragging the one she must have hit with the mace after I got out of the car."

"Were you speeding?"

"What!!!!"

"Relax. You were, judging by the position of the car. But that's not important. I want you to come with me and give me your best description of those midgets. This is important! Your speeding isn't. Are you catching my drift?"

"Yeah Officer. Anything I can do to help. No problem." Saul accompanied him back to his cruiser, happily realizing this wasn't about him as he always assumed everything was.

The other Statie and Fredricks conferred out of earshot of everyone else. They compared the descriptions of the suspects and they matched.

The Statie said a chopper was being fueled in Plymouth when he left the barracks and should be here shortly. "Let's call in our findings and go from there. We need a perimeter set up on Great Neck Road, Rt. 28 and the road to Willowbend to seal these guys in. But we're out of cops for the moment, what about you guys?" asked Fredricks.

"We'll see what's available."

"Colleen?" called Fredricks, "Can you make sure no one touches that arrow? We're out of cops for the moment but I'll send someone by."

52

POMARAT HEARD THE STRANGE wailing of the sirens as the three cruisers pulled into the reception center. They were well into the woods and moving fast passing backyards of numerous hovels similar to the woman whose choice parts were contained in the satchel they carried. They had to get to water! Massot's eyes were watering like they would from the powder they used on Maushop's sons. He could not afford to lose another brave.

She must have been a witch and the young boy they followed into the hole, a shaman. She possessed magic potions and they both were able to avoid arrows. He guessed the wailing of the sirens he heard were her unleashing beasts under her command to come after them. They must get to the river and keep running. Her powers were great! Maybe she was also a servant of Maktahdou, sent here to punish him because of his earlier thoughts that Maushop's god may be greater than Maktahdou.

Meanwhile, Saul followed Colleen into the reception center after the cops had gone to their cruisers to go to their appointed positions. Colleen lit up a Winston Light on the way, and Saul asked, "Can I use the phone to make a few calls?"

"Yeah, sure, knock yourself out. Let Mr. Kaufmann use the phone," she instructed the front desk clerk who was back at her post, "and go outside and make sure no one touches the arrow in the column!"

"What?" asked the confused clerk.

"Watch that arrow in the column and make sure no one touches it! Understand?

"Yeah, okay."

Kaufmann promptly dialed up his lawyer and insurance company in that order. Then he called the pro shop to have them adjust the tee time of his group. "No problem, Mr. Kaufmann."

Colleen on the other hand was a celebrity in the back office and no one noticed her smoking inside. The inquiring minds all wanted to know. They all were filled with questions. Her lateness was off the table. Once the story was out, she'd be pursued by the press. Also, Matt Fredricks would use it for an excuse for a reunion of sorts. Things worked out after all. Though it would become a pain in the ass after the novelty wore off.

The braves on the other hand had reached the river. Pomarat ordered Massot to open his eyes and hold his breath. He had the other two dunk his head in the river and hold it till he signaled. Three dunks cured the blindness but not the sting. Massot waived the other two off saying his sight was back, but stayed on his knees and cupped water to his eyes. Eventually the sting dissipated and he could function normally.

"We go!" commanded Pomarat, "We must move fast!"

The Mashpee River had been designated a protected area and had few hovels abutting, thus reducing the temptation of mischief. But eventually it would intersect Route 28, the secondary major east-west artery on the Cape. When the braves reached it they would have to decide to pass through a strange metal culvert under the highway or cross the thruway with those screaming beasts flying by.

53

A BEAST WAS LYING IN wait, its blue antlers flashing wildly on the road above the culvert. Pomarat didn't like the culvert. It was obvious there would be an ambush on the other end. He halted his braves. "Sarkem and Hysko, you will go left and right a great distance, then you will cross the hard path to the woods on the other side. Wait until no blind beasts are coming to cross. Do not be seen! Once across double back to this point on the other side. There will be a human there who is waiting for us. Kill him! Then signal us with a whippoorwill call. I will bring Massot through the tunnel and we will continue north."

Sarkem and Hysko did as ordered. Pomarat and Massot moved closer to the culvert. The beast with the flashing blue antlers was dark blue with white writings on its side. Pomarat heard and saw other beasts continually passing it by in both directions on the path above. Their number amazed him. They seemed endless. He wondered how long it would take Sarkem and Hysko to cross the path.

Sarkem would be delayed, as he confronted a long straight sight line on the hard path and going further a large circular path fed by several paths otherwise known as a rotary. If Pomarat was amazed by the traffic on Route 28, he would be catatonic after seeing what Sarkem saw at the rotary. Sarkem decided to return and report he could not cross and why.

Hysko however, found a bend in the path with thick brush and limited sight lines in each direction. He watched the passing of the beasts for several minutes, gauging their speed and the distance across the path. For someone with such short legs his judgment would have to be perfect. There were metal guard rails on each side of the path. He could hurdle the far one but would either have to roll under or hop over the one in front of him. With his bow and quiver, he decided over.
He checked the placement of all his paraphernalia and took two steps back from the rail and waited. Then came the opportunity! Clear in both directions! Go!

He took two steps, hands on the rail, legs leaping to the side and over. He went on a dead run, little legs scrambling to cross the road and to hurdle the guard rail on the other side. Halfway across an eighteen wheeler beast carrying gasoline came barreling down on him from the east! "Shit," screamed Hysko pumping his legs as hard as they would go.

The driver of the big rig saw something, he didn't know what. His mind said kid. He slammed on the brakes and could feel he was going to lose his rig on the curve. He had been going too fast. The kid or whatever was clear so he let up on the brakes but the rear was sliding. He tried to right the skid as the rear of the trailer smashed the rail

Hysko had initially hopped over. At the same instant, Hysko hurdled the guardrail on the far side crashing into the pucker brush. He heard the deafening screech as the rear of the big beast scraped the rail. The driver now confronted the added problem of approaching traffic. He tried to get back to his lane but one vehicle clipped the end of the rig sending shards of metal across the road. Hysko got to his feet on the other side and ran as fast as he could through the underbrush back to where the culvert was without the benefit of a path. Pucker brush scraped his flesh, but he had screwed up, he was not unnoticed, the noise of his mistake was continuing.

Getting back in his lane caused him to bounce off the other guardrail, and then he saw the flashing blue lights! "Fuck!" His correction for the guardrail hit led him directly at the cruiser! "Nooooo!" the driver screamed as he slammed the brakes, but in reality there was nothing more to do. He was going head on into the cruiser and an approaching vehicle was about to broadside him … a propane truck!

54

POMARAT HEARD THE INITIAL scrape of the guardrail, the subsequent clip of the vehicle and the bounce off the far guardrail. By instinct he pushed Massot in the culvert and followed. On the other side of the culvert, the Statie who had questioned Mr. Kaufmann, left his ambush position and climbed up to the road to see what was happening. That was a mistake he would not live to regret! Hysko was almost to the other side of the culvert. Sarkem was almost to where Pomarat had given him the order. Timmy, Amos, Vern and Brett were in the parking lot at the tennis courts trying to come to grips with their unexpected reunion. Mr. Kaufmann was finally checking in at the pro shop. Colleen was sitting in her basement office in the Reception Center wondering now what? They all heard the explosion! All of Mashpee heard it.

The gasoline truck slammed into the cruiser, the propane truck simultaneously hit the gasoline truck resulting in a mega explosion heard all over Mashpee! The Statie who had been waiting in ambush had reached the guardrail at the precise moment of collision. His body parts showered Hysko who was sent to kill him. Mr. Kaufmann asked the golf pro at the desk if that was thunder. Colleen wondered, "What the fuck was that?" and went upstairs. Sergeant Sikes closed his eyes and let his chin fall to his chest as he awaited the calls with no one in the station except Bogger, and he'd take a hundred to one odds at this point, Bogger had nothing to do with any murder.

Pomarat grabbed Massot and ran out of the far side of the culvert, not expecting but prepared for someone on the other side. Flaming gasoline was now barring any return from which they came. All they found on the other side was Hysko covered with blood and body debris of the Statie who had been waiting in ambush. "Where's Sarkem?" asked Pomarat.

"I don't know" answered Hysko expecting him to be approaching from the west.

Sarkem was forty feet from the culvert when the force of the explosion knocked him on his ass and was almost beheaded by debris from the two trucks that crashed. Now he had to deal with a wall of fire as a result of the gasoline draining over the entrance to the culvert. Sarkem said screw it and ran up to the road, crossed it and ran down the other side. No one noticed as they were preoccupied with starring at the fireball in front of them. He caught up with his band. Sarkem tried to explain the rotary, but Pomarat waived him off saying they must get away from here.

Amos looked at older Vern when the explosion occurred and said, "That's them! They're here! Fuck, look at you! You're old. And Brett ain't fat. This is too much to take in."

"Yeah, well you and Timmy are still thirteen and dressed like hicks!"

"What was that explosion?" asked Brett.

"Fucking them! That's what." Even though Brett now towered over him and was built like a linebacker, Amos still talked to him like he was the chubby fat boy he met at the marketplace which was weeks ago for him and over twenty years for Brett.

"What happened to the trap door?" asked Amos staring at Vern.

"I started dismantling it." answered Vern without hesitation. "Did you happen to notice the new development approaching the hole in your travels? There's a four-unit condo planned to sit right on top of the hole. I needed time. I didn't want some land clearer tripping over it before it was time for the bulldozers. I was going to get the rest of it tomorrow, then all hell broke loose. I was buying time. Then I hunted down Brett in the phone book."

"What do ya mean, 'hunted down Brett'? You mean you guys haven't been back here together every year waiting for us?" asked Timmy realizing this was the first time old Vern and old Brett had seen each other in a long time.

Vern and Brett looked at each other, each wondering how to explain what happened after they disappeared. How their lives had changed and things moved on.

"Fuck this ain't good," said Timmy.

"WAIT! Relax," stepped in Amos looking at Brett and Vern. "Do you guys like the way your life turned out?"

"Come on, we to got chase the Pukwudgees!" insisted Timmy impatiently.

"Let's think first! Seems like the monkey's pulled the cork out of the constipated pigs butt and I don't know how the four of us can get it back in with all the havoc they started," mumbled Amos starring directly at Vern.

1968 WITCH POND
&
THE LAND OF LEGEND

55

THEY EXITED THE HOLE and it was late. "Fuck! What time is it?" asked Timmy.

"Past suppertime, the sun is low and it's the near the end of August," said Vern. No one had a watch.

"How do we explain where we've been?" questioned Timmy looking for an excuse.

"Just tell 'em you were playing tennis with me," said Brett.

"What about us, me and Amos?"

"Ah … well … I don't know," Brett said frustrated, knowing the tennis excuse wouldn't take in the Wampanoag community. "Haven't ya ever been late for supper?"

Yeah, don't worry about it. We'll figure something out," said Amos as he began covering up the hole and stashing the ropes and spike.

"I know! I'll give you a $20. Say an old woman broke down on the way back from the beach," rattled Brett, pleased by his new idea, "and she gave you $20 for changing her tire!"

"That's not necess …"

"That's a fantastic idea, Brett!" finished Vern cutting off Amos and snatching the twenty knowing they had at least another hour or so till they'd be expected home.

Amos let it go. "Let's meet here tomorrow. Bring the same stuff."

"Why?" asked Timmy, "I thought we were going to seal this hole."

"With what, shovels and rakes," asked Amos? "We need dynamite or a backhoe to seal this hole! You know anybody who can get us that? And even if we could destroy the tunnel, what about 'Satan's orb' down there? That would still be there and I get the feeling the tunnel would still be there in a future time. Look, we know no one between Sarah's time and ours has used the tunnel because of the mesh cover put there by Sarah. But someone or something before Sarah's time could be still going in and out of the orb, trying different holes and just hasn't gotten to one between our times yet. Then again … someone in between our times … could be doing the same. Or someone from the future … Fuck! I don't know! We gotta find out more is all I know."

"So we're going back in," surmised Brett.

"Ya," said Amos.

"I gotta get going," said Timmy, "I'll see ya tomorrow."

"Fuck Amos, your head's going faster than a laundromat washer on spin cycle," said Vern, "Come on, we'll come back tomorrow."

"Yeah, he's got my head spinning," said Brett as he turned and left.

Amos finished covering the hole.

Vern got their bikes, "I'm gonna go back and see Sarah, I think she likes me."

"NO YOU'RE NOT!"

"I'm just kidding, though she is gorgeous isn't she?" said Vern thinking 'Yeah, I am'.

"Yeah she is," said Amos grabbing his bike.

Vern would revisit her that night ... in the safety of his bed ... and would imagine much more than a caress of the cheek and a kiss on the forehead.

56

THAT EVENING AT THE O'Rielly residence, Mary said, "Where have you been Timothy!?"

Timmy responded, "Playing tennis at the New Seabury tennis courts with Brett!"

"And who is this Brett?"

"A friend of mine I met at Callahan's awhile back. His parents are members at the clubs there."

"Jesus, Mary and Joseph! Don't you go getting all-uppity, remember where you come from. Don't be tellin' the neighbors what you've been doing. Now go wash your hands, you're filthy and you missed supper. Colin! Timmy's been playing tennis at New Seabury!"

Colin Sr. was watching TV in the living room. "Ask him if he can get me out on the Ocean golf course on Saturday yet! I'm only allowed during the week with my non-resident status." He took another sip of his Budweiser, chuckled and turned up the sound as Mary began her indiscernible mumbling.

That evening at the Simmons' residence, no one was home. A note with a twenty was on the counter. It said that his mom and dad had gone to the Popponesset Inn for dinner and that he should go down to the marketplace and get a pizza. Brett pocketed the twenty and gouged himself on cookies, pie, chips, soda and candy.

That evening at the Otis residence, nothing was out of the ordinary. Mom was cooking supper. Dad was not yet home. And the boys came home at the usual time.

All the boys went to sleep that night reliving their day's adventure in their mind. Vern's night was especially special due to his remembrance of Sarah's warm touch. The next day they would all be back at the hole, hoping for new adventures to occupy their next evening's thoughts. Little did they know, those thoughts would be nightmares.

57

AMOS BROUGHT HIS BOW and arrows in addition to his paraphernalia from their previous visit. The others returned with their stuff. Brett had replaced his glass jar with an over the shoulder deerskin wine satchel from his parents' concert going days. His time alone last night had been productive … he had searched the cabinets and cubbies that were plentiful around the house. He also found a small can of lighter fluid that he stuffed in his back pocket.

Amos began clearing the debris off the hole and tied Timmy's rope to the oak. "You know which hole we're looking for?" asked Timmy.

"No, but I know the vicinity of the one I want to try. Somewhere to the left of the hole with the 'SS's?"

"How far?" asked Vern.

"Don't know. It's a crap shoot."

As they were repeating yesterday's journey down the hole, Timmy casually asked Brett, "Hey, why would my mom tell me not to get all uppity when I told her I was playing tennis with you?"

"Cause to Popponesset people, we are uppity. My parents have money and they flaunt it. I bet the Popponesset people are considered uppity to Vern & Amos's parents."

"Are we Vern?" asked Timmy.

"Nah, we don't think about 'em less they get in our way. You Yankees have been squeezing our land for centuries! But it's only temporary. That's what our old man says."

"But I'm Irish and a diehard Red Sox fan!" blurted Timmy.

"Not the baseball team, the people who came here on boats. He calls them Yankees," clarified Brett.

"We drove here in a car, from South Boston. So why are we Yankees?"

"Your ancestors! Your ancestors came over on a boat," said an exasperated Vern wondering why he had been dragged into this discussion.

"Come on. I'll set up the stake and tie off the rope. You guys look for Sarah's hole," said Amos putting an end to the discussion.

58

THEY ALL SCANNED THE array of holes surrounding them and moving. They stood back to back, each responsible for a quadrant of space.

"This is futile!" yelled Brett. There are a zillion holes!"

"Keep looking," said Amos.

The boys stood, then finally sat, back to back, gazing at the endless shifting maze of holes from floor to ceiling for over an hour.

"So where we going to go when you pick a hole, Amos?" asked Timmy.

"Hopefully … the land of legends."

"Why there?" pressed Timmy.

"Because I don't think anything happened around this hole between Sarah's time and ours, and probably nothing between her time and when the Pilgrims landed. Nobody was in this area on a regular basis. Yeah some Indian could have stumbled upon it by accident but I don't think so. She ended up in prehistoric times when she tried a hole. A pterodactyl attacked her! In the interim, there was the ice age. After the ice age came the Wampanoag. We have legends, which must relate to our history and our beginning. You and Brett only have a little over 200 years history here. We have thousands. I want to find the Wampanoag beginning and see if this hole was something they knew about."

"Wow, you think a lot, don't you? How do you know all this shit?" asked Timmy.

"I read. Somebody in the past knows about this thing. It could be the legends. It could be God or Satan or fucking aliens. I don't know … but I want to."

"I just want to know Sarah better!" injected Vern getting a chuckle from Brett.

"Hey? How are you gonna converse with the legends if we find them? I mean, we brought the English language, which you are using, so do you know ancient Wampanoag language?" asked Brett.

"Yeah sure we do, mom speaks it all the time"

Amos looked sideways at Vern wondering where this was going.

"Well say something in Wampanoag!" demanded Brett.

"Okay … Fuck you!" said Vern.

"Fuck you?!!! That's Wampanoag?"

"Yeah."

"No it isn't. That's a French-English term."

"Well who the fuck ya think taught them? They stole it from us."

"What does it mean in Wampanoag?"

"It means – Fuck You! We invented the term, you stole it. The meaning is the same."

Amos was now laughing.

Brett looked at Vern and saw the smirk on his face and asked, "You're shitting me, right?"

"Don't know … 'shitting me' isn't one of our phrases."

"Asshole!"

"That's one of ours though."

59

"THERE IT IS!!!" YELLED Timmy breaking the frivolity. "THE SS!"

Amos focused on where Timmy was pointing and saw it. It was four rows down from the top of the globe and would move to the right, as always.

"Shoot an arrow in it Amos! Let's go back and see Sarah!" said Vern.

"Nah-ah Vern. We're going back further. Everybody look up from that hole … look for one that's slightly different … like it's been used or nicked as if someone scrambled out of it in a hurry."

Brett, getting the concept, looked straight up. "Hey look! That one straight overhead has a bunch of nicks around the edge!"

"That's the one … the one she went into!" said Amos after checking it out. "So now … let me think …" Amos's mind raced. He roughly calculated the number of holes going to left and up from the 'SS' hole to the hole with the nicks. He divided by three and added the result to the 'SS' hole while he was fastening the rope attached to the anchor they had planted in the floor of the orb. He had his target. It was in the second row up from Sarah's hole 270 degrees to the left. It was an educated guess. The holes shifted as they had done since who knows when … it moved one space to the right. He aimed his arrow at a hole and let it loose. It lodged somewhere in the hole. "That's where we're going! Come on!" said Amos as he dropped the bow and grabbed on the rope, gently.

"So that's the hole for the Legends?" asked Timmy.

"Don't know," answered Amos, "but it's my best guess. I don't think there will be any dinosaurs here though."

"I'd sort of like to see the dinosaurs," ventured Brett.

"No you wouldn't. They'd pounce on you like an abandoned candy coated apple at the Barnstable County Fair," replied Vern.

"Fuck you … There! Now there are three of us who can speak Wampanoag. Timmy? You know 'Fuck you'?"

"What? Cut the shit. This is serious!"

"He hasn't mastered Wampanoag yet, Vern." Vern and Brett laughed but inside were apprehensive of what they were about to get involved with.

"Are you guys coming or what?" asked Amos.

They all grabbed the rope and just as Sarah had said, the hole was at their level when they exited the orb … Satan's orb. They scrambled up the tunnel, just like the one in their time and Sarah's time. When they exited the hole, the flora and fauna seemed the same yet younger, smaller and less dense.

"Let's take a walk," whispered Amos.

"Where?" asked Timmy.

"To where Vern and I live. If we're in the time of legends we should see something," said Amos.

"Amos, what makes you so sure this is the right time?" asked Vern.

"I'm not sure, but it feels right. Besides, we take a walk, we look around, if nothing happens, we go back to the hole and try another one."

"How do we find our way back," injected Tim, "what if there are no roads to follow in this time?"

"I've been breaking branches on the way since we got out. I suggest you guys do the same. There probably won't be any roads but we got the sun. Vern and I know the lay of the land."

60

AS THE BOYS REACHED what was now the intersection of Red Brook and Great Neck Rd., but then was two small trampled paths, they heard a pair of agonizing screams to the southwest. Screams of torture! Screams of pain!

Pomarat and his braves heard the same screams and turned in their direction. He could guess what had happened. There was no smoke. Maushop had returned! Their comrades had not followed orders. "Shifat nodketein!" shouted Pomarat. "Let's go! Quickly!" The braves ran north. The boys heard their voices, and then saw them coming out across a small clearing.

The two parties of four saw each other at roughly the same moment and both froze! "WHAT THE FUCK?" said Brett.

"KILL THEM!" said Pomarat.

"RUN!" said Vern.

Pomarat nocked his bow and raised it pointing at Timmy.

Amos pushed Timmy to the ground as the arrow flew over his head, "PUKWUDGEES!"

Amos nocked his own arrow and shot at Pomarat grazing his Mohawk as he shrugged his shoulders. Vern scooped up Timmy under his armpits. Massot and Sarkem had pulled their bows off their shoulders and were pulling arrows from their quivers to load. Hysko ran two steps and hurled his tomahawk at Vern. Timmy grabbed his shillelagh at both ends and lifted it quickly over his head deflecting the tomahawk. Brett grabbed several BB's out of his pocket, loaded his slingshot and fired, creating a shotgun effect startling Massot and Sarkem thinking they had been stung by wasps.

The four boys bee-lined back to the hole after this initial incursion with the midget Indians in close pursuit. The boys were bigger and had longer strides. "What the fuck are Pukwudgees!?" screamed Timmy running.

"Little evil fucks, I'll explain later … run!" yelled Amos. Even fat Brett could outrun the Pukwudgees on a short run, especially with periodic arrows flying by. They got to the hole and scrambled in and out pulling their rope and arrow with them.

"They're gonna track us to this hole," panted Vern peering down the tunnel now in their time.

"We're gonna stop 'em! They'll be freaked by the orb for awhile. Get anything that will burn! Branches, leaves, wood!" commanded Amos. "Brett, you got that lighter fluid?"

"Yeah, here."

Vern and Timmy threw everything they could get their hands on down the hole. Amos drained the can on the debris and waited, listening. "Quiet!" he commanded.

Everyone stood around the hole in silence … waiting.

Then he heard that strange language rising from their hole and the sound of approaching bodies in the tunnel. He tossed a lit match in the hole resulting in an immediate flair up and fire. Amos heard the initial screams and sounds of retreat. He smiled. "More shit in the hole, keep the fire going!"

The boys kept a steady bonfire going with debris from around the site. "Now what?" asked Timmy.

"We keep it burning for awhile" answered Amos. "I think they retreated and will choose another hole, thinking they'll flank us. But they'll pop up in another time."

"Is that good?" asked Vern.

"No, I fucked up" answered Amos, "We've unleashed the Pukwudgees on the world, though not in our time."

"So now what," asked Brett?

"I'm going to find out where they went" answered Amos.

"How?" quipped Vern.

"I'm going to track them."

"By yourself?" asked Timmy.

"Yeah"

"I'll go with you" volunteered Timmy.

"Why?"

"You saved my life when you knocked me down!"

"I gotta think about this" said Amos sitting and admiring their fire.

Vern asked, "What the fuck happened, what were those screams before we ran into those midgets?"

"My guess is we stumbled upon the exact moment when Maushop came back and discovered his sons dead and Pukwudgees in his hut. These four were probably also responsible in some way," answered Amos.

"Do you know this or is it legend?"

"Legend, but you heard the screams. That was probably Maushop ripping the Pukwudgees' arms and legs off as he did to the giant bird," said Amos.

"We should go back to that hole and find Maushop and have him help us track down the Pukwudgees," stated Vern.

"If the stories are true, I don't think he could fit in the tunnels. Besides, there's always a chance he'd think we're Pukwudgees and rip off our limbs. It's not like we can converse with him," sighed Amos.

"Yeah, I don't think 'Fuck you' will go over that well in his state of mind," injected Brett looking at Vern.

"So what now," asked Timmy?

"It's still early," replied Amos, "We got to seal this hole. We need 2 by 4's and boards, an ax, a sledge hammer, a saw, hammer and nails and one of those latches you can attach a padlock to, … and a padlock."

"I ain't got any of that shit," said Brett.

"Then you stay here and keep the fire going till we get back," responded Amos. "What about you Timmy?"

"I can get a saw, ax, sledge and the hammer and nails … and oh yeah, a padlock."

"Good! Go get them. We'll meet back here in a couple of hours. Vern, you and I will get the 2x4's and planks from Dad's wood stock and a latch from the hardware store. Brett, give us some money."

Brett didn't even ask but reached into his pocket and gave them a twenty. Then he proceeded to gather shit to keep the fire burning in the tunnel. He didn't want any Pukwudgees popping out while he was alone.

"Brett, you okay with this?" asked Vern. "Don't let that fire die. Keep it fed. We'll be back. God knows what those little fucks are thinking. Don't give them the option of coming up this hole!"

"I got it! I got to get more shit. Get going and hurry back!"

Amos and Vern then headed to town and Timmy headed to Popponesset.

As they peddled away Vern asked Amos, "So much for experiencing the 'Time of Legends'! Fuck I wanted to see the shit they been telling us about. Instead we saw trees, a few evil midgets and ran home. By the way, how we gonna get all this shit back here?"

"We get eight foot lengths and strap them tightly in two places to the cross bars on our bikes with rope."

"So what am I going to be when I grow up?"

"WHAT?"

"Man, you think everything out in no time! How do you do that?"

"Don't know … it just happens. We'll get the latch first."

61

TIMMY ARRIVED AT HOME. Luckily no one was around, probably at the beach. He quickly gathered the tools, stuck some in a knapsack and lashed the longer items to the crossbar of his bike. Vern and Amos looked like a pair of Sanford & Son's trucks carting their materials back down Great Neck Road. Timmy arrived first and the twins an hour later.

"Brett! What the fuck? You'll have the fire department down here!" said Timmy as he arrived witnessing a huge bonfire over the hole.

"Too much?" asked Brett admiring his work. "I wasn't taking any chances. I didn't want those things coming up while I was alone."

"Yeah, but the smoke! People could see the smoke and think the forest is on fire."

"I'll stop feeding it for awhile then."

"Good idea!"

The twins arrived and quickly unstrapped their wares.

"Wow! How the hell did you ride that shit back?" asked Timmy.

"It wasn't easy," said Vern, "everybody was looking at us like we stole the stuff."

"We got to wait for those flames to die back down the hole," stated Amos. "In the meantime, we got to saw these 2 by's in half and hack a point on one end of four pieces with the axe. Jesus that's a big fire! You nervous, Brett?"

"Yeah a little. I was here alone. I just wanted to make sure."

Timmy cut the studs. Amos hacked points on the pieces and Vern drove the pointed studs into the four corners of the hole with the sledge hammer when the fire was reduced to embers. They used the remaining planks and studs to fashion cross braces and a trap door. Finally they attached the latch and applied the padlock. Timmy gave the key to Amos.

"We'll meet back here tomorrow … early! At sunrise!" The boys got home by supper and were all were back at sunrise. That night Amos took his dad's .22 caliber pistol and loaded it.

62

AMOS SURVEYED THE OTHERS. "Look, I've been thinking about this last night. Timmy I don't think you should come with me."

"Why!!!" exclaimed Timmy. "I'm ready! I'm not scared!"

"It's not anything like that." explained Amos calmly, "Whoever goes in that hole, whether it is me and you or just me, could be gone for awhile. If we're gonna finish the job we may not be back here today … this time … now."

"What does that mean Socrates?" asked Vern now concerned. "Why won't you be back today?"

"Cause we or me have to track these midgets and they have a big head start … or not. I'm not sure how this thing works yet. But I do know it will be in another time, whether before or after our time. So there's a good chance we may not be back today, tomorrow or weeks from now … or maybe even ever."

"Fuck …" exclaimed Brett, the message sinking in. "You'll be missing and we'll be here! Oh wow! This ain't good."

"Right … and I think if there is only one of us missing, it's easier for the rest to stick to a story … Timmy. That's the only reason I think you should stay," said Amos looking Timmy in the eyes.

"But there's four of them and only one of you! They've been doing this shit for years … you need a second set of eyes!"

"Yeah, but if I just disappear, Vern can use the 'runaway' excuse. If you and I disappear at the same time … things get more complicated for them," said Amos.

Timmy thought about it. "Wait a minute. No one knows we know each other!"

"Willie at the Marketplace may," said Brett, "he saw us when we first met and a couple of times thereafter."

Timmy's shoulders slouched in resignation. Despite Willie being Irish and from Southie also, he wouldn't say shit to the cops but would tell his brother Colin about the meetings with the twin Indians and the rich fat boy. And Colin would go around the law to find out what happened, and that could be dangerous.

"There you go Timmy," said Amos feeling the discussion was done but not feeling really great about doing this alone.

"No! Here's what we do," bellowed Timmy drawing on all his yet untapped brain cell, as he would not be denied this adventure. "Brett, is your mother at home?"

"Yeah, of course! Eh … I didn't check before I left. Why?"

"Go home. If she's there stick with her the whole day. If not, go to the tennis courts and play or hang around with the girl at the counter. In other words, have a continual alibi. If we don't get back in a reasonable time, keep being where someone can say you were there."

"Yeah, but what about your brother if you don't get back?" countered Brett.

"Say you haven't seen me since you whipped my ass in tennis. That would ring true since I told Dad I was playing tennis with you. He might take a swing at you because of the ass whipping thing, but now you know and can duck if he does."

"Shit! You're saying I should piss off your brother, Colin?"

"Yeah, but it takes you off the suspects list. It gives you and me a legitimate split point!"

"But we never played tennis! What if he questions the staff at the club?"

"He won't! He's intimidated by the clubs. He won't go there."

"Hey, Einstein! What about me?" asked Vern. "Me and Amos go everywhere together. What do I say? And that question goes to you, Amos too since you seem set on going it alone. In that case, I'll be getting the third degree from mom and dad. Why did you run away? The runaway excuse ain't worth shit. Why would you run away?"

Amos didn't like this. Daylight was burning and time was moving on. 'THINK!' he thought to himself.

"Fuck! This is gonna waste time, but it will work," commanded Amos. "Timmy?"

"Yeah?"

"If I tried to buy a pack of cigarettes from Willie, would he sell them to me?"

"No way! He'd tell you to fuck off."

"Perfect. Timmy you leave first. Go to the marketplace and wait for me and Vern to show up. We'll be right behind you. Wait outside the store. We'll show up and talk with you and I'll go in and ask him for a pack of Marlboro's. He'll tell me to fuck off. I'll come outside and say 'Come on Timmy, I know where we can get some butts, Vern wait here.' I'll say it so he can hear. Timmy and I will go back to the hole."

"So I'm going with you!" exclaimed Timmy foreseeing Amos's plan.

"Yeah."

"Fuck yeah!" yelled Timmy happy to be going.

"What am I doing!?" yelled Vern.

"And me?" asked Brett, seemingly being left out of the scheme of things.

"RELAX! ALL OF YOU! Listen, cause the next part is very important!" said Amos, exasperated. They all looked at Amos as they stood by the hole.

"Brett, you wait here at the hole for me and Timmy to come back after making a scene for Willie. I'll give you the key to the padlock. Timmy and I will go after the Pukwudgees and you shut the trapdoor but don't put the padlock on. Leave it right here – CLOSED BUT NOT LOCKED," said Amos looking Brett in the eyes pointing to the ground next to the latch. "If we come out I want to be able to find it and attach it fast! You understand?"

"Yeah, but…"

"What am I doing?"

"WAIT, VERN! Let me deal with Brett first! Brett, again, you shut the trap door and don't lock it. Leave the lock on the ground. This is so we can get out if we come back today or tomorrow."

"What if you don't get back tomorrow?" asked Brett.

"First things first. Keep the key safe. If we do come back today or tomorrow we'll find you. But Brett, after you close the trapdoor … go home and hang out with your mom. If she ain't there go down to the tennis courts and be seen – all day. Then go home. You'll need an alibi like Timmy said, but don't go to the marketplace today because that's where Vern will be and I don't want Willie associating you with us."

"Soo, what about me?" asked Vern.

"You wait outside the marketplace for us to come back."

"How long?"

"All day."

"All day?"

"Yeah, all day, periodically go in the store and buy a drink. I want you to stay in Willie's sight so you're not a suspect. If we get back today, we'll come get you. If we don't, go home and tell momma I went off with Timmy and said I'd be back but didn't."

"Fuck me! This sucks! Now I got to be some great actor with mom and dad! I can't do this!"

"YES YOU CAN! YOU GOT TO! Or else you're fucked!"

"Thanks Amos. I'm fucked whether I do or don't. We'll see. Fuck me this sucks."

"You can do it Vern. I need you to do it! You understand?" Amos looked Vern in the eye.

"Yeah, I guess so, but it still sucks."

63

BEFORE THEY LEFT FOR the Marketplace to try to buy cigarettes, Amos yelled "Wait!! One more thing …"

"WHAT???" yelled Vern hating having his mind interrupted while preparing for his role in this sham.

"If we aren't back in a couple of weeks, you and Brett have to put the lock on the trap door and come back every year about the same time to see if me and Timmy are trying to get out!"

"What the fuck??? If you don't come back??? If you don't come back, the shit will hit the fan! You better get back or I'm screwed!" said Vern realizing that nothing was certain when you went in the hole.

"We'll be back! We'll be back! But we need a backup plan in case something happens. If we're not, be at the hole at this time of year. We'll do three slow knocks on the door followed by two quick ones," said Amos trying to calm Vern.

"I'll be here," said Brett realizing he had dodged a bullet and became invisible again as he was with the 'The Pool Man' incident. Brett had acquired a knack for being invisibly involved which would serve him well later in life.

"LET"S GO! I'll figure it out!" screamed Vern. He hopped on his bike and peddled to the Marketplace.

"Brett, you know what you're doing?" asked Timmy.

"Yeah, pretty simple. Stay here, get the fuck back here every year and don't fuck around. I got it easy. Vern's got a lot to deal with."

64

WHAT THE BOYS DIDN'T know was that the Pukwudgees were out before they completed the trapdoor … in the year 1992. Vern's dismantling of the trapdoor was inconsequential in the scheme of things. Time of day remained pretty much constant no matter which hole you selected. The Pukwudgees, after being repelled by the flames, retreated back down the tunnel and regrouped inside the orb. Pomarat looked at the innumerable holes everywhere. When they were chasing the boys it was simple … follow their tracks into and out the orb. Since they were so close behind the holes had not shifted yet. Now the holes moved!

Quickly he shot an arrow to the right of the hole he believed they had just exited. The other braves wondered what he was shooting at. Pomarat realized something wasn't right and needed a point of focus. Gazing around, a sense of apprehension was creeping up his spine. Glancing at his braves he could see in their eyes the same was happening to them. Again the holes shifted! "Fest mu ta?" whispered Hysko.

Pomarat saw them all look to him. He looked for his arrow, it had moved right. Enough! This place was strong magic and they must get out NOW! These boys they were chasing were not to be underestimated and had strong gods assisting them.

He shot another arrow forty-five degrees to the right, which lodged in the wall next to a hole three rows higher than the row they came in. He commanded Sarkem to retrieve his first arrow and headed for his second. Hysko and Massot followed him glancing over their shoulder at Sarkem hoping nothing popped out and devoured him from the multiplicity of holes. Sarkem also seemed to have the same fears as he sprinted to the arrow, yanked it and sprinted back to the group. He was so frightened he hadn't noticed all the other holes except the one by the arrow had disappeared.

"Ya tha som tey fa, seta fustum. Askom da tum yon kidee!" said Pomarat pointing his finger and making an arc back to where the second arrow was. He had told them they would go out this hole, flanking the boys and proceed back to the right and attack. The braves were relieved. There was a plan! Best of all they'd be out of this horrible hole. Pomarat exited the membrane and went to grab his second arrow. Instead of being three rows higher, it was now at waist level and there was one hole not many! Hysko, Massot and Sarkem penetrated the membrane and now noticed the same. Sarkem looked back into the orb and also saw no other holes … anywhere. "Ahmatt!" he whispered.

Pomarat heard the word we'd translate as Black Magic. He quickly marked the dirt surrounding this hole not knowing if it would help if they were forced back here. He scrambled up the tunnel with his braves staying as close as they could without bumping their heads in his rear.

There was no sign of fire as they went through the tunnel and Pomarat came out with caution to a place similar to where they went in, but different. When they had exited the hole they began their ninety-degree arc expecting to ambush the boys. But there were no signs of the boys. No tracks … nothing! This should not be! Pomarat decided they would hunt for food, make more arrows and resume their pursuit in the morning. He would use the night to digest what they had seen.

65

VERN AND BRETT FOLLOWED the script to the letter. Brett found a match at the tennis court after placing the padlock and key by the trapdoor when Timmy and Amos went in. He also bought sodas and yakked it up with the staff at the club. At four-thirty he went home to his mother and her cast. Dad was back in Boston, but would be back on Thursday night due to his mom's condition. Dad had hired a house-maid to deal with the domestic tasks during the week. In the past, dad had only come to New Seabury for the four-day member/guest or other special club events. Now he came every weekend for the remainder of the summer.

Mom spent her time at the beach, drinking and sunning herself and listening to her cronies' talk of their exploits with the new "Pool Man". Mom figured, even with a plaster cast, she could still seduce the new "Pool Man" but then there was Maria – her constant servant hired by her husband. Besides, because of the incident he had fired the "Pool Man" and hired the "Pool Care Experts". The guy who now tended their pool had a beer gut, was older than her husband, wore denim cut-offs and a Budweiser T-shirt.

There were always the cabana boys at the Beach Club but that would mean going to their place. This was not acceptable. A cougar dragged her prey back to her den where she knew there would be no distractions of roommates coming in or the prying eyes of frat boys in the next cottage. This summer had become a bust! 'But there's always next year', she thought, like a pitcher facing a season ending injury.

Brett had hoped things would change, but instead he returned to find his mother sleeping off the day's cocktails on the couch and Maria cheerfully asking him if he would like something to eat. He liked Maria. She was cute and always smiling.

Vern, on the other hand had a tougher part to play, a part that would extend a lifetime. Vern put on an Oscar performance. He was about to leave Callahan's late in the afternoon but decided to buy a pack of gum before he left, insuring Willie knew he was still there. He placed a pack of Juicy Fruit on the counter and rummaged around in his pocket for money. Willie probed as expected. "So your friends didn't come back?"

"Fuckin' assholes. I'm goin' home. When they come back, tell them I was sick of waiting."

"This ain't Western Union, Tonto. You deliver your own messages. I'm out of here in fifteen minutes. But I have to agree with you, they are assholes."

"Never mind, I'll probably be back tomorrow with at least one of the assholes."

"I hope not," responded Willie, dinging the register, depositing the change and shutting the draw with authority.

As Vern rode away on his bike, he thought Act 1 went well, now he had to deal with Act 2 – Mom and Dad! God he hoped Timmy and Amos would come flying down the road on their bicycles, but that didn't happen.

66

VERN GOT HOME. OF course the first question from Mom was, "Where's Amos?"

"Don't know. He took off with Timmy and told me to wait at the Marketplace and he didn't come back … left me waiting there."

"Why are you two hanging out at New Seabury? Where did they go?"

Vern realized he was now under cross-examination. If he could get through Mom, F. Lee Bailey would be a breeze.

"Don't know."

"Don't know or won't say?"

"Mom …"

"Don't Mom me! Supper's going to be ready soon … what's going on? AND VERNON, DON'T YOU LIE TO ME OR I'LL BRING YOUR FATHER INTO THIS DISCUSSION!"

Act 2 wasn't going well. Vern had to give up something. The cigarette thing would do. If Amos returned shortly, he'd be in a world of shit even though Dad smoked like a chimney, meaning dad would be in a world of shit also. Meaning a swipe to Vern's head out of the blue when he least expected it for ratting out his brother and dragging him into it. God knew what it would mean for Amos, but Amos wasn't here and he said he knew I could handle it. Well I'm handling it and Amos will have to handle the fallout if he gets back here.

"You can't tell Amos I told you!"

"Told me what young man!"

"Promise me!"

"Vernon, you're in no position to demand ANY promises!"

"Okay, okay! Amos tried to buy cigarettes at the marketplace and the guy at the counter wouldn't sell him any."

"Thank God for that! Then what?"

"Amos said 'Come on Timmy, I know where we can get butts.' Then they left and told me to wait there and they'd be right back."

"Where did they go? Where is Amos getting cigarettes or is it this Timmy kid?"

"Timmy's not from here he doesn't know where to get shit."

"VERNON! DON'T USE THAT LANGUAGE WITH ME!"

"Sorry mom …."

"Is that how you talk now? Hanging out in New Seabury? Who is this Timmy kid?"

Vern's head was spinning, too many questions too fast. It was tough to lie. Lies can come back to bite you. "Timmy's not from New Seabury. He's from Popponesset. He's summer people. We met him fishing."

"You and Amos never mentioned him before."

"Mom …"

"Who's this Timmy kid from Popponesset? Why is Amos finding him cigarettes? What's Amos getting from him? Booze? Money? What? Start talking young man?"

"HE'S NOT GETTING ANYTHING!!!! THEY BOTH LIKE

SMOKING!!! They think it's cool or something."

"What about you, you like smoking?"

"No!"

"Where do you think they went?"

"I don't know. Amos doesn't tell me everything, probably cause he knows I'll break down like a two dollar watch under your questioning."

Vern received an open hand blow to his cheek.

"Don't you be flip with me, young man! There'll be no supper for you till you find your brother! Now get!"

Vern jumped at the opportunity to get off the stand. Unfortunately for his dad, he picked the wrong time to come into the room with a lit butt in his mouth inquiring when supper would be ready.

"THIS IS ALL YOUR FAULT! I TOLD YOU NOT TO SMOKE INSIDE THE HOUSE!"

Vern left quickly to look for Amos, knowing Amos was not in this time. He'd stay out all night using some of the money they had gotten from Brett to eat. Home was no place to be with Mom on the rampage and Dad under attack with no clue as to why. This shit storm would not end till Amos showed up. If Amos didn't it would be directed at him. If he did, it would be directed at Amos, and that would be Amos's problem. But that would be tomorrow … except at the O'Rielly residence.

67

AT 7:00 PM SUPPER was ready. Timmy was late, no problem. He had been late before. At 7:30, Mrs. O'Rielly was getting nervous. "Colin Jr., where is Timmy?"

"I don't know ma."

At 8:00 PM, Mary O'Rielly had enough. "Colin Jr. go out and find your little brother."

"MA, I got to meet my friends at the Marketplace!"

"Well then ask your friend Willie if he's seen Timmy! He's at the store all day."

"Okay ma, I will." Colin Jr. had a mission and an excuse to extricate him.

"Timmy will show up, he's probably out screwing around with his friends fishing or playing ball and lost track of time," added Colin Sr. from his recliner watching the Sox.

"It's eight o'clock! It's getting dark!" shouted Mary from the kitchen trying to be heard over the TV.

"He probably latched on to one of those rich little New Seabury teases and lost his senses. It happens when you're that age," chuckled Colin Sr.

"Mother of God! Just watch your game. You're no help."

68

COLIN JR. HOOKED UP with his friends at the usual spot, in the remotest edge of the Marketplace parking lot. Sean Murphy, as usual brought the beer. He had been working at the package store at the rotary for a couple of years and had learned who the dopes were and who was sharp. When the dopes were in charge, he'd stash cases by the dumpster and load them his car when he left. Willie supplied cigarettes. As a result the Irish teens from Southie were always well stocked.

Colin Jr. and the rest of his cronies were "the muscle". This had been as a result of their reputation in their South Boston neighborhood where they periodically got the call from the "higher ups" to take care of some foreigner or outsider getting too close to some guy's Irish Rose daughter. When they got the call, they did it well. No fanfare, just a good old fashioned masked, ass whipping … plenty of blood, not life threatening, just sending a message, which worked 99% of the time. When it didn't, the elders would step in. With Colin Jr. on the job, that happened once in a blue moon, which was better than expected by the elders.

As a result, his peers in the neighborhood feared Colin Jr. "Hey Willie, come here," said Colin after cracking a beer. A chill went up Willie's spine even though he outweighed Colin by 100 pounds but all those pounds were fat and Colin's were muscle. "You seen Timmy today?" asked Colin with no threat in his voice.

"Yea, he was here early with those two featherheads he's been hanging out with."

"You know where he is now?"

"No, one of the brothers came into the store looking to buy cigarettes. I told him to screw. He went outside and told Timmy he knew where they could get butts and told his brother they'd be back. He and Timmy took off on their bikes, and the other one waited outside the store all day. They never came back while I was there. Just before I punched out, Tonto was pissed they hadn't come back and took off."

"What time was that?"

"Five."

"Gimme some change, I got to call home."

Willie gave him all the change in his pocket gladly thinking he was off the stand. Colin stuck the change in his pocket and started to head for the pay phone at the Marketplace. But then he stopped. "Did the brother say anything?"

Shit he wasn't off the stand after all. "Yeah, he asked me to tell his brother he went home if he showed up. I told him I was off work and leaving and to deliver his own messages." Willie fidgeted with his free hand in his pocket but with no change to jingle.

"Any idea where this Indian kid would go to get cigarettes?"

"Ehhhh, no. Even Sean can't get butts at the rotary packie, and he works there. The only place I can think of is that shitty little general store by the town hall. That's in injun territory. Maybe he has a connection there."

"It doesn't add up. I'm gonna call home. Sean, can you give me a ride around town when I get back?"

"Sure Colin, no problem."

Colin went to the pay phone and called home. "Ma, it's me."

"Oh Colin, did you find out anything?"

"Yeah Timmy went into town with one of those Indian kids he caught the fish with."

"It's not like him to be late for supper without telling us."

"Yeah mom, me and Sean are going into town to find him. He's probably having supper at the kid's wigwam cooking out or something. We'll find him."

"Okay Colin, give me a call when you do and don't stay out late. I don't like this!"

"Don't worry mom."

Colin walked back to the group. "Well the evening's fucked cause of my little brother. I'm gonna kick his ass when I find him. Willie! Where do these twins live?"

"I don't know!" Willie is back on the stand after a brief recess.

"You DO KNOW what the brother looks like don't you?"

"Yeah, sure."

"You're coming with me and Sean. Mikey, you come too and keep Willie company in the backseat."

Fuck this sucked. Willie had expected to spend the night drinking and chasing tail as they usually did. Now he was being called upon to ID an injun in Indian territory, at night, among probably many other Indians with Mikey riding shotgun. Mikey was Colin's right hand man in Southie when doing "errands" for the "higher ups". Mikey was bigger and more muscle bound than Colin, but less sharp. Colin took very good care of him, and he would do anything for Colin. Colin knew the formula for rising in the ranks in Southie.

"Mikey, grab the case," ordered Colin.

The four of them hopped in the car and headed for town.

As they sped away from the marketplace, Colin cracked a beer and turned to look back at Willie. He raised an index finger to his lips and said "Sushsss … we're hunting Injuns!" in a poor imitation of Elmer Fudd. Sean and Mikey cracked up. Willie tittered and cracked another beer. If those fucking twins showed up tomorrow he would tell them to screw. He would never serve Indians again. Screw Callahan. Let him fire me. If they found them tonight and Timmy wasn't with them … God help them. I never signed up for this kind of shit, but now I'm all in … that's what happens in Southie. But this is 70 miles away! Shit, who knew?

Vern didn't know. He was so thrilled to escape his mother's cross-examination and his father's resulting retribution. Little did he know while he was riding around killing the night, the A-team of the Winter Hill Mob was on the way to cruise his neighborhood looking for him.

69

VERN DECIDED TO GO back to the hole. He could make himself seen around town asking if they'd seen Amos, which would enhance his cover on the off chance they didn't come back. But he wasn't into that at the moment. He assumed the role of an optimist, feeling he would run into Amos on the way back to New Seabury and Amos would tell him why he and Timmy were delayed. The world would be right.

Vern peddled into the rotary from Great Neck Road North just as the Irish boys were entering from Great Neck Road South. This should have been fortunate for him since it was a rotary and they'd always be 180 degrees away from each other. However, Willie was gazing out the window regretting being so close to Colin when a member of his family was missing. He was usually just the "funny" guy who cracked them up, not the link to finding his brother. He was not part of the banter between Mikey, Sean and Colin, he was the identifier, required to point out a target. He was not sure he'd be able to do it if confronted by multiple Indians at a distance. In something as important as finding a little brother, his performance could have a major impact on dictating the course of his future.

So he gazed out the backseat window, sipping his beer as they entered the rotary. About 45 degrees in he caught the sight of a dark-skinned boy peddling a red bike around the rotary towards the road from which they just came. He was frozen but a moment. Sean and Mikey were laughing about something he wasn't paying attention to. Colin was laughing along with them. Willie's arm flayed out and hit Mikey causing Mikey's beer to spill. "THAT'S HIM! THAT'S THE BROTHER!" screamed Willie pointing across the rotary.

Sean reacted too late and continued on Great Neck Road North. "FUCK, WILLIE! MY BEER!" yelled Mikey.

"That's him! We got to go back! Sorry about the beer."

"Sean, turn around! Head back towards home!" commanded Colin.

Sean slammed on the brakes sending the car in a 360 degree fishtail. Thank God traffic was light or there would have been a major accident. They sped back into the rotary pursuing the Indian racing down the road from which they came. Willie was relieved. He had done his job without having to venture among the savages. Everybody lost some beer with Sean's hard 360.

Vern heard the squealing tires in the distance but had no idea it had something to do with him. He continued peddling down Great Neck Road South. Then he noticed the sound of a car accelerating from behind him. He glanced over his shoulder and noticed the wide array of headlights bearing down fast. Could be they were going to New Seabury, but it just didn't feel right. He turned his bike down a dirt path off the road to see if they would pass. He heard the screeching of brakes as they reached the path, and then he knew they were after him. SHIT!

He knew this path would take him back to Route 28 and no car could follow. But there was little ambient light and he'd have to walk his bike up the path from here otherwise he'd be running into bushes.

"Get out of the car Willie!" yelled Colin.

"What?"

"Get out of the car and follow him up that path! Make sure he doesn't double back! If he does, sit on him till we get back!"

"It's dark! How the fuck am I going to see him!"

"Fuck! Get out of the fucking car and do what I say!" screamed Colin.

Willie jumped out and ambled up the path not sure of his mission. Just when you think you got it made, you don't he thought as he proceeded up the barely visible path.

"Sean! Head back to Route 28 towards Falmouth. The path has to come out there," commanded Colin.

Vern heard enough of the conversation with Willie, and he knew what their game plan would be. Time to be an Indian.

70

VERN QUICKLY WALKED HIS bike half the distance between Great Neck and Route 28, lifted it over his head and made a 90-degree left, slowly wading into the underbrush as not to make a sound. Willie's reluctance to venture into the darkness left him standing in the middle of the path, sipping his beer, about 10 yards from where he was dropped off and about 80 yards from Vern. At about 50 yards into his journey off the path, Vern heard what had to be Willie's friend's car screech into the back of the gas station where the path exited. He kept moving deeper into the woods. The 'friends' had to be Colin, and some guy named 'Sean' who was obviously the driver and God knows who else. Vern hadn't expected to have to deal with these guys until tomorrow at the earliest. Actually, he hadn't figured to be dealing with them at all, as he expected Timmy and Amos to be back by now. I guess Timmy's mom was as forceful as his in driving them out of the house on a mission. Vern kept moving increasing the distance. He briefly paused to lower the bike and rest the cross bar on his shoulder.

"Sean, you got any flashlights!"

"Yeah, yeah there must be one in the car somewhere."

"Where the fuck is it?"

"I don't know … somewhere. Let me look around."

"Mikey, check the glove box and under the seats! Sean! Open the fuckin' trunk!"

"Yeah, yeah," Sean fumbled with the keys and finally found the one for the trunk.

Vern could hear the conversation in the distance over the periodic chirping of the late night summer insects. He kept moving deeper into the woods, now moving faster as his rustling would be out of earshot of Willie.

"I got one!" said Mikey producing a flashlight from under the driver's seat. He flicked it on shining it in Sean and Colin's face.

"Give me it!" commanded Colin irritated.

They proceed down the path. "WILLIE! ARE YOU THERE?"

Willie heard Colin's scream, and waddled another ten yards up the path. "YEAH, I'M HERE! HE HASN'T COME BACK! HE'S GOT TO BE HEADING YOUR WAY!"

"No fuckin way. He'd be here by now," said Colin to no one in particular.

"You think he got here before us?" asked Mikey.

"No, I think he went off the path. Grab the rest of the beers, and follow us." Colin proceeded up the path with the flashlight trained on the path.

71

Vern was back on Great Neck Road peddling his way to the hole, long before Colin realized he was no Daniel Boone and there was no way he was going to track down an Indian in the woods at night. He and his troop went back to their car. He yelled for Willie to get his ass up the path to the gas station. Willie ambled up the path lighting matches along the way till he could see the lights of the gas station. He was worried about ticks and it was comical how he'd light a match and it would immediately extinguish as he moved forward.

"What the fuck you doing, Willie?" asked Mikey.

"I couldn't see shit, you guys had the flashlights."

"Get in the car. We're going to that shit ass store to see if they've seen Timmy," intoned Colin, "The brother will be back to the reservation eventually, we'll catch up with him then."

Vern continued back to the hole and planned to stay there the night hoping Amos and Timmy would come back soon. They didn't, not that night or what seemed like forever until 1992. Lives changed.

Vern's life went down the toilet. Brett's life took off in a new direction of success. Mrs. O'Rielly became a basket case. Colin rose in the ranks of the Winter Hill organization taking his cronies with him, except Willie who decided to get out of dodge, get a hospitality degree from Johnson & Wales and take a job as a hotel manager in Southern California. He could see the writing on the wall and had no desire to be making any similar nighttime romps in the swamps of Dorchester where the stakes would be higher. Mr. O'Rielly spent more time at the corner bar near their home in Southie, wishing to reduce the number of times he had to hear over and over again how if he had … Timmy might still be here.

Mr. Otis noticed his .22 pistol was missing and searched the boys' room and the yard. He eyed Vern's waistband whenever Vern was home. He asked Vern once if he knew where his pistol was making sure he was in a position to see Vern's face and eyes when he did. Vern's eyes and face revealed he didn't have a clue as to the whereabouts of his gun. He didn't know Amos had taken it. Now Mr. Otis assumed Amos took it and was on an adventure that would lead to no good.

Mrs. Otis took every opportunity to point out that Mr. Otis' smoking around the house was responsible for all this. Mr. Otis guessed otherwise, and kept his mouth shut. Mr. & Mrs. Otis separated five years later with Vern alternating his time between both, moving from one to the other when pressed about how he had to change his life. Vern had lost his desire to change his life, if Amos came back that would take care of itself.

1992 NEW SEABURY AND BACK

72

SIKES' LINES BEGAN RINGING. Instinctively he hit the button on an open line and picked up the receiver before all lines were filled with incoming calls reporting the massive explosion, the details of which was being filtered into his head in the background over the police radio. "We need fire and ambulance crews, NOW! …". Fredricks, Dimitri, and the other Mashpee cops were asking on the radio what happened and what were their instructions. Bogger was also asking from the jail cell. Sikes said to himself, 'You all tell me, I don't fucking know what the hell happened.' He took a deep breath, and dialed human resources at Town Hall.

"Mashpee Human Resources, how can I help you?"

"Janie, it's Sgt. Sikes at the police station."

"Billy! What the hell was that explosion? What's going on?"

"I'll tell you later. I don't know yet. But I need you to call everyone with the police department in, officers and clerical. Tell them to report immediately. If they ask questions, say you don't know - just get their butts to the station."

"But …"

"No buts, don't worry about 'no' answers or excuses, just keep going down the roster. I gotta go now, talk to you later."

Janie looked at the receiver and debated in her mind what she should do. Should she try and find her boss or just do what he asked? If this was important as it sounded, she'd never find him in time. Come to think of it she hadn't seen him today, or yesterday. She went to the file cabinet containing the Police Department active employees, grabbed them all and plopped them on her desk. She dialed up Arthur Addams …Sikes picked up the radio, "Fredricks, what's you location? Report …"

The chaos slowly revealed itself to Sikes from multiple conversations. Suspects were still on the run, the Staties may have suffered causalities and there was a major accident on Route 28 involving a gasoline and a propane truck. Also, there were two homicides and an attempted homicide in New Seabury. Okay, Terrific! Sikes started dialing the Captain as he came barreling into the station. Sikes hung up the phone. The Captain screamed, "Billy, what the fuck is going on???" Billy gave him everything he knew. "Get everyone in!"

"In progress, sir."

"Who's that back in the fuckin' tank asking all the questions?"

"Bogger."

"Rayburn?"

"Yeah, he was at the scene of the first homicide but in custody at the time of the second."

"Should we cut him loose? He's bugging the shit out of me with his yammering."

"Probably, based on what has transpired since we brought him in. I don't think he's a suspect, but he may have seen something of value."

"Okay. Bring him out."

Sikes went back and unlocked Bogger's cell, "The Captain's letting you go but he wants to ask you some questions."

"So I'm not a suspect?"

"Just come on."

"Phil! Sorry about this! Have you been treated okay?" The Captain had shifted into a combination politician/Lt. Colombo mode.

"Yeah, I'm okay but a little shocked."

"I know, I know. Sorry I wasn't here sooner."

Sikes cringed, but he could see the drill. The Captain even began assuming Peter Falk's demeanor as Colombo.

"Phil, before you go, I need to know what you saw at the site. It could be critical to the investigation."

Phil hitched up his pants, feeling important again forgetting about his earlier treatment. He proceeded to describe to the Captain what he had seen that morning.

73

POMARAT AND HIS BAND continued on a course north along the river. He wished to be away from this chaos as soon as possible. The red headed witch's magic was proving to be extremely powerful; it may have been a mistake to send Massot after her. He made a mental note to avoid all fire heads in the future after his failures trying to dispatch Timmy and Colleen. As they ran he asked Hysko, "You're covered in blood. Is that from the warrior, waiting to ambush us? Did you kill him?"

"No, no one was on the other side. If he was, he must have went up to the sound from the screeching beast and the beast killed him."

"We under estimated the power of these beasts when they get angry. We must avoid them in the future."

"This one was very large!"

Sarkem tried to interject and tell about all the beasts he saw at the rotary, but again was waved silent by Pomarat as a new sound filled the environment. WHOMP, WHOMP, WHOMP, WHOMP, WHOMP, WHOMP, coming from the sky! Pomarat squatted and the rest followed his lead, looking to the sound. The WHOMP blended with a humming as a huge metallic bird passed over their head to the site of the crash. They saw it but a moment through the treetops, but it was enough to cause a fear in their hearts, which could best be capsulated by a line from the 'Wizard of Oz', "Toto, I don't think we're in Kansas anymore."

"What was that???" asked Massot, the fear evident in his voice.

"We must go!" said Pomarat not wishing to address the question at the moment. Maktahdou had his giant crows. This bird was faster and more intimidating. Can this also be a servant of the red witch? She looked me in the eye and raised her middle finger! A curse? A spell? Pomarat didn't know. The other braves couldn't know he didn't know. He commanded his band to pick up the pace, they must get back to the Great Marsh.

The State Police chopper out of Plymouth circled over the crash, the remaining Statie on the ground radioed the suspects were heading north. Officer Fredricks piped in over the radio, "They'll probably be sticking to the Mashpee River up to Mashpee-Wakeby Pond."

"Who's this?" asked the pilot.

"Officer Fredricks, Mashpee PD."

"You play hockey with the Guns and Hoses at Gallo?"

"Affirmative."

"Your name Matt?"

"Affirmative?"

"I played with you guys a couple of times, Jack Reed. How do you know they're going up the river?"

"That's what they've done to get to this point. No reason to believe they'll change their course unless you spook them. I'm going to proceed up Great Neck to Town Hall so cruise the right side of the river. If they get spooked they'll head toward the road."

"Roger that, heading there now. You still play Thursdays?"

"Affirmative."

"Maybe, I'll see you then and we can compare notes on this cluster fuck."

Jesus Christ, thought Fredricks. He recalled Reed as a thirty plus cop who still thought he was playing to make the Bruins. The Guns & Hoses played a collection of 30, 40 and 50 year old local ex-college and high school players who were good natured and out for a good skate. The intent was to have a few beers afterward, go to work the next day and not end up in the hospital.

Reed sped his chopper up the river planning to travel up and down it till the perps were spotted or he had to refuel. Pomarat heard the WHOMP, WHOMP again and ensured his band was under cover of the oaks that lined the river. The giant bird came and went and came again, slowing their progress as it passed over and over again just above the treetops. Pomarat and his braves continued north between each pass of the giant iron bird.

Pomarat was deep in thought. He was out of his element. He had doubted Maktahdou at a time when he needed him most. He needed him now to be rid of this flying monster. He decided the only way to get back in his good graces was a sacrifice, human blood of an innocent. He must look for an opportunity. The WHOMP, WHOMP, was coming back. They instinctively found cover. However a momentary glint of sunlight reflecting off Massot's long slicing knife in his britches caught the attention of Reed. Instead of the WHOMP, WHOMP, fading into the distance, it was now returning. Pomarat commanded his braves to seek better cover, the beast had seen something. The braves made themselves invisible like a squirrel when it knows a hawk is present.

The iron bird hovered over their location, Reed scanning the ground below. This gave Pomarat a chance to study his predator. There was a human inside! Same as the iron ground beasts! No doubt a servant of the redhead witch who had bested him. He needed to make a sacrifice, but must wait till the beast left or risk being devoured. The beast sat on the area for about five minutes but it seemed like an hour to the braves. Finally, it veered back to its southern course. Pomarat decided to vector west of the river and rejoin it closer to the big pond. He hoped the iron bird would stay close to the river long enough for him to find a suitable sacrifice. The braves broke on a dead run through the woods, away from the river. It wasn't long till they came upon another hovel located on a dirt road off Great Neck Road North. There was a human in the yard gazing at the sky, no doubt following the noise of the great iron bird. The human was female. 'Perfect!' thought Pomarat.

74

CARMELLA OTIS' LIFE HAD finally settled into a comfortable pattern, as much as it could for someone whose one son had vanished mysteriously and the other as a result, had never capitalized on the athletic talents God had given him. Also, she had separated from her husband, yet he had not sought the comfort of another woman that she knew of, and was always still there when she had a problem and left when the problem was solved without pressuring her to take him back. She still loved him, but didn't know if she could take him back without the case of Amos being resolved. Nor did she know if he would come back.

But on this day, she had been distracted from her regular routine of tending the garden, by the explosion that all had heard, then by the helicopter going back and forth flying so low. Something was happening out of the norm. The pattern of the helicopter indicated it was looking for someone. Someone probably related to the commotion. It was probably not a good idea to be outside if that was the case, and she decided to go inside. She first gathered her gardening implements and brought them to the shed, placing them in their racks. While she was doing this Pomarat lead the braves into her hovel.

He commanded Sarkem to watch for her return. He decided to kill her inside and do it himself. He could not risk the iron bird interrupting his sacrifice, even though the human controlling the bird had seemed convinced his prey was along the river. But that could change. Pomarat took Hysko and searched the rest of the hovel, making sure they were alone. It didn't take long since it was a two-bedroom ranch. They returned to the open living area where Sarkem stood watch out the back door. Photos much like the ones he saw in the old ladies hovel back by the pond sat atop the hearth. In them he saw two of the four boys they had chased into the hole the other day! The ones that were twins! And the woman outside was hugging them in the photo. Was this their mother? But she looks so much older today than in that thing on the hearth. He also noticed a photo of a large man with a bow, with his foot on a carcass on a deer. Was he the father? A hunter? Where was he now? Had Maktahdou lead him to this particular sacrifice? A sign that he had not forsaken him and provided him with revenge of an innocent soul? Sarkem hissing at the door indicating the approach of the woman interrupted his thoughts. No time to process! Instinct must take over!

Pomarat signaled his group to get out of sight. He moved behind the wall separating the living room from the dining area until she had come far enough inside. He had signed his braves to stay put … he would do this one.

Carmella came through the backdoor intending to wash her hands. Sarkem was in a cupboard with the vacuum cleaner, Massot was under the dining table and Hysko was behind the sofa in the living room. She turned on the faucet and placed her hands underneath. Pomarat stepped into the kitchen and uttered a low growl, "Are you prepared to die bitch mother, for your wayward pups!" Hysko peaked over the couch at Massot under the table, both having no clue as to the why of their rambling chief. Sarkem could only twist his head like the RCA Victrola dog, hidden in darkness of the cupboard wondering what the fuck his chief was talking about.

Carmella turned keeping her wet hands over the sink, her left hand seeking the butcher-block knife rack behind her. "Why are you in my house?" she asked in a non-threatening tone. Pomarat did not miss her hand moving to the knife holder similar to the one at the Finch residence. He stepped forward forcefully throwing his stone tomahawk, hitting her square in the forehead drawing blood. Carmella felt the room spinning, but managed to withdraw a large chopping knife from the rack as she went to the floor. She tried with all her might to maintain her consciousness and break her fall and maintain her grip on the knife. But Pomarat was on her fast grabbing his tomahawk again and smashing it on her hand.

With the commotion, the other braves popped out of their hiding places to assist their leader but instead stood there with their mouths agape witnessing his anger in sacrificing this woman. He needed no assistance, nor did it seem like a good idea to interrupt him and put their own lives in danger. He seemed possessed. They had never witnessed such fury. After the blow to the hand releasing the knife, he struck her on the face and body multiple times over and over again with the crude stone implement. She laid there moaning in pain, blood streaming out her wounds with Pomarat straddling her watching her pain. He had intense desire to rape her in her last remaining moments of consciousness but he could feel eyes upon him.

He got up taking the chopping knife, her blood on him. Looking down on her slowly moving moaning body, he was pleased. He looked at the shocked eyes on his braves' faces, smiled and slammed the chopping knife into the woman's chest and left it there. "Let's go."

"Our luck will change now!" he told his braves. They nodded. Although, they said nothing to each other, they each were reminded in graphic fashion why no one in the tribe challenged his authority. He was a lunatic liable to fly off the handle at the drop of the hat, a lunatic with skill.

Their luck had in fact changed. The iron bird had vanished, going to Hyannis to refuel. They proceeded unabated to the great pond. They were half way to their home by the great marsh. Their chief was extremely confident and in good spirits. They felt a modicum of relief, which was always welcomed.

75

"WHAT'S TODAY'S DATE AND time now?" asked Amos urgently.

"It's about 11:30 AM, August 29th, 1992," answered Brett seeing this was important to whatever was rolling around in little Amos's head. Amos had a better grasp on this time shit than the rest of them though he and Vern had years to try and figure it out. They hadn't and obviously hadn't devoted the time to the problem that they should have. He felt guilty now that after a few years, they had lost focus that Timmy and Amos were still out in time-space somewhere. And now, 24 years later they were back and he and Vern were unprepared.

"So it's a day later than when those assholes chased us in the hole?" Timmy jumped in.

"Yeah," said Amos digesting the info. "I got an idea. We got to get out of this parking lot. You got anywhere we can go?" Amos looked at Vern then Brett.

"We can go to my place! It's just down the street. Same place you did the Pool Man, remember?" laughed Brett wishing to do what he could to make up for his indifference over the years.

"Yeah, of course we remember! It was a few weeks ago!" yelled Timmy. "Fuck this is weird, seeing someone we know in another time period!"

"Calm down Timmy, we'll sort it out and come up with a plan when we get to Brett's place."

Amos told Timmy to go with Brett and he would go with Vern in his truck.

Timmy was in awe of Brett's BMW and its dashboard asking questions about the evolution of cars on the short ride to Brett's place. Amos hopped in Vern's truck and asked how mom was. "Mom's fine," said Vern. "She split with Dad after you disappeared. Blamed it on him, cause he smoked in the house."

"What the FUCK! Cause he SMOKED?!"

Vern became uncomfortable, now he would have to explain the disintegration of the family as a result of his answers to questions of Amos's disappearance. "I'll tell you about it at Brett's."

"NO TELL ME NOW!" demanded the 13-year-old brother to his 37-year-old twin.

Vern proceed to explain the answers he shot out when he returned home without Amos and that he told her Timmy and Amos went to get cigarettes and she connected Dad's smoking to Amos's fate. Amos slumped in the seat of the truck as they pulled up to Brett's. He put his face in his hands like a drunken man trying to rub himself back to sobriety. "I'll fix this," he mumbled "I got an idea." He paused and took his face out of his hands, looked at Vern, "I got to know what's happened since we left and how you two feel about it!"

"Okay, let's go inside."

Brett's place was the same yet older - like Brett and Vern. The shrubs had matured to the point of being overbearing. They all went in. Vern noticed there seemed to be no one at home. The voice he had spoken to on the phone was nowhere in sight. Brett asked if anyone would like a drink, thinking alcoholic, forgetting the age of Timmy and Amos but needing a stiff one for himself, due the recent events. Vern would love to start drinking but knew it was too early if he was going to deal with all of this. "Got any coffee or a Coke?" asked Vern, "I called you earlier and a woman answered."

"You mean Vicki? She said she was going shopping today. I guess she left. I can make some coffee it will take a minute. You guys want something?" Brett asked looking at Timmy and Amos, glad that Vern had mentioned soft drinks.

"A soda if you got it," replied Timmy.

"Coffee's fine," said Amos and added, "Check out the house and make sure Vicki is gone. She shouldn't overhear what we talk about."

Fuck, that little shit Amos was ... no, is smart, thought Brett. His mind is always turning. "No she's definitely gone. Her car isn't here." Brett grabbed the scotch off the bar and headed for the kitchen. "Sit down, make yourself comfortable."

"Where's your mother and father?" shouted Timmy to Brett in the kitchen. "Any chance of them stopping by?"

Brett belted back his first scotch while hitting the button on the coffee maker which it was a policy of his house to refill with water and coffee after cleaning so it would be ready with a touch of a button. "No they're divorced. She found out why he stayed up in Boston in the summer, and divorced him. Of course, she was planning to run off with this Frenchman to Monaco so the timing was calculated." Brett poured another. "The house is mine now. I was well taken care of in the financial fallout. Dad's shacking up with a middle-aged blonde in L.A. No one's going to be popping in if that's what you're worried about."

"Shit!" whispered Amos to no one in particular and then thought about Timmy's parents. Timmy was unaware of the conversation between Amos and Vern on the way over.

Brett came back with a carafe of coffee, soda and his third scotch. The past that he so successfully essentially purged from his thoughts was now manifesting itself in his living room. Things had been good. He was rich, built, handsome, had a life of fun and beautiful woman. Mom and Dad were an occasional perfunctory Christmas card and phone call. Now his fat fuck past was sitting on his living room furniture looking at him. His weeks with the boys had been the most exciting in his life and his meeting them had made this life he had possible. Dad had to move to the Cape that summer to take care of mom due to the injuries unwittingly sustained as a result of Brett's plan. By Brett's reckoning that is what kicked off the events that hastened the inevitable divorce.

Then there was the disappearance of Timmy and Amos, which he was questioned about, but not long due to the foresight of the plan concocted by Amos and Timmy to remove him from suspicion. Vern on the other hand had it much harder. He poured coffee for Vern and Amos and gave Timmy his Coke. Then he settled in his recliner with his scotch and said, "Now what?"

76

AFTER THEIR TALK, CAPTAIN Miller put his arm around Phil's shoulder and led him to the door, "Phil you're information may be instrumental to solving these homicides! I am so sorry you were detained so long, but I was tied up at budget meetings with the selectmen. You of all people with the Conservation Department know how onerous that is. We can't get the funding! Right?"

Phil nodded in agreement not knowing why.

The Captain continued, "And when an environmental disaster or a crime wave like we're experiencing now happens … who do they look to solve the problem? That's right! You and me! They send us out to extinguish a blazing inferno with a squirt gun and then wonder why we couldn't contain the problem. You know what I mean, don't ya Phil? It's got to be harder for you guys to get funding. Isn't it?"

"Well yeah, they don't …"

"I know! I know exactly, we face the same shit day in day out. Look, I got to get the info you gave me out to the troops. It's critical. Please, in the meantime, I need you not to talk to anyone about these crimes … especially the press." Miller sticks out his hand at the door and looks Phil straight in the eye as he shakes his hand, "The stuff you gave me is invaluable, but I wouldn't expect less from a fellow enforcement officer. IF ANYTHING! I mean ANYTHING else you remember comes to mind … call me!"

"I will." Phil shook his hands vigorously and left the station hitching up his pants with a renewed sense of importance. Half way to the parking lot he realized his truck wasn't there. Now what? He looked at the door and Miller wasn't there. Shit? His truck must still be at the crime scene. 'How do I get back to my office? I can't go back … these guys have their hands full.' Finally he decided to walk back to Town Hall. It was only a mile or two. Another successful mind conversion by Captain Miller.

"Fuckin'-A Sikes! Is that guy weird or what?" says Miller rejoining Sikes at the desk. "What's the situation now?"

Sikes overheard the Captain's conversation with Phil, and realized why Tom Miller was the Captain. "Fuck Tom, it's a nightmare, two homicides, a horrific crash of two fuel trucks on 28, a decapitated state cop as result and the recurring theme is midget Indians. What did Bogger tell you?"

"Midget Indians. Also, mentioned seeing two young boys. How soon till the call-ins get here?"

"Fifteen minutes I guess."

"Okay, terrific! Should we call up the DPW?"

Sikes laughed and looked at the Captain grateful for breaking the tension. Then Matt Fredricks' voice brought it right back over the radio.

"Sikes?"

Sikes grabbed the mike, "Yeah, what's up Matt?"

"Another homicide, Carmella Otis, at her home on the dirt road off Great Neck North. Alert the State chopper. She was beaten and stabbed." Fredricks had been checking any roads on the right side of Great Neck Road North.

"Any other info?"

"Small foot prints around the door, knife from her kitchen in her chest. Her face is caved in from what seems like some sort of blunt instrument."

'Fuck', thought Sikes. "Secure the site Matt. Help is on the way. Hopefully."

"Roger."

Miller went to the wall map of Mashpee, marking the sites of the homicides and incidents. "Billy, call Sandwich PD, they'll be out of our jurisdiction shortly. And see if you can raise the Wampanoag tribal council on the phone. Maybe they can give us some info on any midgets in the tribe." Miller turned to go to the can and stopped … "Ah Billy, we got to see if we can get in touch with Vern and let him know …"

"He was here a couple of hours ago, come to think of it. He was trying to sneak in to talk to Bogger. Dimitri kicked his ass out. I'll call DPW and see where he's supposed to be and look everywhere else when we get the manpower."

Miller stopped, his fly already halfway down, "You think he knows something about all this?"

"Now that I think about it, yeah maybe."

"Send the first call-in to look for him and tell him I need to talk to him … now." Miller resumed his march to the can unzipping on the way.

77

VERN AND BRETT RECOUNTED the events immediately after the disappearance and, as best as they could recall, what had happen in their lives and the world since then. Amos and Timmy listened with rapt attention, overwhelmed by the consequences of their actions. “Anybody know anything about my family?” asked Timmy finally.

Vern started, “Like I said, your brother Colin was tracking me down like a rat with his friends the night you didn’t come home. I lost them and went back to the hole hoping you two would show and it would be over. The next day I went home got some stuff and lived in the woods till Labor Day passed and I knew he was gone for the summer. Then I went home and told my mom I couldn’t find Amos. I tried to keep track of your family, especially Colin. Over the next couple of years, Irish guys from South Boston would show up in the local bars, strike up a conversation with one of the locals, initially about sports. They’d buy the guy a beer and the conversation would go to ‘ever hear anything about the Irish kid and the Indian kid that disappeared?’ Then they’d ask, ‘What about the Indian’s brother?’ At that point, the locals would clam up realizing what was going on and just say I had went downhill and turned into a drunk that probably lived in the woods.”

“Your brother only visited me once,” piped in Brett. “I stuck to the script you gave me and said I hadn’t seen you since I beat your ass in tennis. He proceeded to punch me in the mouth and said ‘So he didn’t beat you in tennis, he probably couldn’t beat you in figure skating or a brownie bake off either. If you do see him, tell him to get his ass home’. Then he left and I never saw him again.”

“Fuck, sorry. Did it hurt?” said Timmy with almost a smile on his face.

“Yeah it fucking hurt, but all my teeth were intact and I was glad I got off easier than Vern.”

“He never caught up to me,” said Vern “but I was constantly looking over my shoulder.”

“You think my brother is connected?” asked Timmy. The question was sincere, he had no idea his brother might be.

“I’d say so,” said Vern. “There are still guys randomly popping in asking questions. That tells me he’s not only connected but he must have risen in the ranks. He must be pushing 40 now and he still has guys coming around.”

“What about my mom and dad,” asked Timmy?

"They still come down here in the summer. Your mom goes to the beach and church. Your father goes to the golf course in town and the bar at night. I know this 'cause my friend is a local cab driver and has a deal with him. He picks him up at 7:00 PM and returns him home at 10:30 PM. Your dad pays him a flat rate of $1,000 a summer. It's a good deal for both," said Vern looking into his empty coffee cup.

"Shit, he never did that. Going to the bar every night," answered Timmy looking lost.

"So what you're saying is everything is fucked up if we disappear?" interjects Amos after listening to their narratives on the world without them.

"Basically … yeah," answered Vern.

"Well … not for me … I mean I wasn't really affected by your disappearance, except for a punch in the mouth," said Brett thinking that things couldn't be better.

Amos looked at them. "Where are the Pukwudgees now?"

"Somewhere near the center of town based on the sound of that explosion," said Brett.

"So what do we have for weapons? I have a .22 pistol," said Amos. "What do the cops that are chasing them have? A lot more than us. Any ideas on how we catch them? Brett, you got any weapons, Vern … you?"

Vern and Brett looked at each other, realizing they had nothing and they had abandoned their responsibility to keep up the vigil or at least research on what they may have to deal with. The horse was out of the barn and they had been asleep.

Amos continued, "The cops may eventually take down the Pukwudgees, though I doubt it. That still won't bring back the two people, maybe more they've killed. And what about that construction site … and the hole! We need another plan. We can't change the fact the Pukwudgees found the hole but we can change what happens afterward."

"What are you thinking Amos?" asked Timmy snapping out of his confusion as to his family's fate.

"I think we go back and do it over … together … the same age."

"If we go back we won't be the same age!" said Vern

"Not you two, me and Timmy."

"Oh …" uttered Vern trying to figure this out. "What's that mean for me and Brett?"

"I don't know about Brett, except for not getting hit in the mouth by Colin. But for you, maybe you'll do something with your talents and not have to deal with me missing."

"How does that stop the Pukwudgees?" asked Brett really thinking 'Wait a minute what does this mean to me?'

Amos noticed Brett's second thoughts. "Brett, nothing's going to change. Timmy and my disappearance seems to have had no impact on your life. Except … if we go back, we'll have to keep in touch with you until 1992. By August 27th we have to have something in place to permanently stop them from coming out of the hole.

"But won't the four of us staying in contact … ehhhh … change things?"

Timmy leaped out of his chair, grabbed Brett by his now broad shoulders and slammed his knee into his crotch as Brett was reclined in the chair.

"You selfish fuck! People are DEAD!" screamed Timmy as he wildly punched at Brett's head. Brett caught completely by surprise doubled over with his arms in a defensive posture as intense pain shot up his groin. Brett could have easily tossed him across the room, but the pain in his groin was intense and he was totally caught off guard. Luckily Vern and Amos were immediately on Timmy, pulling him off.

"Cool it Timmy! Cool it!" whispered Amos as he applied a half-nelson on Timmy. Vern took a position between Brett and Timmy in case Brett recovered from the blow and went after Timmy. But Brett wasn't going anywhere soon … the knee had made a direct hit.

"Fuck!" he groaned as he held his groin.

Amos had calmed Timmy and gradually released his hold and said, "Look, we're going back! We got to fix this! Brett, I'll make sure your life remains like it is, but you gotta help … now … today."

"Christ, Timmy why did you do that?" asked Brett as the pain subsided.

"Because everything's fucked up cause of what we done and now you don't want to help fix it," panting as he cooled down.

"I'll help! I'll help! I'm just overwhelmed by the whole thing. I owe you guys. Just humor my questions. Frankly, I'm scared about changing my past … and future."

Amos seeing the situation had calmed down asked, "Vern, when did Colin and his friends start chasing you?"

"I don't know, about 8:30 or 9:00 at the rotary."

"We got to get back before 7:00 to call off the dogs," said Timmy, "cause Mom probably got Colin all fired up and then he'd have to round up his friends to find you."

"So we got to be in the hole before seven. What time is it?" asked Amos.

Brett looked at his Rolex, "Almost 1:00."

"Good, we have some time. Which one of you can get info the quickest on what's been happening in town with the Pukwudgees? Vern?" asked Amos knowing the answer.

"What you thinking, little brother?"

"I came out before you!"

"Yeah, but right now I'm older squirt and I'm enjoying the moment." Vern smiled and so did Amos.

"Go try to find out what is happening and get back here before 5:00."

"What do you want me to do?" asked Brett.

"Tell me everything you can remember that's happened between 1968 and 1992. Tell me history. What big things happened in between? What would be the best way to make money? We can use it to make sure your life is the same and get the stuff we need for our next meeting with the Pukwudgees … yesterday to you … 24 years for me and Timmy."

78

THE PUKWUDGEES REACHED THE southern shore of the great pond without further incident. The shoreline was vast, and dangerous, now being dotted with hovels similar to the areas from which they had come. Things had changed! Pomarat surveyed the situation to decide their best course of action. Passing by all these hovels would slow them down, however if they could find a canoe … that could speed up the journey. But the risk would be high if the iron bird came back. They would be in the open.

Pomarat squinted and surveyed the coastline more closely. Many of the hovels had a wooden structure extending into the water with what obviously were strange looking watercrafts of some sort next to them. Maybe they could take one and row to the north end of the pond, keeping close to the shoreline in case the iron bird returned.

The first hovel they came to had a small 26' cabin cruiser tied to the dock. Pomarat told his braves to stay put on the shore as he went up on the dock to investigate. He checked the hovel for signs of life and seeing none ran down the dock to the boat. He knew before he did, it was much too large for his braves to maneuver quickly if the iron bird appeared. But he was curious nonetheless, as there may be something useful. How could you paddle such a craft? The concept of an outboard motor was foreign to him and the twin 75's on the back were a mystery. The owner of the craft had removed all the electronic gear such as the radio and fish finder. Pomarat had no clue anything was missing. However, a finely varnished oar on hooks under the gunwale caught his eye.

He hopped into the boat and took the oar from its hooks and placed it on the deck. Then he saw another oar under the gunwale on the other side of the boat. He placed that on the deck also. He surveyed the inside of the craft and saw nothing else of value. If they could find a smaller craft, the oars may be useful. He climbed back on the dock and retrieved an oar in each hand and ran down the dock to his party. The size of the oars made him look like a two-fisted pole-vaulter.

He gave the oars to Massot and Sarkem. Hysko was glad there were only two. Pomarat motioned them to follow as he proceeded up the eastern shoreline. They passed several more hovels with boats tied to their docks. Most were smaller than the first, but they were not what Pomarat was hoping for. At the next hovel, he stopped and raised his hand and crouched. Pulled up on the shore out of the water was what he had been hoping for … a canoe … not as crude of those of his tribe, but a canoe in shape nevertheless. However in the canoe was a very young Wampanoag girl lightly crooning to her doll as she rocked gently in the rear seat. She seemed to be imagining she was sailing around on the pond.

Pomarat surveyed the area and signaled retreat to the cover of a storage-shed on the property they had just passed. Silently the braves retreated unnoticed by the adorable three-year old who continued crooning away lost in the warmth of the day and the quite of the lake. Once behind the shed, out of site of the little girl, Pomarat outlined a plan.

Hysko would go and quiet the girl but not kill her. She could be of use if a sacrifice was needed later. Hysko did not like the idea of sacrificing her. He loved her crooning and saw her as a beautiful child. But he kept these thoughts to himself and nodded remembering Pomarat's last furious outburst. Pomarat stated he would push the canoe to the water after Hysko had the girl secured and quiet. Sarkem and Massot would go to both ends of the canoe with the oars and do the rowing. They would go north staying close to the shore but far enough out to make a straight line to the northern most part of the lake without navigating any coves. He looked at his braves making sure their eyes indicated they understood the plan. Satisfied, Pomarat looked at the hovel up from their position and saw a woman behind a small square of clear material similar to invisible door they encounter at the home of the old woman with the cat. All the hovels had similar clear material in many places. He watched her for a moment. She must be the mother of this child. She would glance down at the canoe periodically, then her attention was focused on whatever she was doing. The hovel was far enough from the canoe that even if his timing was off and they executed the plan smoothly they would be well in the water before she could reach them. A mother protecting her cub was not something to be underestimated though. If she did happen to become a problem, Pomarat would be ready.

He signaled his men to be set and watched the window. There! The woman checked the canoe. The babe was still rocking and crooning. The woman returned her attention to what she was doing. Pomarat signaled Hysko to go! He looked at Massot and Sarkem as if to say, "Don't screw up!" Pomarat then followed Hysko towards the canoe on a run. Sarkem and Massot followed him, each dragging a six-foot oar ensuring they did not drop it or get it caught in the underbrush.

Hysko hopped in the canoe and wrapped an arm around the girl and a hand over her mouth but not before the girl was able to let out a shrill squeal. She had been awoken from her crooning trance when she heard the trampling sound from her left. No sooner had Hysko silenced the girl and was seated behind her, he felt the canoe being moved to the water by Pomarat. Sarkem and Massot hopped in the front and the back of the canoe. Pomarat hopped in behind Hysko and the girl.

The shrill squeal did not reach the auditory senses of the mother but they did connect on a subliminal level, which has yet to be explained on a scientific basis. Mothers seem to sense when their cubs are in distress. Theresa Williams glanced up. She was still rinsing a pot. Usually she would look up after rinsing the pot and drying it off and before beginning washing another item. "ABBY!!!!!"

She saw these four … she wasn't sure what. Kids, midgets, Indians, kids? What were they!? She burst out the back slider running to her child screaming, "Abby!!!! Stop!!! Abby!!!!" By the time she reached the shoreline, the canoe was forty feet off shore. "BRING BACK MY BABY, YOU BASTARDS!"

Pomarat was standing in the canoe facing her. He had removed his bow from his shoulder and was aiming it at her. Fortunately, Massot and Sarkem were still trying to adapt six-foot oars to be used as three-foot paddles and Pomarat's footing and aim was unstable. Pomarat almost went over the side while trying to aim but quickly righted himself by grabbing the side. He decided to sit down till Massot and Sarkem got the hang of it, though he didn't like it.

Theresa was in a panic now. Should she swim after the canoe or follow on shore or go back to the house and call the police. The swimming option was eliminated when Pomarat seated himself and resumed knocking his arrow and pointing at her direction. Besides, if they went to the center of the lake she would surely drown. She couldn't let her baby get out of sight! She would follow them up the shoreline, keeping them in sight and scream for help all the way hoping a neighbor was home and would call the police. "HELP! HELP! THEY'VE TAKEN MY BABY!" she screamed keeping her eye on the canoe.

By now the canoe was well from shore. Massot and Sarkem had learned to choke-up on the oars and were paddling smoothly. Pomarat relaxed his bow, seeing the mother was following them on the shoreline. This would be a problem if the iron bird returned. Not only would he have to consider the iron bird but also a delirious screaming mother if they turned to shore. He instructed Massot and Sarkem to head for the western shore instead.

Theresa noticed the subtle change in the heading of the canoe. "NOOOOOOOOOO!" she screamed. Should she go back to her house and call the police or keep the canoe in sight? She quickly glanced up the beach looking for signs of life and back to the canoe going ever further across the pond. She kept running up the shore through the backyards alternating her concentration from the shoreline to the ever-shrinking canoe.

She came to a yard where a solid fence ran to the shoreline. Without hesitation she ran into the water to get around it. On the other side was an elderly woman tending to her garden. "Help me!" Theresa screamed. The woman, not having her hearing-aid on, barely heard her and turned. She was surprised out of her quiet moment by this dark-skinned woman who had appeared in her backyard out of nowhere. The woman's face showed extreme distress. She was pointing back out on the lake begging her to … Mrs. Wellington reached to turn on her hearing aid in time to catch "… my baby!"

"What about your baby, dear?"

"Kidnappers took my little girl! They're in that canoe going across the lake! I need to call the police!"

Mrs. Wellington fumbled in the pocket of her gardening apron for her distance glasses. This is going too slow … "Do you have a phone?"

"Why yes dear it's in the house. Where's the canoe?" Mrs. Wellington asked getting her glasses in place.

Theresa wasn't waiting, she ran up the slight incline into the house seeking the phone assuming there would be one near the kitchen. And there was … on the wall, with an extra long extension cord. Theresa dialed the Mashpee police.

"Is that dot a canoe?" asked Mrs. Wellington, pointing and turning only to see the stranger running into her house.

79

"POLICE." SIKES LISTENED TO the distraught woman tell her story on the other end of the line. His heart said fuck, his mind said where the fuck is Reed. "We'll have a chopper and cruisers on the way, Mrs. Williams. What is your location?"

Theresa eyes darted around the kitchen for something. There! Mail! She picked up an envelope. "94 Lakefront Drive, but the canoe is heading to the other side of the lake!"

"Stay put, we'll get someone out to you and someone to the other side of the lake. The chopper will pinpoint the canoe's location."

"Thank you!" she stated with heartfelt gratitude of a mother who was helpless to help her child.

Sikes hung up the phone wondering how he was going to fulfill his promise. He had no officers yet! Then the first call-in showed up. And logical thinking returned to replace temporary anxiety. "Hey Nelson, go across the quad and get the fire-rescue boat and anyone the fire department can spare, if anyone. Launch at the Town Landing at Mashpee Pond and head north along the western shore. Look for four midget Indians in a canoe, they've kidnapped a little girl. They are also suspected in multiple homicides."

"What?" asked Nelson wondering if this was a joke?

"Do it!"

"I got to get in my uniform."

"Fuck the uniform, wear the badge on that shirt and pretend you're a detective. Make sure you bring your weapon and radio. Now go! We'll get you better info when the chopper gets here."

Sikes picked up the radio. "Reed, come in. I need you."

Sikes waited.

"Roger, where to? I'm back in the air."

"Mashpee Pond. Our targets are now in a canoe, crossing to the western shore. They have a hostage. A three year-old girl, Abby Williams. Stay high and radio their location when you get there."

"Fuck! Roger that. Be there in five." Reed decided to fly the treetops till he got to the pond and then ascend. He wanted to muffle the sound of his approach as long as possible not to spook the midgets.

Tom Miller came out of his office. “Hey, I just saw Nelson run out of here. Is he going to hunt up Vern?”

“No. We got a kid taken hostage on Mashpee Pond in a canoe. I got to call Sandwich PD.”

“Is there anything I can do?” asked Miller realizing it was time to be a police officer and not a bureaucrat or a politician.

“Yes, go out to 94 Lakeshore Drive and pick up Mrs. Williams, she’s the kid’s mother who called in. Monitor the radio. When we get the kid back she should be there.”

“How are we getting the kid back, what’s her name?”

“Abby, and I don’t know yet. Nelson’s getting the fire department boat and Reed’s coming fast with the chopper. And I won’t know till I talk to Sandwich PD if they got anything.”

“Okay, call them and keep me posted. I’m on my way.”

Two more call-ins came. Linda was dispatched to the west side of the pond to the 4-H camp figuring that would be the best place to maneuver up and down the western shoreline on foot or by car. David was sent out to find Vern and bring him to the station. Sikes called Sandwich PD.

80

ABBY LOOKED UP AT Hysko who held her secure in his short but strong arms. She looked him squarely in the eye and said, “I know what you are!” Hysko, smiling, looked at her not knowing what she said but liking the soft tone of her sentence. “You’re Pukwudgees!”

He heard the word ‘Pukwudgees’, but had no idea that he was a Pukwudgee - no more than a Brownie would know it was a Brownie or a Pixie would know it was a Pixie. These were names given them over time as stories were passed down. If she had said Itchiwan, he would have recognized it. They were the Indians of the Marsh in English, but the Itchiwan in his language. But then she continued, “I know Pukwudgees. Maushop is going to crush you!”

Hysko’s eyes widen, Pomarat’s head swung around. Massot and Sarkem glanced at the little girl and paused in rowing. She uttered the name Maushop. A name! Never manipulated by language. He was Maushop to them and Maushop throughout the ages up to this little girl. Did she know him? Did she know they had killed his sons? Was she a witch?

Pomarat then heard the faint return of the iron bird from the east. She was a witch! Maushop! The summoning of the iron bird! Yes this small one was not what she seemed! The western shore was within reach. Time to take action before the iron bird was overhead.

Pomarat tapped Hysko on the shoulder and yelled at Sarkem and Massot to row to shore! This was a challenge with the long oars. He looked at Abby … the witch. Hysko saw the look on his face and knew this would be bad. Pomarat stood over Hysko as he held Abby in his arms, indicating to hand her over. Hysko released his embrace on the child but did not offer her to Pomarat. Nevertheless, Pomarat reached over, grabbed her little arm and tossed her over the side like a Frisbee.

Hysko was in shock. He had come to like the little girl. He looked up at Pomarat with open mouth. Pomarat only pointed to the tree line on the eastern shore. Hysko looked and then heard the faint approach of the iron bird, yet he glanced back to water to see the fate of the little one.

81

VERN DROVE TO THE police complex figuring that would be the best place to get caught up on the events of the day. David was just leaving on his mission to find Vern and there he was! "Hey Vern! Sikes needs to see you."

Vern got out of his truck, "Why?"

"Don't know, just told me to find you and bring you here."

"What did I do?"

"Nothing I know of, I think he just wants to ask you what you know about these midget Indians causing havoc."

"I don't know anything about midget Indians."

"That doesn't matter, I just got to get you back to see Sikes. Know what I'm saying?"

"Yeah, Dave. Relax, I'll go see him. Come on, you can take credit for the collar."

"Fuck Vern. That's not the point. As far as I can see the town's turned upside down and this is my assignment."

"I know man. I'll go in."

Vern walked up to the desk, Sikes was busy in conversation with Reed in the chopper. "How do you know?"

"Look I came in low to muffle the sound. When I got to the pond, I raised up, and located the canoe. There are only four people in the canoe. No child! They're almost at the shore by the 4-H site."

"You sure there's no child!"

"Definitely affirmative!"

"Fuckin' buzz 'em hard! Slow their progress. If they get to land, they'll be hard to catch."

"Roger! I'm gonna sit on that canoe and scare the shit out of them!"

Sikes clicked off and saw Vern standing before him.

"Dave says you want to see me."

Sikes eyes dropped, and then slowly rose. He got up from his chair and came around his desk and looked Vern in the eyes. "I got something to tell you."

Vern got nervous, not knowing where this was going.

"Vern, your mother has been murdered." Sikes watched Vern closely not knowing how he would react. The chief was en-route to Mrs. Williams so the duty fell on him.

Vern was in shock, "What??? How???"

"You ok?, have a seat at my desk." Sikes took his arm and pointed to the chair.

"No I don't need to sit Billy, I got to go to her."

"No Vern, don't. She's gone. There's nothing you can do out there. Wait here until the captain gets back. You'll only disturb the site and hamper our ability to catch these bastards."

"What bastards?"

"Look Vern, we've had multiple homicides in the town. The suspects always come back as four midgets dressed as Indians. If you can give me any info, any info on who they may be, please fill me in."

Vern looked at the floor things were out of hand, his mom … never had he thought she would cross paths with the Pukwudgees. This was his fault maybe for keeping his secret shut up all these years. "I got to go out there Billy."

"DON'T! Remember your mother as you last saw her!"

"I got to find my Dad then."

"I'll send David to find him, you stay ..."

He was cut off by the radio. Vern left.

82

"BILLY! REED HERE. I'VE lifted off the canoe. I can't sit on them. I see the little girl in the water. She's paddling. I don't want to kick up the water. They're heading for shore just south of the 4-H campground. I called Sandwich PD. They got two cruisers heading to the location. I know you're shorthanded."

"Thanks Reed, I got an officer going to 4-H. May be there now. Keep an eye on the girl."

"Linda where are you?"

"Just pulled up at the cafeteria at the camp."

"Nelson what's your 20?"

"Getting the boat in the water at the landing."

He'll never get there in time thought Sikes. "Linda?"

"Yes sir?"

"Did you hear my conversation with Reed?"

"Yes sir."

"I want you to proceed through the woods on foot down the shoreline and get to the little girl, Abby."

"Yes sir."

"The suspects will be coming your way. Try not to be seen by them. Do not attempt to engage or stop them, your priority is getting to the girl and seeing her to safety. Understand?"

"Roger that sir. I'm muting my radio."

"Linda, if they do see you, use deadly force ... no warnings! Understand?"

Linda never had heard Sikes last order. She was well on her way through the woods and had already muted her radio. The thought of the child in the water made all his instructions unnecessary.

Vern was long gone before Sikes realized Linda's radio was muted.

"Nelson!"

"Yes sir?"

"Get that boat in the water and get your ass up to 4-H to back up Linda!"

"Yes sir, I understand."

83

THERESA'S EYES NEVER LEFT the canoe even though it was so far away. She picked up the sound of the approaching chopper at the same time as Pomarat. Then she watched in horror as something small was hurled into the lake. She ran to the street planning to run home and get her car knowing that little thing was Abby. Tears were running down her cheeks but her only thought was to get to her baby. Chief Miller saw her running down the street as he drove up Lakeshore Drive and pulled over. "Mrs. Williams? Get in. I'll get you there."

84

ABBY FELT HERSELF FLYING through the air and realized she maybe shouldn't have said anything about Pukwudgees or Maush-op. She tucked in her little legs and hit the water holding her breath and closing her eyes. She sunk two to three feet into the water. She extended her arms and legs and opened her eyes. Gradually she floated to the surface and began dog paddling. This was the first time she did this without water wings or mom standing by. She could see the shore, and heard the helicopter overhead. But years of Water Babies and Toddler Tadpoles had taught her to focus on getting to the edge of the pool or momma's arms. Momma isn't here so the beach would have to do. She began humming and calmly paddling to shore. It was a long way but she would keep humming and paddling and before you know it, she'd be there she thought.

85

LUCKILY FOR LINDA, THE chopper was lifting and her ears could tune into the surroundings … a little bit … the whomp whomp whomp of the chopper was still present in the background. Although this hindered her senses it also served to camouflage her clumsiness when stepping on branches and causing noises. The underbrush was thick in places, providing some cover but much of the area was pine barrens with a thick needle ground cover and open areas under the canopy of the pines.

The girl was in the water. She had to get to her. Somewhere between her and the little girl, they'd be coming ashore and Sikes wanted her to avoid them and get to the girl. She knew the girl was the priority, but based on the landscape, avoiding an encounter with the perps may not be possible. She un-holstered her sidearm, checked that it was loaded and the safety was off. She scanned the woods toward the shore line, saw no movement and made a beeline for the shore some thirty yards south of her position through the pine barrens.

Sarkem and Massot were dragging the canoe up onto the shore. Pomarat was surveying the woods. Hysko was standing knee deep in the water, looking for signs of the little girl on the water. Pomarat angrily ordered them to move and proceeded into the woods. The iron bird was hovering overhead. He was intent on getting deep into the woods out of the sight. They set on a run leaving the canoe behind until Pomarat came to a dead stop. He had spotted Linda. Without hesitation, he knocked an arrow and fired it in her direction some twenty yards away.

Linda felt a sharp object glaze off her left shoulder causing a slight pain and a red coloring to appear on her uniform. She glanced in the direction of the shore and saw the four midget Indians. The one in the lead was readying for another shot. Shit! She instinctively went to the ground and rolled to the nearest pine. This threw Pomarat off. Now he needed to look for the target and aim. Sarkem and Massot were pulling their bows off their shoulders looking to acquire the target, which at this point only Pomarat had a bead. Linda peered around the pine tree. In the back of her mind she was thinking of the little girl in the water and the urgency of her mission. She raised her department issued side-arm and unloaded the full clip in the direction of her attackers.

The rapport of the nine rounds shocked the shit out of the four Pukwudgees. Even Pomarat lowered his bow as something whizzed by his ear and caused blood to flow down his neck. He put his hand to his ear and saw that it was bloodied but his ear was still there. Sarkem screamed as a meatball sized portion of his shoulder exploded from his body. Hysko ran to Sarkem's aid clamping deerskin from his satchel on the bloody hole. Massot wildly shot an arrow in Linda's direction and rushed to help Hysko get Sarkem out of danger. Linda watched Massot's arrow fly off to her left and ejected and reloaded another clip.

Pomarat had seen enough. Witchcraft! He screamed at Massot and Hysko to grab Sarkem and follow him north. They ran. That woman had a thunder stick that could be deadly. They had no answer for it. Surely it was witchcraft brought on by the child he had thrown into the water. She was in league with Maushop! She now commanded the iron bird and the witch with the thunder stick! Hysko secretly hoped his unwillingness to give up the little girl would be noticed by her but he knew deep down inside his efforts were superficial and not worthy of merit.

Linda saw the perps running away and for a moment debated whether she should unload another clip in their direction, but she needed to get to the girl and this was her last clip. She ran to the shore and saw Abby paddling away about twenty feet from shore … humming. Linda ran into the water and swam to Abby. Abby wrapped her arms around her neck and said, "Did you shoot those Pukwudgees? I heard the gunshots."

"Yes dear, I scared them away. Let's get you to your momma."

"Momma's on the other side of the lake. That's where we live, on Lakeshore Drive."

"Don't worry sweetheart. You're safe now. Momma will be here soon," said Linda as she hugged Abby tight and waded out of the water. She also un-holstered her sidearm again knowing she had a trek to get back to the cruiser. She hoped her brief time in the water hadn't deadened her powder. She turned on her radio. "Sergeant Sikes? You there?"

"This is Reed. Where are they?"

"Heading north. The girl is safe with me."

"Roger that. I'll try and find them."

Reed flew over Linda's head on the treetops trying to pick up the trail of the Pukwudgees.

"Linda! You okay?" came Sikes voice over the radio.

"Yes sir. I have Abby. She seems okay."

"I'm fine, tell Mr. Sikes to get my momma."

Sikes heard the little girl's voice in the background and smiled for the first time today. "Tell her momma's on the way, the Chief has her in his car and will be there shortly.

"Sir?"

"Yes Linda?"

"I unloaded a clip at the perps and have one clip left, but I went into the water to get Abby so I don't know if it's any good. I have to follow the path the perps took to get back to the camp and my cruiser."

"So you engaged the suspects?"

"Yes sir, they spotted me and nicked my shoulder with one of their arrows."

"Are you okay?"

"Yes sir, only a flesh wound."

"How serious?"

"Sir it's a line from the Monty Python movie. I'm fine. I fired off a clip and think I hit one maybe two, but they all fled the scene to the north."

"Okay, don't take any chances. Proceed slowly to the camp. Your clip may not work. We don't want to take any chances with Abby. We'll come to you. Nelson and the Chief should be there shortly."

"Roger, sir."

"Good job Linda."

86

ONCE OUTSIDE THE STATION, Vern ran to his truck. It was a short drive to his mother's place. He had to go there, see what happened and convey that information to Amos, no matter how horrible. Amos and Timmy were now the only chance for a do-over. Now their little escapade in 1968 had resulted in consequences that had hit closer to home than was acceptable. His life being screwed up was one thing … it was just his lot in life. But his mother …

As he pulled into the drive, Fredricks popped out of the house with his hands raised frantically indicating he should stop! Which he did, and got out of the truck. "Stay there, Vern! Don't come any closer!" commanded Fredricks now pointing at him.

"Matt, it's okay. Sikes told me what happened. I got to see for myself."

"I just got off the radio with Sikes. He said you'd be coming here and not to let you disturb the site."

"Matt, Matt, I got to see for myself so I can find my dad and tell him exactly what happened."

"Fuck Vern! You don't want to see her. Please. I promise you, you don't want to remember her this way."

Vern was now face to face with Matt, "If what she suffered is as horrible as you and Sikes say, the least I can do is to see it AND REMEMBER HER THAT WAY, so when you catch these guys … and bring them to trial … there will no doubt in my mind when I plead for their execution before the Judge!"

Matt grabbed Vern's shoulder, "Okay … put your hands in your pockets and don't take them out while you're in the house. You can't touch anything, especially your mom – no matter what emotions come over you! The only smoking gun we have in this murder is fingerprints. It may be the only chance for a conviction. You understand?"

"Yeah, I do."

"Okay, follow me and don't go ahead of me. Understand?"

"I won't."

Matt led Vern into the house. As they approached the kitchen, Vern saw the pool of blood and his mother's lifeless body with her beautiful face caved in and the chopping knife standing in her chest. His eyes filled with tears, a hand came out of his pocket to steady himself on the edge of the sofa.

"Vern! You okay?" asked Fredricks noticing immediately Vern was on the verge of losing it. Vern was sobbing now.

"Come on let's go," said Matt softly while firmly putting his arm around his shoulder and leading him back out. Vern didn't resist. Once outside he began wiping his eyes with his sleeves.

"I got to find my dad."

"You gonna be okay to drive?"

"I'll be fine in a minute or two, but I dread trying to sleep tonight."

"This is my card."

"Your card? You guys have cards?" asked Vern trying to get himself under control.

"Yeah we have them to give to informants and witnesses and anyone who may have information. If you need anything or get hammered and need a ride, call me."

"Yeah Matt, I'll do that." Vern went back to his truck. He would not be trying to find his dad. He had to get back to Amos and press their need for a do-over.

87

AMOS AND TIMMY LISTENED intently as Brett spit out bits and pieces of what had happened between the years of 1968 and 1992. The retreat from Vietnam, the hostages in Iran, an actor becomes President and with the convincing bluff of a fictitious missile defense system, brings an end to the Soviet Union and tears down the Berlin Wall. Also, just recently the collapse of the rental real estate market due to the 1986 tax reform.

"We need a book to bring back covering 1977 to 1991," said Amos rubbing his chin.

"Why?" asked Timmy.

"So in 1992, we have the ability to stop them from coming out of the hole … to do that we need money, a lot of money," answered Amos.

Brett understood what Amos was looking for. "I'll go to the library and see what they got that I can take out. Something small enough for you to take back. But you'll probably need the whole library."

As Brett's BMW left, Vern's truck sped down the road into his driveway. Amos and Timmy were inside the house looking at any printed material Brett had inside the house. Vern ran inside. Amos saw the look on his face. "What?"

"The fuckin' Pukwudgees killed mom! Just this morning! Brutally! They caved her face in! I saw it! It's my fault for not telling her what happened!" Vern broke into tears kneeling and burying his face into his brother's arms. Amos embraced his larger brother's body which was convulsing in heavy sobs.

"It ain't gonna happen, Vern! We're gonna fix it! I promise you we're gonna fix it!" said Amos trying to calm his brother. In his mind he was thinking 'we really fucked up, I hope this works.'

88

MASSOT AND HYSKO HELD up Sarkem and ran north through the brush. His shoulder was bleeding profusely despite the hastily applied deerskin bandage. Pomarat took up the rear knowing the servant of Maushop was behind them with a thunder stick and the witch child. Yet again he had failed by not killing the child. Other innocents would correct this, but not now. His group must seek safety. He had come to the realization that this was not his time. The killing of Maushop's sons had somehow set in motion a series of events that catapulted him to another place, a place vaguely similar to his own but not. This was too much to digest with one of his men wounded and on the run. He had to get them back to the salt marsh … home. Hopefully following the long known trails would not result in running into more strange hovels and iron beasts. But this would not be the case. It was wishful thinking. He heard movement to the east in the woods. He commanded the others to continue north, he would catch up. Pomarat ran with them for ten yards and crouched facing the noise and listened with bow ready and arrow in place. The witch servant of Maushop had veered off to the east toward the direction of the sounds.

Linda broke her radio silence. "The suspects are heading north through the woods. I'm headed west back to my cruiser. Is there anyone coming in my direction?"

"Affirmative Linda, there are four Sandwich Officers coming towards you. They're on this frequency," answered Sykes, "Officer Browner you got that?"

"Yeah Billy, we know she's coming this way. One of us will stay with her till the mother arrives and three of us will pursue the suspects. Where do you think they're heading? If we don't catch up to them shortly they'll be crossing into our territory."

"No idea Bobby, no idea. Either the State police or us will get your department everything we know as soon as possible, but I don't even know what we really know at this point. It's chaos here and we're undermanned. But they are vicious little shits so don't hesitate to use lethal force."

"Got it, Billy. I see Linda and the girl. Gotta go. Out."

Bobby and Billy played hockey together on Thursday nights and had become good friends. Next time he saw him he'd have to remember to tell him the dick in the chopper was the guy who occasionally showed up and went head hunting. He remembered Bobby who was an excellent player, had forestalled such an attempt with a well timed raised elbow which 'accidentally' hit Reed's jaw before Reed could make full contact. Bobby apologized profusely saying "Jesus, I didn't see you coming. You okay?" The side-glance he gave Billy indicated he knew exactly where Reed was.

Pomarat heard the chatter of humans in an incomprehensible language and the responses … human, but not. Far away. Pomarat was new to radio communications. Was this how Maushop communicated with his servants? Though he couldn't see them, he figured there were three to five humans other than the woman with the thunder stick and little girl. He knew enough. He was out manned, time to retreat. He ran north to catch up with his men.

Bobby met Linda at her cruiser. "Great job Linda. This must be the brave little girl. You alright honey?"

"Yes sir, they were Pukwudgees!"

Bob Browner was a Sergeant like Billy. He was initially going to leave one of his men and chase the suspects himself. But based on the girl's response he changed his mind. "Honey what's a Pukwudgee? Linda, you're bleeding. You okay?"

"Yeah, only a flesh wound," she said with a smile.

"Monty Python, right?"

"Yeah."

"Give me Abby, I want to hear about her adventure. Abby, you know I have a daughter your age. Adams, can you look at Linda's wound and make sure it's treated. You two pursue the suspects and listen, DON'T HESITATE TO SHOOT TO KILL, these guys are extremely dangerous and responsible for multiple deaths. Understand?"

"Yes sir."

"So Abby what is a Pukwudgee?" returning his attention to the little girl with a smile.

"They're EVIL! They do bad things."

"What kind of things?"

"They kill babies! They killed Maushop's sons and Maushop crushed them."

"Where did you learn about Pukwudgees, honey?"

"Momma read me the stories, and the storytellers at the Pow-Wow would tell us about them too."

"Abby, you have been a GREAT help in this investigation! Adams, how's Linda's wound?"

"All set sir, just a graze, all patched up."

"Linda would you mind taking Abby and wait for her mom? I have to get her important information into headquarters. Adams, go back up the other guys." Abby beamed with pride having been so useful.

Bobby handed off Abby to Linda and walked to his cruiser deep in thought. Myths, legends … imitators popped into his mind. How the fuck could four midgets find each other and decide they were going to be these Pukwudgees of legend? And how did they develop the abilities to pull it off? Whether they're the real deal or imitators, they'd be operating from the same play book.

"Hey Billy, come in."

"Yeah Bobby."

"I spoke with the little girl. This may be something or it may be nothing. I know you got no one at the moment, but maybe you can call the library and have them do some research on Pukwudgees. I think they are some sort of Wampanoag legend and we may have four Pukwudgee wannabes living out some sort of fantasy."

"What?"

"Look Billy, I don't know what a Pukwudgee is, but there is an Indian legend out there about them, and you know how nut cases love to imitate this kind of stuff. Based on the girl's story and everybody's description of them, it may be a lead as to what they'll do next. We need to know where Pukwudgees go, because these imitators will probably be heading there."

"Okay Bobby, I'll call the library and the tribal council and relay this to the Staties. You can relay it to your own department."

"Thanks Billy! Keep me posted."

Bobby called the Sandwich PD and informed them the four midget killers were crossing into their jurisdiction and he needed someone to contact the library and get any info they had on Pukwudgees. When asked why, he said it seems we have imitators living out a fantasy. Bobby knew they were heading north and not in Sandwich yet. Jurisdiction was not really an issue any more since Mashpee called them in. "Adams, you there?"

"Yes sir."

"Have you caught up with the others?"

"Not yet."

"When you do, tell them I'm driving up to Perch Cove to intercept them and be aware I'll be in front of them."

"Roger that sir."

Bobby told Linda to sit tight that help was on the way. He jumped in his cruiser and headed up Rt. 130 to Perch Cove.

89

BRETT'S BMW SCREECHED INTO the driveway. He jumped out and ran to the house with several large books under his arms. "I got a fucking bonanza!"

"What did you get?" asked Timmy his eyes lighting up from Brett's obvious excitement.

Brett dumped the three books on the table like a hunter dumping a deer carcass in front of a starving tribe. "Gentleman, these books will serve as a road map for investing over the last 20 years. It's the history of the stock markets, commodities markets and currency fluctuations. If you two fucks go back with these we can get enough money to make sure this doesn't happen."

Vern was the first to take interest for obvious reasons. He had just witnessed what would happen if something else didn't happen.

"You got to have money to make money," said Vern. "We won't have any when Amos goes back."

"I know! I know!" answered Brett. "I will! It can get us started! Not enough though. So you guys will have to improvise to make more. Vern … you have to be the athlete you were meant to be. Hopefully you'll make the big time. Timmy, your brother obviously becomes a power in the Irish mob in Boston. There must be some way you can generate some scratch from that. And Amos … you're the smartest of us all … you handle the money using these road maps to carry out the plan, whatever it may be."

"Brett, there's a lot of 'ifs' in this plan," said Amos.

"I know that. You and Timmy are the ones going back. You two will have to orchestrate the plan. Me and Vern will be clueless, like we were when you found us today. You two will have to convince us to buy into it all over again."

"Shit, he's got a point Amos," piped in Timmy. "Hey Brett, why don't you give us a thousand to get started?"

"Yeah, yeah, I got that!" He went into his bedroom and returned with ten crisp hundreds and handed them to Timmy. Timmy glanced at Amos eyes wide.

Vern eyebrows raised and commented. "Shit man, you got that kind of scratch in your house? Fucking Amos, remind me about this when you get back. This house is an easy target."

"Fuck, give me those bills Timmy," said Amos as snatched them out of Timmy's hand. Timmy's mouth was agape as the small fortune left his grasp. Amos examined the bills. There it was under Benjamin Franklin's face – 'Series 1988'. "Here Brett, these are worthless to us and will probably get us arrested."

"What???" yelled Timmy.

"The bills weren't made till twenty years from our time," said Amos to Timmy.

"Shit!" said a dejected Timmy.

"What time is it?" asked Amos rubbing his forehead, his brain scrambled from all this information.

"5:30," answered Brett.

"Timmy, we got to go." Amos picked up the books and handed one to Timmy.

"You can't let anyone see those books! Especially me." said Brett.

"I know that better than anyone," answered Amos.

"Bring back Mom," pleaded Vern.

Amos weighed the enormity of that request. "Vern, I'll have to convince you I saw you in the future when I see you again. And when I see you again, there won't be anything from the future you remember. I don't know how I'm gonna keep you on the straight and narrow."

"Fuck Amos, prior to you disappearing, my only goal was to make the NFL. If you're back, I'm on that path." Vern looked around Brett's house and then looked at the books under Amos arms. "Show me those fuckers and I'm sure I'll be convinced, I'm not a dunce."

"Brett, give me and Timmy a ride to the hole," said Amos looking at his brother. "We gotta go!"

90

BROWNER SPED TO THE last cul-de-sac in Perch Cove nearest the lake. Pomarat heard the engine of his iron beast. The beasts were to be avoided especially in their crippled state. He headed for the shoreline again willing to risk a confrontation with the beast in the sky rather than those on the ground. He knew the narrow inlet was here and if they could find a canoe they could traverse the lake and be on the other side in no time … hopefully before the beast in the sky could react.

'Maktahdou, we need your help,' he thought as he hoped for the availability of a watercraft.

Browner proceeded toward the lake his weapon drawn. As he entered the woods he hit the transmit button of his radio twice to signal his men on the ground he wanted to talk if they were able to communicate safely. "Sergeant, Adams here. We're all together now and we can hear movement and voices ahead."

"I'm coming in from the last cul-de-sac in Perch Cove, which would be to your left."

"Roger sir."

"Yeah, just be sure you have a clear sight line if you decide to shoot."

"Yes sir," as if I need to be told thought Adams.

They were so close that Pomarat and his braves heard the conversation from behind and to the left. Pomarat didn't like this. Surround sound spooked him. Pomarat silently signaled Hysko and Massot to head to the lake. They were supporting an ailing Sarkem. At the shoreline Pomarat's prayer was answered. There lay a large canoe made of materials foreign to him on the shore. He signaled his braves to get in. He heard the iron bird in the sky, but it was behind him and inland searching the forest. The braves loaded Sarkem into the canoe and hopped in. Pomarat covered their rear.

Henry Addison was fishing twenty yards up the shore from his canoe. He came here often to fish the inlet. All fish passed thorough it going from the upper to the lower pond and back. It was a good spot … many beauties. He heard the grating fiberglass makes when being rocked or disturbed on shore despite the endless drone of the helicopter that had been flying around for a while now. Henry was retired, living the dream of daily fishing excursions whether lakes, surf or on the open ocean. Earlier today he heard the explosion from the center of town, the seemingly endless sirens, and the chopper. He had fish to catch and could watch the news later or read about it in the paper. Unfortunately, he was about to become part of the story.

At the sound of grating fiberglass, he glanced over and didn't know what he was seeing. There were three small people getting in and fiddling with his canoe. 'What the fuck?' he thought! Are they kids or midgets? "Hey! What are you doing with my canoe?!" These would be Henry's last words excepting a gurgle.

Pomarat was at ready. When he heard "Hey!" he wheeled around locked on Henry and sent an arrow through his throat. Hysko was in the canoe laying Sarkem in the middle. Massot was pushing the canoe to the water. Massot stopped at the sound, pulled his bow off his shoulder and launched a kill shot in Henry's chest as he staggered holding the arrow in his throat. Pomarat was now at the canoe pushing and commanding Massot to get in. The surround sound recommenced.

"Adams, move in!" commanded Browner. "They're at the water."

"Roger sir!" The three bee-lined for the shore, weapons drawn.
"If you get a clear shot, take it!"

91

THE FOUR SANDWICH COPS reached the shore simultaneously. Browner saw the canoe almost halfway across the inlet. The fisherman lay 20 yards up the shore on his back with two arrows protruding from his now motionless body. "Nathan, go check on the fisherman! You two open fire!"

Browner, Adams and Lundquist opened fire on the canoe crossing the inlet. Pomarat commanded Massot and Hysko to crouch low, as the thunder sticks let loose a barrage. Bullets flew over their head. Browner slowly acquired a head target just above the rim of the canoe. The target, Pomarat, was also drawing a bead on Browner with his bow held horizontally. Both being so intent on their target failed to notice the fast approach of Reed's chopper swooping down low from the tree tops over the canoe kicking up the water. Both had fired simultaneously, both missed their marks due to the impact of the rotors on the atmosphere surrounding the canoe. "Fuck!" yelled Browner. Pomarat issued a similar expletive in Itchiwan.

"Reed! Unless you can sink that canoe or blow it out of the water, lift up! Your rotors are fucking up our aim!" yelled Browner into the radio.

With the far shore approaching, Pomarat ordered Hysko to turn the canoe parallel to the shoreline when they beached and both of them to lean to tip the canoe so it serves as a shield.

"Fuck I'm gonna land on these bastards!" replied Reed.

"Negative! Negative! Pull up! Look at the shoreline! You got trees!"

"Shit!" was what Bobby heard as Reed realized he fucked up. The blades of Reed's chopper clipped branches of a sagging oak hanging by the shoreline and sent it into a sideways spiral. Although Pomarat's command for flipping the canoe was meant to shield them from the thunder sticks, it gave them the good fortune of not being eviscerated as the tail rotor of Reed's chopper swung into the water.

Hysko and Massot grabbed Sarkem and dragged him on shore. Sarkem was losing consciousness from his wound. Pomarat watched the chopper sink halfway into the inlet. The sight line to the far shore was blocked by its mass. He commanded Hysko to head north into the woods. Pomarat decided to wait and watch the demise of the iron bird. Maktahdou had answered his request! He watched the semi-submerged body of the iron bird to see if the human inside would emerge. His thanks to Maktahdou would be the sacrifice of this human.

"This is Browner, Sandwich PD, we got a state chopper down on its side and in the water at the Mashpee-Wakeby inlet on the Sandwich side. Any available units go to the Ryder Conservation Area for assistance." Browner kicked off his shoes and holstered his weapon. "Adams flank left up the shore. Lundquist go right. See if you can see those assholes and cover me." Browner dove in the water. It was a long swim but he couldn't chance there being no cruisers nearby and Reed unaided.

Adams and Lundquist had moved to a point where they could see only one midget standing on the far shore. Pomarat had his bow at ready waiting for the human to emerge from the iron bird. He could hear the wailing sirens of the ground beasts off in the distance probably coming to the aid of the bird. Then he heard a whizzing over his head simultaneously with the rapport of a thunder stick. Instinctively, he crouched low. Another thunder stick from the other side of the chopper sounded. Two humans on the far shore were now in his sight line as he was in theirs. Sarkem was in bad shape. More ground beasts were coming. The human in the iron bird may already be dead. A voice in the back of his mind said in native language, 'We gotta go!' He fled into the woods after Hysko and Massot.

1968 REDO

92

BRETT DROVE THEM TO the hole, or at least as close as his car could get to it without coming close to the crime scene. Vern came with them. They all got out and tramped through the underbrush till they reached it. "Okay, once we go in," began Amos, "you guys got to get those studs and cross braces out of here and cover the hole with shit."

"How …" started Brett.

"Shit Brett, you're a big fuck now … use a sledge hammer!" chided Timmy.

Brett over the course of his life had achieved a sense of self-confidence and swagger as a result of his short experiences with these three boys. But now being face to face with them again with them being thirteen, his self-confidence had disappeared. "I don't have a sledge hammer," he said. Of course he didn't, he was rich. The only tools he probably had were slot and Phillips head screw drivers, a hammer and pair of pliers, all in the kitchen draw with scissors, a tape measure and other essential implements of day to day life with no heavy lifting.

"I'll get the sledge hammer," interjected Vern looking at Amos. "Why? … What are you thinking Amos?"

"I'm thinking anything can happen. Timmy and I could be dead before we live 24 years to get back to this point in time. You and Brett back in 1968 may lose interest in our plan after awhile and we may not get it done. Tomorrow or the next day, the cops will be back scouring all around that crime scene for answers and anything we can do to delay them from stumbling across this hole is worth a shot. But do it today! Cause I guarantee you they'll be back in force sooner than you think."

"Okay." Vern embraced Amos. "Save mom."

"I'll try."

Timmy looked at Brett, "Your balls okay?"

"Yeah."

Amos and Timmy vanished down the hole with books from the future in hand.

Vern looked at Brett. "Get me back to my truck. I'll get a sledge and we will do this now."

"What's going to happen to us, Vern?"

Vern got in the passenger door. Brett got in the driver side. "Well what do you think?"

Vern laid his head back on the headrest, with eyes closed. "The best I can guess since I was never as smart as Amos, is you and I will wake up tomorrow and be thirteen again and back in 1968 without a clue as to what happened over the past 24 years or today. Hopefully, Amos and Timmy will convince us of this future and we'll help to make a better one."

"Vern, I'm scared!"

"Brett, don't be. We'll get a sledge. Remove the remaining wood. Then you and I will go out. Get surf and turf and get hammered with your spare cash since it will be no good when we wake up tomorrow. Then you'll get us some fine broads. And we'll have the time of my life. Then we'll pass out, and wake up 24 years ago." Vern opened his eyes and looked at Brett. "Sound like a plan?"

"Yep! What else can we do?"

93

AMOS AND TIMMY WERE back in their time. "What are we going to do with these books," asked Timmy.

"Shit, another problem I hadn't thought out."

"Relax … we just got to find a place to stash them where they won't be disintegrated by the weather."

"You got any ideas, Timmy? Time's running out. It's about six and we gotta get back before our parents start freaking."

Plastic bags weren't a common commodity in 1968. "Hopefully our bikes are still here and we can go to my house and stash them. Then I'll find a suitcase in the basement and tomorrow we can bury them or something," answered Timmy.

"I don't know man. If these books fall in the hands of anyone, the future of the world could be fucked. I don't like the idea of taking a chance of Colin seeing us stash them."

"Yeah, you got a point. Seems like Colin's always in the shadows seeing me do shit I shouldn't be doing and holding over my head."

"What about going to Brett's?"

"Without having a chance to convince him about what happened in the future? What if he runs with the books, realizing what they are and leaves us holding our dicks trying to block the hole in 1992?"

"May be a problem ..." pondered Amos rubbing his chin. Fuck! Time was running short! Amos was hoping to get back home before Vern spilled his guts about smoking and Timmy's mom unleashed the dogs of war (Colin) looking for Timmy. "We're running out of time. We got to go to Brett's. You'll go up to the door. He'll see you and figure out a way to come out because we're back. Then I'll scare the shit out of him about what we saw in the future and tell him to hide the books till we come back tomorrow."

"He'll fucking look at them before tomorrow."

"No he won't! And if he does look at them he won't do anything with them."

"Why?"

"Cause I will tell him if he looks at them he will be signing the death warrant for my family, him, you, and the world as we know it. And if the books are not here tomorrow, I will come looking for him with this ..." Amos pulled his .22 pistol from his waist band.

"Fuckin'-A, Amos, you sure you're not Irish? Cause you sure sound like the guys from my neighborhood."

"Yeah, I'm sure, I don't turn beet red from a day in the sun. This is our only option. We have to scare the shit out of Brett and get back home as soon as possible. The more we delay, the more shit to clean up."

94

BRETT WAS HOPING AMOS and Timmy would be back soon and everything would be okay. Mom was passed out in her bedroom and Maria was in the kitchen doing whatever when there was a light knock on the door. Brett didn't know if he heard it or not, but then it was repeated but louder. He went to the front door and looked out the spy hole. Timmy! He's back!

He opened the door. "Timmy!"

"Yeah it's me. Amos's up the street. We gotta talk."

"You're back! What happened?" asked Brett too loud for Timmy's liking.

"Shut up! Follow me!" Timmy's eyes shifting to inside.

"Don't worry, mom's passed out and Maria's in the kitchen."

"Fuck Brett! Just do what I say! The shit's hit the fan!"

Brett closed the door behind him and followed Timmy to Amos.

"What happened?!" asked Brett to the two of them.

Amos took over the conversation. "Timmy and I have to get home fast! We've been to the future and seen what happens to you and Vern if we don't. And it's not good!"

"What happens to me?"

Timmy smirked, having seen Brett of the future and recently kneed him in the nuts for just such a question.

"Never mind, get it through your head we have to act fast! No time for questions. I'll explain everything tomorrow morning when we meet. Now … I need a place to hide these books …"

Brett craned his neck to get a look at them.

"DO NOT LOOK AT THESE BOOKS!!! YOU HEAR!!!"

"Wh …"

"NO, FUCKIN' QUESTIONS! I will explain everything tomorrow! Tonight is critical! We need to stash these where there is no chance anyone will find them tonight. No one can see what's in them, especially not you! If you or anyone does, people die … understand?"

Brett's face went pale. "Yeah," he responded weakly. As his mind raced wondering what the fuck happened. What did they see?

"You got a place?"

Brett thought hard, looking back at the house and the yard. "The fucking garage!"

"What?"

"The fucking garage! There's a drop down ladder that goes to the attic over the garage. Nobody's been up there since we bought this place."

"That will do," said Amos. "Get us in there."

The garage was detached with a side door entrance. Brett brought them in and pulled out a crate to reach the cord to the drop down ladder. "Give me the books and I'll put them up there," said Brett.

"No Brett, I'll place them up there, face down, a certain way known only to me. If they've been looked at or disturbed in any way when I get them tomorrow … I will know. Then based on what I've seen in the future, I will have to use this …." Amos showed Brett the pistol in his waistband. Amos scrambled up the ladder and vanished from sight for a few seconds and came back down without the books. He refolded the ladder and pushed the spring-loaded trapdoor shut.

"There's a lot of dust up there. I'll know if anyone's been up there," Amos said looking at Brett. "We'll be back tomorrow. Go in the house and stay there tonight."

Brett was curious but scared. He decided to heed Amos's advice and just watch TV and wait for tomorrow. But his night was mostly sleepless as the contents of the books ate at his curiosity. But his fear of Amos and his gun kept him in his bed.

95

"JESUS, AMOS, YOU SCARED the shit out of me! Is it true about the dust and shit?"

"Sort of. Brett bought it, so who cares. Let's get the fuck home and cool the immediate fires."

"Yeah, see you tomorrow."

Timmy and Amos pedaled furiously to their homes to head off the cluster fucks that were yet to come. Timmy and Vern would avoid theirs. Amos would not by mere minutes.

96

TIMMY GOT HOME LATE for dinner but long before Colin was unleashed.

"WHERE HAVE YOU BEEN, YOUNG MAN?!!" demanded Mary.

"Ma, I lost track of time. Sorry."

"Wash up, your dinner is cold. Maybe next time you'll keep better track of time." Mary was secretively relieved that Timmy was home. She went to the kitchen to prepare him a plate as opposed to sending him to bed hungry. Colin Jr. took advantage of her absence to send a message to Timmy.

"Look asshole, you better get home on time. I don't want mom cutting into my time having to find out where the fuck you are. Understand shithead?!"

"Yeah, yeah, fuck off."

Colin Jr. cuffed him with a backhand as Colin Sr. walked in the room. "HEY! What's going on?"

"Nothing," said Timmy.

"Nothing, just screwing around," said Colin Jr.

"Fucking fine Irish lads, just monkeying around? Just keep in mind, you're in the house. If you have something to settle, go outside! Understand?"

"Yes sir," they answered in unison looking at each other knowing the matter was settled and the message conveyed. Dad seemed not to pay attention to shit, but if he did it was wise not to bring him into the matter at hand. You could sense his temper was there though you never saw it, unlike the raw Colin Jr. who had yet to learn to control it.

Things settled to normal at the O'Rielly residence. Colin Jr. hooked up with his friends as usual with no special mission. Colin Sr. retreated to the Laz-y Boy with a cold one and listened to the Sox. Timmy ate his cold supper and went to his room in anticipation of tomorrow. Mary did the dishes and listened to the radio comfortable knowing her family was accounted for.

At the Otis residence, things were not as tranquil.

97

VERN HAD GOTTEN OUT of Dodge by the time Amos returned and Amos's dad had just received mom's vengeance when Amos appeared.

"WHERE HAVE YOU BEEN, YOUNG MAN?!!!!"

Amos immediately knew he was too late. Dad was screwed. Vern had screwed. And now he was screwed. But he looked at his mother's face and smiled realizing this was the first step in insuring the horrible fate that would befall her would not come to fruition. "I was with Timmy."

"Timmy who?"

"O'Rielly. Why?"

"I'll ask the questions!"

"Yes mam."

"What were you and this Timmy doing?"

"Nothing."

Amos received an open hand smack to the face, which he hoped would not come but knew it would.

"Don't you lie to me young man, your brother told me what you two were up to."

"Ma ..."

"Don't you Ma me, what were you doing?"

"Trying to buy butts," said Amos wishing to get this charade over with so he could find Vern.

"Cigarettes?"

"Yeah."

Another open hand blow to the face.

"Give me them!"

"We didn't get any, no one would sell us any," Amos braced for another blow.

"Don't lie!"

"I'm not lying!"

Carmella Otis looked him in the eye and saw he was telling the truth and decided future interrogations about Timmy could wait. "Go find your brother, and bring him back for dinner."

Those were the words Amos was hoping for. He knew exactly where Vern would go and he would be able to find him and get him to buy into the plan. Dad however was on his own though he would do his best to minimize the fallout.

98

AMOS CAUGHT UP WITH Vern after he went through the rotary. Of course this time there was no junior Irish Mafia pursuing him into the woods due to Timmy's timely return. "VERN! VERN!"

Vern slowed and looked over his shoulder. He hit the brakes. "You're back!"

"Yeah I'm back. Let's go somewhere where we can talk."

"Where's Timmy?"

"Home."

"Do we have to go back to the hole?"

"Not tonight, but first thing tomorrow. All of us."

"Did you go home?"

"Yeah."

Vern looked down.

"Yeah, I caught shit for the butts story and so did Dad. No big deal. We got to talk. Timmy and I saw a shit storm and we have to stop it."

"What did you see?"

"Come on. Let's go to the pond by the house. I'll tell you everything. We got to be close to home. We got to be up early tomorrow."

Amos and Vern peddled back towards home through the rotary as Colin Jr. and his cronies ... Mikey and Sean were entering the rotary with a full case in the car. Willie had not been invited due to Timmy's timely return. "Hey, fuckin' injuns on bicycles! We get any points for hitting them?" yelled Mikey.

"No leave 'em alone," said Colin Jr. "Let's find some broads."

Amos and Vern peddled back to the pond by home never seeing the car with Colin pass them by. At the pond, they sat at the shore and Amos began.

"Vern, Timmy and I saw the future."

"How far into the future?"

"Twenty four years."

"Yeah ... so"

"The Pukwudgees get out and a lot of people die ... one we love."

Vern tried to process this and focused on the 'one we love'.

"Who?"

"Mom."

"NOO!"

"Yes, but we brought back the tools to stop it. Stop it all."

"What tools?!"

"A road map to ensure it does not happen."

"What happened?"

Amos proceeded to explain the extent of the carnage inflicted due to the emergence of the Pukwudgees and what they had to do to stop it from ever happening. He also pointed out that they were responsible for this since they had led them to the hole.

"Wow," was all Vern could muster. They sat staring at the pond deep in thought. "So, I ended up working for the DPW?"

"Yeah, but that ain't gonna happen! You aren't going to be carrying the weight of my disappearance, mom and dad's separation, or being hunted by Colin. Now you can focus on being what you always wanted."

"What are you going to do?"

"Fucking study finance and economics and tell Brett where to put his money with the help of the tools we brought back."

"What about Timmy?"

"I don't know. Timmy's brother is more connected in the Irish mob than he realized. Future Brett thinks he should use that. I'm not so sure."

"What does Timmy say?"

"We haven't had a chance to talk about it yet. But fuckin' Timmy is fearless ... and reckless, I'm sure he's willing to jump in with both feet. But, if we try to reign him in will he listen?"

Vern looked at Amos and Amos continued, "He will while he's here, but next week they'll be going back to Boston. Then who knows what he'll do? Let's go home and deal with this tomorrow."

"What are these fucking tools?"

"I'll show you tomorrow."

99

THE FOUR BOYS WERE up at the crack of dawn with little prompting. All except Timmy had spent hours in bed lying awake. Timmy was relieved that his parent's life would not turn to shit, and Colin Jr. would not be endlessly looking for Vern. Brett tossed and turned as the secret stash in the garage called to him, however Amos's cryptic warning kept him in his bed. Vernon replayed Amos's story over and over again in his head wondering if he could be the football player everyone expected him to be. He got the impression that mom's life depended on it. Amos was focused on one thing. Where the fuck am I going to stash those books so I can access them without being discovered. As he had drifted off, no answer came to him.

Amos and Vern met Timmy at the hole. "Timmy! So glad to see you! Amos told me the shit I was in for if you didn't get back."

Timmy hugged Vern. "Yeah, I guess my brother is well on his way to being connected. I thought he was just another local tough ass."

"We got to get Brett," interrupted Amos, "and bring him back here. I don't know how long my threat can overcome his curiosity. Timmy, you go get him."

"What about the books?"

"Leave them there for now."

"What if he starts whining?"

"Tell him, Vern and I are waiting next door. That should do it. We'll go back for the books after we tell Vern and Brett all about their future and what the results were."

Timmy pedaled to Brett's house.

"We going to follow?" asked Vern.

"No it's not necessary. Timmy can handle it. We need to use the time to talk some more. The tools we brought back are histories of the stock markets, commodities and currency fluctuations for the future. It's a key to becoming very, very rich."

"Shit, so … let's get rich!"

"Jesus! This is why we didn't go with Timmy. I need you to be in the same boat." Amos grabbed Vern by the shoulders, "We are thirteen years old! You know how to buy a stock? Play commodities? What a commodity is even? And what the fuck do you do with currency fluctuations? Do you know?"

"Ehhhh no, maybe we can find someone ..."

"No fuckin' way! NO ONE BUT US FOUR CAN BE IN ON THIS! UNDERSTAND!"

"Yeah, yeah ... no? I have no clue. What do we do?"

Amos ran his hand over his head, "I don't know yet. I'm thirteen. I do know if we become rich, famous and known that the tools may become worthless because history will change and the books won't be the new history. Get what I'm saying?"

"Yeah, sort of."

"Okay. This is the goal ... we have to make enough money before August 1992 to buy all the land around this hole and seal it forever with concrete so those bastards don't get out and kill mom. We got to make millions and millions according to Future Brett. To make money you need money. We have none. Brett does. Enough to get started. But we can't use it till Brett's 21. So we only have 15 years not 24. I got to figure out how all this shit works in the meantime. According to Future Brett we don't even have 15 years, maybe 10 to 12 due to complications in buying the land and getting the permits to pour the concrete."

"So what the fuck are you saying?"

"Future Brett gave us the roadmap. Present Brett doesn't have a clue. Future Brett doesn't think we can make enough unless you contribute through football and Timmy does what may not be good for Timmy in the long run."

"What about you?"

"I got nine years to figure out how all this money shit works and keep you, Timmy and Brett on the path."

"So I got to play football and get to the pros?"

"Give it your best shot and in the meantime back me up."

"If we can't use the books for nine years, how are you going to hold off Present Brett from jumping the gun? Based on what you told me last night about Future Brett, he turned out pretty well off. Maybe he tries to jump the gun since he has the money."

"I hadn't figured that out. I need a place to stash the books but have them accessible so I can study them."

"Shit! What about the box we got buried back home, where we stash the Playboy's?"

"Damn! I forgot about that!" Amos had his missing link to the plan. Vern and he had buried a waterproof cooler on a remote portion of their property to store valued items such as Playboys and an occasional can of beer. They hadn't used it in awhile but it still would be there. "What made you think of it? You been stashing stuff in there lately?"

"Yeah, new Playboy's."

"How new?"

"A couple of months ago."

"You didn't tell me?"

"I would have eventually ... but ... you know ..."

"I know what?"

"Well ... two's company three's a crowd ..."

"Shit, here comes Timmy and Brett! Let me do the talking."

Vern was relieved wondering whether Amos would accept the idea of having sloppy seconds with Miss May.

100

"SO BRETT, DID TIMMY fill you in on the way over?" asked Amos giving Timmy a look indicating he knew Timmy didn't tell him shit. Timmy was smiling behind Brett.

"No, Timmy wouldn't tell me shit! Can you tell me what the fuck happened now?"

"Yeah sit down. You didn't look at the books did ya? Cause I'll ..."

"No I didn't look at them! You scared the shit out of me."

"Sorry about that. I had to. You told me to, 24 years in the future."

"What ...?"

"Come on sit down, I'll tell you what happened." Amos sat followed by Vern, Timmy and Brett. "Yeah, you told me twenty-four years in the future not to trust you ... with the stuff he was giving us to bring back. You said you couldn't trust you at this age to follow the plan you created to undo the mess that happens."

"Ehhhh ... what's all this "U" shit ... you mean "U" is me?"

"Exactly! Let me tell you what happened!"

Amos proceeded to relive all the horrific events leading up to their meeting with future Brett and Vern with Timmy adding color commentary. At the point where they met at the tennis courts, Amos paused and Brett jumped in, as he knew he would. Up to this point everything was relayed as it was or will be … or maybe from this point in the re-telling he would have to selectively limit the info on future Brett.

"What was I like?"

"Can't tell you."

"Why?????????"

"You told me not to."

"Why the fuck not?"

"Not sure, you said you'd ask that and only you would know why." Timmy sat in awe, amazed at Amos's handling of Brett. Brett's mind was now in a matrix wondering why he would feel that way about himself.

"Forget about that for now," said Amos while Brett's brain was in overdrive. "Future you gave us the plan to keep all our families from being totally fucked up or dead! Brett, THIS IS YOUR PLAN! You told us when to tell you what and when. You grow up to be very smart and able to see what needs to be done, just like last week when you had the plan for your mother and the pool boy."

"Yeah but look what happened!"

"Yeah, your Dad came back here and the pool boy was toast. You don't have to sit all day down at the Marketplace unless you want to."

"Yeah, I guess everything worked out for the better …"

"Exactly! And the future you is smart, successful and built like a brick shithouse!"

"I'm not fat?"

"No, you also told me to tell you to stop eating like a pig and play more tennis and work out. You said you'll get more girls."

Timmy was maintaining a straight face, barely.

"More girls?"

"Yeah, your future girlfriend looks like Raquel Welch!"

"Really?"

"Yeah, really!"

"So what do we do?"

"Simple, you do what I tell you that you told me to tell you to do.

We have to make enough money to buy the land all around this hole before 1992. We have to seal it over with concrete, block the exit of the Pukwudgees forever and save countless lives."

"So this is my plan?"

"Yes. You told me all the roadblocks to doing it and how long it will take."

"How much?"

"How much what?"

"Money to do all this."

"Three to four million."

"What the fuck????? For what? Where do we get it?"

"Relax, you told me how. The land containing the hole is large! In 1992, someone's going to buy it and be digging up this area to build condos."

"What's a fucking condo?"

"I don't know, but they will be building them."

"So what do we do now?"

"You and Timmy will be going back to where you came from in a few days cause school's going to be starting. The first thing we do is exchange addresses and phone numbers. If it turns out you're not coming back to the Cape next year for some reason you both have to let me and Vern know. If something happens to Vern or me, we'll let you know. We got to stay in touch with each other no matter if you're here in the summers or not.

We still have to monitor the hole every summer in the last days of August because if we're successful in closing the hole, we got to make sure they don't double back and pop out between now and then."

"Hey Amos," interrupted Vern, "what if they come out before now?"

Amos hadn't thought of this scenario in his sleepless night when his young but very intelligent brain had been in overdrive concocting this presentation to Brett. Amos looked at Vern with a blank stare and in his mind was thinking 'Didn't I tell you to follow my lead? Couldn't this wait till we were alone?' Amos looked down and looked up at Vern. Vern's mind said 'oops'.

"Good question, Vern. You tell me why that hasn't happened."

"Ehhhh … I don't know," answered Vern realizing the best answer was no answer.

"I know! I know!" said Timmy raising his hand like he was already back in school.

"Christ Timmy! This ain't school! Why?" Amos smiled at his fellow traveler to there and back knowing he always had his back.

"Cause if they did come out before, we probably wouldn't be here having this fucking conversation!"

"Exactly!"

"Fuckin' A, circle gets the square!" screamed Timmy.

"What?" asked Vern.

"Hollywood Squares, it's on TV," answered Brett trying to be helpful.

"I told you, we don't have a TV," responded Vern.

"I forgot," said Brett apologetically.

"Let's get back to what we got to do," interrupted Amos.

Amos reinforced keeping in touch, and monitoring the hole in late August. Then he said, "But right now, we go back to the garage and I get the books and do what I got to do with them,"

Amos cast a glance at Vern which said 'Don't talk!!!!'

"What are you going to do with them?" asked Brett.

"Can't tell you."

"Wh ..., never mind ... I know, I told you."

"Yeah. Look, we'll all meet tomorrow at the Marketplace and we'll figure out something fun to do until you guys go back home. We'll forget about this until next year."

Brett thought about this and bit his lip but still spit out, "But you won't forget about this till then, will you?"

"No I won't, you entrusted me with the plan and now you're showing me the person that you will be."

"Is that good or bad?"

"Good."

"Good."

They all went to Brett's garage and Amos retrieved the books. Amos and Vern went back to their 'territory', or home, and left Timmy and Brett behind until tomorrow at the Marketplace. Brett watched them go, sort of relieved that he wouldn't be tempted by the books being up in his attic. "So, Timmy does my girlfriend really look like Raquel Welch?"

"No Amos lied."

"What?"

"She kinda reminds me of Alice the Goon from Popeye."

"No!"

"Just kidding!" smiled Timmy. "She was fantastic! Of course you were built like a linebacker not a marshmallow."

"Shit…"

"Look, we never should have gone down that hole. You wouldn't believe the shit we unleashed by doing it. A lot of people die. You came up with a way to prevent it. We got to follow your plan."

Timmy saw the 'What happens to me look' though Brett learned to keep it to himself. "If we didn't come back, Colin would have beat the shit out of you, tomorrow or the next day!"

"Is Colin connected like Amos says?"

"I guess he is, I never knew for sure. But knowing our neighborhood and seeing what we saw, he's not someone you want to fuck with."

"What about you?"

"I'm his brother, he'll knock me around but he won't hurt me or me him."

"What do you want to do for the rest of the day?"

"Wanna go down to the Marketplace and fuck with Willie?"

"How?"

"I don't know, we'll figure it out when we get there. Willie fingered Vern when we didn't come back. He also fingered you and that's why Colin came after you."

"Fuck! After all the money I spent there!"

"Doesn't matter to him, it's the owner's money, unless he's skimming, in which case he wouldn't finger you. Come up with a plan like the one we did on your mom."

"We can't!"

"Why?"

"Amos said we'll meet there tomorrow. If we fuck with Willie, you and I may not be able to come back there tomorrow."

Timmy thought about this and said, "Yeah you're right. Let's go down the beach and see what's going on."

"Where, Popponesset, the Irish Riviera? I'm not in the mood for a bunch of shit from your brother and his friends."

"Can you get me in the New Seabury Beach?"

"Yeah, we're members."

"Well let's go there, we can look at the big titted, Jewish and WASP babes!"

101

VERN AND AMOS HEADED home, Amos pedaling hard to keep ahead of Vern. He didn't want to talk about today's events till they got back and the books were stashed in the cooler in the ground.

"Amos, I know I screwed up! Slow down," yelled Vern.

Amos peddled harder, "We'll talk when we get to the cooler" yelled Amos over his shoulder. "You better beat me there if you're ever going to be any good at football!"

Vern realized he was in a race … no, a test by Amos, the master manipulator. Vern had always dominated Amos in physical contests, while Amos dominated him with grades and brains. Vern put his head down and pedaled harder closing the gap fast and passing Amos as they entered the rotary.

"LOOK OUT!" screamed Amos now behind him.

Vern looked up just in time to see the car coming fast into the rotary to his left. Vern slammed the brake, the rear wheel slid sideways and barely grazed the rear bumper of the car. Vern righted the bike without notice of the driver and pressed ahead hard. Another car was exiting the rotary ahead. Vern slammed the brake and pressed across the rotary egress in front of a closely following car.

Amos had stopped at the entrance of the rotary, watching Vern's jukes and jives, regretting his taunts not realizing they were so close to the rotary. He now regretted egging on Vern. But Vern, with his series of moves was through the rotary and on his way home, while he was left to carefully negotiate his way through rotary traffic. By the time Amos got through the rotary, Vern was long gone. Amos peddled to their pond. There was Vern sitting on a log. "Where the fuck have you been?" he asked.

"Admiring your moves," answered Amos, dropping his bike and

heading to the cooler with the books. Amos placed the books in the cooler and covered the hole with leaves and dirt. "Now we can talk."

"About what?"

"You and me."

"What about us?"

"We got to stick together on this until 1992. We can't rely on Timmy and Brett being back here every year till then. I know Timmy will do his best to be here every summer but Brett I don't know. Their being back here every year depends on their family not finding a better place to go in the summer. Hopefully, I instilled enough curiosity in Brett to see what his grand plan is."

"Was it his plan?"

"Yeah, it was basically. But he didn't tell us not to tell him the plan and all that shit."

"So what da we got to do?"

"I have to do everything I can to figure out what those books say and how to take advantage of it. You have to play football and get a scholarship and hopefully make the pros. If Brett doesn't come back every year, I don't know if we'll have the money to pull this off. Maybe the three or two of us can, with money from other stuff such as your football career and Timmy's Irish mob shit, but I doubt it. Anyway stay away from the cooler with Playboys ... we don't want to attract attention to it. Plant another cooler somewhere else."

"You think Timmy's cut out to be a mob guy?"

"Not really. But who knows. I hope not."

"What about me and the pros?"

"I don't know, never seen the pros just read the papers. You can try though and see what happens. We got 24 years, and I don't know shit yet. But I do know I can figure something out."

"So what are we going to do for "fun" tomorrow at the marketplace until they go back, Mr. Brainiac?" smiled Vern.

"I'll sleep on it. You got any ideas?"

"Yeah, I do. Let's bring them home and show them how we live, hunt, who we are, who they're saving, meaning mom. We've been living in their world since we met them. Let's give them a taste of ours."

Amos leaned back against a log and pondered this idea. It wouldn't hurt for them to meet their mom. They'd have to feel her out first. It would be harder for them to walk away from saving someone they knew. "That's a good idea. But mom thinks Timmy's a bad influence on me."

"This will give her a chance to change his ways and size him up. You know she'll try to do that."

"Yeah, we'll warn Timmy in advance. This may work. Let's ask mom if we can have them over for lunch and have some of our food."

"We better ask her now, so she has time to figure out some good 'Indjun' food."

Amos laughed, "Yeah."

102

BRETT AND TIMMY HAD spent the remainder of that yesterday ogling the teenage beauties at the Beach Club. Timmy thought some of the moms were knockouts also. Brett had asked Timmy, "So you're saying I get girls like these in 1992?"

"See that built guy over there talking to the four broads?"

Brett looked and saw a chiseled body and hair the same color as him, "Yeah, what about him?"

"That's you in 1992."

"You're shiting me right?"

"No I'm not. See the fat fuck sitting in the chair sipping a Budweiser all by himself over there?"

Brett shifted his gaze to the left. The fat guy was eyeballing the broads Mr. Chiseled was chatting while sucking down his beer. "What about him?"

"That's you if you don't stick with the plan 'future' you gave us."

"So what's the plan?!!!"

"You start getting in shape."

"That's it???"

"That's it for this year, we'll give you next year's plan when you come back next summer."

Amos asked their mom if they could they could bring Timmy and

Brett home for lunch. Mrs. Otis was caught off guard. "You want to bring them here?"

"Yeah," said Amos, "I want them to see us ... experience how we live. We see how they live all the time but they never come north of the rotary except to get back to the highway when they go home."

Mrs. Otis looked at her boys seeking any sign that they were up to something but saw nothing but sincerity. That sincerity was driven by their desire to make sure she was not killed in 1992. "Okay, so should I make peanut butter and jelly sandwiches?" she asked knowing that's not what Amos had in mind.

"Nooooo ma. Make something they never had in their world. Something that's us."

"That's us? You mean Wampanoag?"

"Yeah! Exactly!"

"What else you trying to do here, Amos, besides introduce your new friends to the Wampanoag culture? I can see that brain of yours spinning."

"I want you to meet Timmy and Brett and see they aren't the bad influences you think they are."

Mrs. Otis looked hard at her son. Her heart filled with pride. He was so aware and confronted issues head on when they arose. She wanted to hug him but instead asked, "Have Timmy and Brett agreed to come north of the rotary?"

"No, I wanted to ask you first."

"Do you think they will come?"

"I know Timmy will, and if he comes Brett will too."

Vern nodded in agreement.

Mrs. Otis knew there was something deeper in their motives, but had no clue as to what it was. Whatever it was it was important to them and they were sincere.

"Okay, but get back here quick if they decide not to come. No sense wasting food."

The four boys met at the Marketplace as agreed. As usual they looked to Amos for the plan of the day. "So what are we doing?" asked Timmy.

"You ever go hunting?" asked Vern.

"Hunting? Are you serious?" responded Brett.

"Yeah, I'm serious. It's fun," answered Vern.

"What are we hunting with, rocks? We don't have any guns," said Brett.

"We have bows and arrows."

Amos and Timmy glanced at each other as this debate continued.

"Bows and arrows? I never shot a bow! It's not even hunting season!"

"Brett, we're Wampanoags, hunting rules don't apply to us. We can hunt anything anytime."

"No shit? But what about Timmy and I, we're not."

"Look we'll go into our woods north of the rotary if it makes you feel better."

"North of the rotary???" Brett was becoming uncomfortable.

Timmy jumped in, "Come on Brett this is an adventure! Where's your balls?!"

"Haven't you two had enough adventure?" answered Brett now including Amos.

"Take it easy Brett," said Amos. "Yeah Timmy and I had an adventure, but this in no way compares to that. This is fun. We go out and look for game. We teach you two how to hunt. Most likely we'll see nothing, but it will be fun being out there looking. Maybe, just maybe, we'll get lucky. That's the fun of hunting. And afterward we can have lunch at our house."

"What are we waiting for?" asked Timmy.

"Brett?" asked Vern.

North of the rotary? Brett didn't like the idea. Then the idea of 'future' Brett spoke in his head 'Christ man, a week ago you're going down a fucking hole in the ground and popping up in God knows where! Now you're sweating going with your friends to someplace in the here and now? Fucking buck up man!' "Okay," mumbled Brett.

103

THEY PEDDLED THROUGH THE rotary. Amos and Vern were on their regular route home, Timmy in third was looking forward to new vistas. Brett, bringing up the rear, was thinking, 'Lions, and Tigers and Bears, Oh my! – Courage …' But basically, north of the rotary looked like south of the rotary. When they came to Amos and Vern's house, it looked the same as the homes in Popponesset with a lot more land. So much so, you couldn't see the neighbors' house. Amos and Vern bypassed the house to a shack in the back. There they dismounted leaving their bikes on the ground. Timmy dumped his bike on the ground as the twins had, but Brett dismounted and kicked out his kick stand leaving his bike upright … 'till he walked toward the shack and it fell over.

Amos and Vern emerged from the shack with two bows and two quivers filled with arrows. They offered them to Timmy and Brett. Timmy took a bow and quiver. Brett asked, "What about you guys?"

"We only got two," said Amos, "and we hunt all the time. So now you two can try."

"You're coming with us? Right?" asked Brett tentatively taking the bow.

"No, we're going to point you over there and wait for you to come back," said Vern, "Of course we're going with you!"

Timmy had already knocked an arrow and shot at a tree, which he hit.

"Hey Robin Hood, wait till we get into the woods," said Amos.

"Practice," smiled Timmy.

"Looks like you don't need any practice."

"Let's go! What are we hunting anyway?" asked Timmy ready to go.

"Elephants," said Vern sarcastically.

"Easier to hit than Pukwudgees, ay Amos?" asked Timmy.

"Yep and easier to find."

They spent the remainder of the morning traipsing through the woods. Vern and Amos knew the chance of killing anything was slim and none. Brett was as stealthy as an elephant walking on bubble wrap and Timmy was constantly trying to shush him. But his shushing had the same effect as Brett's tromping. Any animals that had been in the area were long gone before the boys could get near them. That didn't stop Timmy from firing an arrow at anything he perceived could be something … a rock suddenly in a sunbeam in the forest, a chickadee darting off a branch, anything that moved or made a sound. Amos and Vern knew early to keep out of the 180 degree arc of Timmy's vision.

He was wired and had a hair trigger.

But as far as Amos was concerned, that was okay since his main objective was getting Timmy and Brett up here to meet their mom and hopefully have a stake in saving her beyond just their friendship with each other. He believed it would be harder for them to lose interest over the years in saving someone they met and liked as opposed to 'just a friend's mom'. He also knew how charming his mother could be and was counting on it.

Finally Amos asked, "You guys hungry?"

"Yeah!" said Brett getting tired of the hike with weapons and starting to get really hungry.

"But we haven't seen anything yet," pleaded Timmy.

"Why is that Timmy?" asked Vern.

Timmy considered this and knew the answer. Brett was as subtle as a fart in church. He never considered that he was as unpredictable as a downed electrical wire in high winds.

"Never mind, you guys need some training and that ain't going to happen on your last day here," interrupted Amos. "Next summer, Vern and I will teach you like our dad taught us and by the end of the summer you two will be pros. Now let's go back and get something to eat."

"Fine with me," exclaimed Brett.

"Hey Brett, remember what I told you at the beach, cool it on the eating," chided Timmy, pissed that the hunt was over.

"Yeah, yeah I will. Leave me alone."

Mrs. Otis stood in the doorway with her arms crossed. Like the animals of the wood, she heard them coming a half-mile away and smiled at the chatter. "You boys bring me back anything to cook?" she asked with a sly smile as Vern was putting the bows in the shed. Brett looked at Amos fearing that Mrs. Otis was depending on them for lunch.

Amos replied, "No mom, we ain't got nothing."

"Don't say ain't, say we haven't got anything …"

"Yes mam."

"Timmy shot a rock!" chimed in Vern coming out of the shed, "But we figured it would take us too long to chisel out the meat."

"Vernon!"

Timmy was turning red, not the usual red he turned in the summer.

"You boys go in and wash your hands. I cooked up something dad caught the other day."

The boys entered going past Mrs. Otis. Vern got lightly cuffed in the back of the head as he passed causing him to smile. Brett and Timmy followed Amos to the bathroom absorbing the fine odors coming from the kitchen. Brett and Timmy never experienced anything like it. They were intoxicating. Brett was in heaven and didn't know why, only that it smelled sooooo good and it was meant for eating.

They all sat at the kitchen table while Mrs. Otis prepared each a plate. "So where are you boys from?" she asked as she brought the plates to the table.

"South Boston, Mrs. Otis," answered Timmy.

"Concord" said Brett eyes wide at the feast appearing in front of him.

Amos looked at Vern and smiled. Sea bass, steamers, fresh picked corn on the cob, fried potato slices with bacon and a pie baking in the oven. Wow! Mom went all out. Fucking A' this was better than when Dad's relatives came over. Amos's grin was ear to ear as he looked at his mother when she laid his plate before him and she gave him a subtle knowing wink. His heart was filled with love and pride. She looked back at the boys and said, "Dig in before it gets cold."

Timmy and Brett obliged with no hesitation. This was a heaven of food. The sea bass melted in their mouth, seasoned like nothing they'd ever tasted. The corn was small white kernels, so tender and luscious like nothing that came from the supermarket or the local farm stands. And the potato slices with bacon … indescribable.

"So I understand you're going home tomorrow?"

"Yes mam," answered Timmy and Brett between mouthfuls.

"My boys tell me you've been having a good time together this summer. Will you be coming back next summer?"

Timmy's eyes immediately went to Amos's which wasn't missed by his mom. Brett said "Yes mam, we have a house down here. We come every year."

Carmella now knew Amos and Timmy were the leaders and Brett and Vern were the followers. What they were up to she probably would never know. She didn't believe it was anything evil, but it was secret.

"Yes mam, we do too," chimed in Timmy, a day late and a dollar short.

Amos knew his mom. She had baited the trap and hooked Timmy and by default, him, hook line and sinker. Timmy's glance confirmed to her that they were up to something. Now she would periodically be probing him waiting for his guard to be down. The apparent innocent inclusion of "a good time together" in her question had caused Timmy to instinctively react. It was going to be a long twenty plus years, figuring out how to make millions while being on guard for mom's subtle booby traps. But the objective made it worth it. It struck him as ironic that in trying to save his mother, her actions may become a speed bump in accomplishing it.

104

"WAS YOUR LUNCH OKAY? You want some more blueberry pie."

"No Mrs. Otis, that was great! If I eat anymore I'll burst!" said Timmy leaning back from the table.

"Can I have another," asked Brett tentatively. "I never tasted a real blueberry pie. Mom gets her pies from the bakery or the grocery store."

"Sure you can Brett." Mrs. Otis cut him another slice, which was gone in no time.

Timmy looked at Brett scoffing down the pie and wondered how long it would be before he decided to become an Adonis. Maybe never, now that he and Amos were back. Maybe they would have a bad effect on him. Shit this could be complicated. "Mrs. Otis, can we help you clean up?" asked Timmy before Brett would have a chance for thirds.

"Thank you Timmy, but no. You boys go out and enjoy the rest of your day together. I'll manage fine."

The boys went outside. When they were a sufficient distance from the house, Amos said, "We'll ride back with you. Let's go back to Sarah's at Witch Pond."

They sat by the crumbled rocks that were Sarah's chimney and relived their summer of adventure together, vowing to keep to the plan that future Brett had handed down to Amos, though Brett was still unclear to what a lot of that plan was/is. Their splitting up for the final time that summer was awkward at best. School and winter would be a big let down from the adventures they had shared.

As they rode back to their homes they were all engulfed in their own thoughts. Timmy was reliving the wonderful feast he had at the Otis's. Brett was doing the same but thinking, 'okay, that was real food, now I can give up the junk and start focusing on becoming future Brett.' Amos's brain was aching to start digging into the future books and researching their meaning, but first he'd have to figure out a safe way of doing that. Calculation and planning was a weary and endless task. Vern was thinking of Sarah Screecham with her beautiful blue eyes and flaming red hair. His afternoon by her crumbled hearth brought back the memory of standing by her erect hearth in his skivvies with an erect hearth of his own.

1992 CONTINUED

105

THEY RAN NORTH TO known paths they had traveled many times, but the paths were gone. Pomarat knew they were there but time had made them different. The ground had changed but the horizon hadn't. They ran where the paths should be which were at certain points overgrown. But at other points, there was a hovel that hadn't been there.

When they were long past the wailing sirens and in the cover of the woods, Pomarat indicated to hold up. Sarkem's wound was not life threatening but had been bleeding profusely and had to be stopped. Pomarat lit a small fire with the flints in his satchel. He wrapped deerskin on the end of a stick and held it in the fire. He looked at Massot and Hysko and told them to hold him and cover his mouth. When the skin caught hold, he removed it from the fire and laid the flaming skin to Sarkem's shoulder. Sarkem let out a muffled scream under Hysko's hand and passed out. Pomarat inspected the wound making sure it was fully cauterized.

Bobby got to the semi-submerged chopper and managed to free an unconscious Reed before his head was under water. He would live but would not be skating for awhile as he had sustained a broken leg and arm. He dragged Reed to shore, and tried his radio. Dead. He yelled back to Adams on the far shoreline. "GET ME AN AMBULANCE!"

"ALREADY DONE, SIR!"

Bobby tended to Reed in his semi-unconscious state. "Take it easy. The ambulance's coming."

"I fucked up," muttered Reed in a haze.

"Don't worry about it," said Bobby thinking 'Yeah you did, cowboy!' But he kept it to himself. He stood up and looked at the far shoreline. Lundquist was still there trying to provide cover if the Pukwudgees came back. He yelled over, "WHERE'S ADAMS?"

"GETTING YOUR CAR AND COMING TO YOU!"

'Fucking Adams is a regular Radar O'Rielly. He always seems to be one step ahead of me,' he thought then yelled, "HOW'S THE FISHERMAN?"

"DEAD."

"HAVE NATHAN STAY WITH HIM. YOU DRIVE OVER HERE."

"WHAT ABOUT YOUR COVER?"

"THEY'RE LONG GONE! I'D BE DEAD IF THEY WERE STILL AROUND. GET OVER HERE! AND BRING MY SHOES!"

Lundquist left his position to go back to his car. Bobby decided he would take Adam's car when he arrived and pursue these bastards. Adam's could wait for Lundquist. Then he looked at Reed who was out cold. He removed his boots, Reed stirred when he felt his broken leg move. Bobby tried them on, close enough. He removed the radio from Reed's shoulder. "Radio check."

"Go ahead Radio check. Who is this?"

"Officer Browner from Sandwich PD."

"State barracks in Yarmouth."

"I'm with Officer Reed, he's unconscious but okay. It looks like he has a broken leg and arm. His chopper is down in the water. He's onshore and there is an ambulance coming. I'm taking his boots, gun and radio. Mine are toast after going in the water to pull him out."

"We've been listening to the radio. Thanks. Quite the cluster fuck there?"

"Yeah, I can hear the ambulance coming. I'll be leaving to follow the suspects."

"Where they heading?"

"North to Sandwich from the Ryder conservation area. If you can spare anyone, send them."

"Reinforcements coming from the Middleboro, Bourne and Plymouth barracks."

"If I get any info where they are, I'll let you know."

106

POMARAT KNEW IF SARKEM was to recover there would have to be a significant blood sacrifice. Blood to replace blood lost. He could not afford to lose another warrior, especially now. He continued through the yards of hovels that should not be there. Hysko and Massot carried the unconscious Sarkem. Then they came upon even stranger terrain! Expansive green grass neatly trimmed. Pomarat held them at the edge of the wooded area separating them from the yard of hovel and this green expanse. They heard a ping and then something slice through the air nearby and hit with a thud fifty feet in front of them. It was a white round orb the size of a small rock which could fit in the palm of a hand. Pomarat surveyed the field and saw three similar orbs dotting this field of green. He looked to the right and saw four humans mounting two small white beasts similar to, but much smaller than those they had encountered. They were heading in their direction.

One individual in the group stood out. In his bright yellow polo shirt, madras shorts and gigantic close to 400 pound orb-like body, he was like the living presence of the sun itself! This human was HUGE! Blood to replace blood and plenty of it! Pomarat indicated Massot and Hysko should lie Sarkem down and be ready to attack. The two white carts came to a stop twenty yards from Pomarat and his group. Irwin Goldstein went to the white orb farthest to Pomarat's right. Howard Robinson went to the other orb near that. Ray Shaw went to the orb farthest to their left and Walter Rollins, the sun itself approached the orb nearest Pomarat. All carried shiny metal sticks. Ray Shaw being farthest forward on this par 5 18th hole struck a cavalier pose with one hand on his hip and the other on his five-iron which he placed on the ground like a walking cane. "Well Gentlemen, your only chance of winning the day is to carry the pond! You going for it or are you laying up?"

"Fuck you Ray!" said Goldstein, "I'm going for it! If you win today the least you can do is buy a fucking round for a change."

Shaw chuckled and thought, 'You'll be in the pond for sure, you fucking ambulance chaser.'

Goldstein addressed his ball, adrenaline pumping, and proceeded to duck hook it into the pond. He slammed his club to the ground. Pomarat made motions to Massot and Hysko. Hysko was to take Goldstein, Massot ... Shaw. He would take Robinson. Then they'd converge on Rollins.

Robinson stated he was playing it safe and hit to the left of the pond. Rollins waddled up to his ball saying he was going for it.

"You do that, big man!" said Shaw.

Rollins calmed himself and envisioned the trajectory of the ball.

Using all the skills he had acquired taking lessons and reading golf magazines with an endless parade of pros rehashing the same old golf tips, he smoothly hit the shot. The ball sailed into the sky. All watched even Pomarat and his men though they had no clue what these four were doing. The ball landed on the edge of the green, 200 yards away and commenced a long slow roll to the flagstick. As it got to the flag-stick, it disappeared from view.

Robinson and Goldstein let out a "FUCKIN A!!!!"

Rollins gave a huge smile to match his body width in disbelief. The shot of a lifetime! 'Oh my God!'

Shaw turned away in disgust thinking 'Fat Fuck!' just in time to see a maniacally looking half-naked midget Indian signal two other half naked midget Indians. As Massot's arrow approached his heart, a thought flashed through his head, 'Did I sample the drugs I've been supplying the rich youths of Sandwich this morning?' Falling to ground dying, he thought … 'No … but wish I had.'

Robinson and Goldstein turned to see what Shaw's reaction to the once in a lifetime shot was. "AHHH! LOOK, SHITHEAD FAINTED!" laughed Robinson. Robinson was old, and in between chemo treatments with questionable eyesight. Goldstein however, had the eye for detail of an ambulance chaser.

"Howie, I think he has an arrow in his …" And then Goldstein had an arrow in his and fell to the ground with a gurgle as his eyes rolled back in his head.

"What," said Howie as he turned to Goldstein? "What the fuck!" Now Goldstein was out cold. He approached Goldstein's body and saw the arrow. Pomarat had sensed his target disorientation and un-knocked his arrow. Instead he charged with fury and a nine-inch blade taken from the Finch residence. Before Howard Robinson knew what was happening, Pomarat had eviscerated him from balls to chest cavity in one fell stroke. He immediately smelled the sickness. This victim was of no use to Sarkem. He turned to the giant orb-like human.

Walt was still savoring his once in a lifetime shot. His biggest sports achievement prior to this was receiving his participation trophy in Little League. He turned to see Shaw's reaction and instead saw the rest of his foursome all dead on the ground and three little Indians looking at him. His mind said 'RUN!" He did – and it was comical. He had all the grace of a scared hippo trapped in a Pump and Jump.

Pomarat ran up and hammered his sternum with his tomahawk. The pain was intense. But survival instinct kicked in and he wildly swung his 5 wood towards his attacker, forgetting that his attackers were midgets and as a result, the club passed harmlessly a foot over Pomarat's head. The force of the swing caused Rollins to lose his balance and fall to finely manicured fairway looking up at the maniacal grin of a half-dressed midget Indian. He wanted to swing his 5 wood back at his target, but his heart gave out and he suffered a massive heart attack. Pomarat was about to slam his tomahawk in his head but hesitated, as he saw his eyes roll back and life rapidly fade out of them. Strange! The huge human just died. From fear? Had Maktahdou intervened?

Pomarat yelled at Hysko and Massot to bring Sarkem here, now! The blood would be fresh. They ran back to the wood line and gathered up their comrade, "Wake up, Sarkem, we have medicine."

Sarkem's arms were around their shoulders as they dragged him to the fallen buffalo. He was drifting in and out of consciousness. Pomarat told them to lay his head next to Robert's throat. Pomarat withdrew Finch's knife. He slapped Sarkem awake. "Drink!" He slashed the main artery in Robert's throat and grabbed Sarkem's head forcing his open mouth to the gushing flow blood from Walter's artery. "Drink, drink deeply Sarkem. This will replace the blood you lost!"

Sarkem sucked on the wound like a baby suckling its mother's breast. Pomarat held his head there. The flow was long as Rollins had fell on a slight incline with his head below the rest of his enormous body. Hysko and Massot watched in awe and wondered if this would work. They did not hear the two electric golf carts pulling up to the eighteenth tee two hundred and fifty yards behind them. But they did hear the click of the brakes and chatter of the four occupants as they walked to the tee. Hysko and Massot turned to the noise. Pomarat looked up still holding Sarkem to the wound.

"What the fuck is going on down there?" asked the first member of the foursome looking down the fairway. The others took notice.

"Why the fuck are they all lying down?"

"What are those midgets doing around the big guy?"

"Hey!!!" yelled one of the four.

Pomarat yelled at Hysko and Massot, "Take position, ready arrows!" Hysko and Massot assumed a position between the buffalo and Sarkem with bows drawn.

"What the fuck, they got bows and they're pointing them at us."

"Anybody got a car phone?"

"Yeah, but the battery's dead."

"I only got a beeper," said another of the group.

"They can't reach us from there."

"Yeah, but I think those guys in the fairway are dead. We got to do something!"

One of the group had served in the military surveyed their situation. They had two golf carts with windshields and roofs. There were four of them, and three standing midgets and one on the ground. Good odds. "Get in the carts. You guys go wide left, we'll go wide right. At 150 yards converge on them keeping your windshield pointing at them."

"Then what?"

"They'll fucking run long before we get there."

"Ehhhh ... if they don't?"

"Fuck we're bigger than them. Grab your drivers now, and keep your windshield between you and them. If they don't run, run them over and beat them with your drivers."

The military man had never actually served in an active engagement in his service and failed to factor that electric golf carts top speed was 20 to 25 mph without an incline. Also, that his adversaries were tested warriors and had bows while they were out of shape middle-age men with golf clubs.

Pomarat watched the approaching golf carts and their obvious flanking maneuver. "Hold till they get close, flank them and fire." Pomarat looked down to Sarkem and saw he was awake and drinking. He took Sarkem's head and clasped it to the side of the buffalo's neck. "Hold tight Sarkem and drink deep, I will be back."

Pomarat pulled his bow off his shoulder, leaving Sarkem to handle his nourishment. He saw the two carts were close. He had made a gamble the approaching humans didn't have fire sticks since the four lying dead didn't have them. "HOLD!"

One of the guys in the cart flanking right said, "Ehhhh ... they're not running. They're aiming at us!"

"I'll keep the windshield in the line of fire!"

"I don't have a good feeling about this," he replied as he nervously fingered the grip of the driver.

In the cart flanking left the passenger echoed similar concerns to the military man who was driving.

"They can't hit us through the windshield relax."

The two carts bore down on Massot and Hysko, each drawing a bead on the left and right carts.

"HOLD!!!" screamed Pomarat. When the carts were within ten feet of Hysko and Massot, Pomarat screamed, "Kristen!!! Ma!!!" Massot and Hysko leaped out of their stationary position to the right and left and let loose their arrows. Massot's found the chest of the military man and Hysko's entered the ear of the guy who said 'Ehhhh' in the right flanking cart and came out the other ear …an inch from the eye of the driver of the cart. Both carts rolled slowly to a stop, one as the result of the military man's foot sliding off the pedal and the other because of the initial horror of the driver. That shock wore off when he saw the third little Indian charging him with a bow with arrow knocked in one hand and a knife in the other screaming in an indiscernible language! "Massot! Get the other one!"

Right flanking driver slammed down on the gas pedal. Left flanking passenger made a dash for the pond with his club still in hand. His eye caught the dead fat guy with another little Indian sucking at his neck like a vampire. He ran for his life thinking 'Fuck! Vampire midget Indians! This can't be real.' But reality struck in the small of his back as Massot's arrow pierced his skin. He stumbled and dropped his club but survival kept him running for the pond, adrenaline numbing the pain. He made his leap as the second arrow scraped his scalp. He felt himself under the water and swam as far as he could hold his breath, making a move slight right so his resurfacing for air would be unpredictable.

Right flanking driver's cart started to gain speed but not before Pomarat managed to climb on the back of the cart and scampered between the two golf bags. Right flanking driver heard the rattle of the clubs, glanced back into Pomarat's maniacal eyes. He swerved the cart as Pomarat grabbed his hair and lashed Mrs. Finch's slicing knife across his throat. The driver's foot pushed the pedal to the floor as blood gushed like a fountain. The cart went up the side of a mogul lining the edge of the fairway and flipped rolling back down, coming to rest on its side.

Pomarat found himself under the 220 pound right flanking driver who was bleeding profusely and a spaghetti mangle of golf clubs that had fallen out of the bags. He was on top of the head of the guy who said 'Ehhhh' and Hysko's arrow through 'Ehhhh's' brain was now in his right bicep. Pomarat was the pickle in a Double Whopper, buried between two masses of meat with special sauce dripping down all over him.

Hysko initially gave chase after the runaway passenger until he heard the commotion of the cart roll over. He did not see Pomarat so he ran back telling Massot to watch for the passenger in the pond. Hysko noticed Sarkem was no longer sucking the blood of the dead buffalo and appeared to be sleeping. Sarkem could wait. He ran across the fairway as fast as his little legs would carry him. When he got to the cart, he could hear the grunting and exertion of Pomarat as he tried to extract himself from the sandwich he was in. Hysko surveyed the situation and crawled in. Bracing his legs on the inside of the roof of the cart, which was now on its side, he pushed the body of the driver with all his might into the floor board revealing his chief. Being free of the weight, Pomarat ripped his arm off the arrow with a grunt. "Get me out of here, Hysko!"

Hysko dragged his chief from the cart and patched his arm with a leather swatch. Pomarat said, "We must go. Get my bow. I'll get Sarkem." Pomarat realized it was time to retreat in all due haste to their homeland. He was wounded and Sarkem was wounded. They needed reinforcements.

Massot intently watched the water surface with bow drawn and aimed at the expected line of resurface. Right flanking passenger resurfaced to get air, but not where Massot expected. Massot hastily redirected his aim and fired, but was late, as right flanking passenger gained the air he needed and went under and swam for the far side of the pond.

Hysko gathered Pomarat's bow, slung it over his shoulder and surveyed the landscape. Massot was standing at the edge of the pond seeking his target and Pomarat was trying to rouse Sarkem to get him upright with one good arm. Then he focused on the golf cart with the dead military man in the driver's seat. Ever attentive, Hysko had noticed that both drivers had had their hands on a cylindrical thing and kept their legs and foot on the things by the floor. Pomarat said he wanted to leave. In their current state, only he and Massot were fully mobile. If he could command the white carts, it would make their trip to marsh easier. If he couldn't, they'd be slow moving snails for the beasts with flashing blue antlers. Hysko ran to the military man's cart and pulled the dead man out of the driver's seat. He sat in the cart and handled the wheel. He noticed the front wheels tried to move when he turned it ... reins! There were two metal pedals on the floor. They were there for a reason. His legs were too short to reach them. Shit! He looked around. The bags on the back! He jumped out of the cart and pulled a putter from one of the bags and hopped back in the driver seat.

Pomarat had reached Sarkem and looked for Hysko. "Hysko! Come! We must go!"

Hysko heard the chief but focused on the cart. Grasping the putter by the head he pressed the handle to the metal pedal. The cart lurched forward! He removed the handle from the pedal but the cart kept rolling. He pushed it against the other pedal, and the cart stopped abruptly almost slamming him against the windshield. 'Stop and go! And the wheel was the way to steer! HE UNDERSTOOD! He composed himself. Pressing gently on the go pedal the cart moved forward and he used the wheel to steer to Pomarat and Sarkem.

Pomarat looked up in shock as he saw Hysko in the mini beast coming at him and Sarkem. His initial thought was the mini beast had consumed Hysko. He raised his tomahawk at the approaching golf cart preparing to shatter the windshield and extract Hysko from the belly of the beast. Hysko saw him ready to charge and he slammed on the brake! "NOOO! Pomarat I control the beast!" He jumped out of the cart and held up his hands. Pomarat lowered his tomahawk, confused.

"Watch! We can use the beast to go home!" Hysko hopped back in the driver's seat and drove up to the right of Pomarat and stopped. "We'll put Sarkem in the beast! You and Massot can ride in the back!" Hysko ran to the back of the cart, surveyed the two sets of golf clubs and saw they were strapped in. His first impulse was to hack at the strap, but he noticed matching latches on each side. He pulled at a latch which released the strap and then did the same with the other. He tossed the two bags of clubs to the ground making space for Pomarat and Massot. Pomarat seeing this hauled Sarkem into the passenger seat and hopped on the back of the cart holding on with his good arm. Hysko jumped into the driver's seat and drove over to Massot who was fixed on the pond.

"Massot! Come now!" ordered Pomarat.

Massot reluctantly turned to the command giving up his spot where he expected his mark to resurface. What he saw caused momentary shock. A golf cart, rapidly approaching with Hysko driving, Sarkem and Pomarat riding. Hysko had tamed a mini-beast!? He looked back to the water … his mark resurfaced but was out of range. Damn! He obeyed Pomarat's command and hopped on the cart though he still had doubts about Hysko's ability to control the mini-beast. As he did, he noticed two more mini-beasts had reached the tee above. Hysko and Pomarat saw this also, time to go. Before Pomarat gave the order, Hysko was driving away from the other mini-beasts towards the 18th green. The foursome arriving on the tee had been drinking beers all day and pulled their drivers and proceeded to the tee. "What the fuck!" said one as he was going to tee his ball. "There's fucking bodies all over the fairway!"

"You got to be shitting me! What should we do?"

"I don't know man. There's fucking seven bodies. That's two groups. If we go down there, we may be the third?"

"Look! There's a golf cart driving by the green. They must be going to the clubhouse to report this."

"Soo, should we finish?"

"ARE YOU FUCKING NUTS? Let's go back to the clubhouse. We'll go back up 17. This round is over. I'm not going down there."

As they we're driving through the community back to the clubhouse, the shitfaced foursome was confronted by the soaking wet maniacal right flanking passenger waving his arms.

"HELP ME! HELP ME!"

"What the fuck?"

"Should we stop? Maybe he's the killer, man."

"Maybe he isn't and he needs help."

"Who was leaving in the golf cart then?"

"Fuck this! I'm stopping!" Red hit the brake, jumped out of the cart and grabbed his driver cocking by his ear like Reggie Jackson waiting for a pitch.

"WHO THE FUCK ARE YOU? WHY ARE THERE BODIES ALL OVER 18? TALK MOTHERFUCKER OR I'LL CAVE YOUR SKULL IN!"

Right flanking passenger stopped his approach to the carts and tried to process Red's anger. "WAIT! I WAS PART OF THE FORESOME! I ESCAPED!"

"ESCAPED FROM WHO?!" said Red cocking his club.

Right flanking passenger was about to describe the horror he had seen but looked at the drunken foursome. They would never believe the truth about midget Indians. Instead he concocted one they would believe. "A bunch of teenage thugs attacked us on the fairway. They robbed and killed my friends and the group before us. I jumped in the pond and swam to the other side. They took one of our golf carts and screwed. They had knives and bows and arrows. I think a couple of them are hurt! We got to get back to the clubhouse and call the police."

Red un-cocked the driver. "Get in and drive! I'll be on the back and watching you. We're taking him back to the clubhouse!" he announced to the others as if he were addressing his armies on the field. Right flanking passenger relaxed realizing he would finally get back to people who were not hammered and had phones.

107

ADAMS DROVE UP AND Browner was at his door. "I'm taking the car! Stay with Reed till Lundquist gets here, then take the car from Lundquist and follow me."

"Follow you where?"

"I'll be going up Cotuit and then down Farmersville. Monitor the radio … I'll keep you updated on my '20'."

"What shall I tell Lundquist to do?"

"Have him stay with Reed. If the ambulance is there, take him with you."

"Got it."

Browner hopped into the cruiser and drove off. He adjusted the volume of the radio looking for local transmission knowing anything the Staties had would be second hand. "This is Officer Browner, any info on the suspects?"

"Negative," responded dispatch at Sandwich HQ.

"Billy, you got any info from the library or the tribal council?"

"Yeah, Dickey Samuels from the council is bringing in Amanda Renyard the chief historian for the Wampanoag nation."

"Does she know anything?"

Billy looked at the radio and raised his arms, "How the fuck do I know," exhausted from the day's events, "she's fricken 89 years old, it may take her a week to get here."

Bobby laughed, "Billy, relax they're in my territory now. You're on clean up now. Give me call if Ms. Renyard has anything of value. If your shift ever ends, have a six pack on me."

"Believe me I will. What a cluster fuck!"

Browner was turning onto Farmersville when Sandwich dispatch broke the silence. "We got a call from the Hollybush Country Club."

"Yeah, what is it?" clicked in Browner.

"A guy who was playing golf claims there were midget Indians killing golfers on the 18th hole of the club."

"How long ago?"

"Just now."

Browner floored it turning on the antlers but not the siren till he needed a blip to get a driver to wake up. The Hollybush Country Club was a short distance up the road. He pulled in to the gated community. The guard had just gotten the call from the clubhouse about the midget Indians. He came to the door and raised the gate. "Officer, I just heard! Those Indians drove out of here about ten minutes ago on a golf cart."

"Did you see where they went!" asked Bobby.

"They took a left on Farmersville."

Browner knew the guy was a hired gatekeeper. He had no time for questions. The guard wasn't armed and his job was to check people coming in not those going out. He probably just figured it was a bunch of dressed up rich kids taking daddy's golf cart for a joy ride. Billy broke the radio silence, "Bobby, Mrs. Renyard is here she says the Pukwudgees were believed to live in the marshes by Sandy Neck!"

"That was quick. I guess she's still got her fastball."
"She sure does."
"We could be close Billy. I know where I'm going now."
"Be careful these guys are killers."
"No shit? I'll keep you posted."
Bobby u-turned out of the Hollybush Country Club. Ten minutes on a golf cart. They aren't far. "All units the suspects may be on Great Hill Road heading to the marshes by Sandy Neck."

108

HYSKO WAS DRIVING THE cart up Great Hill Road with Sarkem passed out in the passenger seat and Pomarat and Massot perched on the back with their heads on a swivel. They had passed a general store with no iron beasts, but one was now coming from behind … a soccer mom in a family assault vehicle, with five nine and ten year old future soccer participation trophy winners strapped dutifully in the back of the Plymouth Caravan singing songs not taking their impending game as important as mom who now noticed the golf cart in the road ahead.

'Shit!' She thought, 'what the fuck are these kids doing in the road with a golf cart? I'm gonna be late for the damn game!' She slammed on the horn and went to pass.

Hysko looked over his left shoulder, unknowingly turning the wheel in that direction, putting them in the path of the accelerating family assault vehicle. Hysko screamed! Massot screamed! Soccer mom screamed! The five future soccer participation trophy winners broke off their song and looked forward. Pomarat saw what was coming and hopped off the back falling to the pavement. Hysko tried to slam the putter handle on the brake but missed. Mom cut the wheel hard left but could not avoid hitting the front of the golf cart. Metal versus plastic – metal wins.

The front shroud of the cart shattered in pieces and the cart went into a roll throwing Hysko onto the unconscious Sarkem's chest, both landing on the pavement. Massot pin wheeled, his back slamming the asphalt. Soccer mom's airbag deployed knocking her back in the seat and the assault vehicle coasted into an oak tree on the side of the road. Now the five dutifully strapped in future soccer participation trophy winners were screaming!

"MOM!" screamed Danny sitting in the passenger seat, the airbags now deflating. Mom was pressed back in her seat with eyes closed but popped open at "MOM!" She gathered her bearing and saw her son was okay and look in the back seeing the remainder of the squad was fine but shaken. Then she looked for the golf cart which was further up the road on its side. Clearing her head, she noticed three of the kids in the cart scattered in the road. Two were moving … one was not. "Danny, kids, stay in the car." She opened her door and glanced at the crumpled front end of the Caravan. She circled around the back of the van to go to the kids in the road and came face to face with the fourth kid with bow drawn. But he was not a kid, he was a … midget? Dwarf? Munchkin?

She may have been able to decipher the answer to that question had she more time, but she was a redhead and a kill shot to her heart made the puzzle irrelevant. Pomarat knocked another arrow in his bow making his way to the door she had exited to finish off the screaming siblings of the red headed witch.

Bobby flipped on the siren seeing the accident and overturned golf cart up ahead. He keyed the radio, "We've got an accident on Great Hill Road. It is the perps, the Pukwudgees! I need back up, people down!"

At the sound of the siren and then the flashing blue lights, a groggy Hysko and Massot gained their feet and scrambled to draw their bows. Sarkem wasn't breathing and probably dead. Pomarat slammed the driver door shut; the siblings would have to wait. Browner sized up the situation. Two unstable Pukwudgees to the right and a very alert one to the left by the driver's side of the van. All with bows drawn at him.

"Fuck it." Bobby hammered the accelerator and ran into Hysko and Massot as their arrows deflected off his windshield. Their bodies flew into the air while the cruiser's tires crushed Sarkem's lifeless head. Bobby slammed on the brakes hard and turned to the right performing a 360. He slammed the brakes by the back of the van and there was Pomarat with bow drawn. "Pitiful" he thought. He shoved open the driver side door and exited it low behind it. Pomarat held his shot as his eyes met Bobby's behind the glass of the door. He had just seen Hysko and Massot rendered immobile in the street, maybe dead. Sarkem was definitely dead. There was a man behind that invisible shield, and he was a warrior of his equal.

"DROP THE BOW!" yelled Browner behind the door.

The words were unintelligible to Pomarat. The kids were sniveling in the van beside him, but he could not afford to break his glance from Browner. He then saw he had a shot at Bobby's boots below the cover of the door. Bobby saw his eyes shift down and tensed. He shifted his feet right and fired as did Pomarat ...

1968 TO 1992 - THE YEARS BETWEEN

109

THAT FALL BEGAN THE first year of high school for the boys. For Timmy it meant a new building about a half-mile from the old building … both had crosses over the entrance. It also meant going back to the bottom of the food chain, being a freshman. He however had an advantage having heard how Colin went through the same drill and handled it. Not only that, he was Colin's brother and that bought him leeway but not a complete pass. Timmy's experience in the summer of '68 gave him an attitude, which projected him to be crazy … no fearless. Timmy had few problems after the day Danny O'Hearn, a wanna be junior, confronted him at the first dance of the fall semester. Danny had been sucking a bottle of Thunderbird prior to the dance.

"Hey Red!" yelled Danny coming up from behind Timmy when he was talking to a group of friends, as local band was belting out '*Fire*' by Arthur Brown.

Timmy turned and started to say "Hey Dan …" when he was greeted by a fist to the face. "What the fuck was that for?" yelled Timmy now on his back on the basketball court. Timmy's friends stood in shock not knowing what to do. The music was blasting and the gym was dark.

"Cause you're fucking ugly and queer. Now pay me two bucks or get the fuck out of here."

"Yeah sure Danny, I didn't know. Got the money in my pocket!" Timmy held his arm out as a sign of submission as he raised himself from the floor. Danny was wearing a smirk of dominance looking at Timmy's circle of friends daring any of them to interfere. Timmy, back on his feet looked down like a beaten puppy and reached in his pocket for the two dollars he always carried with him as his older brother taught him. It was roll of wrapped nickels that he closed his fist around. "Can I pay you in change?" he asked feigning nervousness.

"Oh no, oh no, oh no, you gonna burn!" sang the lead singer.

"Yeah, yeah cough it up," said Danny figuring he now had an easy mark for any future school events for the next two years, 'He must be queer,' he thought. That was Danny's second to last thought for the evening as Timmy ripped his fistful of wrapped nickels from his pocket with his knuckles curled around them. He landed a vicious right cross to Danny's temple. Danny's last thought for the evening was 'Fuck!' Timmy was on him as he fell to the floor slamming his head again as it rebounded off the hardwood. He was about to go for thirds when he realized Danny was out cold. Timmy got up, and said to his friends, "I gotta go. I'll see you later. Give me some time."

"Fire, to end all you've become. I'll feel you burn!" continued the singer.

Timmy went out the gym doors and left the building. Timmy's friends stood in a close circle around the lifeless body of Danny hoping to delay notice by the dance chaperones as long as possible. The gym was crowded. The chaperones were on the perimeter not paying attention, talking to each other. But the confrontation had not gone unnoticed by nearby upperclassmen. When they were sure Timmy had to be clear of the building, his friends dispersed to areas elsewhere leaving the view of the convulsed Danny open to those who had no clue as to what happened.

"Help, someone's fainted!" screamed a sophomore girl.

Two male chaperones came running, being sure to leave their punch on the table since they contained more whiskey than punch."What happened?"

The question went unanswered as all such questions do in Southie. A few students knew but weren't saying anything, but soon many would know and Timmy's stature would grow, as someone not to be fucked with, much like his brother Colin. Danny was in the hospital for three days with a concussion. On his third day, Colin bearing a get well card with a two-dollar bill visited him. "Hi Danny."

"Sorry Colin, I was drunk. I should have known better," said Danny, now scared for his life.

"No problem Danny. But now my brother's welfare is tied to yours. You know what I mean?"

"Yeah, yeah."

"No, I don't think you do," replied Colin squeezing his hand tight, any tighter would break a bone.

"I do, I do," seethed Danny feeling the pain.

"I mean nothing happens to Timmy, not by you or anybody. You are now responsible for his well being. If he gets run over by a tourist, I come looking for you. Understand?"

"Yeah."

"Good, there's two bucks in the card for your efforts, Timmy didn't know you had a toll booth. Get well soon, I need you looking out for my brother." Colin released his grip and left. Danny had wet his bed.

110

BRETT'S HIGH SCHOOL INDOCTRINATION was less eventful. He was a chubby rich kid in a school of rich kids. At least on the Cape he had more money than his friends did. Here everyone had money. He was disadvantaged by being chubby. Over the first few weeks of school he saw where the wisdom of future him was right. Being fat sucked. The pretty girls wouldn't give him the time of day. In a sense he was invisible to them, hard to believe for a person his size.

He could play tennis though and decided he would go out for the team in the spring. He knew strategy and technique from his years of lessons at the club from the pro Buzz Conforti. That was half the battle. The other half was athleticism, which up to this point was unnecessary since he had a killer serve and could place the ball in such a fashion so he wouldn't have to move far for a return. But at private school such as this, he knew that everyone going out for the team would probably similarly schooled in technique and strategy. To that end he made up his mind he would heed Timmy's revelations and would use the time between now and then to slim down.

In the fall, he went out for the cross-country team knowing he wouldn't make it but he learned the trail through the woods. He started running the first 200 yards and walked the rest. Of course he was one of the first to be cut. But he'd run/walk the trail every school day gradually increasing the distance he actually ran. When the snows of winter came he asked his dad if he could start using the weight room at his dad's club. His dad was shocked "You want to use the weight room?"

"Yeah, I'm going out for the tennis team this spring."

"Okay, son. I'll arrange it. I'll get Ernst to set up a regimen for you." Dad was glad his son was taking an interest in something other than food. "You think you can make the team?"

"Yeah, I'll make it."

"You know that cross-country escapade cost me $20."

"Yeah but it saved you twice that amount in Twinkies, Cupcakes, and Yo-Ho's."

"Yeah, I noticed you're not eating as much. Keep up the good work and you will make that team."

And he did make it. As a freshman, he was third seed on the team and rose to second seed by the end of the season. He was no longer invisible to girls.

111

VERN MADE IT AS freshman also, as the starting halfback on the Falmouth High football team. Mashpee didn't have a high school and their kids attended school in neighboring Falmouth enduring long bus rides each day to and from school. Coach Gilligan had heard of this kid from Mashpee with amazing agility and speed. The stories didn't do the kid justice, probably due to the fact the people telling them didn't possess the vocabulary and experience in the sport to fully describe what they saw. Gilligan never had a kid with such instincts. Prior to the snap his eyes were surveying the defense and this didn't stop until he was brought down or in the end zone. The kid ran like a chased rabbit, turning on a dime and bursting into the open.

He thought to himself, 'I got Gale Sayers! Holy shit, I got Gayle Sayers.' Of course he kept this to himself, as state titles floated in his head. The kid was like a sponge at practice sucking up everything he said. And he wasn't a wise ass. He could sense a kid with a quick wit underneath the "Yes, sir" demeanor. He took him aside after a practice and said, "Vernon, I want you to beef up a little so you don't get hurt."

"Yes sir. How do I do that?"

"Lift weights three to four times a week on alternate days."

"Where can I do that sir?"

"Can your parents get you a set of free weights?"

"No sir, we don't have much money. My Dad has a rear axle in the garage, would that be good?"

"I'll see if I can find someone who doesn't need them anymore. Don't worry about it for now." Gillian decided to hit on some old alumni whose kids were beyond needing free weights anymore. The following Saturday morning he dropped them off at the Otis's. Carmella thanked him profusely for taking an interest in her son and asked him if he'd like something to eat. The coach said, "No, thank you, is Vern around?"

"No sir, he's bicycling to school for practice this afternoon."

"He rides his bike all the way to Falmouth?"

"Yes sir, on the weekends there's no bus and Mr. Otis needs the truck for work."

Gillian thanked Mrs. Otis for the hospitality and she thanked him for the weights and wished she could give him something to eat. Gillian drove back to Falmouth. Practice was still three hours away. The kid had been doing this for the last two weeks. The first game was next Saturday afternoon at New Bedford. Vern would probably be pedaling at 7 or 8 AM to catch the ten o'clock bus to New Bedford. And he never said anything to him. He had already made up his mind. Vern was starting the first game. He'd be damned if his starting half back would be dispensing all that energy prior to game time and then doing it again after the game. Again he'd lean on the alumni. He wondered who else on the team was from Mashpee and needed a ride.

As a result of this eye opening visit and Gillian's organizational skills, a group of mothers and fathers were commissioned to ensure those who didn't have rides to practices and games, got them. The results of his efforts were evident in their first game. Falmouth rolled over Bishop Fenwald 42-7. Vernon Otis rushed for 230 yards with four TD's. A star was born. Visions of state titles danced in Gillian's head. But the kid would have to bulk up because the competition would get stronger as the season went on and if they got to the state tournament, they'd be facing physically stronger teams from around Boston. Shit, Vernon could be his ticket to a higher level of coaching, maybe college or at least state college.

112

SIMPLY PUT, AMOS WOULD become a library rat as long as the weather permitted him to make the long trip on his bike to the Falmouth Library on Saturday. As much as he wished he could go see Vern play, Saturday was the only day he could go to the library since it was closed on Sunday and there was school during the week. He and Vern spoke about this and Vern understood completely. Mashpee's small library was limited and didn't have the resources he was looking for.

Amos realized that going out to the pond and studying the books from the future after school wasn't going to work. One, the days would be getting shorter. Two, it would be getting colder. Three, his parents would start wondering what the hell he was doing out in the cold and the dark. One Saturday, when his parents went to Falmouth to see Vern play, he decided to cut a hole in the floor of the closet in his room. Since their house had a crawl space and not a cellar, this should work well. The floors were wide finished pine boards overlaid on sub-floor. Crafting an invisible hatch would have to be a work of art. Amos had pre-thought out the entire process required to do it and what he would need. He scrounged or acquired what he needed well before that day. Since they would be bringing Vern home after the game, he told Vern to drag out coming home as long as possible. As soon as his parents left for the game, he went into action much like the TV show 'Mission Impossible' which he had never seen since they didn't have a TV.

He cut two pine boards flush to the molding through the underlayment on all sides. Of course they fell to the ground leaving a hole. Earlier in the week he had cut and predrilled holes in a 4" wide pine board he found in the barn that he would use as a lip on three sides of the hole. He had two hinges. He ran outside and unsecured the entrance to the crawlspace and set it aside. Grabbing a flashlight, the boards, screws, hinges, a cabinet handle and a screwdriver, he dropped to the ground in the crawl space from his room. Lying on his back he turned on the flashlight and surveyed the space under the house. There was about two and a half feet of clearance. There was also an abundance of cobwebs and some small mammals scampering away from him. "Shit!"

He shinnied into the cobwebs so he could lift the cut floorboards through the hole back into the closet and slide it aside. Then he screwed the 4" shim around the hole and attached the two hinges. He stood up in the hole in the closet, flipped the cut floorboards over and screwed in the cabinet handle. He also drilled a hole through the underlayment between the two pine boards through which he inserted a wire tied to a t-bar, which would serve to lift the door from the closet. Now came the hard part.

Amos flipped the floorboards over and lay back in the crawlspace. Using the cabinet handle he jockeyed the floorboards into place. Repositioning the flashlight, he started the screws through the hinges into the underlayment of the two boards. The four screws started, he grabbed the cabinet handle to keep the boards from rising while he drove each screw home. Working in this position, screwing without pre-drilled holes was difficult. One arm's strength was working against the other. The first screw was relatively smooth. The second was more difficult. Half way through the third he had to lay back and rest his arms as the muscles were aching. After a few moments, he resumed and managed to bring it home. Again he laid back to rest his arms before attacking the final screw. His hand with the screwdriver was shaking from exertion. He noticed the flashlight bulb seemed to be dimming. "Shit!"

He went for the last screw. His shaking hand knocked it loose before he could lodge the screwdriver in the Phillips slot. It bounced off his chest on to the dirt floor. "Fuck! This ain't good." He rolled on his side, frantically looking for the errant screw. When batteries were going, they went relatively fast. He gently swept the ground with his right hand. This wasn't good. Then his middle finger felt metal … or was it a rock? It was a rock. Panic start to sink in. Then his mantra counteracted! "DON'T PANIC YOU IDIOT! YOU HAVE MORE SCREWS IN YOUR POCKET!" He reached in his pocket, pulled out a screw and placed it on the head of his shaking screwdriver. Using both hands he guided it into the started hole. He shifted his left hand to the handle and drove the screw with his right. The muscles in his arms burned. The flashlight was losing power. He was determined to bring it home. Each turn of the screw was excruciating. But he finally did. He collapsed in exhaustion. The light dimmed further. The job was done but he had to get out of the crawl space. No time to rest. He tried to push up his newly crafted trap door, but his arms were numb. "I gotta get out of here." He had no strength left to lift the door. He looked down his body past his feet and could see light at the entrance to the crawl space. He'd have to get there through the spider webs and those that lived here … the rats.

He grabbed the flashlight, the motion dimming it further to where it was pretty much useless. He rolled on his stomach and began crawling to the exit. He could feel more webs engulfing his face and used his hand to rub from neck to chin. "Gross!" He knew the feeling would be continuous until he got out so he continued crawling like an infantry recruit scrambling under barbed wire.

The flashlight went out, now he had to worry about the rats. The last thing he needed was to be bitten. God knows what diseases they carried. But there wasn't time to worry about that. Time was running out. If Vern didn't slow them down, it could be less time than he calculated and he had a lot more to do to cover his tracks. He kept moving forward through the webs. He felt something scamper over his right arm and then his left hand. It seemed like it had kept moving and didn't stop to bite. That was it! Amos started screaming as he resumed his crawl, hoping to disperse any fellow rats that were around. The tactic was successful as he reached the entrance.

He jumped to his feet and started wildly rubbing the webs from his hair, neck and face. God knows how many spiders came with the webs and were exploring his body. He rubbed himself all over hoping to knock them off. He couldn't reach his back so he flopped on the ground and slid around on it hoping he crushed them or knocked them off. He got up and surveyed his clothes. He was a mess. He re-secured the entrance to the crawl space and hoped there would be no need for anyone to be poking around in there for a long time. He'd have to tell Vern to keep his ears open for any talk of maintenance under the house by their parents. Now he had to finish the job at hand. He was running on borrowed time. He'd have to get the cooler with the books, put it in its new hiding place, replace the tools, clean the work area, replace the junk that was in the bottom of the closet, shower, change his clothes and find a way to clean the ones he was in later. If Vern hadn't found a way to slow them down, they'd be pulling into the driveway at anytime now. Thankfully for Amos, he had.

113

IN HIS FOURTH GAME of the season, Vern put on a performance that would attract attention of people from over the bridge. To date Falmouth was 3-0 and facing a Southeastern Mass powerhouse, Brockton. No one in Eastern Mass thought Falmouth would be 4-0 at the end of the day. But Vern vaulted himself to regional attention. Two hundred eighteen yards rushing, four TD's … two rushing, one receiving and one kick return leading Falmouth to a 35-17 win. The Cape Cod Times wanted an interview with Vern, but a reporter from the *Globe* was in his face first. Vern looked at the Times reporter and winked holding up a finger to say 'I'll be right with you'. The *Globe* reporter, needing a one liner for the high school summaries in the Sunday *Globe* asked "Vern, did you ever imagine you'd be so instrumental in defeating Brockton as a freshman running back?"

"I wasn't sir."

"What do you mean? 200 plus yards 4 TD's? Why do you say that?"

"Coach called the plays, Steve our quarterback executed them, and the rest of the team blocked. I just ran for my life."

"Yeah, ok."

The *Globe* reporter flipped his book closed deciding to get back to Boston well before deadline and maybe get an early start on clubbing tonight. The one line would read "Vern attributed his amazing performance to his coaches and offensive line," leaving the quarterback, receivers, and fullback on the cutting room floor.

The Times reporter stepped up. "Vernon Otis, my name is Jack Ryan, I work for the Times."

"Yeah I know. I've read your reports."

"Off the record, why did you give the *Globe* guy nothing?"

"Cause he pushed his way in and didn't introduce himself."

"Yeah, but the *Globe* has a lot of exposure."

"Yeah, it does. But nobody reads about high school games except the parents. At least you guys write stories about the games. They do paragraph summaries."

"So what's the story of this game, Vern?"

"The story is the one liner I gave the *Globe* guy. All week the entire team and coaches worked hard to give me a chance to do what I do."

"And what is it you do?"

"I run as fast as I can and avoid players on the other team. We all got jobs to do, like you have a job to do. And we did it well today as you usually do with your stories."

"Okay Vern, I'll see you after the next game then?"

"You bet, Mr. Ryan."

Vern shook his hand and went over to his parents, "I got get back into the locker room, okay?"

"Yeah, sure son, we'll be here," said his dad beaming with pride.

Vern dragged his ass in the locker room showering and getting dressed. The coach told him "Good game." His teammates were slapping him on the back. In his mind, he was hoping he was doing a good blocking job for Amos. As it turns out, he did. When he and his parents got home, Amos was all cleaned up, doing his homework at the kitchen table.

"Amos, you missed a hell of a performance by your brother," said his dad going to the fridge and grabbing a beer.

Later that evening he and Vern went out to the country store. Amos told him of his day's events and Vern his. When they got home, Amos showed him his work in the closet. "The books are here and now I can go full tilt. You got to cover my ass and if you ever hear of dad having to go under the house, we gotta get the cooler out of there. Understand?"

"Yeah, good job, Amos."

"You too, you saved my ass."

Vern smiled.

114

IN THE SUMMER OF '69, they hooked up again thanks to the organizational efforts of Amos who sent out letters setting up a meeting on July 1st at Callahan's. They all had big smiles when they saw each other. "Fuckin' look at you guys!" hollered Vern pointing at Brett and Timmy.

"Yeah Vern, I read about you in the *Globe*," smiled Timmy. "And you too Brett, though I usually don't follow tennis."

"Yeah well you should start, what's the name of that papist school you go to in Southie? We may be playing you next year."

"Our Lady of Nasty Gansetts, and we don't have a tennis team," laughed Timmy. "Seriously though, you lost weight."

"Yeah at rich kid school, I found out fast it sucks to be fat."

"AMOS!" said Timmy as he gave him a hug. "Why you being so quiet?"

"I was just soaking this reunion in."

"Amos has been studying and planning," said Vern.

"Yeah I can see that by the look on his face," said Timmy looking Amos in the eye. "What's the plan? You getting anywhere?"

"I am. I think we can pull this off if we keep in touch over the next twenty-three years. That's going to be the hardest part."

"What da ya mean," asked Brett.

"We got a whole summer, we'll talk about it and I'll explain. In the meantime let's catch up on what we been up to this winter."

115

AND TALK ABOUT IT they did. In the summer of '69 they spent many nights around a fire at Witch Pond discussing their lives, and thanks to Amos, focus on what they had to do. Timmy provided beer. How he got it he didn't say nor was there a need to ask. During the day they did what their families expected of them. Brett sharpened his game at the Tennis facility. Vern worked out and did chores. Amos studied and did chores. And Timmy went to the beach and looked for chicks and conducted business. Occasionally, they all got together to fish, hunt or hangout on the beach. They talked about the orb and all agreed that it would be unwise to take any more trips through it. Vern wished he could make another trip. His mom's life came first.

The years went by. At Labor Day they separated. By July they were together again … for the next three years. Then came the college years. Major football programs heavily recruited Vern. He ended up selecting Syracuse based on the success of previous running backs that had come through their system … Brown, Davis, Little, Nance and Csonka. Brett went to Yale as his father had. Amos went to Wharton on a full boat scholarship based on his grades and essay on how the fluctuations in various markets impacted each other. Carmella Otis was beaming with pride over her boys.

Timmy O'Rielly went to Suffolk University in Boston for a degree in political science. Timmy was schooled in the shadow of the State House to learn the machinations of state and local governments and how to find the wheels that needed to be greased in order to accomplish future Brett's plan … and maybe a few of his own.

In June of 1973, when they met after their first year of college and having all told their stories of their experiences, Amos ask Brett, "So did you do as I say and ask your dad to give you access to a portion of your trust fund to invest?"

"Yeah, he told me the market sucks and now is not the time to be screwing around with money."

"Did he give you access to any of it?"

"Yeah $10,000."

"Whoa, how fucking big is that trust fund if he thinks $10,000 is play money?" asked Timmy chuckling.

"I have no idea, man. But I can call the broker and tell him what to do with the $10,000. But I can't touch the money."

"Fantastic!" said Amos. "I'm gonna tell you what to tell your broker to invest in and by next summer your dad will be asking you to invest his money and probably give you access to more of yours."

"You sure? How do you know?"

Vern and Timmy laughed and chimed in together "Future you told us!"

"I'm getting sick of being the only one of us who doesn't know what you two brought back."

Vern said, "I ain't seen it either Brett, but I don't want to. The only one who's really read them is Amos. And if he says trust me, I trust him. Future you gave the books to Amos and Timmy. Timmy never read them. Only Amos has a brain big enough to know how to handle what's in them."

"I'm getting sick of future me telling me what to do."

"Future you was a very happy guy," said Amos "and he wanted to make sure that this time travel shit didn't screw that up for you."

Brett thought this over. Things were going well after all. He was slimmer, going to Yale, and made their tennis team. And the broads were noticing him. 'Maybe future me knew what he was doing and I should follow his advice.

"Hey I got a grand," chimed Timmy, "can you invest that too?"

"No we can't Timmy." answered Amos. "We got to wait three years till we're 21 to be doing that. Otherwise, everyone will want to know where you got the money. You ready to answer that question?"

"Err, well, here and there … ya know."

"Yeah, I think I know. But imagine saying what you just said to someone in a suit and you being you. Know what I mean?

"Yeah, I'd be opening a bag of shit."

"Exactly. Where is the money now?"

"In a secret place in my house."

"Man, you got to get that in a bank. Open an account, and slowly phase it in it."

"How slowly?"

"About $100 to $200 a week."

"Okay."

"Be careful! Don't get in over your head Timmy. You know what I'm saying?" Amos looked Timmy in the eye while saying this.

Timmy paused, glanced down and then met his eyes, "It's part of where I live. My brother Colin's a good teacher. He's got my back and I got his. If I'm not part of the program, I'm fresh meat. You know what I mean."

"Yes, but not really. I've never been there."

Brett had a tremendous urge to ask what they were talking about, but his instincts told him not to interrupt. Vern knew but didn't really know like Amos.

Amos told Brett what to do with his $10,000. The market was down in 1974 but rebounded tremendously in 1975. Brett's $10,000 increased to

$15,000 despite the market nosedive in 1974. In 1975 Brett's father gave Brett control over another $50,000 and secretly told his broker to take a half million of his investments and mirror his son's movements in the markets.

116

IN THE SUMMER OF 1976 they met for the last time as dependents on their parent's tax returns. Amos had graduated from Wharton Summa Cum Laude and had offers for tremendous jobs in New York City. Instead he took a job with a major brokerage firm in Boston much to the delight of the firm. The kid landed two clients right out of the box. The first was Brett Simmons a Yale graduate who had investment control of a half million dollars of a trust fund which after a few months would grow to a million as more funds were released to his investment control. And the kicker was Brett couldn't draw down the funds till ten years from now, though he could always switch brokerage houses. Amos was confident that wouldn't happen.

The second was his brother Vern, a graduate of Syracuse who also just happened to be drafted in the fourth round of the NFL draft, a promising prospect. Amos's third client a few months later was Brett's father, a big fish. His fourth client was a political science major from Suffolk University named Timmy O'Rielly with $20,000 to invest. Amos's 20th client was himself after he received his generous bonus in January.

For the next ten years things were good. Vern was always near the top of the pack of rushers in the NFL but nearing the end of his career. His contracts had increased substantially over the years and he had picked up a number of endorsement contracts due to his humorous personality. He was never ostentatious in his spending which made him a hero to his fans in the rust belt city that he played and in his home state of Massachusetts. He was loved in both and would never have to pick up a check in either and was sought for numerous public speaking engagements. The networks were courting him to be an analyst when he retired because of his quick wit and appeal to the common man.

Brett and his dad watched their portfolios grow. Brett learned about real estate development. Dad's client base was cut back to those willing to pay the highest rates, leaving him time to travel the world and savor the younger ladies in a multiplicity of countries thus finding the fountain of youth. Mom also found it, bouncing from their homes in Concord, New Seabury, Boca, Vail and Aruba with an occasional jaunt elsewhere.

Amos made money hand over fist for himself as he always followed the advice he gave to clients. His reputation was increasing. More of the firm's clients requested him based on the word on the street. The firm increased the fees for his services and increased his bonuses. Amos realized it was time to slow down. No one was as good as he was without some divine intervention.

Timmy was a different kind of client. He brought his money to be invested in cash in a Zero Halliburton suitcase.

"Don't you have a bank account?" asked Amos one day.

"Yeah but I'm trying to keep my earnings under the radar, know what I mean."

"Yeah I do, and it scares me. You're not getting in dangerous shit are you? I mean this isn't more than simple numbers shit? Cause if it is, we got more than enough money with our investments to date to accomplish what we set out to do."

"Relax Amos. It's a byproduct of where I grew up. It has nothing to do with what you and I went through. I'd be in the same place if we'd never met, probably with a different broker making less money and not having a clue. With Colin and I's inclination for vengeance we attracted the attention of the hierarchy of Southie. We do simple tasks and they pay us well."

"So it is dangerous stuff."

"Not completely, we get to run our own gigs with no vig. We just have to go and scare people every so often. Our rep is growing so now the situation is usually resolved with little need for violence. We just show up and say what needs to be done."

"Shit man, you know you two got a fucking target on your back! There are people out there that think they'll improve their station in life by taking you out. And they're not the people you're currently intimidating. They're the ones you intimidated or beat up in the past. They're the ones who work for you and want your action. They could even be your bosses, if you get too good at what you do or screw up one time."

"Amos, I saw the Godfather movies just like you, it ain't like that. It's Boston, we're small time."

"Yeah but human nature is the same no matter what the stage."

"Stop worrying man, I'll be okay."

"I'm gonna worry. We got enough money to do what we set out to do. There's no need to put you in this position."

"Colin and I got it covered. We'll be fine. Relax man." Timmy gave Amos a hug and walked out of his office. That would be the last time that would happen.

117

IN 1987, BRETT CAME into Amos's office. "It's time Amos!"

"I'm doing fine Brett, how are you?" said Amos with a curious smile on his face.

Brett laughed, "Yeah, I'm fine and fuck you. It's time."

"For what?"

"We're buying the property!"

"Now?"

"Yeah."

"Why, what's happening?"

"Remember you told me a company was gonna build condos on the site."

"Yeah."

"They're here investigating the site for condos. We gotta move now!"

"And? ..."

"They want to move with a massive condo project and the town planner is totally against it! He's a dyed in the wool conservationist! We're gonna top their bid to create ... get this ... a park dedicated to preserving Wampanoag history!"

"What?"

"Yeah! We'll put a concrete pavilion over the hole with statues of Wampanoag legends on top. Maushop, Pukwudgees, giant crows ... you got to help me here. We'll have fog machines, storytellers similar to Plymouth Plantation. We got Sarah Screecham's ruins. We can have actors relate the stories! We'll recreate scenes from the land of legends. The town will love it! Anything to avoid more condos! We could just come in with a conservation buy, but this plan allows us to close the hole and create something!"

Amos leaned back in his chair and commenced thinking as this information ran through his already overtaxed brain. "Soo … who wants to build the condos?"

"A bunch of Italians from Boston, they formed this real estate development company. They've done projects in Mass, Florida and one in Vegas."

"Italians from Boston?"

"Yeah."

"Brett, do you have any idea who we're bidding against?"

"Yeah, that's where you come in."

"ME?!!!"

"Yeah you. You're Wampanoag right?"

"Soo …?"

"Ever heard of the Mashantucket Pequot Tribal Nation?"

"I've heard of the Pequots."

"They're making hay in Connecticut. They got tribal recognition three years ago and opened a high stakes bingo casino there with an asian front man. And now they're looking to build a real casino. The Mashpee Wampanoags can follow their game plan. You soap box the idea to the tribe and the Italians will drop out."

"They won't drop out, they'll kill me!"

"I've talked to the planner, there are so many wetlands exceptions and vernal pools on the land, that the plan they submitted will never fly."

"They were building the project when Timmy and I came out of the hole! How did they get past the vernal pools and wetlands exceptions then?" answered Amos slumping in his chair."

"BECAUSE THE OPPOSITION DID NOT HAVE ANY BACKING FROM THE WAMPANOAG NATION! Get that and they have no shot."

Amos considered this. He would research what the Pequots were doing. This could work. Mom and the others could be saved. He needed time. "Brett, tell the planner you've talked to the Wampanoags and they need time to assemble support."

"Fuckin yes! Let's go have a drink."

They left Amos's office at 50 State Street and went for a drink at one of the bars nearby. When they left the bar they shook hands. Amos said, "You know when I last saw Timmy, I had this feeling I may never see him again. I thought it would be because something happened to him. Now I'm wondering if it is because something happens to me."

"Nothing's going to happen to you, yeah they're Italian but the days of the Godfather are gone."

"Maybe, but if anything does happen to me and Timmy, you got to stay close to Vern."

"Why do you say something like that?"

"Cause I feel like I'm doing something wrong. It seems like Timmy and I by going in the hole, seeing the future and then you and Vern, violated some rules of natural order. Now Timmy and I seem to be something that was not to be. We wouldn't be who we are now if we hadn't chased the Pukwudgees down the hole."

"Who would you be?"

Amos pondered the question, "I'd be a smart kid with a promising future in a major corporation, not a superstar with the books of knowledge. Timmy would probably be like his dad, a man of principles making an honest living watching the Sox's and playing golf."

"Yeah, but that's not how it turned out. So now we got to deal with the cards that we were dealt. We got to prevent the carnage that resulted and make the best of it."

Amos looked at Brett. "Fuck! If anything happens to me and Timmy you got to stick to the plan."

"Nothing is gonna happen!" Brett gave Amos a hug and they parted.

118

AMOS SUCCESSFULLY RALLIED THE tribe after researching what the Pequots were up to and informing them of the potential of the land they held nearby. Plus a site similar to the Plymouth Plantation would only serve to enhance their stature as a tribe. The tribe came out in full force in support of Brett's group and in protest of the Italian development company's condo project. Vern also made an appearance and spoke at a crucial planning board meeting using his charm and wit to emphasize the importance of Brett's project to the Wampanoag children and the Town of Mashpee. His appearance caught the attention of the network news stations in Boston.

Marcello Magotti, the head of the development company, watched the news clips from his home in a Boston suburb. "We ain't gonna get this project," he said after flicking off the TV. "The project's dead, withdraw the plans and cut off funding."

"I'll get right on it," said John getting up from the couch. "What about this Indian kid who organized the Indians."

Marcello laid back in his recliner. "He's a high priced broker, very successful. My first impulse was to do a hit and run. But if he's backing this stupid ass project, he must be on to something. I think I'll pay him a visit and maybe become a client. The Indians are making a move in Connecticut. I smell them making a move here. Nice touch though, getting his fucking high profile brother to give that speech."

"Soo … what do you want me to do?"

Marcello sipped his drink and said, "Kill the project and get me an appointment with the kid."

119

THE PROJECT WAS FULLY permitted by late 1991 and would be completed in time for its opening in the summer of 1993 barring any delays, complete with its concrete pavilion and statues. They would name it "The Wampanoag Cultural Village," but only two of the four would be there for the ribbon cutting.

Amos reluctantly had accepted a meeting with Marcello at Amos's office in Boston after the town had denied Marcello's project.

"Mr. Magotti, how can I help you?" asked Amos coming out from behind his desk to shake his hand in a sign of deference.

He had told Timmy that Magotti asked for a meeting, and asked if he had any tips. Timmy told him he was probably looking to see what you were up to and probably get in on the action.

"There's no action," said Amos.

"Tell him the project was worthless but critical to laying the foundation to getting a casino on Indian land five to ten years from now."

"Fucking casino? This is Mass, fucking Connecticut only gave them a Bingo parlor. Mass is so tight-assed they won't grant casinos until hell freezes over."

"Yeah, but I hear a casino is in the works there. Trust me, if all the gambling money starts flowing to Connecticut, fucking Mass will speed up the process. 'Gentlemen! We got to protect our mamby pamby jobs!'" said Timmy in an animated voice.

"What???"

"Didn't you ever see 'Blazing Saddles'? The 'GOV' says that to his staff."

"I didn't see it."

"Fuck man, get out of your office and enjoy yourself. Rent it, it's got to be the funniest movie of all time."

"Thank you for seeing me Mr. Otis, call me Marcello,"

"Call me Amos, please have a seat." Marcello took the chair in front of Amos's desk. Amos sat in the other chair in front of his desk as opposed to the one behind it. This didn't go unnoticed by Marcello. He liked the respect this successful colored person was showing him. The kid had been brought up right.

"Amos, I'm going to be up front. How the fuck are you going to make any money on that project you pulled out from under me?"

"Marcello, can I be frank?"

"Yes, yes," said Marcello waving his hand in a circular 'come on' fashion.

"We're not. Neither were you if your project got passed."

"What do you mean?"

"Can I offer you a drink? This may take awhile."

"Do you have any wine?"

"Merlot?"

"That would be nice."

Amos poured them both a glass of Merlot from the bar in his office.

"Have you heard about the Tax Reform Act of 1986 passed by

Reagan?"

"Yes."

"No one seems to realize what it means for real estate on the Cape ... vacation property."

"What does it mean?"

"At some point in the next few years the real estate market on Cape is gonna crash. Your project would have been dead in the water with no buyers."

"Why doesn't anyone see this?"

"Because they don't read. After a few years of doing their tax returns, they will have realized this. So will everyone else."

"So you saying you were just saving me from myself?" asked Marcello with a smirk.

"Not at all, I'm laying the foundation for the Wampanoags' recognition as a tribe. You know what's going on in Connecticut."

"It's a fucking bingo parlor!"

"Now it is. It's their first step to becoming a casino. Our project is our first step in getting one for the Wampanoags in Mass. It enhances our tribal recognition."

"How do I get in on this?"

"Don't know. Your tribe knows more about casinos than my tribe. We're just trying to get one."

Marcello let out an honest belly laugh.

"I like you Amos. I want to become a client and talk some more."

"I would like that. And maybe you can help my tribe realize our goals. But I must tell you, come 1992 I am retiring as a stockbroker. Then I'm going into real estate."

Marcello looked at him with a raised eyebrow, "I thought you said the real estate market was going to shit."

"I did. And what is the fundamental law of investing?"

Marcello smiled, "Buy low, sell high."

"Yep."

Marcello was enamored with this kid. He finished his wine and gave him a hug. "I wish I found you a long time ago."

120

TIMMY AND COLIN WERE commissioned to tone down a Guido making a move into Southie unbeknownst to his bosses in the North End. They left him with a concussion and a fractured kneecap on A Street and called his family to pick him up. Timmy and Colin retired to a bar on L Street to have a nightcap. Timmy left after one. Colin stayed. Danny O'Hearn happened to be walking down the opposite side of L Street at the exact time Timmy left the bar and turned right to head home. Danny had a significant buzz going when he saw him. He ducked out of sight. If Timmy was heading home he knew the route he'd take.

This was his chance for pay back! His stature in the neighborhood had been worth shit since that blow in the gym. The bottle of whiskey he had consumed that evening had buried his common sense and elevated his testosterone. When Timmy turned right on 4th, he ran across L and paralleled on 5th. He would run two blocks and cross over to 4th and wait for Timmy to go past. He waited, out of site at the corner of 4th and N Street. He heard footfalls approaching. Timmy crossed N Street with hands in his coat pockets briefly glancing left and right for traffic, which was non-existent.

Danny ran up behind him and shot him in the back. "Where's your nickel roll now, fuck face!!!"

Timmy spun as he fell to the sidewalk one hand still in his pocket. Intense pain seared his chest as he struggled to see his attacker through eyes that were begging to fade out. Danny made that easy by standing over him pointing his gun in a shaking hand. "Pay back's a bitch, isn't Timmy?" he said preparing to put a another in his head.

"It will be!" seethed Timmy as he fired his .45 from inside his coat pocket ripping a hole in Danny's thigh. Danny screamed. His gun fired a shot that went left of Timmy's head and ricochet through a window. Lights started popping on in the residences around the intersection. Timmy's lights faded out. Danny ran as best he could, drunk with an injured leg bleeding profusely. Luckily he was able to make it home. His wife was a nurse and the bullet had just past through flesh.

"I got to take you to the hospital!!"

"NO, no just patch me up!"

"I already did! You passed out! But you lost a lot of blood!"

"I'll be okay, let me sleep."

"What did you do?! There has to be a blood trail leading right up to the house! Why did you have a gun in your pocket?"

Danny passed out again.

Eileen took his coat with the gun and hung it in the hall closet. She grabbed a bucket, mop and flashlight. She filled the bucket with water and bleach and proceeded to engage in some late night mopping following the Hansel & Gretel trail of drippings Danny had left behind. Starting at their stoop she quickly cleaned to the nearest intersection two blocks from their home. Hopefully, if the cops followed the trail of blood, they'd believe whoever they were chasing got picked up in a car. 'Fucking Danny! What the fuck did you do now!' she wondered as she lugged her bucket and mop back home. 'Fuck you, you bastard! If you jeopardize my career, that's it!'

At the bar on L Street, Johnny Sullivan had a police scanner in his office and a monitor connected to camera that gave him a view of the patrons and the staff. He happened to be in his office to hear "That shooting at 4th and N … looks like a hit. Man down. Get us back up."

"Need an ambulance?"

"Negative the victim's dead."

Johnny looked at the monitor. Colin was still at the bar but Timmy wasn't. 'Shit,' he thought. He left his office and approached Colin. Colin saw him coming. He knew about the monitor and scanner. It was one of the reasons he, Timmy and their peers frequented here. When Johnny came out of his office something was up.

"Where's Timmy? Is he in the can?" asked Sully obviously unnerved.

"No, he went home. Why?"

"Somebody's dead at the corner of 4th and N and they think it's a hit."

"Fuck!" Colin stormed out of the bar. Sully took his tab to the office. If Timmy was okay, he'd expected it to be settled. If Timmy wasn't, he'd be expecting an appropriate gratuity at the next Christmas.

Colin ran up 4th. He could see the flashing blues the minute he had turned the corner. Yellow tape lines had already been set up. He knew every cop in the district. He passed under the yellow tape and saw Timmy lying in a pool of blood. He went to grab Timmy's lifeless body but Sergeant Murphy saw him coming and wrapped him in a bear hug before he could get there. "Colin! He's dead! If we're ever gonna catch the bastard, the body can't be disturbed."

"Let me look at him Murph!"

"NO! Colin he's dead," said Murphy squeezing him tighter. "What you're gonna see if you look at him is he was shot in the back. He never knew it was coming."

Colin struggled to break loose. But Murphy was too strong. He whispered in Colin's ear, "Timmy evidently shot the bastard before he died. There's a blood trail leading up 4th. There are no detectives here yet and my job is to secure the scene. You know what I'm saying?"

Colin relaxed and Murph relaxed his bear hug. "Try holding off on notifying my parents until tomorrow. I want to tell them first."

"I'll do that Colin."

Colin tapped Murph on the shoulder and Murph released his grip. "Thanks," said Colin as he proceeded up 4th following the trail of blood.

Murphy returned to controlling the crime scene, knowing he protected the evidence as well as earning himself a little something extra in his Christmas envelope from the locals. He looked down at Timmy's lifeless body and thought, 'How the fuck did someone get the drop on you! I got to pay more attention.'

Colin's head was thumping with rage. Over the past ten years, Timmy had been able to control that rage with a few well-placed words. Now Timmy was gone and the rage was back in full force. He followed the blood trail up N to East 2nd. There it stopped. He crossed 2nd. Nothing. To the left was the park. If he went in there he'd never find him. He crossed N. Nothing. Back across 2nd. No blood but wet in patches. He continued east, more wet spots every few feet. It hadn't rained. He started walking faster, up ahead he saw her unlocking the door and picking up a bucket and mop and going in. 'Fucking Danny!?'

Eileen didn't notice Colin down the block. She shut the door. She took the mop and bucket to the back foyer and would rinse it out tomorrow. She'd check on Danny and cleaned up the spots in the house. The fucking sofa he was on would have to be trashed. But she couldn't do anything about that now. She went into the kitchen and got the Lestoil and a sponge.

If Timmy were alive he would have said, "We know who it is, we'll come back and get him tomorrow". But Timmy wasn't there. Colin tried the door. She hadn't locked it. He slipped in and silently closed it. Danny was passed out in the living room with his leg bandaged, blood all over the sofa. He heard her down the hall in the kitchen. He slipped into the darkness of the dining room.

Eileen came into the living room and checked Danny's pulse. It was good. Maybe he would survive this. She muttered, "If you survive this Danny, I'm getting a divorce. I've had it with your drunken shit. Fucking asshole! I work sixty hours a week and you get drunk and bring back pocket change." She started cleaning the blood spots on the carpet.

Colin came out of the dining room and whispered, "He won't survive this, Eileen."

She yipped in surprise. Colin was on her with his hand on her mouth, the bottle of Lestoil spilling across the floor. She looked into his eyes in fear. 'What the fuck did Danny do???' ran through her head.

"You're a good wife Eileen. Will you promise me not to scream if I take my hand off your mouth?"

Eyes wide she nodded, "Yes."

He gently removed his hand but still straddled her. "Danny killed my brother tonight, shot him in the back."

"Timmy? Why? Why would he do that?"

"Timmy decked him in high school when Timmy was a freshman. I thought that was behind us but I guess it wasn't"

"In high school???"

"Yeah Danny was an upperclassman and tried to shake him down. He picked the wrong guy. It was before he met you. It was before Timmy got in the business."

Eileen rolled her eyes and started sobbing. She grew up here and knew the rules. "Are you going to kill me Colin?"

"No Eileen, you're a good person. Look at all the fucking shit you had to go through tonight thanks to that drunken shit on the couch. Your Dad and your brother work for the same people I do. You know what I'm saying?"

She knew what he was saying. She, her Dad and her brother were at risk if she didn't cooperate. She also knew Colin, her Dad and her brother could put an end to this nightmare if she cooperated. She nodded her head and started sobbing. Dad and her brother had always thought Danny to be a worthless shit and she'd be damned to show them they were right. Though over the years, she came to realize they were right, but she'd be damned if she'd give them the satisfaction of admitting it. Now this! It was time to surrender. She couldn't take anymore nights of Danny sneaking into bed drunk, just before dawn when she had to get up and get to work. He'd be in bed till the afternoon and start the cycle again.

"Calm down Eileen," said Colin gently. "Everything will be alright. I'll make sure of that. Understand?"

"Yes," she said between sobs.

Colin got up off her and extended his hand to help her up. As she got to her feet, Danny started coming awake. Through the haze he saw Colin and his wife. He instinctively reached for the gun in his coat pocket. But he no longer had his coat on. Colin made sure Eileen was securely on her feet and put Danny back to sleep with a roundhouse right to face. Eileen let out another yip. He held her. "I got to take care of this. We're going to go in the kitchen. You have any duct tape?"

"In the draw in the kitchen."

"Pillow case?"

"In the linen closet in the hall."

"We haven't got a lot of time. The detectives will be arriving at the scene and there's a chance they'll follow the blood stains and wet stains if they haven't dried yet. What's your father's number?"

"Why?"

"I need him and your brother to get over here and clean up this mess and protect you if the cops pick up the trail. After I call them, I'm gonna put a pillow case over your head and tape your mouth, hands and ankles and lay you on the kitchen floor. Then I'm gonna get Danny out of here. This is the story in case the cops get here before your father. Danny came in shot and passed out. You patched him up and were cleaning up when someone threw the pillowcase on your head and tied you up. You don't know anything else. Got that?"

"Yeah," visibly shaken.

Colin dialed her father. Someone answered after six rings. "Who is this?" asked a masculine voice obviously awoken from sleep.

"Jackie?"

"Who wants to know?"

"Colin O'Rielly."

Jackie woke up fast. "What is it Colin?"

"I need you now. And your son, if he's available."

"Where?"

"Your daughter's place."

"What!"

"You're shit ass son-in-law killed my brother tonight!" He gave a few seconds for that to sink in. "I need you and your son to get over here and clean up or run interference. Your daughter is fine. Say hi Eileen."

"Hi Da, I'm okay, but you got to get over here and help. Colin's not going to hurt me."

"Jackie, Danny's out cold. I'm taking him out of here. The cops may be coming here tonight 'cause Danny left a trail of blood. Timmy managed to wing his leg." He explained his plan of binding his daughter and what Jackie had to do depending which way it went.

Jackie sat in his boxers in the kitchen trying to digest all that he just heard.

"Jackie…? Jackie…? You there?"

"Yeah Colin."

"You, your son, and Eileen are clear. I don't hold you responsible, I swear. But I need your help NOW! Understand? NOW!"

"Yeah, I'll be there."

Colin hung up. Jackie was never so scared in his life. He'd have to rely on Colin's word. His daughter's life was at stake as was his. Should he call his son? Fuck! He knew that Danny was shit.

Colin gently taped up Eileen. "You okay? Can you breathe okay?"

She nodded yes.

"Your Dad will be here soon. Remember the story! I'm leaving, okay?"

She nodded not liking the darkness but accepting it as a portal to a new life.

Colin threw Danny's unconscious body over his shoulder and left through the back door, down an alley and the three blocks to his and Timmy's home. A normal scene in Southie … a man lugging his friend home after a drunken binge. But instead of tucking his friend in bed, he duct-taped his mouth, hands and legs and put him in the trunk of his car. Colin went back to Eileen's checking the street in front. No new cars except Jackie's truck. He walked down the street. The wet was gone as well as the blood. He walked further and looked at the intersection of N and 2nd. No blue lights. He was relieved yet also upset that Boston's finest had put so little effort into finding the killer of his brother. Then again maybe Murph was buying him time and didn't alert them to the blood trail. Colin went back to Eileen's and came in through the back. Jackie and Eileen were scrubbing down the living room hardwood floors. They both jumped up when Colin entered, Jackie instinctively getting between Eileen and Colin. "Colin! I'm so sorry about this!"

"Jackie, fucking relax! I'm not holding any of this against you and your family! I told you that!"

"Yeah, yeah, I know but …"

"No buts, where's Jackie Jr.?"

"I couldn't get a hold of him. He's probably out boozing somewhere."

"I think we're in the clear here. Danny's gone, understand?"

"Yeah sure," he said not giving two shits about what happened to Danny.

"Eileen, you'll be okay. I'll make sure of that. You'll be better off than when you were supporting that loser. Stay close to your Dad. You hear?"

She nodded.

"Jackie, I got to make a phone call. Then I want you to get Jackie Jr. or someone you trust to get this fucking couch out of here and burn it down at the warehouses tonight. Not tomorrow, TONIGHT!"

"I can help him get it out to the truck," said Eileen.

'God, I love this woman,' thought Colin. "Here's five hundred bucks, go down and get a replacement tomorrow." He handed her the five bills and left for the kitchen phone. He dialed a number few people had. The voice at the other end said, "Talk! This better be fucking important I AM SLEEPING!!!"

"It's Colin, have you heard?"

"HEARD WHAT? You take care of that job?"

"Yeah, the job went fine, no problems."

"SO WHAT THE FUCK YOU CALLING ME AT THIS HOUR FOR?"

"Timmy was killed tonight in Southie."

The voice at the other end became more alert, "The wops?"

"No a fucking asshole he punched out at a high school dance, Danny O'Hearn."

... "Jackie's son in law?"

"Yeah. I'm at Danny's house. Jackie is here taking care of Eileen. Danny's toast, I got him in a trunk. Everything's under control."

"Fuck me. It's fucking late. You're not going to do anything to Jackie and his family, are you?"

"Fuck no! They had nothing to do with this. I need Billy Reagan to get his boat fired up and I need Mikey to meet me there. Is this possible?"

"What do you think? There'll be a boat and fuck if I know if I can find Mikey. You handle that. So do I have to worry about anything?"

"No everything is covered."

"Good. Goodnight, sorry about Timmy. He was a good man. I'm glad you wrapped it up. We'll talk when things settle down." The line went dead.

Colin made another call.

"Yeah?"

"Mikey? Colin."

"Yeah man, what the fuck?"

"I need you now at Billy Reagan's boat. Bring about eight of those cinder blocks in your yard and any rope you got."

"What the fuck time is it?"

"Time to get up!" said Colin hanging up knowing he'd show. Thank God Mikey was home and asleep. Then again he looked at the clock which was pushing 4 AM. Hopefully Mikey was functional.

Colin let himself out the back door. Jackie and Eileen felt relief. "Are we gonna be okay da?"

"Yes, Eileen I think we are," he said as he hugged her. She sobbed into is shoulder as she did when she was a little girl. "Did ya hear what he said over the phone?"

"Yes da."

"Who do you think he was talking to?"

"Him?"

"Yeah, him. We're okay but we gotta get this couch out of here and over to the warehouse before dawn. You up to it?"

"Yeah," she wiped the tears from her eyes and got her coat from the closet. She was about to close the door when she remembered the gun. She took a pair of mittens from the bin, removed the gun from Danny's coat with a mittened hand and offered a mitten to her dad to take the gun. "We got to get rid of this too."

Dad took the gun without the mitten and stuck it in his pocket. "I'll take care of it, let's get the couch. Once we get rid of it, I'll get your fricken brother over here to finish cleaning up. You can come home and get some sleep. Not this one, our one."

121

COLIN WENT BACK TO his house. He proceeded to the shed and grabbed a machete, small sledge, a hunting knife and whatever rope was there. He went back to the car, threw the stuff in the back seat and checked the trunk of his car. Danny was awake, eyes wide and fearful. The duct tape was still intact. He was struggling to plead his case to Colin through his taped mouth, but it only came out as "mmmmmmm". Colin looked down at him with a cold stare, no emotion, no curiosity as to what he was saying. He shut the trunk. He went into the two-floor house he had bought with Timmy and got a case of Buds out of the fridge. He then locked the door went back to the trunk and opened it. "MMMMM!!!" He slammed the case of Buds down on Danny's face.

"Time to go fishing!" He drove to the marina where Billy's boat was docked. Billy had the boat running and ready to go. "Sorry to inconvenience you Billy," said Colin shaking his hand.

"No problem man. I usually go out at this time anyway. It's a good thing the boss got in touch with me or I might have been out fishing for the day."

"Well this is your lucky day, you got a charter, you'll make more than you make all week."

"Yeah, I heard. It's going to be humming down here soon. Others will be prepping to go out for the day."

Colin surveyed the area. All was quiet. "Help me get the shit out of trunk. Is Mikey here yet?"

"No."

Colin and Billy went to the trunk and carried unconscious Danny onto the boat. "We'll put him in the bait box," said Billy nodding his head towards a box at the rear of the boat. They dropped him in on his side but his legs were too long. Billy looked to Colin. Colin took Danny's ankles and bent his legs back at the knee, but it wasn't enough to fit in the box. "Fuck this!" said Colin. He took the ankles and leaned in hard like an offensive guard trying to stand up a nose tackle and pushed! Billy heard the pops in both Danny's knees and a muffled "arr-rhhh" from his mouth as Colin stuffed him in the box and slammed shut the lid. "There," said Colin "a place for everything and everything in its place. Get the beer out of the trunk and I'll get the tools from the back seat."

Mikey's pickup came whipping into the parking lot. More head-lights were following but heading to different slips in the marina. They got the cinder blocks and ropes out of his truck and into the boat. "Let's get out of here," said Colin.

Billy manned the console, "Throw off the lines." Colin and Mikey obliged. Billy's fishing boat left the dock out to the harbor. Colin relaxed for the first time since leaving Sully's. He grabbed a Bud and tossed it to Mikey and opened one for himself.

"It's five AM, you don't have coffee? What the fuck is going on?" asked Mikey, looking at the beer in his large hands.

Colin took a long sip of his beer. "We got to do some disposal work."

"Fuckin who? Or am I not supposed to know?"

"Danny O'Hearn."

"What the fuck could that twerp have done? He was drunk every waking hour."

"He killed Timmy. Shot him in the back as he was going home."

"No! Jesus, Mary and Joseph! I'm so sorry Colin! What the fuck did he do that for?"

"My guess is he was drunk and saw Timmy leaving Sully's and decided to get pay back for Timmy decking him in high school."

"In high school?!"

"Yeah, and I even paid him a visit after it and gave him a warning. I guess he forgot or was too drunk to give a shit."

Mikey opened his beer and took a swig. "Shit!"

"BILLY! GO WAY OUT! AND WHEN WE GET THERE, BLAST SOME STONES! THERE'S GONNA BE SOME SCREAMIN'!" yelled Colin to be heard over the engines. Billy increased the throttle heading into the coming sunrise. Colin tapped Mikey's beer with his, "To Timmy!"

"To Timmy!" said Mikey. "Should I scrub and put on my surgical gear?"

"Yes, Doctor we got some cutting and deep water chumming to do." They chuckled and tapped beers again and sat back pondering life and enjoying the ride to the giant rising ball of fire. They both saw the irony of how things could be going so well and then out of the blue, they weren't. Colin ran his thumb along the edge of the machete and looked at the cooler.

122

AMOS, VERN AND BRETT attended the wake, as did higher ups, the controllers of South Boston and the North End. The Mayor, State Senators and Reps from the district also made an appearance, though most had never met Timmy. They did not wait in any lines. Amos, Vern and Brett assumed their place respectfully in line and would wait the estimated three hours on the streets outside to pay their respects to the family. Colin had instructed Mikey to monitor the line with a couple of the guys. Mikey spotted Amos and Vern and went in to Colin in the reception line and notified him of their presence. He knew Colin made a lot of money with Amos, and Vern was a celebrity. "Yeah, bring them in the back, all three of them. Offer them drinks and food and tell them I'll be back as soon as I can."

Colin took a break from the endless stream of people coming to pay their respects and went to the back room. Amos, Vern and Brett sat apart from the others waiting for their chance to see Timmy and his family. Amos was lost in his thoughts. Timmy was gone. Had he and Timmy screwed up? Should they have come back to save his mother and the others who died at the hands of the Pukwudgees, or should they have pressed on after them. Vern wouldn't have realized his potential but Brett turned out as he had in his alternate life. If they had never gone down the hole and hadn't brought back the books … would this have happened? Amos put his hands to his eyes and started sobbing, catching Vern and Brett by surprise. At that moment Colin came into the room. Everyone rose expecting he had come to see them, but he saw Amos and was perplexed by his state. He never realized Timmy and this Indian brainiac were so close.

Colin whisked past a State Rep and City alderman directly to Amos. "Amos, come on we got to talk." Colin lifted Amos from his seat and took him to yet another back room. He raised his hand to Vern and Brett indicating that he'd be back.

When he and Amos were alone, he said "I never knew you and Timmy were that close."

Amos got himself under control. "When we were kids, he always had my back. When we grew up, I thought I had his monetarily, protecting him from the IRS and DOR. What the fuck happened, Colin!"

Now Colin understood. "Amos, the guy who killed Timmy held a grudge from when Timmy decked him in high school, nothing more. You had his back in what you do. I took care of this high school vendetta. Don't let it eat at you."

"This sucks Colin! No matter what the story is."

"I know man. Come on. I'll take you, your brother and Brett through the line. Then get out of here and have a drink in Timmy's memory."

"There's no need for that. The only people we know are you and your mom and dad. Are they holding up okay?"

"Mom's in a daze going through the motions, Dad can't wait for this to end so he can mourn Timmy on his own without everyone's eyes on him."

"I feel the same way as your Dad, so there's no need to escort us through the line. We'll go out the way we came in. I don't want to see Timmy's body in a coffin. I want to remember him the way I last saw him, Timmy full of life and laughing. I don't want to bring back memories to your mom of when we were kids … here. She's in a daze and that's a good state to be in 'till she's past the funeral. Afterwards she's gonna need you, Colin, to get her through it. Don't underestimate that need. You got to be there."

Colin gave Amos a hard embrace. "I'll be there. Thanks for coming. I'll call you when things settle down."

"Yeah, call me anytime."

Colin escorted Amos back to Vern and Brett. He gave Amos another embrace and patted him on the shoulder. He turned to Vern and Brett and gave them each hugs and said, "Thanks for coming, I really appreciate it". Then he went to the State Senator and the City Alderman.

When he left them, Amos said, "Let's go."

Vern and Brett were confused. They followed Amos and went out the way they came in. When they reached the street clear of the people waiting in line, Vern asked, "What the fuck happened?"

Amos relayed the conversation he had with Colin in its entirety. "Do you guys have a strong urge to see Timmy's formaldehyde corpse?"

"No," they both said without hesitation.

"Did you notice the line we were in? You see any colored people in it?"

"Did Colin say that?" asked Vern.

"No, he was going to escort us to the front of the line. The thought never entered his mind. I thought of that and kept it to myself. Timmy's mother is in a daze. I want her to stay that way till she gets home. Vern, you'll understand this. She's among her tribe, people coming through the line holding her hand offering her condolences. It's automatic and repetitive. The last thing Mary should have to deal with is greeting two darkies who cut in line. Sorry, Brett, you'd be guilty by association. If you wanna go back in line, go ahead. I'm sure Mikey will pull you out again."

"No man. I hate wakes. I never know how to act going through the reception line. What do you say to people you don't know at times like this? For that matter what do you say to people you do know?"

"Then let's get back to downtown and raise a drink to Timmy's memory!" said Amos as he signaled his car he was ready to go. They sat quiet in the back seat, Amos told the driver to go to The Wharf on Atlantic Ave. It was a long narrow bar on the waterfront, popular on weekends but populated by a few regulars during the week. They found a booth away from the regulars. The waitress that handled the tables happened to be coming back from a smoke. Weekdays generally sucked as the regulars sat at the bar and no one occupied the tables. The owner and the bartender made sure she got a cut of the bar sitters if it was a slow night.

But Mr. Otis was a regular who never sat at the bar. He valued his privacy and usually took a table as far away from people as he could find. And if she managed to steer patrons to tables away from him it would result in a Benjamin tip even if he only had one beer. He'd come in and bury himself in his work. The few superficial conversations they had, made her think he was a really nice guy with a heavy burden. He was obviously a very rich guy, but he was so down to earth. He had never hit on her, though she would love that to happen. He just wanted his space after a period of chit chat and tipped royally if that happened. Things were looking up this evening. He came in with two friends! No one would get near them. She'd see to that.

"Hi Mr. Otis, how are you tonight?"

"Hi Kathleen," said Amos.

Only Mr. Otis and her parents called her Kathleen. Everyone else called her Kate or Katy.

"Kathleen, this is my brother Vernon and this is a close friend Brett."

"Nice to meet you," she said with a twinkle recognizing Vern immediately never having suspected that the football star/TV commentator and Mr. Otis were brothers. Now that they were together, side by side, she realized they were twins! And the Brett guy was a hunk. "Can I get you guys something to drink and a menu?"

They ordered their drinks. When Kathleen returnèd, Amos thanked her and said he needed some space. Kathleen knew to make sure the last tables filled were those near them, though she doubted she have any problems on a week night. "I'll see to it Mister Otis, let me know if you need another."

Amos nodded and smiled. Amos picked up his drink as did Vern and Brett, "To Timmy, our brother, friend and someone who always had my back. May he be in Heaven before the devil knows he's dead."

"Where did that come from?" asked Vern.

"You don't remember? I was paraphrasing the words on the shit stick weapon he bought with him when we went in the hole."

"Oh yeah, the Shillelagh!" said Brett.

They clicked glasses and drank. Then Vern and Bret looked at Amos basically for guidance. "Nothing changes, we proceed as planned," said Amos meeting their eyes.

"No, something has changed. Timmy isn't going to see August 29, 1992, though he did, when he was twelve," mumbled Vern now looking into his glass. "It's like … I don't know … like we're fucking around with things we shouldn't and now we're like Mickey Mouse as that Sorcerer's Apprentice trying to correct a major fuck up."

"Mom and others … that's what we're doing!" said Amos grabbing Vern's arm, "We stick to the plan!"

After looking into Amos's eyes, Vern realized Amos was right … for Amos. God knows what would be the result of that plan for those that carried it out.

"Brett, I hope the fuck this plan of yours works out," said Vern.

"I hope I was as smart as you say I was Amos," responded Brett nervously.

123

AMOS WAS ALWAYS THE man with a plan but Vern had one also which he revealed to no one, not even Amos. He was retired from the game, collecting fees for speaking engagements and doing an occasional gig on talk radio or on network TV doing games.

Amos gradually withdrew from the brokerage firm, transferring his clients to trusted brokers who would never be as successful as him, but would manage a good return for them. During his hiatus, he would initially focus on "The Wampanoag Historical Village Project" with Brett who was overseeing the engineering and construction. Amos, with consultation with the tribe, focused on design. Whereas The Plymouth

Plantation devoted one living exhibit to the Wampanoag and the rest to the Pilgrim settlers, their project would be devoted to the history of the Wampanoag with one exception, a recreation of Sarah Screecham's cabin by the pond at the insistence of Vern.

There would be dance and drum demonstrations, nightly Fire Ball games, ongoing canoe races on Witch Pond where the visitors would be the contestants, archery and black powder ranges, farming demonstrations, and feasts of clambakes, venison and game birds.

Brett had started an excavation company for this project. He would personally supervise all earth moving and laying of the concrete operations for the pavilion project in his jeans and work boots. He never envisioned himself mucking around in the dirt with Caterpillar D-8's no more than yards away. He personally interviewed all the equipment operators and foundation-laying employees for the project. He emphasized that the Pavilion must be in place by the first of August so the rest of the Village could be completed by the following summer.

The pavilion was laid and awaited the statues without incident by August 25th, only three days before the Pukwudgees. However, the other exhibits awaited approval of the Cape Cod Commission much to the consternation of the Wampanoags, the citizens of Mashpee and the local papers. Amos and Brett could give a shit. The pavilion was in place. As far as they were concerned they had accomplished their purpose. The hole was blocked! Brett and Amos met at an upscale restaurant on the Cape to celebrate their accomplishment. They shook hands and were escorted to their table. "We did it!" said Brett.

"Yeah, let's sit down," said Amos.

After they exchanged pleasantries and received their drinks Amos leaned over the table and said, "I haven't heard from Vern since July."

"Shit, he's a busy guy with TV and all."

"You seen him on TV lately?"

"No, but it ain't football season."

"Brett, I'm his brother, a twin. He went in the hole. I know it. I feel it."

"He didn't tell you?"

"No."

1992 TO 1720 TO 1992 TO ...

124

AFTER TIMMY'S FUNERAL, VERN went to work on his plan. Timmy was dead, and no matter how good Brett/Amos's plan was, Timmy was gone and if their plan worked mom would be fine as well as all the others. Or would they? Maybe mom would be hit by a random car crossing the street. Amos was convinced if they followed Brett's supposed plan, all would be okay. But what Amos hadn't figured was that our fates are in the hands of the daily decisions we make and we don't know those decisions are coming till the instant we make them. The decision to go down the hole and the resulting tragedy would be averted with the laying of the Pavilion. However, our actions in this life as a result of our decisions could create other tragedies for which we had not planned.

Vern developed his own plan. It ate at him since he was thirteen when he made a promise to Sarah. He would see it through. The future Timmy and Amos had witnessed would not come to pass after the Pavilion was laid. Though neither saw Timmy's future coming. He was making his own decision … his own future.

Vern visited his current employers in radio and TV in New York and told them he'd be going on hiatus for a couple of years to travel the world. They tried to talk him out of it but he used his charm, saying he'd be back older and wiser with tons of funny filler to keep viewers tuned in to those blow out games and those days on radio when there were no sports stories of note. Then he became a collector, buying black powder flintlock pistols, rifles, ammunition, replica bows and arrows, flint, knives, hooks and fishing line. He visited numismatists and purchased a number of gold coins of various dates. He also bought sundresses and flip flops taking a rough guess at Sarah's size. He needed one last thing … a rope, not like Timmy's clothesline rope or the rope he and Amos purchased at the hardware store, but an invisible rope, a rope which only he could see.

He cruised the streets of Manhattan seeking out those specialty electronic shops that seemed to frequent every block. He found what he needed at the corner of 42nd and 5th. "Can I help you sir?" asked Vinnie, a well dressed key holder with slicked back hair.

Vern glanced at the narrow walls of the store lined with every sort of electronics up to the ceiling, "Hi, I got a cabin in Vermont ..."

"Hey I know you! You're the guy on TV who does the football games! You played too! A running back right?!"

Vern held up his hands. "Yeah, you got me, Vernon Otis." Vern held out his hand looking to shake. "I need ..."

Vinnie grasped his hand in both of his shaking vigorously. "Mr. Otis, anything you need! Anything! Just ask Vinnie!"

"Thanks Vinnie," said Vern being used to these types of encounters, "I appreciate it! I'm looking for something I don't know what you call it."

"Hey we got it! If we don't, we can get it! Ya know what I mean!"

"Yeah, fantastic! I got this rustic cabin in Vermont back in the woods. No electricity, everything runs off a generator."

"You need generators! We got generators! Not here of course, the shop's too small. But we got generators that can power a ..."

"No man," interrupted Vern raising his hands, "I got a generator! Hear me out!"

"Sorry! Go on. I'm always jumping the gun, ya know what I mean."

"When I go up there's no lights on. What I need is a lantern."

Vinnie was chomping at the bit to interject, but stopped short when Vern held up his hand.

"I need a battery operated lantern to put in the window that I can activate with a remote control from as far away as possible. That way I can drive up to a lighted cabin and easily find the switch for the generator inside. You know what I mean?" said Vern parroting Vinnie.

"Yeah, yeah, high tech," said Vinnie scanning the walls looking for the answer. "Give me a minute here," Vinnie went over to the computer at the counter and signed into AOL, and waited while the computer waited for a dial tone ... and waited. "Fucking computers! We'll do it the old fashion way" Vinnie thumbed to the index of the catalog on the counter and looked up lanterns – pages 367 to 370. "Here we go!" said Vinnie flipping to page 367. Meanwhile, the computer reported 'The AOL connection had timed out, try again.'

Vern scanned the walls of boxes upon boxes looking for lanterns among all sorts of electrical gizmos. Vinnie scanned the descriptions of all the lanterns in the catalog. On page 369, he found it! "I got it! Now let's see if we got it in stock." Vinnie scrambled to get rid of the internet connection screen and into the store's inventory program, only to get, 'Are you sure you want to Leave AOL?'

"Fuck me! Yes! Yes!"

"You say something Vinnie?" asked Vern examining a box on the bottom shelf toward the back of the store.

"Ehhhh, I found what you need in the catalog, now I'm trying to see if we have it," said Vinnie with his concentration focused on the computer, waiting to be able to bring up the inventory program. Windows 3.11 was supposed to be so much better than the DOS systems, but it wasn't fast enough when you had a celebrity customer in the store.

Vern had what he was looking for – a battery operated lantern with a remote control with a supposed range of 200 feet. He plopped it on the counter. "This what you're looking up Vinnie?"

Vinnie looked up from the screen. "Yeah man … maybe, I didn't finish looking it up!"

"I'll take it!"

"Great! Let me look up the pri …"

"Vinnie! It's here on the box! $19.95"

"Oh, well I'll ring you up then." Vinnie rang in the sale and collected the money from Vern, deflated that he had been no help at all. Vern saw that despite all his efforts, the energetic Vinnie he met when he entered the store was now a shell of himself.

As Vern was set to leave, he said, "You know Vinnie, ya got to get your head out of that screen. Instead of fucking around on the computer when no one's here, check out these walls, know what's here. Be aware of your surroundings. People are too pre-occupied with looking in those screens for answers when the answer is right in front of them."

"You learn that playing football?"

"No, I learned that growing up a Wampanoag."

A 'wampawhat?' thought Vinnie as Vern left the store?

125

VERN MONITORED THE PROGRESS of the Pavilion project from a modest home he had purchased under a realty trust in the Fells Pond sub-division near Witch Pond. It was a short walk to the far side of the Fells Pond and a several hundred yards further through the woods to Witch Pond. He monitored the activity daily from afar. Late in the afternoon of the 21st the CAT D-8's showed up. That meant the next day site preparations for the pouring of the Pavilion would start. Earth would be moved and the hole would be forever closed. Time to go! The goalie hockey bag he had purchased was ready with his purchases over the past weeks. He made sure the car he bought was filled with gas in the driveway. The trip to the hole would be on foot and hopefully there would be a similar trip back.

Vern outfitted himself in clothes he imagined would be the dress of Wampanoags in the 1720's, which was basically a buckskin cod piece for this time of year. He also threw a buckskin shirt and pants in the bag in case he didn't get back as soon as expected. He put on a sweatshirt and sweatpants for appearances on the walk to the hole and in a pinch he could use them for warmth if the nights got cold in the woods in 1720. He did one last check on the items in his bag. Satisfied he left the house around 10 PM. He placed his keys on top of the front driver side tire of the car. Hoisting the bag on his shoulder, he left for the hole. 'Fuck I hope no one's out walking their fucking dog!' he thought as he proceeded through the subdivision in the dead of a hot night in sweats with a hockey bag over his shoulder and barrels of muskets and bow poking out. Being a football star and TV personality only went so far. Luckily he ran into no one but he did hear a screen door slam as he exited the subdivision and proceeded down a path along the pond. Hopefully the person had his dog on a leash if he had one.

The three quarter moon lent enough light to get him to the far end of Fells Pond and allow him to pick a path through the underbrush to Witch Pond. However, the moonlight would not be enough to find the well hidden hole when he was in its vicinity. He pulled out a flashlight when he came to the first of several engineering stakes indicating the extent of the Pavilion. He shined to the left and right looking for the other stakes. The hole would be near the center of their perimeter. The stakes were tipped with orange ribbons which made them easy to locate. He walked carefully toward the middle. As he got closer he ran the beam over the ground looking for subtle differences. Fucking leaves everywhere. The branches they had covered the hole with were somewhere under them. Vern put down the duffel bag and squatted shining the beam back at the stakes and gauging the distance. The leaves were something he hadn't anticipated despite all his planning. He wondered whether the master planner, Amos would have if it was his plan. Nah, he was a financial genius now and for that matter Vern was a football player and funny guy on TV. They both had lost their fastball at being Wampanoags. That was fine for Amos but not for him. He was going back to a time where that may be his only advantage.

He was definitely near the center. He pulled a long knife out of the bag and got on hands and knees, and began stabbing the ground ahead of him. He moved forward till he deemed he was too far from center. Then he moved two feet to the right and followed a path parallel to which he came, stabbing as he went, each time finding solid ground. When he reached the area of his original starting point, he crawled four feet to the right and started a course parallel to the original course but on the other side. The next cross traverse would be six feet, but would not be necessary. Halfway down the line, his knife sunk down with no resistance. He brushed back the leaves … branches! He found it! He grabbed his hockey bag and parted the branches. He slid the bag in and he went in waist deep brushing leaves around and over him.

At the path surrounding the orb, he opened the bag, pulled out the lantern and went back up the hole, placing it far enough in so it wasn't visible from the path or from inside the orb without being lit. Back on the path he tried the remote. The hole lit up with a glow of diffused light! He tied the end of a rope to one of his larger knives and reached far into the hole and dug it in at an angle away from the orb. He took the rope and hockey bag and walked into the orb … and waited for the hole to shift left. It did and he hit the remote. Fantastic! The signal penetrated the orb and the glow from the lantern was enough to be visible through the translucent glow of the orb. He turned off the lantern and followed the rope back to the hole. He removed the knife. He inspected the area around the mouth to the hole for any visible marks in the dirt he may have made going in and out of the hole. He smoothed them with his palm making the hole as virgin as possible to the naked eye. Satisfied he went back into the orb, tied the rope to an arrow, withdrew his bow from the bag and hit the remote lighting the lantern. He shot an arrow into the hole to the left of the one with the lantern. He clicked off the light and followed the rope to the hole. He found traces of collapsed earth four feet from where the surface should be. Examining it with his flashlight he saw grey hardened granules of concrete mixed with the dirt. Probing his arrow into the dirt he hit solid! The pavilion was in place! He went back inside the orb and repacked his bag. When was this hole? Tomorrow? Next week? Next year? There was no time to do an Amos like analysis of the data nor did he have the ability to do so.

He had one more thing to do … mark a number of holes to the left of the hole he had just exited. Following the procedure he had used in the last hole he found all the holes to left were blocked. He was going to mark them with random numbers, letters and symbols. Instead he wrote 'Dead End' and had himself a chuckle. On another 'No exit!' And another, 'Dumb asses this way!' "Fucking idiots can't read anyway," he said to no one in particular. Satisfied he sat down in the orb and looked for the hole with the four 'SS's. He craved a beer, reached into his bag and extracted a Bud. Maybe another tomorrow, if he hadn't found Sarah … wait, tomorrow would be the 22nd. In five days the young version of him along with Amos, Brett and now dead Timmy would be here. Vern didn't think being here with a young version of Vern would be kosher with this orb thing. One of them couldn't, right? Unlike Amos, he hadn't focused on this part of his plan yet. What about Timmy, would he be here or not because he is dead? Now he knew why Amos would bury his face in his hands and say he had to think. Vern's life had been one of acting on instinct and Amos's one of acting on logical thought. Now he had put himself in a situation where both would be required while suppressing his urge to see Sarah as soon as possible.

126

THAT NIGHT HE SLEPT in the orb ... not well. The pressure of the thoughts of ifs, ands, and buts crammed his brain. The constant drone of the orb itself denied him sleep 'till pure exhaustion took hold and closed his brain. Six hours later he awoke. The drone of the orb quickly snapped his brain to focus as to where he was and that he had no immediate plan how to carry out his original grandiose plan. What time is it? He looked at his watch ... 1:15. AM or PM? He flicked the lamp and picked a hole to the right and climbed up. He did not need to disturb the covering; he could see the light through it. It was the 22nd. What now? Should he contact Sarah before the younger version of him arrived, or after?

If before, she'd have no reference of him or their last conversation. If after, he'd have less than 18 hours to convince her he had come back for her before Pukwudgees and his cohorts were running hither and fro through the orb. It would have to be after. If he tried before, she may suspect him of being just another local looking to get laid. And if he told her what he knew about her sister/brother ... he may end up with a molten ball in his head, being mistaken for an extorting member of Hannah's crew.

He would wait five days then. However, in four days the boys would make their first voyage into the hole. They'd leave and come back the next in search of Sarah. In the meantime, he would have to get out of the orb and kill time. He sat and considered putting his head in his hands as Amos had done so many times before. Unlike Amos he found no answers in doing so. Which hole should he choose to venture out in? If he chooses the wrong one would it be the end of him, leaving his carefully planned hockey bag full of goodies for someone to discover and change the course of history. He searched the orb and found the hole with the "SS" markings. He thought of going a couple of holes to the right of that hole. He would safely be before the time of convergence, but how much before? Time, time, time! This time shit was driving him nuts. He did not have Amos's patience for dealing with factors and logic. Wait! "TIME!" the final stanza of a Chambers Brothers song clicked in his head followed by "Yeahhh!" Fucking go left young man! Just far enough left into future Sarah so he could leapfrog all this shit which was about to go down in orb central. No dealing with midget me and friends or angry little Indians! This was perfect! He wouldn't have to wait five days to find Sarah! Hopefully she'd be hoping for his return as he promised when he left.

Time to crack another beer! He may not need the other four if he was able to quickly find her. He gazed at the 'ss' hole sipping his beer. Okay, how far left was far enough? Amos would be doing all sorts of calculations based on probing the hole for the one with the correct numerology. Vern instinctively decided 'three' was the right number. So right he decided to stick his two empties in the bag as opposed to being left in the orb to be gathered up when he came back. If all went well he'd be back tomorrow.

He raised his bow and shot an arrow into the third hole to the left. He left the orb with his bag. At the top he found Sarah's mesh of reeds. Carefully he pushed them aside to create minimum disturbance and climbed out. Squatting, he looked and listened surveying 360 degrees around his position. Sarah's cabin was still there and the hearth was smoking! Hopefully she was cooking more of that lovely stew. There was no sign of anyone outside. He gathered his bag and headed for cover in the brush and sat surveying the cabin. It was warm out and he considered abandoning his sweats for just the cod piece and going native. Then he recalled Sarah's comment on their weird dress when he first met her. The sweats would lend credence to him being an older version of the young Vern. He pulled a pair of flint lock pistols from his bag and stuck them in the band of his sweatpants making sure they weren't cocked as he had preloaded all the weapons he had purchased. He threw a satchel of balls and flint and a powder horn over his shoulder. Why he did, he didn't know, as he had no intention of shooting her just gaining time to hold her at bay while he explained who he was. He knew she might be similarly armed when they met.

He decided it was time. He rose to approach her cabin unsure of his plan once he got there. A thunderous pair of blasts rang out to his left! "Fuck!" He instinctively hit the ground thinking Sarah had spotted him first and unleashed both barrels in his direction. Instead he saw her burst out of the woods on a beeline for her cabin. He looked behind her for a pursuing animal but instead saw what had to be a pissed off client desperately trying to reload his musket on the run with a look of fury in his eyes. 'Shit!' this may be the end of the Sarah he and Amos had learned from tales around the campfire.

Vern pulled a musket from the bag and drew a bead on the upset john. He had him dead to rights when Amos's voice entered his mind. "Don't! That may be our great, great, great grandfather!" Vern re-aimed and fired a blast at a tree directly in front of the john. The john dropped his powder and rifle as bark splatter into his face. The john fervently rubbed his eyes trying to clear the particles that obscured his vision. Vern took advantage of this moment to grab the spent musket by the barrel and charge the blind john. Swinging it like a bat, he struck john in the back of the knees. Before john knew it Vern was straddling him with his knees on his arms and his musket across his throat.

"WHY ARE YOU CHASING THIS WOMAN?!" screamed Vern.

The john's eyes weren't clear enough yet to see Vern's face or dress and he couldn't bring his hands up to clear them or ease the sting of the bark. Squinting and wishing to relieve the pain he bleated, "I wanted her and she said, 'No More'!"

"Fuck me!" said Vern as he pulled his fist back and clocked the john into unconsciousness. Vern thought if this Indian woke up and remembered what he had just said, then Indians would have originated the word 'fuck' as he had jokingly told Brett and Timmy. Also, his theory of how Sarah died might have happened ... if not for him. Damn! He was a regular selective self fulfilling prophet of his own bullshit. He looked over his shoulder at the cabin for signs of Sarah. No doubt she ran inside and watched this incident and was reloading thinking, 'Not another one!' Convincing her of who he was may take awhile and he couldn't risk john waking and fucking up the moment.

Vern positioned himself so he could keep his eyes on the cabin while he hog tied, blind folded and gagged john with strips of john's clothes. He chuckled, thinking of how john would explain the tattered condition of his wardrobe to his wife when he came home. Knowing Sarah, she may be already trying to flank him using the cabin as cover to come up behind him. That would take awhile, so he finished his task and retrieved his bag and went to the cabin guessing she would not be there. Just in case he withdrew a pistol from his waist band and entered the cabin saying softly, "Sarah?" He heard nothing. He dropped the bag by the hearth where a stew was cooking. He removed his sweats and stuffed them in the bag. He ladled himself some stew and took a seat awaiting her return. He knew she would have seen him come in and wondered if she would abandon her cabin avoiding confrontation or would decide to confront him head on. He was betting on the latter as Sarah was not one to walk away in fear from the meager possessions she had accumulated in her lifetime. And it was a bet he would win. Luckily she evidently had spent significant time debating what to do, so that Vern had been able to fill his belly with her stew.

He heard her pistols cock outside the cabin. He felt her gaze from the outside the window as he sat on the stool facing the hearth. He counted to three and swiveled on the stool, knowing she'd be coming through the door.

"WHAT ARE …"

"Yee doing in me house," he finished looking her in the eyes as she came through the door with pistols aimed, and his laying on the ground on either side of him.

Flustered she searched for words as he had finished hers. All she could up with was "SPEAK!"

"It's me, Vern. We met before … when I was thirteen. I promised to come back for you. I'm back."

She came closer and studied the stranger. He made no move for his weapons and hers were on him. Three years ago she was visited by youngsters who knew the workings of Satan's orb. She had not ventured into the orb since their departure making it more difficult for her in dealing with the men who came seeking their pleasure. She did recall young Vern, his manhood at full attention showing no shame at it being so. So sweet. So innocent. And his promise to come back now registered. "STAND!" she commanded wishing his hands further from the pistols on the floor. Vern stood gazing at her face. She was more beautiful than when they had last met, older, yet younger than his age now. He smiled.

"Can you see the young Vern in me?"

For the first time in her life Sarah was disarmed. No words came to her. Yes there were traces of the youngster Vern in his features and manner. This was a lot to comprehend. She was unarmed, though she still had her pistols aimed at Vern's chest.

"When I left I asked you to tell me something no one else would know so you would know it was me. And you did."

"AND!!!" she blurted not so confident as before.

"Okay, before I say it, know that when we met I was with my twin brother Amos, Timmy with the crimson hair and fat Brett. Do you remember them?"

"Iye," she replied in a state of consciousness she had never experienced. All his words rang true so far, though she had to drag these memories from the back of her mind as every day demanded the full attention of that mind to survive.

Vern could see her eyes on him but focused inward, though her hands with the pistols remained steady as a rock. So Vern let it out slowly, "Your sister Hannah, is really your brother and only you and Bellamy know that. You said if I told you this you would know it was me."

Sarah let her pistols fall to her side and looked closer at Vern. "It's really you?"

"YES!" he said with a big smile wishing to embrace her but mindful of the pistols at her hips. "I came to take you back with me, as I promised."

Sarah looked Vern in the eyes and saw the love or lust or whatever lived in the hearts of men. Her guess was it was sincere. She dropped her eyes to the ground and walked past him and sat on the stool which Vern had just risen from. She crossed her arms across her lap with pistols still in hand. Vern sat cross-legged on the floor directly in front of her. She again looked in his eyes for signs of falsehood and saw none. She placed her pistols on the ground by Vern's. "So, young Vern, not as young now, speak more for I am at a loss for words or action. What does this mean?"

Vern tried to chose his words carefully, "I've been thinking of you since the day we met. To you that would be maybe three or four years … to me, twenty four years." He paused, waiting for this to sink in. "There is so much to explain."

"Ye waited twenty four years to come back!?"

"Yes, with good reason."

Vern explained how Amos was set on finding the time of legends after what she had told them of her experience. He told her they went back in the orb the next day and found what Amos was looking for and unfortunately unleashed Pukwudgees on their time 24 years later. He related how they had prevented them from coming out in 1968 and how Timmy and Amos went back in to kill them and how he and Brett were left behind to watch the hole ... for twenty four years. He continued, finishing the entire story of how he and Brett had lead two lives but had no memory of one of them except for what Timmy and Amos chose to tell them. Throughout the telling, Sarah was captivated. She studied Vern's face and eyes throughout for signs that it was just that ... a tale, not to be believed like the tales the Indians that sought her favors would tell. There were no such signs, only an underlying sense of urgency. When he concluded stating he was here to fulfill his promise to her, she dropped her gaze, put her face in her hands and thought long ... like Amos had done so many times. When she finally returned his gaze she began asking the questions that had run through her head in that time of meditation. "Ye want me to go in that evil hole again?"

"Yes. We'll be in and out and will not be able to go back in."

"Because after, ye friends will have blocked it forever."

"They have already, at least for our lifetime and longer if their park is a success. I've marked a hole just before that happens."

"Will ye friends be waiting for us when we come out?"

"No, they don't know I came back for you."

"Even Amos?" she asked arching her eyebrow.

"Even Amos, though I think he has guessed it by now."

"Where will Brett and Timmy be?" For the first time she saw in Vern's eyes that he was hiding something.

"Brett lives about a mile in that direction," said Vern pointing to the east. Sarah did not know the term 'mile'.

"Timmy?"

Vern looked down. Here was the falsehood he was hiding. She quickly checked the windows suspecting he may be lurking outside as he had on their first meeting.

"Timmy died a few months ago," said Vern still looking down.

Sarah pondered this news. "How did Crimson die?"

"He was killed by an enemy of his from his youth in Boston."

"Like the stories that are told of me two hundred years from now of which Amos would not tell?"

'Trap,' thought Vern. "Maybe, I don't know. There is no history of your death, except for stories passed down."

"Maybe today was the day I was supposed to die, but ye just saved me."

"I don't know. Maybe it was, but I don't know. He's tied up outside. I have to let him go sometime. Do you think he'll come back if I do?"

"No. I saw what ye did. He is a coward at heart. He may think ye are me husband and will be waiting if he comes back."

Vern looked in her eyes at the word 'husband'. She saw that. Saw that he wanted to be that, but where? Here or his time? "Why did ye not use that evil hole to save yer friend Timmy instead of me?"

This caught Vern completely off guard like a blitzing safety coming through the center. The thought that he could use the hole to save Timmy never entered his mind. It hadn't because he was alive when it happened. What would happen if he traveled to a time in his lifetime? Would he implode under the old adage, you can't be in two places at once. Now it was he who put his face in his hands. The power of the orb was maddening. Wondering the 'what ifs' could lead a man to madness. Throughout his life he had only focused on it for the purpose of being with Sarah. Amos had seen the possibility of the orb in 1968 and saw a different 1992. Amos had used that power once for the purpose of saving their mother and the area from the events of a 1992. Vern raised his head from his hands and looked at Sarah. "My desire to be with you was the only thing strong enough to consider using that orb again."

Sarah saw the sincerity in his eyes. Young Vern had grown up to be a very handsome older Vern and he still exhibited the sweet sincerity she saw when they first met. She desired to ask Vern many questions. But the instincts responsible for her survival in this world were screaming in the recesses of her brain. Not about Vern, but about the trash outside that had tried to kill her. He was a loose end that had to be dealt with. She had never had to kill a man … yet. But she came close to doing so today. She had fired on the run with intent to kill but with aim hindered by being so. "I wish to speak more about ye plan, but we must first deal with him outside."

"We let him go right?" asked Vern not sure what 'deal with' meant.

"Yes Vern, but ye must scare him so he does not return!"

"Okay, be like a wife and do not speak unless I ask."
"I understand."

127

SARAH GRABBED HER PISTOLS leaving Vern's and rose from the stool. Vern realizing he was only in a buckskin cod piece and not his sweats arose. It would be a good costume for intimidation rather than his sweats. What else could he use? He smiled at Sarah and squatted by the hearth. He placed his hands in the cooled ash farthest from the fire and rubbed his face creating a pale death like appearance similar to the character in that old movie "Black Orpheus". This would be good! He'd scare the shit out of that fucker.

He picked up his pistols, went to his bag and got the large hunting knife. "Let's go."

They approached the john who was now awake and struggling to get out of his binds. Vern held out his palm for Sarah to stay back. Vern crouched next to him as he lay on his side working at his ties. "Are you going somewhere?" he whispered in the john's ear. The john stiffened and froze at his voice still blindfolded. Vern cut the ties on his feet and grabbed him by the hair and stood him up. He waited for the man to be able to feel his feet under him and support his weight. When he was stable, Vern removed the blindfold. He struggled to adjust his eyes to the light and when they did he saw the visage of a death. Fear came into the man's eyes.

"Why don't you speak in our language?" the man cried.

Vern hit him with an open backhand sending him back to the ground. Then he grabbed him by his hair and brought him to his feet again. "You have no permission to ask questions here! I speak the language I chose and they are many for I speak in tongues!" Vern proceeded to rattle off a litany of gibberish in French, Spanish and German. Languages he had taken in high school or was exposed to in movies. If the john had been versed in language he would have heard "The pencil is on the table. My name is Jose. Hail to the fatherland," ending with "Bee aye bay. Bay e bee. Bee eye bicky bye bee oh bo!" The john trembled in Vern's grasp. He was truly the devil!

"See that woman you tried to kill?!" he twisted the john's head so he was looking in Sarah's direction. "She is my wife and I will gut you like a deer and leave you to be feasted upon by crows if you come to these woods again! I am a Brown of the Cleveland tribe! We do not make idle threats. Do you understand!?" Vern ran the tip of his blade from crotch to under the chin, hard enough to leave a dribble of blood.

The john shook his head with overkill showing he understood though he had no clue as to what a Brown was or knowledge of a Cleveland tribe. "Good," said Vern as he let go of his hair. Vern went and picked up the man's musket and slid it through john's wrists that were bound behind his back. "Hold this to your ass!" He pressed his tied hands to his backside so the gun did not slide through to the ground. "Now go home and never come back. I've given you your gun. Do not let it fall to the ground till you are far from here. If it does fall, do not stop to pick it up as I will be following and you will not get home. Understand?"

He was about to ask for his satchel of balls and powder but saw Vern's grey face harden at his hesitation and nodded saying "Yes! Yes!"

"GO! AND NEVER RETURN!" Vern fired a pistol over his head. The john ran like a Tyson chicken trying to escape the axe man … his bound hands pressing the stock of the musket tightly to his ass cheeks, desperately trying to keep it from falling. Losing his satchel was bad enough, but he could never explain the loss of his musket to his wife. It was the means to feed his family.

"Wait here," whispered Vern. He followed chicken running man about a hundred yards and sure enough john turned and looked back. Vern promptly fired another round into a pine tree nearest his face almost causing him to lose his balance and his grip on his rifle. Stabilizing himself he bent at the waist trying to reposition his gun in his butt cheeks. Once he did he continued on his awkward run.

"I TOLD YOU NOT TO STOP! DO IT AGAIN, IT WILL BE THE LAST!" Vern watched him for another two hundred yards and returned to Sarah.

"Did I scare him? Can we talk now?

128

THEY WENT BACK TO the cabin. Vern placed his weapons by his bag. Sarah placed hers on the table. "Ye may wish to go to the pond and cleanse your face," she said. Vern remembered he looked like a Voodoo priest with his ash covered face. He smiled and ran down to the pond and dove in. He emerged from the water rubbing the ash off and submerging again. While he was gone, Sarah took the opportunity to examine Vern's bag and its contents. She at first was fascinated with the material of the bag itself … like nothing she had seen. Then she remembered clothes of the four young boys and those of Vern when he came to her rescue. She also made note of the armory in the bag … of her time but not really – too new.

"What are your questions?" asked Vern standing in the doorway, water glistening on his skin, seeing what she was doing.

She was startled and turned seeing his backlit vision. It was unlike her to get caught. She had let her guard down. Maybe the death she had saw in Amos's face that day was supposed to have happened today and now she was on borrowed time. She went and sat on her stool and looked at Vern, he was beautiful. "What is yer plan, Vern?"

Vern walk to his bag and took out two of the remaining four Buds. "Have you ever tasted beer?"

"Beer? What is beer?"

"This is beer! Ale? Grog?" he said holding out one of the cans.

"I've tasted ale an' grog, how is that ale?"

Vern popped the lid and took a sip. "Taste," he said handing it to her. She looked at the small hole in the top of this tin vessel and carefully sipped.

"It be mild."

"It be all I got right now," said Vern as opened his and took a drink. He sat on the floor in front of her. "I came to take you back with me to my time as I promised."

"I remember that Vern. What is it like in yer time? Not like now I imagine."

"Yes things have changed. There have been many inventions that do things unimaginable in this time!"

"What things?"

"Make life easier. For instance we have carriages that move without horses. They use oil like you use to light lamps to create power to move forward."

Sarah looked down. "I would be like a new born babe in a grown woman's body in such a world. I would be an outcast, a simpleton. Here I survive on my instincts and knowledge. In yer world I'd be defenseless."

"You will never be defenseless! I will always protect you."

Sarah paused and looked at him. "Always? Ye must have a woman in your time. Do ye have a wife?" she probed thinking he might be like all the men she had contact with.

"No wife. I have seen you as becoming my wife for twenty four years."

"Ye know nothing of me Vern except for the stirring in yer loins as a young man. I may yet be a she-devil for all ye know, the kind those men come down here to escape from for an afternoon."

"Are you?"

She looked to the ceiling and after a moment said, "I think not but I know not what men would think if they were witness to my daily behavior."

"If you come back with me I promise I will always protect you even if you turn out to be a she devil. I made a promise to you twenty four years ago and I kept it! I will do the same with this promise."

"So if I agree to go back with thee, we are married?"

"Yes."

"I agree. We are married." She took a long drink of her beer and placed it on the floor. She smiled at Vern, rose, and took his hands helping him from his sitting position. She pressed her body to his and kissed him deeply. Then she led him to her bed in the corner of the cabin. That night Vern lived the dream that he had for the last twenty four years. As a movie is never as good as the book, the experience far exceeded the dreams and went on and on till exhaustion gave way to sleep with two bodies lying in warmth as one.

129

AN AROMA FILLED HIS head as he awoke to an empty bed. The aroma was good … breakfast. Something was cooking in the pot on the hearth, but he had no idea what. He did not see Sarah anywhere in the cabin and wondered if last night was but another dream. He went to the hearth to sample the goodness when Sarah came back with his soaking wet clothes. "I washed ye clothes, they should be dry enough after the noon sun."

"You're gonna love washing machines and dryers."

"Of what do ye speak?"

"Machines that wash and dry your clothes, so you are free to do other things!"

"What other things?"

"I don't know, read books. Watch TV."

"I have no books. What is 'TV'?"

Vern realized this was going to be tough without the actual appliances to do a show and tell. "When we go to my time I can show you all these things."

"Then tell me Vern, yesterday ye spoke of Putwudees and they being the reason for ye closing the hole. What are Putwudees?"

Shit! Yesterday he assumed she knew. He had told her of the carnage they created but not what they were. "They're called Pukwudgees. Sarah, Pukwudgees are ... I don't know ... small Indians of ancient legend. They are trouble makers. Legend says they killed another legend's sons who were giants. We found out firsthand how evil they were. Given the chance they brutally killed my mother and many others."

"But ye stopped this from happening by using Satan's orb to block them from doing this!"

"Yes."

"Tell me what these Pukwudgees look like."

He described them as best he could based on that day they chased him into the hole and also based on what Timmy and Amos had told him about the other 1992.

Sarah face dropped. She looked Vern in the eye and said slowly, "They're here."

"What do you mean, 'here'?"

"About two days after ye were last here, they came out of the hole. I kept watch on the hole thinking ye may come back. Instead they came out. Four of them, they followed yer tracks to my cabin. I watched as they made a mess of me home. Then they left and followed yer tracks back to the hole. They went in and came out several times. Then they came back and headed north. Several days later three came back, went in the hole, but not for long. They came out and talked at length and left to the west. They haven't returned. But three others came back several weeks or more from the north, and didn't go in but headed south."

Vern was in shock. "They are here?"

"Iye."

Fuck! Another algorithm where he could use Amos's help.

"I've not seen their tracks anywhere in the area since they left that day."

"Where do you think they went after they were here?"

"Back to their people me think."

"Their people? What people? Pukwudgees?"

"Some say there are tribes of natives in the marshes by the great waters that only venture out to trade. Short, like your Pukwudgees. They call them Itchiwan."

"Itchiwan?"

"Iye, I hear they are a peaceful people, not like the four you describe. Vern took a moment to swallow this. He looked at Sarah, his face lacking the self-confidence he had always displayed since the day Amos had returned from the hole and changed his future from being a drunken DPW worker to being an NFL star with a promising broadcasting career. Now he saw their folly in venturing into the hole, to find Sarah, to find Legends, and most recently to find their … no his desire. They thought they could master their destiny. But they couldn't. Every entry into the orb resulted in subtle changes to the future and in this case, the past and thereby the future. They had opened Pandora's Box and their attempts to close it may have created more problems.

"Tell me ye thoughts Vern. Ye seem troubled at this news."

"I am Sarah, I am. These Itchiwan are peaceful and these four are evil. They lived hundreds or thousands of years ago and would have been long dead by now had it not been for us being tempted by the hole. Now they have jumped time, not to my time but to your time and now maybe to some other time. Excuse me for rambling but it is the only way I can figure this out without my brother. He was always the one to puzzle out the possible outcomes of new information."

"Keep talking, ye will find yer answer."

"Yeah, it is helping," said Vern realizing things were becoming clearer the more he talked out loud. "I worry that these four or now six, will change the history of the Itchiwan in some way that will change the world I am bringing you back to. Should I follow and kill these three, four or six or should we stick to my original plan not knowing what has changed in the world as result of leading them to this time. The leader of the four is powerful and truly evil and probably has taken over leadership of the tribe. This shit he did in the time of legends is probably happening now. God knows what that mischief means for current and future generations!"

Sarah smiled and straddled his lap facing him and gently took his face in her hands, kissing his forehead. "Vern, ye are a good man. I will go with thee to yer time and see yer magical machines. Ye worry too much about the past. It has been three years and I've heard of no troubles with the marsh people. Black Bellamy is an evil man much like the leader of yer band of Pukwudgees. How has his actions shaped yer life? The three that went south looked like they were wounded, covered with blood and hurt. They never came back. Maybe they are dead."

Vern felt warmth, "I … I don't know."

"Nor will ye. Should we hunt yer Pukwudgees or my Bellamy? I know not where to find the Itchiwan, there are many marshes. Nor do I know if Bellamy and my brother are even in the waters surrounding here. Thee are not a killer of men Vern. Ye had opportunity to do so to the man yesterday, but did not. Ye are a good man, but ye are a strong man. I say it's time to go … to yer time."

By the time they finished making love it was past the noon sun and Vern's clothes were dry.

THE ROAD TO SANDY NECK

130

POMARAT SAT IN THE middle of the orb with Hysko, Sarkem, and Massot anxiously awaiting instruction. The four boys had stalled their pursuit with fire. He had tried to flank them and found the holes with strange lettering blocked. He didn't know what the lettering meant, but it was obviously a trick by the boys to keep them occupied while they got away. And he had taken the bait! They were mocking him. Now what?

He hated the maddening changing positions of the holes. He studied the holes not only to the left but all over. He saw the hole with markings! "ss" on four corners. He also saw a hole with a simple "Z". Which was a sign from Maktahdou?! He picked the Z hole. He told his men to wait in the hole as he went up the tunnel. Once outside he saw one set of tracks not four and those tracks, though old, came back to the hole. Another diversion! These boys had delayed his pursuit again. These boys were good, and should not be underestimated.

That left the "ss" hole. They all went out this hole with no resistance. He found the boys tracks, though days old. They followed them to a hovel, which they proceeded to ransack and wait. Nothing. He went outside and noticed the boy's tracks leading back to the hole and those of a woman or larger boy. Could this be their chief? He surveyed the area. Nothing. No ambush in waiting.

He knew if he continued his pursuit of the boys, his judgment would be secretly questioned by his men. He had already lost two braves to Maushop and now these boys had led him around in circles. "Back to the tribe!"

Hysko, Sarkem and Massot exchanged glances of relief and followed Pomarat north. Their travel was uneventful but something did not seem right. They all were starting to realize this was not right. The paths had changed. The hovel at the pond was not there when they first went in the hole. Pomarat pressed forward. Only by getting back to his home encampment could he unravel this spell the boys had cast over them. Their travels brought them past more hovels which had not been there when they had traveled south to kill Maushop's sons. They ransacked the first three killing anyone they found in the vicinity. Loaded down with booty, Pomarat decided they would make wide arcs around future hovels they encountered. However, they came across something else which he could not resist … a campsite.

The red haired fair skinned man had caught sight of them as they had him. He proclaimed loudly, "Gentlemen of short stature! Welcome! Come have a drink if ye are willing to trade. And I see ye are loaded with goods! Natives are always welcome at O'Hearns! Liam's the name, whiskey's my trade! Sit! Sit!" He motioned for them to go to the stools by a table sitting outside his tent with a big shit-assed grin.

Pomarat glanced back at his men and indicated he wished them to comply and sit at the table. He also signaled them to follow his lead. Pomarat was wound tighter than a rubber band on a balsam airplane. A red head! Pale skin! Revenge! He returned Liam's shit-ass grin and pointed to the table as Liam had.

"Sure Chief, drinks all around! What do ye got to trade? Ye from around here? Drink! Drink!"

Pomarat had no clue what he was saying but knew he was bartering and knocked an arrow in his bow holding it out horizontal as if offering it in trade. Pomarat was going to put an arrow in his throat but decided he wanted more from this red headed demon. He smiled placed the bow on the table and signaled for Liam to take it over and over again.

Liam scratched his crotch, and gave a reserved smile. "Chief, no offense but I don't have a market for midget bows. What you got in those satchels your braves are carrying?" he asked pointing at the satchels by the others at the table.

Pomarat raised his eyebrows and smiled and commanded Massot to open the satchel. He motioned Liam to have a look. Massot saw the signal and opened the bag. Liam bent over to look in the bag.

Immediately, Pomarat was on him with his tomahawk and beat him on the head over and over again till he was barely conscious on the ground. He stopped, looked at his prey trying to fend off more blows weakly with his hands. He took out his cutting stone and crudely eviscerated him taking an internal organ and stuffing it in Liam's mouth.

"Drink!" he mimicked as he watched life fade from Liam's eyes. Pomarat grabbed a bottle of whiskey from the table and took a long draw. His eyes widen and watered as the fire hit the back of his throat. He dropped the bottle wishing he could expel the fire liquid but it was beyond expelling as it sent fire down his esophagus and into his stomach. His face contorted. His braves looked at their chief with mouths agape wondering if he had been poisoned. Pomarat gasped for air and sat, his eyes looking to the sky. The fire in his belly was subsiding. He shook the shock from his head and looked at his men and saw the shock in their faces and grasped the situation. He was fine. He had taken too much of the fire water too fast. To counteract, he grabbed the bottle he dropped and took a small sip from the liquid remaining therein. He put his head back and closed his eyes savoring the warmth as the liquid passed through his body.

He smiled and pointed to the other bottles indicating he wished his men to partake also. They all looked at each other for an indication for what to do but found no answers as none were leaders, only followers. The braves shuffled over to the stock of bottles and each grabbed one. They all took tentative sips and Massot and Sarkem swallowed. Hysko spit out the foul tasting liquid. Pomarat laughed. Pomarat, Sarkem and Massot took more sips of the curious liquid. Hysko went back to the table capping his bottle and taking a seat. Before long Pomarat was slurring and stumbling about, Sarkem and Massot were laughing. Hysko was nervous. They should not be laughing at the chief. Pomarat did not seem to notice. But Hysko knew Pomarat always noticed everything.

"Let's kill something!" screamed Pomarat out of the blue. Sarkem and Massot screeched in agreement. Hysko was terrified. That liquid had possessed them. Pomarat gathered his weapons and ran north. Sarkem and Massot took awhile to realize where they had left theirs, soon found them and followed. Hysko looked at their loot and the red headed peddlers possessions and was torn between following or guarding their loot. This was bad. That liquid was bad. He decided to follow knowing he was the only one currently capable of shooting a straight arrow. He gathered his bow and set off north.

Pomarat was several hundred yards ahead and came across a Wampanoag hovel. He screamed in rage, bent on bursting inside and massacring everyone therein. However, he tripped over a tree root, fell and knocked himself out. The occupant of the hovel came running out with a large knife hearing the scream. He saw the unconscious Pomarat sprawled on the ground. He approached cautiously with knife raised. Sarkem and Massot came stumbling from the woods with bows drawn and fired two arrows, both off the mark. The man sensing the danger charged with knife raised as the two drunken braves fumbled to knock another arrow. Sarkem sensing the bow was futile dropped it and took his tomahawk and charged back swinging wildly. The man side stepped the blow and watched Sarkem fall flat on his face. Massot was next charging with tomahawk. The man again sidestepped and stuck out his foot sending Massot flying to the dirt. He went to lunge his knife into Sarkem when an arrow caught him in the throat and another in the heart. He fell harmlessly on Sarkem pinning him to the ground. Hysko emerged from the woods. Pomarat was down. Sarkem was under the man unharmed and Massot was slowly getting to his feet but stumbling while he did. Hysko looked to the hovel. A woman had come out with a bow and arrow knocked, surveying the scene as he was. She saw him, fear in her face. She drew back the arrow but he was faster, his arrow hitting her heart. She fell. A baby cried from inside the hovel. Hysko's heart sank in sorrow. But he dutifully approached the hovel, checking it out for older children. There were none, only a babe in a crib crying for a mother who would never comfort him again. He put down his bow and picked up the child cooing a tune in an attempt to coax the babe back to sleep. The babe looked up at him with wide eyes, eyes of trust of one being comforted at a time when he was awakened with noises of turmoil. Gradually those eyes grew heavy and returned to sleep. Hysko gently placed him back in the crib.

His chief had totally fucked up thanks to this evil liquid and now it was up to him to clean up this mess. All his party were under the influence of the magic liquid and lying on the ground. Their booty was back at the red head's camp. Massot, groggy stood in the doorway. "We should kill the child."

Hysko turned, "No!!!" he hissed as to not wake the child. "Go tend to Sarkem and Pomarat!"

Massot was shocked at the force and command of Hysko's words. He obeyed and tried to help Sarkem get out from under the man's body falling several times in his attempts. Finally Hysko came over and grabbed the man by the shoulder and rolled him off with a look of disgust at Massot. He went over to Pomarat. He was out cold. Hysko turned him over and poured water from his sack on his face. Pomarat came to, groggy. Seeing the face of Hysko he asked what happened.

Hysko proceeded to explain the failure of the attack and how he had rectified it. Pomarat asked, "Massot and Sarkem?"

"Alive, but not right in the head."

Pomarat laid his head back feeling the throbbing. His mind tried to digest this information. "Is there anyone left in the hovel?"

"Yes a baby!"

"Kill it!"

Hysko heart was beating hard. He had just bailed out the band thanks to their stupid behavior. "NO! The babe will be left."

"Are you now the chief of our band Hysko?" asked Pomarat raising an eyebrow? Hysko recognized the look and knew he must be careful with his words, though if acted immediately he could probably put an end to Pomarat in his current condition. But one never knew with him. Hysko chose his words carefully.

"No! You are chief. I was alone. All of you were poisoned by the fire water. I prayed to Maktahdou, and I killed the occupants of the hovel. He told me to spare the child."

"He told you to spare the child?" asked Pomarat watching every muscle in Hysko's face.

"Yes! He stopped my hand as I was about to end its life!"

Pomarat saw the lie in his eyes and filed it in his mind. "We go back to the camp with the firewater, gather our loot and head north tomorrow. No more hovels or firewater 'till we find our tribe."

Hysko nodded knowing Pomarat had not bought his story. Both he and Pomarat would be keeping an eye on each other.

131

VERN PACKED UP HIS stuff and showed Sarah the clothes he had brought for her. Sarah smiled. "Ye were pretty confident in yerself, to spend ye money for these dresses."

Vern chuckled, "No, I came prepared for anything. Back in my time I have plenty of money."

"Are ye saying thee be a rich man back in yer time?" she asked smiling but subtly probing.

Vern sensed the probe. "Yes I am, but in due time Sarah. You will have a lot to digest in my time. Gather what you wish to bring. I will tell you everything without overloading you. It must be gradual. Tonight we go back to my time."

132

THEY FOUND THE ITCHIWAN in the remote areas of Sandy Neck. Outlying sentries confronted them with their bows drawn. Pomarat recognized none of them. "Who are you?"

The two sentries looked at each other. "Who are you?"

"Pomarat, Chief of the Itchiwan!"

The two looked at each other. They had a chief. This man was a stranger with three other strangers. "Drop your bows. We will bring you to our camp."

"I DROP MY BOW FOR NO ONE!" yelled Pomarat as he quickly raised his bow and unleashed an arrow in to the heart of the sentry that spoke. The moment Pomarat raised his voice Massot shot the other sentry who had begun raising his bow. Hysko and Sarkem scanned the area for other braves with bows ready, Hysko noting Pomarat's rage when confronted with insubordination. Massot had gut shot his sentry, Pomarat's sentry was dead. Pomarat went to the dying sentry, "Why did you question the chief of your tribe?"

"Our chief is back at camp, you are not our chief!" responded the sentry. The Itchiwan were a peaceful tribe. They posted sentries in case the white man came to encroach on their territory, which was sparse. In 20 years the white man never did except for a random trader who was sent on his way with no argument. The last thing the sentry expected was an attack by Itchiwan.

Pomarat gave him a drink from his water satchel. "I am your chief, Pomarat! Though I do not recognize you or him," he said pointing to his fellow sentry.

The dying sentry spit the water back into his face and hissed, "POMARAT IS A LEGEND! YOU ARE AN IMPOSTER! POMARAT LIVED MANY HUNDREDS OF YEARS AGO! HE

KILLED MAUSHOP'S SONS AND ABANDONED US LEAVING US TO BE SCORNED AND EXILED BY THE WAMPANOAG TRIBE! YOU LIE!!!!!" The sentry expired with his last words but they were not lost on the others.

Pomarat sat back on his haunches. There was a lot to consider. Legend? Hundreds of years ago? Exiled by the Wampanoag? What had those boys done to us? THE HOLE! It was magic. Whose magic, the Red Witch? Hysko, Sarkem and Massot watched the face of their leader, Hysko closer than the others. Pomarat felt their eyes. He slowly rose from his haunches. No time to ponder, time for action. "Maushop has poisoned our tribe against us!" he bellowed. "We must take our tribe back to its greatness."

Massot and Sarkem were all in. Hysko did his best to indicate the same. He knew Pomarat knew his heart wasn't in it. He would not sleep till this played out.

133

"YOU READY SWEET PEA?" asked Vern that night as they approached the hole with their belongings.

"Sweet Pea? What is the meaning?"

"It's a term of endearment. Let's go!"

They went down the hole into the orb for what would be the last time. As they settled in the center, Sarah asked, "Which hole?"

"Watch," Vern grabbed the remote from his bag and pressed the on button. The hole illuminated. He fired an arrow to which he had previously attached a thin wire line. "This is our hole! I told you we'd be in and out of this thing. Let's go."

He went into the hole first and reached for Sarah's hand. He pulled her into the hole, her foot scraping the edge. Vern grabbed the lantern on the way out. When outside, he showed the lamp to Sarah. "See this beauty? This was my lifeline if things went wrong and the Pukwudgees were in pursuit. Tomorrow or the next day, the hole will be closed. God knows what has happened as a result of unleashing those bastards in your time."

Sarah looked around though it was dark she could see that her cabin was not where it had been. Then she spied a large yellow thing made of iron. She gasped and pointed, "Vern! What be that?"

Vern chuckled realizing he would be handling these questions over and over again for awhile. "That Sarah is a large dirt mover, one of the machines I warned you about. There are many, many more machines to see. Don't worry. It can't do anything unless a man controls it. Even then it moves slowly. Come on. Let me take you to my chariot."

"Chariot?"

"Yeah, car."

"What is 'car'?"

Vern grabbed her face in both hands and kissed her forehead. "Sarah, relax! Trust me. This is my world. I will protect you with my life. The machines will not hurt you."

Vern grabbed her hand, "My home and car is on the other side of the pond over there."

"Home?"

"Not really. I just bought it for tonight, for me coming back for you."

"Bought it?"

"Yes, I'll have them sell it when we get to my place in Maine."

"Ye have another place in this Maine?"

"Shush … yes you'll see."

"Ye must be very rich Vern. Are thee a pirate in yer time?"

"No, I'll tell you what I am when I can show you what it is. In your time, your men did not make money doing what I did. As close as I can put it is to tell you I entertained people."

"Were ye a jester?"

Vern started to say no, but thought of his TV contract and said, "Sort of, but you will see and judge for yourself."

They arrived at his home, with car in the drive packed and ready for Maine. He found the key on the tire and opened the trunk and threw the bag in. "Come inside," he said to Sarah leading her in to the house. When he flipped on the lights, Sarah gasped and her hand went to her chest. "Sarah!" he yelped, "You alright?"

She saw the polished hardwood floor, the rugs, and the strange furniture, not to mention the instant light. "Iye!" She gathered herself, "Ye must be a king!"

Vern muttered 'Fuck'. "No not a king. You will see that this is a nice, but not a palatial cabin in our time." Vern had brought her in the house to show her VHS videos of what he did. But now he realized it was too much too soon. Vern took her hand and led her to a sofa in the living room off the foyer. "Sit here, I gotta get some things." Sarah's eyes were darting everywhere taking in her surroundings. Vern knew he had to get out of here fast, or they would be staying here.

Vern found a box and grabbed a bunch of VHS tapes from his bookshelf. He also grabbed a camera and put them in the car. He retrieved Sarah from the living room. As expected she had left the sofa and was examining everything in the room with open mouth and hands. "Sarah, time to go," he said gently not wishing to startle her.

"Why? There be so much here!!!"

"My other place is better for us now." Vern took her hand, turned out the lights and locked the door placing the key under the mat outside. He led her to the car and opened the door. "Get in."

Sarah examined the inside and was hesitant. Vern understood. He went to the other side, got in and extended his hand to her outside. "Come, it's safe."

Hesitantly, she entered and seated herself next to Vern. "This is like a horse drawn wagon without the horses," he said while he reached across her and pulled her door closed. She tensed being enclosed in this metal machine. "It's okay, relax. Now I'm going to make this carriage move. There will be a noise then a hum. Then it will move. I am the one moving it. Okay?" Sarah nodded unsure of his words.

Vern started the car. Sarah tensed. The lights came on, lighting the driveway. Sarah gasped. "This is normal!" said Vern as he pulled out of the driveway. Sarah felt the movement and grabbed anything she could find. Vern lightly pressed on the brakes stopping the vehicle on the street in front of the house. "See? I control this carriage. Do you like music?" She nodded, scared. "Okay." Vern cranked the volume on the radio all the way down, turned it to channel 107 which was the local classical channel. He slowly increased the volume and Mozart gradually filled their space. "See, I control this!" She tentatively smiled as music softly filled the space. "Relax. I'm the master of this machine. I will take you to my other home."

"Go forward now Vern." Vern gently moved the car forward and drove out of the Fells Pond subdivision. Sarah's tension eased now believing he was fully in control of this machine, car, carriage or chariot. She would come to realize it was a new world with many names for the same thing. As they drove along, he warned Sarah they would see more and more lights, and to not be afraid. He explained there were many more homes than in her time, something she had already realized in the Fells Pond subdivision – none of it had been there in her time. He continued to explain there would be other cars approaching them with lights, which was happening at the moment. Sarah tensed then relaxed as the car passed harmlessly by. "There are rules about driving cars, you stay to the right. I'm on the right, and he's on his right. All roads are wide enough so if we follow the rules we won't run into each other."

"What if he does not follow the rules, Vern?"

"That's why I have to pay attention, so I can do this!" Vern accelerated swerved right into the breakdown lane and back into his lane. "So until we get to my home in Maine, relax, listen to the music, and by the way, we will be going over a big bridge with lights."

"Like those in London?"

"Yeah, but bigger, with more lights." Vern decided he take the low visual stimulation route to Maine via 495 instead of Route 3. Longer but he'd avoid the lights and skyscrapers of Boston.

134

THEY WALKED THROUGH THE marshes to the dunes of the neck. They could see the smoke from the fires of the camp in the distance near the end of the neck. 'Stupid' thought Pomarat thinking there was no means of escape at the end of the neck from an attack. True in his time, but this wasn't his time. This was their time. Their main source of trade was by canoes across Barnstable harbor. The Itchiwan could see miles of coastline on the bay and monitor activity in the harbor. Should danger come it would come from the sea or the village by the harbor and their means of escape would be the neck. No one ventured down the neck by land. In case they did, sentries were posted. If the sentries failed they had the canoes to go anywhere they wished. In hundreds of years, no one of significance approached from the neck. There was no value to be had. There were deer, small game and coyotes, but there were deer, small game and coyotes all over the narrow land.

Pomarat and his men stopped as they saw two Itchiwan approaching from the village in the distance. Pomarat indicated that they would let them pass. They were half way down the neck, and this was an excellent opportunity to rid himself of Hysko while he did what had to be done. They hid in the beach grass as they let what was obviously relief sentries pass.

"Hysko! Stand guard. We will go to the camp. When they come back after finding their brethren, kill them! Understand?" commanded Pomarat.

Hysko nodded knowing he was intentionally being relieved of the carnage that would be coming to the camp. Pomarat did not trust him anymore. Hysko was not a chief, but he knew the most strategic move would be for him to accompany the band to the camp and stand guard just outside the perimeter. That way he could watch the rear approach and be available if needed in the camp. Pomarat was going to do what he was going to do in the camp and wished Hysko nowhere near. If Hysko couldn't handle the relief sentries when they returned, Pomarat, Massot and Sarkem could handle those which got past Hysko. Pomarat figured Hysko would handle both, as he was a great warrior. But maybe Pomarat would get lucky and one would get rid of Hysko, saving him the task at a later date.

Hysko knew this was Pomarat's plan. Hysko gave the band a half mile head start and then followed. He would guard the rear from the perimeter of the camp, not way out here on the neck. It was time to bring this to a head. His survival depended on it.

135

SARAH HAD HER FACE close to the window as they passed over the Sagamore Bridge. She looked down, "OHHHH, Vern we are so high! I can see lights from cabins down below. Is it safe?"

"Yes very safe, enjoy!"

"LOOK! A GIANT SHIP ON THE RIVER BELOW! IT HAS NO SAILS!"

"This is my time Sarah, over two hundred and fifty years after your time. The days of sail are over except for fun and show." Vern decided to skip explaining it was a man-made canal, not a river. That could wait. Even taking 495, the visual stimulation of neon lights just off the highway, prompted more questions. Thankfully there were long stretches of no lights except the cars on the highway. The day and future shock had taken its toll on Sarah. On one of those long stretches before the Lowell exit she drifted off into sleep to the comforting strings of the London Symphony Orchestra playing Brahms on a Boston classical station. Vern hoped she would sleep till they passed Portsmouth and the coastal areas of Maine. After a few miles he gently lowered the volume a little and hoped some asshole in their travels would not find a reason to lay on his horn. However, he had forgotten about the tolls.

136

POMARAT SURVEYED THE CAMP from the dunes. As far as he could tell there were no armed sentries between his depleted band and the camp. There were however two armed men by the canoes by the harbor and one man on the beach facing the sea. The rest of the men were busy in the camp preparing the game they had killed that morning and the women were busy tending to the children, cleaning and making items that would be used in trade. He could not tell from this distance who was the chief.

He decided on a plan. He instructed Sarkem to go down to the beach and kill the sentry watching the ocean. After he was to go to the position Pomarat indicated. From there he could come to Pomarat's aid if need. Massot was to go to the two sentries on the bay. Massot was to kill them if they tried to come to the aid of their chief. He told them once Sarkem had killed his sentry Massot would go to his position while he, Pomarat, walked into the camp and gained a meeting with the chief. He explained that whoever the chief was, he would not willingly submit to him. But he would try and convince the tribe he was their true leader. Sarkem was to take out any of those braves farthest from the chief that went to gather their weapons. Pomarat would handle any close to the chief. Massot was to handle the two sentries if they moved to come back to the camp. Then he was to come back to the camp. He looked at his two braves, "Understand?"

They both nodded in fear. In their hearts they questioned killing more of their fellow Itchiwan. Pomarat saw the fear in their eyes. In response he said "How easily did we come upon the tribe? Would you follow a chief that allowed the Itchiwan woman and children to be so vulnerable to attack? So weak that their livelihoods depend on trade with the white invaders? Our tribe is in exile. We must bring it back to its greatness!"

Sarkem and Massot nodded, swayed by the logic of his words. Sarkem gathered his bow and headed to the beach. Pomarat and Massot watched his progress. Hysko did also from a half mile behind. He did not know why Sarkem was heading to the beach, nor could he see the camp yet. But he knew whatever Pomarat's plan was, it was set in motion. He assumed a position where he could see Pomarat and the path the relief sentries took. Sarkem did not waste time with chit chat with a fellow Itchiwan. He did what he was told - slit his throat and pushed his body into the gentle surf. The sand crabs and dogfish would feast when the tide rose. Pomarat was right, the Itchiwan had grown weak. It never should have been that easy.

With a glance, Pomarat sent Massot to his position by the sentries on the bay. Pomarat checked his weapons and adjusted his loin cloth. Then he took two eagle feathers and leather band from his side satchel and placed them on his head … the head dress of a chief in his time. He threw his shoulders back and walked down the dune into the camp with the arrogance of a true chief.

Hysko saw they all had abandoned the top of the dune and decided to go to their vacated position. He would have a longer view of the path by which the relief sentries would return once they had found their slain brethren. He would also be able to see what Pomarat was up to. He knew Pomarat intended to take back the tribe. However, he had no idea the strength of the tribe. Judging from the ease which they had handled the sentries, and the fact the Pomarat was moving forward with only two braves, he assumed there was not much strength. This posed a dilemma for him. He saw the look in Pomarat's eyes when he refused his order. If Pomarat reclaimed command of the tribe, it would only be a matter of time before he would find a reason to kill him or just turn and put an arrow in his heart for no reason apparent to anyone else. Massot and Sarkem would never question Pomarat's authority nor come to his aid if it came down to it. He was doomed unless by some miracle, Pomarat failed in his mission to take over the tribe. Knowing Pomarat for so many years, he knew the chances of that was slim and none.

Hysko reached the crest of the dune. His band had left the satchels with their plunder there. He saw the camp. He saw Sarkem in position to cover Pomarat who was just about to enter the camp which was unguarded from this direction or any direction for that matter except the bay. Where was Massot? There ... in a position to take out the bay sentries. He looked back to Sarkem and could see his tracks coming from the ocean. There was an Itchiwan face down in the surf. He turned and scanned the path for the sentries returning. No sign of them. Good, they would probably be of no use to the tribe anyway and he had no desire to kill more of his tribe. He watched from his perch to see how this would play out.

137

POMARAT STRODE INTO THE camp with the gait of a chief. None of the men were armed except for knives in their belt. The women were the first to notice him. Pomarat was well inside the camp before anyone confronted him. Sarkem watched the men heading to Pomarat at the bequest of their woman. Their knives were still in their sheaths. If things went bad it would be like shooting fish in a barrel for Sarkem.

"I AM POMARAT, CHIEF OF THE ITCHIWAN! WHO IS THE LEADER OF YOUR TRIBE?"

The women gasped, one brave went running to a tent on the far side of the camp. If this was Pomarat's time, he would have several arrows in his throat after that proclamation. It wasn't his time. His eyes followed the brave who went to the tent. Then he looked at the Itchiwan gawking at him while they awaited their chief. They were weak! They lost the greatness he had commanded. He would change this.

The brave and an old man emerged from the tent aided by a woman. The brave now had a bow with arrow knocked. Sarkem now had a target should the need arise. The old man sized up Pomarat as he approached. With the woman aiding him he stood before Pomarat.

"Young man, I am Nakim, the chief of this tribe. You claim to be chief of the Itchiwan. Where is your tribe?"

"THIS IS MY TRIBE OLD MAN! I AM POMARAT!"

"Pomarat!!??" the chief scratched his chin and slowly shook his head from side to side then looked Pomarat in the eyes. "Pomarat is a legend!" the old man had a cough attack but continued. "Why were you given that name of all names? He lived many hundreds of years ago. He is responsible for the exile of our tribe by the Wampanoag! We were once great warriors, now we have adapted and become traders, because of Pomarat's adventures. He abandoned his tribe and angered Maushop by killing his children. Pomarat and the remainder of his band that survived Maushop's rage fled this land without warning the tribe they may be in danger. The Wampanoag chief did tell the tribe! He told the tribe to flee like their chief had or they would risk the wrath of Maushop and the Wampanoag people. They would forever call our people 'Pukwudgees'... a term of derision ... evil murderous little thieves not to be trusted. And the tribe fled the Wampanoag wrath and remained in hiding. Our whole culture as a proud nation had changed. When the game was sparse we became the murderous thieves they had cursed us to be in order to survive and also to rebel against the exile the Wampanoag placed upon us. Eventually the tribe tired of running and hiding. That was when visitors came from over the great waters, first in long boats with one canvas and many years later in larger boats with many canvases. We became traders as did the Wampanoag. They stopped hunting us and we stopped bothering them. We both profited from trade with the whites. Now you come here saying YOU are chief of this tribe. Explain that to me young man."

Normally Pomarat would have put in arrow in this old man's heart after the first sentence. But his story fascinated him. When they came out of the hole the landscape had definitely changed. There was a hovel by the hole when they came out but there had not been one when he went in not more than a sun's notch before. He wanted to know more. Pomarat removed his bow and arrows and placed them on the ground. Sarkem watched in horror not knowing what was said or what he should do. Then Pomarat also removed his tomahawk and stone knives and laid them next to the bow.

Pomarat spoke. "Chief Nakim, your words weigh heavily on me. Would you invite me into your tent so we can talk further on what you have said?"

"I can see you're confused. Yes of course, we will prepare a meal and we can talk. But first bring in your band."

Pomarat raised an eyebrow.

Nakim raised his and said, "The one in the dunes to the right with his arrow trained on Baskin here and the one down by the bay watching our sentries. Also the one at the top of the dune, is he yours also?"

Pomarat snapped his head around to his previous position. Hysko! Nakim had eyes everywhere. He had under estimated the old chief. Nakim could see by Pomarat's reaction that the brave on the hill was supposed to be back up the path awaiting the return of the relief sentries. But Nakim's relief sentries had seen the men they were supposed to relieve dead and immediately split, one to the north of the neck, the other to the bayside of the neck and ran to the camp, ran like they had been trained for hundreds of years since the tribe had been exiled. They also reported the deaths of the two sentries and the sentry by the sea and the positions of Sarkem and Massot prior to Pomarat's arrival. But Nakim kept this to himself.

Pomarat had been out foxed by this wily old chief. No doubt he had braves with arrows pointed at Sarkem and Massot should they make the wrong move. As far as Hysko, he could care less, as once again he had disobeyed his order. He pointed directly at Sarkem, and then indicated for him to come. Sarkem hesitated. The brave covering Sarkem arose from the dune grass and launched an arrow landing an inch in front of his head as he laid prone. He now knew why Pomarat wished him to come. He did not drop his weapons but did not knock an arrow. He proceeded to walk towards Pomarat.

"Sarkem, get Massot. Nakim's man will accompany you. We will eat with Nakim when you return." Sarkem set off to retrieve Massot and did not fail to see Pomarat's subtle signal of thumb down while pointing to Massot's position

Pomarat looked to Nakim, "The one on the hill is no longer of my band. He disobeyed my orders and killed your outlying sentries. I banished him, yet he follows. Do with him what you will."

Nakim nodded, that still did not explain the sentry on the beach. "Come to my tent, we will eat. Your men can wait outside when they return. They will be given food and drink. We will talk further, you and me." Nakim indicated to the woman of the tribe they should make Sarkem and Massot welcome, feed them and see to their needs. He called over two braves who were to be the relief sentries and took them aside pointing to the top of the dune. He told them to capture Hysko and why. Hysko saw the pointing and got out of dodge. He didn't know what was going on below but knew it would not end well for him if he didn't take action immediately. Pomarat knew the action he would take after he had a talk with Nakim. Though Pomarat had abandoned his weapons, he had not abandoned the pouch that sat round his waist that contained the powder. He also surveyed what was available in Nakim's tent.

Nakim entered the tent assisted by two women. They seated him across from Pomarat and sat on either side of Nakim. Pomarat surveyed the demeanor of the women and recognized they were more bodyguards than nursemaids. They had hardened faces and who knew what weapons they concealed.

138

SARAH AWOKE WHEN THE bubbly toll taker greeted Vern with "Welcome to Maine!"

"Shush!" tried Vern as he handed her the toll before he realized it was too late.

"Soo sorry sir ..." Vern drove off. Damn they usually just take the toll in a comatose fashion. She must be new. Damn the bad luck.

"What was that thing?" asked Sarah.

"A toll booth."

"What is a toll booth?" she asked stretching her legs coming to.

"You pay money to travel their road."

"And ye paid the toll??? Are they highwaymen??? Are they pirates??? She was just a young girl! Why did ye give her yer coin?"

"It's not highwaymen or pirates, it's the government," then he improvised, "The government is the pirates of today much like the king in your time, but it is the law so you pay. There will be no more tolls."

Soon Vern exited the highway taking the rural routes that would lead to his cabin. Isolated but close enough to towns where he could gradually introduce Sarah to his time. Sarah took comfort in the darkness only illuminated by the 'car' they were in and not the endless stream of machines approaching and the red lights of those going in the same direction.

"We're home," said Vern gently as he pulled into the long drive leading to his cabin.

"Is this another of ye palaces, rich Vern?"

"It's not a palace like the place you saw, but it is a nice place which I bought in case you agreed to return."

"And if I didn't agree?"

"I would return a broken man listening to the blues. I would have the place sold and then I don't know."

"What are the blues?"

"Music for men and woman who are heartbroken and sing of their sorrows." Vern came to a stop by the cabin. "Let's go inside."

"Sad music?"

"Yep."

The cabin was rustic, but not like the one he had described to Vinnie in Manhattan. This one in Maine had electricity. He left the car running with the headlights on facing the door. "Wait here," he said to Sarah as he got out of the car, opened the door and flicked all the light switches inside. Instant light, again! He came back to the car and shut it off. "Come to my Maine palace, I think you will find this more to your liking."

Sarah accompanied Vern inside. It was more modest than the home in Fells Pond, but still a wonder to Sarah. There were chairs and sofas like those of the aristocracy of England but also strange things she wondered what they were. She had seen a similar thing at Vern's other palace but they left so fast, she had no time to experience them. "Vern what are these things" as she pointed to the electronics and lamps that gave off light.

"Sarah, sit," he pointed to the sofa rather than the chair. She sat in the middle of it. He sat next to her. He put his arm around her, "We are now over 250 years in the future. We are husband and wife. I will protect you. More than that, I will teach you about how all those things you point at work and why. But first you must eat and I will cook. Would you like Salisbury Steak, Lasagna, or Macaroni and Cheese?"

"I do not know these foods of which thee speak?"

"I know. But you will learn. And you will never have to worry about where your next meal is coming from. Nor will you have to ever go to the pond to get water. Come with me." He got up and extended his hand. She looked in his eyes and saw only love and adoration. If what he said was true, and she had yet to see any reason it wasn't, she had found her Prince! Never had she dreamed her life would be anything more than a life of constant toil doing what she had to do survive in her modest cabin by the pond. Though before Vern had come, that cabin had been everything to her, the sum total of her accomplishments. She spent every day protecting it. Then came Vern, the little boy who could not conceal his adoration despite having a pistol pointed at his head. He came back a grown man fulfilling his promise to return. She was now in his time. She had given up her time. This may all be a dream, but until she awoke she would enjoy every minute. She followed Vern into the bathroom.

"Your first lesson!" said Vern. "Here is where you get your water now." He pulled up the lever on the sink faucet and water flowed. "Move the lever to the right and the water is cold. Feel." He guided here hand under the flowing water. She felt the coolness. "Move the lever to the left and it gets warm." She soon felt the warmth her eyes widening. "Right good for drinking, left good for washing. There is another of these in the kitchen that works the same way. But the kitchen comes later." He pulled the lever down. The water stopped. "See that." He pointed to the toilet. "No more going outside to … eh … eh, shit I don't know how to explain this in words you'll understand!"

"Just show me Vern."

Screw it, Vern dropped his pants. "It was what you leave the cabin to do in your time. Eh … men stand and do it this way," he stood peeing in the bowl in front of her. When he finished he put down the seat and sat. "Woman do it this way. Men and woman both do the other thing the same way," as Vern stood and pointed to his ass hoping she would understand.

Sarah burst out in laughter, "I understand Vern!" Sarah had had to pee for awhile. She was a quick study. She moved Vern out of the way, lifted her sundress and sat on the toilet and peed. "Leaves?" she asked?

Vern pointed to the roll of paper to her left and unrolled it and ripped and gave it to her. Vern indicated she should then drop it the bowl. She got up dropping her dress. "Now what?"

"Watch!" Vern pushed down the handle and everything in the bowl went away and was replaced by clean water. Sarah's brain tried to grasp what had just happened.

"No more outside?" mumbled Sarah.

"No more outside. These are your leaves, called 'toilet paper'" pointing to the roll.

"Toilet paper." She repeated.

"Now let me show you something else." Vern turned on the shower. "No more pond to bathe except for fun. Take off your dress and come with me." Vern took off the rest of his clothes went in the shower. He held out his hand indicating she should follow. She followed. She felt the warmth of the water and the warmth of Vern's embrace. The kitchen and 'TV dinners' lessons would wait as well as the 'don't say "ye"' lesson and all the other lessons required to bring Sarah into the 20th century.

139

"I AM CONFUSED BY YOUR words," explained Pomarat as more women brought the food in and laid it before them. The two women who escorted Nakim and were seated on either side sat stone-faced with their eyes fixed on Pomarat's. They did not look at the food but only at Pomarat's eyes and hands. Pomarat regretted having to kill them; they would be fine warriors in his camp. But this was no longer his camp, and he was not their leader, they would die before betraying Nakim.

"I can see you're confused young man. Eat and tell me your story," responded Nakim partaking in the feast of venison and shellfish that lay before them.

Pomarat smiled and looked down and then looked up at Nakim. "After listening to your words, I realize you may doubt my story. And if I were you I would. But I am the Pomarat of your legends. Yes, my band killed Maushop's sons. But we did not abandon the tribe. We killed his sons not more than seven suns ago."

Nakim's eyes widened, the women's hands went behind them.

Pomarat continued sensing they thought him to be a madman, "On our way back to our camp, we encountered four boys, two Wampanoag and two like the whites of which you speak. They led us to this hole in the ground, far south of here. We followed them into the hole but were met with fire when we tried to follow their trail up another tunnel out of the hole. In this hole there were many tunnels, almost as many as the lights in the night sky! The center of the hole was a dimly glowing globe! It was magic! We tried many tunnels but they were blocked but we found one with strange symbols. We tried that tunnel and were able to escape the hole. We saw the tracks of the four boys when we got outside and a hovel where there wasn't one when we went in. The tracks went to the hovel and came back to the hole. This was too much magic! We decided to give up pursuit. On our travels back to our tribe we saw things were different. We knew not why. Your words intrigue me. You say I lived many hundreds of sun cycles ago. But the stories you tell of me happened less than a moon ago for me and my band. Have I been bewitched by this hole in the ground?"

Nakim considered his tale and what a tale it was! Pomarat seemed sincere in its telling, which he was since it was what happened. "Pomarat, if you are the Pomarat of legend as you say, then you will realize that I as the chief must consider your words carefully before making a decision on their merits. Would you be willing to bring me to this hole of which you speak?"

"Of course! What I say is true."

"Then we shall visit this hole tomorrow and if what you say is true, I shall tell the tribe you are the true chief and I shall step aside."

Now for the info which he put up with this charade, "Is this camp all that is left of the Itchiwan, Chief Nakim?"

Nakim laughed and sucked down an oyster, "No, no, no young man. Long ago we decided that in order to preserve the survival of the tribe, we should divide the tribe into separate chiefdoms and that all the chiefs would periodically meet and decide on matters on the greater good of the tribe. There are encampments such as this in the marshes and dunes along the coastline from the areas first settled by the many canvassed ships to the tip of the narrow land where the one canvassed vessel first appeared. Now the sons of sons are setting up their own camps in the southern marshes."

Pomarat took all this in, "How do you communicate with all these camps?"

Nakim looked Pomarat in the eye as he feasted on a lobster tail. "You ask the questions a chief would ask. That is good. Are you planning to be chief?"

Pomarat carefully considered the question. "Chief Nakim, you yourself said you would step aside if what I told you was true. I know that tomorrow when I show you this hole you will know it to be so. If what you say is true, the ways of my time are no longer. As a true chief I must adapt."

"YES, YOU MUST!" said Nakim raising his voice and gazing deep into his eyes. "All our men and women from birth are trained to be runners. They can reach the farthest camps in no more than two suns. We also use beach fire signals to the tribes of the north and east if we need help. We are still a great people who have adapted to the times."

Pomarat had what he needed to know. He bowed to Nakim and said "Thank you, tomorrow you will see … " while digging in his pouch and pulling out a fist full of powder which he blew into the eyes of the two women who had relaxed their guard ever so slightly being engulfed in his words. They were blinded and about to die but scrambled for the knives behind their backs. Now Pomarat saw what they were hiding and jumped on the one on the right. As she struggled to find breath, he took her knife and deftly slit her throat. He was quickly on the other woman as her hands went to her throat, not knowing why she was suddenly incapacitated and forever ended her thought as to why. Then Nakim started to emit a death chant but was muted by a knife under the chin up into the brain. Nakim would never see the hole.

Sarkem tried to engage Nakim's man in conversation as they headed to Massot's position but Nakim's man was stone faced and intent on his mission and ignored Sarkem's words while his eyes were always on Sarkem. Sarkem stopped and confronted him now that they were away from the camp. "Why won't you talk with me?! We are only three and you are many?"

"You are four. There is another on the dune," responded the stone faced brave for the first time.

"Him? That is Hysko. He betrayed us creating this conflict between us. He acted without orders."

"Keep moving! No more talk!"

Sarkem raised his hands in the air in feigned frustration and turned to continue to Massot's position. Twenty yards later he intentionally lost his footing on the dune and tumbled into a roll. He came out of the tumble with his arrow knocked and fired into the throat of Nakim's man to eliminate his ability to alarm others. He had another arrow knocked as insurance but it was not necessary as the man gurgled and released the tension on his arrow and fell to the ground.

Sarkem stood over him as he clutched his throat. He knelt and said, "Why would you not talk with me? This could have been avoided." He took the man's knife and thrust the blade under the jaw into the brain, the way you put a lobster out of its misery just prior to boiling. Then he admired the craftsmanship of the blade like nothing from their time. Pomarat was experiencing a similar revelation in Nakim's tent while examining the fine weapons the two women had concealed. Not as fine as the weapons they would have found at the Finch residence, but that never happened due to the boys tinkering with time.

Sarkem took the braves arrows and retrieved his; the fine knife was already in his belt. He had to get to Massot and dispatch the sentries by the bay hoping that their leader had taken out the chief. He had and awaited their return knowing they would accomplish their tasks. Such is the nature of a closely knit band.

Sarkem approached Massot's position and shot an arrow ten feet to the left of his position but forward enough to fall in his sight line. They had used this signal many times before. If it was an enemy, it would have been in his back. Massot turned and saw Sarkem as he scrambled to his position. "Pomarat's in the chief's tent."

"Did he kill him?"

"Don't know, but we must kill those two as planned."

"Why are you here then? Why aren't you watching over him?"

"Pomarat changed the plan and awaits our return. We must move fast I'll tell you what happened on the return. But I don't really know. I only know he is depending on us to complete this and return."

"Should we take them from here?"

"No we must be sure. They have these!" Sarkem showed him the knife. "We will need their weapons and their arrows if we are to be of use to Pomarat."

They ran to the bay and killed both of their brethren with ease, taking their weapons.

140

THEY MADE LOVE IN the shower and Vern introduced her to towels from the closet. When they had dried off he brought her to the kitchen for TV dinners. He took two dinners from the freezer and set the oven. He put them in not waiting for the oven to preheat and set the timer for five minutes longer than the instructions. They would be feasting on Salisbury steak with potatoes, gravy, and a medley of vegetables. In the meantime, he showed her the refrigerator, opening the bottom and taking her hand, he put it inside. She was startled by the cold. "Food goes in here to keep it fresh for a while."

"How is it cold?!"

"Electricity, same thing that makes the stove and water hot, but that lesson comes later. Now feel this." He opened the door on top and guided her hand in. She quickly drew it back. "Much colder, it can make ice. It keeps food good for a long time."

Sarah's eyes widened as they had with all the things Vern had shown her after they had gone in the hole. "Vern, this is too much to understand!"

"Sarah, we have all the time in the world. No one comes to this cabin. In a short time there will be a buzzing sound indicting our dinner is ready. We can eat and relax and talk at length about what you've seen. And when we get tired, we can sleep or learn more or not. It's up to you, when you've had enough for a day, tell me and we will relax."

"What about yer brother and friend?"

"Brett doesn't know about this place. This place is for you and me only."

"What about Amos?"

"Everybody thinks I went to Europe. You just traveled more than 250 years. You need time to adjust. This is the perfect place," he answered avoiding the question.

"Ye said ye would show me why ye are so wealthy and what ye did when we got here. We are here."

"I did. Wait here." He sat her on the sofa in front of the TV. "I'll be right back." He ran out to the car and retrieved the VHS tapes he had taken from the Fells Pond property. The first tape was a collection of highlights from Vern's career that had been edited by his network employer when he became part of their pregame program.

Vern went to turn on the TV, but thought better of it and turned to Sarah as he squatted by the TV. "See this box?"

She nodded.

"This is the hardest thing to explain to you. You will think it is truly magical. But it's not. How can I explain it?" Vern put his face in his hand. Sarah sat wide eyed staring at him and the box. "Okay what is the earliest history you remember?"

"The bible."

"Okay what is the greatest invention since the time in the bible?"

"The machines that make books and weaves fabrics. And … and gunpowder!"

Vernon thought on this and realized for almost 1800 years the human race was basically imbeciles. What it had invented and developed in the last 200 years was mind-boggling when compared. "Sarah, shortly after your time, there was a thing call the Industrial Revolution …"

She looked at him with the rapt attention of a child.

"Damn I am not a history teacher! I don't know how to explain this!"

"Fuck! Just show me!"

"Where did you learn 'Fuck'?"

"Ye said it to the man ye tied up outside my cabin when ye appeared to be frustrated. I am frustrated by yer words, just show me."

"How the fuck close to me were you when I was doing that?"

"Right behind ye in the woods with my pistol pointed at yer head. Ye were too busy looking at the cabin for me."

"Damn. Okay I'll show you. But it's not magic. It was made by men, like me. And Sarah, people don't say ye, thee and yer anymore. They say you and your. Try to do that from now on, only because if you say 'ye' to people nowadays, they will look at you as if you had two heads." Vern went to turn on the TV. Then the buzzer went off, dinner was done. "This is perfect," he said. "Sit on this sofa. You will be introduced to TV while eating your first TV dinner."

Vern retrieved the dinners from the oven and presented her with her first TV dinner. "These are strange plates," said Sarah, eyes all over this strange presentation of food. She was mindful of that fact in order to prepare it, Vern had taken the strange plates from the box that makes ice and put them in another white box that makes heat and now they're ready to eat steaming with no fire made.

"Yeah but we throw them away after. Eat your Salisbury Steak."

"It is named for the town in England?"

"Is Salisbury a poor town?

"All English towns are poor towns except for the palaces of the wealthy."

"Then it probably is since it's basically ground beef loaded with salt, smothered in gravy and formed in an oval instead of in the traditional round hamburger way. Throw in some onion and bread crumbs and form it in a loaf and it's called meatloaf after a great modern day composer. Eat. I'll turn on the TV and join you. The TV is like going to a show in London, you sit and watch. Okay?"

"I've never been to a show but I've heard of them in this country. This is good Vern! I would like to try meatloaf some time!"

"You will. You asked to know about me, well here it is," he slipped the VHS tape that the network had prepared encapsulating his career in preparation of introducing him as a member of the pre and post game staff. He was careful to hit the play button prior to turning the TV. He didn't want to explain whatever channel he had been watching when he was last here. Vern hit the pause button on the remote and sat next to Sarah and dug into his Salisbury steak. Chewing his first bite, he hit the play button and the TV came to life. "This is me … what I do."

He watched Sarah as the screen came to life. She gasped and almost choked on the mashed potatoes she had just put in her mouth. She stopped eating. The tape introduced the newest member to the network commentary staff. "That's you!!!"

"Yes."

"In that box!" she said pointing at the TV. "How?"

"Just watch, I'll try to explain after. This is what I did to make the money I have."

Sarah shut up and watched. Vern scoffed down his dinner as he was starving while she did. After the video was over he hit the off button on the remote.

"Why did it stop?"

"The story is done. I stopped it."

"They pay you money to play a game?"

"Yes, a lot of money."

"Why?"

"It's entertainment, a show. Every Sunday and Monday night people will turn on that box and watch our games while it happens. When play stops they show things to sell people stuff. And people buy the stuff. Also many people bet on the results of the games. This is big business. The people who control the box get money from the people who sell things. They pay the people who run the games for the right to show the games. And those people pay us to play."

Sarah sank back into the couch and thought. She looked at Vern and asked, "Where is Cleveland?"

"Wait here," He returned from the library with a globe which he had since he went off to college in Syracuse. In his freshman year he began marking all the places he went to throughout his life. There were a lot of marks.

He set it down on the coffee table. "This is the world, a map of the world!" Sarah propped herself up and examined it. "You lived here. We are here now," he said pointing to Maine. He rotated the globe, "This is England! You came from there to here," he said rotating the globe back to Cape Cod. He rotated it slightly to the left, "This is Cleveland. See this land?" he ran his hand over the United States. "This is the country you and your fellow travelers and descendants founded. It is now the most powerful country in the world, more powerful than England. In 1776, sixty-six years after I brought you here, it declared its independence from England after defeating them in a war. This country is called the United States of America, USA for short."

"This is true?"

Vern could see she was trying to absorb all this. "Yes it's true, but enough lessons for tonight. Would you like some wine?"

"Ye ... you have wine?"

"I do." Vern retrieved a Merlot from the wine rack and poured them both a glass, and then he cleaned up their TV dinners by putting them in a hefty bag.

"I should be doing that Vern. But I don't know anything in your world."

"Don't worry Sarah, you will. Take it slow, relax and enjoy the wonder of my time. Soon it will be your time."

141

POMARAT TOOK THE TWO knives from the dead women and kissed their foreheads in respect for the way they had served their chief. He peeked out the tent. Life in the tribe seemed to be going on as normal. That was good. He'd await Sarkem and Massot confident they would complete their mission. In the meantime he was hungry. He looked at the food that was presented in the tent. On a whim he decided he wanted something rarer. He looked at the dead Nakim. Good enough. He took one of his new knives and sliced deep into his chest cavity and removed his heart. He held the bloody heart in his hand and was about to feast on it when an arrow pierced the tent close enough to the south facing edge to not harm anyone inside. Sarkem and Massot were here. He had the cover he needed. Instead of feasting on the heart, he held it in his right hand and his bow with an arrow knocked in his left as he exited the tent. Members of the tribe gradually looked up from what they were doing as a murmur went through the camp. Pomarat surveyed their faces. In the Itchiwan language he bellowed, "I AM POMARAT! YOUR TRUE CHIEF! THIS IS NAKIM," holding up the bleeding heart, "HE GAVE ME HIS KNOWLEDGE … AND HIS HEART AS HE WAS OLD AND FEEBLE! I EAT HIS HEART SO HE LIVES IN ME AND I CAN LEAD YOU AS HE DID!" He took a bite of the heart, blood running down his neck and chest.

The camp looked on in shock digesting his speech, except for Baskin, who charged from the right with knife raised. On his third stride, he was cut down by Massot's arrow. Pomarat smiled and took another bite, more blood creating a more horrifying image as he had intended. Two more braves raised their bows from the left and front. Sarkem took out the one of the left before he launched. Pomarat saw the one in the front, let him fire and deflected the arrow with his bow as he stepped to the left. He then knelt grabbing the bow string with the remainder of Nakim's heart still in his right hand and shot his arrow into the eye of the brave who had shot at him. The heart was mush and fell to the ground. Massot then shot the person nearest Pomarat who was a woman who had been preparing food for the chief's tent for no reason except to erase any thoughts of more attacks.

"ARE YOU FINISHED?!!! YOU ARE MY PEOPLE! STOP THIS MADNESS! MY BRAVES ARE WARRIORS SKILLED IN BATTLE! YOU HAVE BECOME TRADERS BECAUSE OF MY ABSENCE! ALL YOU WHO DON'T WISH TO OPPOSE ME … SIT DOWN … NOW!"

Slowly the camp sat one by one. A mother would occasionally jump up to sit down a child. Pomarat had successfully taken back this encampment of the Itchiwan. He walked through sitting members of his tribe observing their faces for signs of future rebellion.

"YOU, YOU, YOU, YOU AND YOU! COLLECT ALL THE WEAPONS OF THE TRIBE!" YELLED POMARAT AT THE WOMEN HE HAD POINTED AT. "YOU, YOU, YOU! PRE-

PARE A MEAL LIKE YOU HAD FOR YOUR CHIEF! BUT FOR THE ENTIRE TRIBE! TONIGHT WE FEAST! TONIGHT THIS TRIBE IS REBORN! TONIGHT I WILL TELL YOU HOW WE WILL RETURN TO GREATNESS!

142

HYSKO SPIED THE TWO braves running towards him after their talk with the chief. They were fast. He threw the satchels of plunder they had gathered far off the path he had taken. He dared not deviate because he knew they were trackers as all Itchiwan were raised to be. He also knew it would only be a matter of time before Pomarat had taken control of the tribe. About a half mile back up the path he stopped realizing there was no way he could out run them. Now he had a decision to make … kill them or surrender and try to convince them that their chief was probably already dead. Neither was acceptable, but a hybrid plan may work. It would depend on his skill as warrior, diplomat and archer. He diverted off the path to a higher dune and took cover in the Rosa rugosa.

The two braves noticed his trail diverging off the path and stopped. They looked in that direction and readied their bows proceeding cautiously. Hysko waited for them to get closer. They would be like shooting fish in a barrel if it was his wish. It wasn't. They were Itchiwan! No more killing. Now the archer … he shot two arrows with minimal time between shots. Each scraped the outside of their left foot. "Lower your bows! NOW!"

They did as ordered. "Now lay them on the ground and lay your weapons next to them!" They did. "Move back ten paces and sit!" When they had, he emerged from his cover. The two runners were worried about their fate.

Hysko walked far enough so their weapons were behind him. "My name is Hysko. I am Itchiwan, I have no wish to kill you, but I won't let you kill me."

The brave on the left spoke first, "We did not come to kill you. We came to take you back to our chief, Nakim. He distrusts the stories told by your chief Pomarat. Pomarat says you killed our two sentries and you are no longer a member of his tribe."

Hysko pondered this news though he was not surprised. "Why does Nakim distrust Pomarat?"

"Because of our dead brother on the beach. Nakim knew because we told him."

"You were the relief sentries?"

"Yes."

Hysko came forward and squatted in front of the two braves. "I did not fire the arrow that killed those sentries. By then I was an outcast because I challenged Pomarat when I refused to kill a Wampanoag babe. Pomarat is in league with the devil Maktahdou! I lied to Pomarat and said Maktahdou ordered me to spare the child. He didn't believe me but had some moment of doubt due to the strength in my words and his situation at the time. Since that moment I knew I was an outcast and dead at his first opportunity." Hysko surveyed their faces, faces of indecision.

Finally he said, "We have wasted much time. We will go back to your chief. You will leave your weapons here; I fear your chief may be dead already." The two relief sentries both nodded without confirming their decision with each other. "Stop at the top of the dune, we will see the situation before we go down to the camp."

The two sentries ran back like the wind, Hysko tried to keep up but realized he couldn't. The sentries reached the top of the dune and stopped as Hysko had commanded. They were in time to see Pomarat emerge from the tent with a bloody mass in his hand which he bit into and all the events which transpired immediately after including the killing of Baskin and an innocent woman. Hysko joined them and watched the events unfold below. "Do you now understand my words?" he asked.

They nodded. "Your tribe is now under Pomarat's control. He will be expecting you to return with news of my death. But I can see you are good men, you will not stand up to his questions. He will see your lies in your face and kill you immediately."

"Our women are down there! And my child!" blurted the sentry known as Fasman.

Hysko looked him in the eye and said, "I can try to kill Pomarat now, but the chances of my arrow hitting its target from this distance is slim. If I miss that arrow will tell Pomarat, I am alive and you failed your mission. Pomarat will seek out your woman and child and kill them or use them for his pleasure. If we run and develop a plan we buy time for your people. Are there more Itchiwan we can rally against Pomarat?"

"Who are you?! Where is your tribe? I have never seen you at the annual council of the Itchiwan tribe."

"You are my tribe, though I do not recognize you. We lived here in the great marsh at the beginning of this spit, not way out here. We left a moon ago to head south, Pomarat wished to kill Maushop's sons. He claimed he was told to do so by Maktahdou. He claimed to be Maktahdou's warrior. There were six of us when we left. We are now four. Maushop killed two. They were careless and disobeyed Pomarat's instructions. We four went on to raid a Wampanoag camp and were coming back to the two warriors we left behind to burn the bodies of Maushop's sons. They were not at the place the paths cross. We backtracked to Maushop's camp and heard his rage as he killed them. Instead of burning the bodies, the fools were feasting on Maushop's food and drinking his wine. By the time they awoke, Maushop had returned. He had them by their feet and swung them over his head and smashed them on trees and rocks over and over again. Our arrows would be useless against such a giant. Pomarat had used magic powder to kill the sons while they slept. Since he dropped his weapons before he entered the tent with your chief I am guessing he used the same powder on him."

Fasman looked at Krat, the other sentry. There was a look of confusion and fear in their eyes. They had seen what happened below, but this Hysko was a madman also. He had relayed the same story their mothers had told them when they were young … of Maushop … of Pomarat … of why the Itchiwan were now outcasts and were called Pukwudgees. These were stories of legend which happened hundreds maybe thousands of full season cycles ago. Now this Hysko is telling them that he and the madman below are that legend. Their weapons were back up the path. They must humor this madman. Fasman focused first and decided to confront Hysko head on with the truth.

"Hysko, the story you have told us is the same story our mothers have been telling Itchiwan children for hundreds maybe thousands of sun cycles. It is a legend. Maushop is a legend. Pomarat is a legend. Stories. How do you explain this?"

Hysko paused rehashing all the strangeness they had encountered since chasing the four boys in the hole and also the hole itself. Hysko watched their faces to see their reaction to what he was about to say. "We fled Maushop's camp before he knew we were watching his rage. On our way back here we came across four boys in strange dress. Pomarat ordered us to chase them. Two were Wampanoag twins. Two were pale skin, one of which had fiery red hair. Pomarat believed he was a shaman, a witch with magical powers. They ran and disappeared into the ground. We followed and found a tunnel into the earth. We went into the tunnel. At the bottom was a rotating glowing orb with a skin around it. Pomarat ran through the skin intent on killing the boys. We followed. Everything changed inside the skin. Inside you saw there were other tunnels beyond counting. And then all the tunnels shifted! We saw the tunnel the boys chose to escape and followed. The boys had made a great fire to block exit. We went back through the skin to try and flank them. And saw all these strange markings on the dirt walls. We tried these tunnels and found them blocked with a hard substance like rock, but not rock. We found a hole with marking like this." Hysko drew an 'ss' in the sand. This tunnel was not blocked. We came out at the same place we went in, but it was different. There was a hovel where there hadn't been one. The boys had been here but their tracks came back to the hole. Pomarat felt this was a trap, if the boy who was a red witch had his way we would be in that hole forever chasing false trails. He decided we would return to the tribe. Along the way I noticed things had changed. The land and its inhabitants had changed. I know not why. It had to be the magic of those boys and their hole." Hysko scanned their faces for signs of acceptance of his story and saw none, only fear they were in the presence of a madman. He took a new tack.

"I can see you don't believe my story. Based on what you have told me, I would not believe it either. But here we sit on a hill. You can see that Pomarat below is a madman?" he looked for agreement. They glanced at each other and nodded agreement. "The three of us cannot change what has happened. If you had killed or captured me and returned to your tribe you would be slaves to Pomarat as your fellow braves are now. You spoke of a council, are there other Itchiwan tribes?"

Krat started to say yes, but Fasman cut him off and said "No!"

Hysko realized he was getting nowhere. He had two choices. Kill these fools and try to find the other tribes himself or continue trying to convince them of his story. He chose the latter. "There is nothing the three of us can do here. And I can see you are not willing to give up your secrets of other Itchiwan tribes. So I will bring you back to the hole of which I speak and you can see for yourself if it's magic. Maybe then, you will help me assemble a force to take back your tribe."

Hysko brought them back to their weapons. He took the arrows from their quivers and put them in his. Then he examined the metal of their knives. It was like nothing he had seen. "Where did you get these?"

"Trade with the whites."

'Whites', Hysko thought to himself. 'Two of the boys had been whites. With tools like these no wonder they took joy in playing with us.'

Hysko put them in his waist band and tossed the empty quivers and bows to them.

"What do we do with these?" asked Fasman.

"Carry them. I have enough to carry. You will get the rest back when I am convinced I have your trust. We will go south to the hole but do not run faster than I do because you are fast but my arrows are even faster." Fasman and Krat looked at each other in agreement to submit.

143

IT BECAME SARAH'S TIME sooner than he ever imagined. If she had been born in his time, she would have been a rocket scientist. She adapted to her surroundings that fast. Vern was amazed, in only months she was a master of the TV, the oven, the refrigerator, the washer and the dryer. Through the TV, her learning was accelerated. She watched it most of her waking hours since the other machines eased what would be her daily toils. Her language changed also to the point where one day while Vern was fishing at the pond on their property, she called to him and asked, "Hey Vern, when we going somewhere?"

Vern thought 'Hey Vern???' She sounded like a person of this century, no thee's and thou's. Vern knew he had to get her an ID. He knew guys in New York who could arrange that. "Where do you want to go?" he yelled totally caught off guard.

"Out. I want to see what they show on the box … no … the 'TV'. I want to go to a supermarket! Is that the correct name? I want to cook for you, instead of putting TV dinners in the oven. I feel useless here!"

Vern knew this was coming. He made the call to New York. "Jessie, I need fake IDs for an illegal alien, license and passport."

"Mexican, a housekeeper?"

"No British … girlfriend."

"Shit Vern, British? I never had to do an illegal from England. Why the fuck do you need me?"

"Because she's off the grid in England, you know what I mean Jessie?"

"No … yah … yah sure. I'll need a photo."

"I'll be there tomorrow."

"Okay."

"And Jessie? This is between you and me got it?"

"Yeah, yeah."

Vern was a good and valuable customer. His NFL player referrals were gravy! They were always looking to paper reliable household staff. Jessie's business depended on confidentiality. His keeping out of jail did also.

Vern hung up the phone and looked at Sarah, "We're going on a road trip."

Sarah's face lit up. "Where?"

"New York City."

"Home of 'The Today Show'!" one of her favorites.

Vern gave her a quizzical glance of surprise. Then he had to think about all the things she had been watching on TV. He had sat with her many times and explained how when they said 'Live' or 'The News' at Noon, Six or Eleven it was happening right now or shortly before now. He showed her how to recognize movies, by the credits rolling on the screen. He told her movies were books come to life and how they made movies with actors and costumes like stage shows in London in her time. They could be stories of the past, the present or the future. They were stories not necessarily real. Then he tried to explain soap operas, game shows and prime time TV shows, but came up short except to say they were entertainment with actors for people to escape from their daily toils.

Sarah had asked, "So they are like the games you played that made you all your money?"

Vern sat open mouthed, unable to answer at the moment. Then he thought about it. Yeah they were to another segment of the population. To beer guzzling men, he was the star, to stay at home moms and wives, Susan Lucci was a star. It took an independent viewer from the 1700's to point this out to him. All those hits and workouts! Shit! "Yeah, I never looked at it that way."

Sarah saw the pain of her words in Vern's face and asked, "What daily toils are they escaping? You have all these wonderful machines! I have no toils now. I can sit here and watch the TV all day while the machines do my work."

Vern opened his mouth to respond but had no answer. New toils had replaced the old toils but he could not explain what they were. But they were real and in terms of the human race, self imposed. "Shit Sarah, you are wise beyond your years and give a fresh perspective to my time."

Sarah had given him a sly smile and said "Judging by the news of these days it seems like the people could use that perspective."

"We should be gone two days, maybe just today. But I want you to know what you been seeing on the TV is not necessarily how it is now."

"Hopefully we will have years for you to explain it to me Vern," she crooned as she caressed his face, "and I will apply the instincts that kept me alive in my time, in your time when we venture out to New York."

So Vern and Sarah commenced their four to five hour drive to the Big Apple. Conversation was light. Sarah would see a billboard or eighteen-wheeler adorned with a popular product of the day and would either recite the by-line of their commercial or sing the jingle associated with the product. After about the fifteenth product Vern laughed and said, "Girl! Your mind is a sponge, it absorbs everything you see and hear, just don't do that around other people!"

She already knew that, but looked at Vern with sad eyes and said, "But why?" wishing to see him struggle to come up with an answer. Then she added "People may think me zany and fun to be with!"

The use of 'think me zany' caused Vern to give her a sidelong glance, "You're busting my balls right?"

Sarah let out a burst of a laugh and said "Duh????"

"'Duh???' where the fuck did you get that? You're becoming a master of slang also?"

"Where did you think I got it? TV! Don't worry I would never 'bust your balls' they bring me much enjoyment. When we are alone I want to be able to say anything and act 'zany' with no reservations. When we are with others I will only speak when spoken to. I will be a perfect lady."

Vern sat back in his seat and smiled and said, "I love you Sarah."

"I know that Vern, don't worry about me. I'll be fine."

Just then an eighteen-wheeler passed them and she belted out "JELLO PUDDING!!!!" like the funny black man with the shaking head. Since she jumped time, Sarah was able to relax for the first time in her life. No more listening for every sound out of the ordinary and being ready to escape with weapons in tow. Food and water are no longer a worry.

144

HYSKO, FASMAN AND KRAT reached the site of the hole as the sun was setting. Hysko stopped them well away from Sarah's cabin and said they will wait and watch. Sarah was way ahead of them and fled the cabin south and would wait and watch also. First the four boys from the future, then the four midget Indians, now three midgets were back. She hoped they didn't ransack her house again. Was this going to be a regular thing now? Should she end this? She only had two shots in her pistols and there were three of them. No, she would wait them out as she would all unexpected visitors.

When Hysko was satisfied that the owner of the cabin was not around, he told Fasman and Krat to follow him. He ran to the hole. It was covered. When he and his band had left for the marshes they had left it uncovered. The owner of that cabin knew something about the hole. The owner could be in the hole using its magical powers. He moved back the coverings. Fasman and Krat saw there was a hole like Hysko had told them. "Let's get this over with," said Hysko, "You go first Krat and you follow Fasman. I will go last and cover the hole."

"How do we know you're not trapping us in this hole?" asked Fasman.

Hysko shook his head in disbelief. He hissed, "I have all the weapons! Why would I drag your sorry excuse for braves all the way back to this hole to kill you?!!!. If I wanted you dead I would have done so back at the marsh. I NEED THE SUPPORT OF THE OTHER TRIBES TO STOP POMARAT! You asked for proof of the hole! Here it is! Go down the tunnel. There will be a light at the bottom and noise. When you get to the bottom, stay there. I will follow and show you what I said is true. Then we will leave the hole and you will bring me to the other camps, knowing I speak the truth."

Hysko's words could not be argued. Fasman looked at Krat and indicated he should go in the hole. Krat looked at Fasman trying to convey his fear of doing so. Fasman, frustrated, all but stuffed Krat in the hole. Krat went in and Fasman followed. Hysko as promised was right behind taking time to pull back the reeds. Why he did, he did not know since these two idiots, once seeing the orb, would be clamoring to get out.

Krat was first to the bottom. He took one look at the glowing rotating orb with the steady hum and tried to climb through Fasman's ass to get out of the hole. Fasman gave him a kick sending him back to the path surrounding the orb where Fasman quickly joined him. Hysko heard Fasman's curse at Krat and joined them. "This is the magic of which I told you! Now do you believe me?!"

Krat nodded 'Yes' wishing to be out as soon as possible. However, Fasman was still looking around. Hysko could see he was not yet a believer. "See the path going around the orb, Fasman?"

"Yes", answered Fasman. "I see no other holes."

"Follow the path, you will return here," said Hysko pointing to the left where Krat was standing. "See if there are any holes."

Fasman hesitated. Hysko was tiring of these clowns. Pomarat was gaining more domination every hour and more Itchiwan were probably dying or worse. He raised his bow and aimed at Fasman's head, "Run! And now I give you permission to use your speed!"

Fasman took off in a full sprint on the path seconds later he was back with Krat and Hysko. "Are there any other holes?"

"No," answered Fasman catching his breath bent over with hands on his knees. He never ran this fast in his life. He never had a deep seated fear chasing him.

"Good! That is what I told you in my story. So that much is true?"

Fasman was busy catching his breath, and nodded in agreement with eyes down. Meanwhile, Hysko grabbed Krat who was focused on Fasman and threw Krat through the membrane into the orb. Krat let out an "EEEE" before he was gone. Fasman rose up to protest but Hysko was already on him and threw him in the orb. Then Hysko pulled the arrow from his quiver which was tied to a long length of twine tied to his thong. He shot the arrow into their hole and marked the hole with a cross slash with his knife. Then he stepped into the membrane.

Krat and Fasman were dumbfounded. They stood in the center of the orb, which had grown ten, no twenty fold of what they had seen from the outside. And there were holes everywhere as Hysko had told in his story. Fasman could not comprehend this as he had just run around the orb and there were no holes. He sat down in the center of the orb and cried. It was too much for his brain. Krat was scared by what he saw and the reaction of Fasman who had been his mentor. Hysko walked up to Fasman and laid his hand on Fasman's shoulder and said gently, "Do you need more proof? We can find the hole that leads to my time. Then you can also meet the legend, Maushop, though he may think you killed his sons. Would you like to see Maushop to believe?"

"NO! GET US OUT OF HERE! WE BELIEVE YOU!" screamed Fasman.

"Gladly!" answered Hysko. "So which hole should we take to get back?" Just then the holes shifted as if on cue. Krat and Fasman had no clue. The holes had moved. Where had they entered? Hysko showed them the twine tied to his thong. "You never enter the orb without knowing how you are going to get out. But first I must show you something. It's too risky to go back to my time but I will show you the holes that were blocked."

"Not necessary! We believe you! Get us out of here. We will take you to the other tribes and verify your story!" The holes shifted again.

"Look down there!" commanded Hysko. "There are the holes with strange markings! Krat! Tie this twine to your loin cloth. You will go check one and see that it is blocked."

"NOOOO!"

Hysko put the twine in his hand, stood face to face close to Krat. "This is not a request!" he hissed. "DO IT! You'll be fine," he assured him now softly. Krat tied the twine. Krat looked to Fasman then to Hysko and wanted to protest.

"GO!!!! WE ARE WASTING TIME!"

Krat went to the edge of the orb and carefully reached out.

Hysko came up on him and threw him through saying "Hold the twine. And we can see you!"

He turned to Fasman, "We'd be here forever if I didn't do that."

He turned back to see Krat's progress and realized he could not see him, only the thousands of holes. The times he exited the orb he had failed to notice this. They had all exited together, usually in haste. Krat had exited the orb but could see Hysko looking at Fasman, but could not see Fasman. There was one hole now with strange markings as Hysko had said. He looked up, down and all around … only one hole. He scrambled up the hole wishing to be free of this evil thing. But the hole was blocked by a hard substance. He dug franticly with his fists but the blockage was not dirt but a hard substance. He scrambled back down to the path surrounding the orb. Now he could barely see Hysko in the orb. He looked left and right on the path, no other holes. Should he run the path or go back in the orb. Hysko though a dim visage was looking in his direction. He'll shoot me if I don't come back he thought. With that he grimaced closing his eyes, and plunged head long into the orb falling to the earthen floor. Looking up he saw Hysko, and FASMAN! He was still here!

Hysko, relieved, asked "What did you see?"

"The hole was blocked with a hard substance as you said it would be. I could not see you Fasman."

"We couldn't see you …" started Fasman but Hysko cut him off.

"I could see you," lied Hysko, "I was closer to the wall. Now we can leave. Bring me to the other tribes."

Fasman and Krat happily obliged wishing to be free of this evil orb. Hysko indicated they should follow the twine tied to his loin cloth. He was right behind them.

145

THEY PULLED UP A block from Jessie's place in Brooklyn. Before entering Vern said, "I'll do the talking."

"Of course Master," answered Sarah doing her best 'Jeanie' imitation with a giggle and a blink like Barbara Eden.

Damn, I have no control of this anymore, thought Vern. Fuck it he thought, play it by ear. Vern approached the clerk at the desk. "Hi, what can I do for you? You've chosen the best prices in town," said the clerk by rote.

"Ya, tell Jessie Vern is here."

"And what should I say is your business?" he asked as trained.

"Fuck, JESSIE YOU BACK THERE? IT'S ME VERN!"

Jessie came out from the back with a big smile. "Good job Jose, Vern here is family. He's okay."

Jose smiled and eyed Sarah, nice … he thought!

"Good to see you man, come back to my office," said Jessie giving Vern a hug and leading them to the back of the house.

"Fantastic, your clerk doesn't have a clue who I am?"

"You're a dinosaur man, kids these days don't follow sports. They spend all day on the computer. You know they can get their porn there. It takes hours to download but it's better than waiting for next month's Penthouse."

"What is 'porn', Vern?"

Vern gave her a glance like 'I told you not to speak.'

This didn't go unnoticed by Jessie.

"You got an English rose there! Vern you devil you!"

"Cut the shit Jessie, I got to get her papered."

Sarah heard this and realized despite all her TV learning she didn't know what getting papered meant. Her confidence in her mastery of modern times waned and decided she should be seen and not heard in the company of strangers.

"Okay! Okay! Come on. Let me weave my magic." Jessie sat down at the desk in his office. "You got a picture?"

"Yeah, here's a head shot." Vern gave him a Polaroid of Sarah.

Sarah thought where did he get that? But kept her mouth shut. Jessie looked at the photo, "This will do. Name?"

"Sarah Otis," said Vern without hesitation.

Jessie looked up from his screen, "Sister, cousin?"

"No, wife."

Jessie pushed back from the desk, "Really????"

"Yeah, really!"

"Shit man! You're famous and on the air! This is dangerous man. You're a celebrity man! You fuck up once or get in the limelight again they'll be all in your backgrounds. Then I'm fucked."

Sarah was lost in this conversation, it was like hearing Chinese. But she recognized the tension. Her decision to shut up was a good one.

"Chill Jessie, I'm not going back to on air. Amos got me set up financially. In a year I'll be a 'who was he'. Just do it and don't worry, I am disappearing."

Jessie considered this, hesitated and said, "I don't know man."

"How much?" said Vern realizing where this was going.

"At least triple the regular ..." started Jessie feeling him out expecting double.

"Asshole!" said Vern.

"Okay double."

"Screw it, I'll give you triple but do your best work."

"You doing Mass or another state?"

The deal was sealed. Vern said Mass. "Social Security on the Passport only, use state numbers on the license."

"Mass ay? Glad you're keeping out of NYC!" said Jessie as he went to work. Twenty minutes later he handed Vernon a license and passport. "Here, I guess this means you won't be sending me more NFL's looking to legalize their housekeeping staffs."

Vern looked over the documents and was satisfied. "Thanks Jessie, there'll be some that keep looking me up and I'll send them your way, but you got to be cultivating some new talent. Like you said, I'm a dinosaur, even if I was still broadcasting. I'm losing my connection to the players."

"Yeah man, I know. I got to sell again, part of the business. Take care of yourself. You know where to find me."

Vern gave him a hug and handed him the payment, "We'll talk again."

"Yeah, nice meeting you Mrs. Otis" he said to Sarah.

Sarah smiled and gave a nod.

When Vern and Sarah were in the car, Sarah felt it was okay to speak. "So do those papers make me your wife in this time?

"Yes they do."

"Why didn't he want to make them?"

"Because I was on TV, and if I went back on TV, he was afraid people would be wondering who this beautiful woman was that I married. And then they'd start snooping into your background and where you came from and how we met."

"Oh … so you're not going to back on TV?"

"Nope, I'm done."

"And you don't mind?"

"Nope I found what I've been dreaming of since 1968."

"You're so sweet," placing her hand on his lap and laying her head on the headrest. "This place does not look like the New York City on television."

"That's over there. See the tall buildings in the distance? That's Manhattan, one of the five boroughs of New York City. We're in Brooklyn, one of the other boroughs. What the hell, we'll drive through Manhattan and get a bite to eat at a restaurant."

"REALLY?!!! Can we go to McDonalds?" asked Sarah bouncing up in her seat.

"Better, I know this place in town."

Sarah was so excited! They drove over the Brooklyn Bridge into Mid-Town. "I've seen this bridge in movies!"

"Yes you have."

They drove to Rockefeller Center and Vern pointed out that it was the place where the "Today Show" is filmed.

"Can we stop?!!!!"

"No … it's the place I sometimes worked also. A lot of shows are shot here. I might run into someone I know. They'll ask who you are."

Sarah was disappointed but accepted this as Vern drove on to an Italian restaurant that he had frequented in the Bronx. "Sarah, you're going to look at TV dinners in a whole different light after you experience the food here," trying to cheer her up.

It was twilight time in the Bronx! He drove up to the storefront with no spaces available and beeped once and waited. The valet came running out opening Sarah's door. She looked at Vern confused. "Get out and wait on the sidewalk," he said calmly as he opened his door and got out as the valet came around to his side.

"Mr. Otis, good to see you again!" said Michael, the youngest son of the owner of the restaurant.

"Good to see you Mike. How's the family?"

"All good, Mr. Otis. Dad's doing the cooking tonight."

"Fantastic! And Mike, you can call me Vern."

"Sorry Mr. Otis, dad wouldn't allow it," he said with a wink and hopped into the car.

Vern joined Sarah on the sidewalk and escorted her into the restaurant. "You're known here?"

"I'm known most everywhere. It's a byproduct of being on TV. Sometimes it's a negative, sometimes a positive."

"Is it a positive here?"

"Oh yeah, my brother Amos made the old man here a ton of money. We're among friends."

They were greeted at the door by Sam Giancarlo's wife, Vicki. She gave Vern a big smooch on the cheek, "Vernon! Where have you been? You don't like our food no more?"

"Are you kidding I love your food! I've been busy in Boston. Now I'm back Mrs. Giancarlo!"

"Vernon! It's Vicki! How many times do I have to tell you this? You're always so polite! Your mother raised her boys right." She gave him a big hug and another kiss on the cheek. She had to be on tip toes to do so. "And who is this beautiful lady?" she asked smiling at Sarah as Sarah smiled nervously back.

"This is Sarah. She is my wife."

Vicki clapped her hands together and raised them to her lips. "Oh my God! I didn't see anything in the papers."

"Yeah and you probably won't for a while, we're coming back from our honeymoon and going back home. I promised her the finest food in New York and here I am."

Vicki looked to Vern and then to Sarah. She wrapped her arms around Sarah and said, "Welcome to the family!" Neither Vern nor Sarah understood this but smiled and hugged anyway.

"I got just the table for you two!" she led them to a private room with a view of the city on the second floor usually reserved for Mafia Dons. Unknown to Vern, they also had another room with a better view if there was a last minute call. "Vincent! Come with me and take their drink order," she said as they were passing through the main dining room which was half full due to the early hour.

"Maria! Handle table six for me. Mama-san calls. Here's their order," he said as he passed the slip to Maria who was exiting the kitchen after a smoke in the alley. Maria rolled her eyes. Vincent always got the V.I.P.'s. She glanced their way as they were going up the back stairs and thought 'That's that sports guy on TV, what's his name? I wonder who the lucky broad is.'

Vicki pulled out a chair for the lady at the only preset table in the room with a long view of part of the Manhattan skyline in the distance. Vern pulled out his own chair and sat. "Enjoy yourselves! Sam will be up to take your order after you've had a chance to enjoy your drinks. She gave Vern's shoulders a squeeze before taking Sarah's hand and saying "Nice meeting you Sarah, you'll always be welcome at our place."

Sarah smiled and as if on cue, Vincent entered the room with drink menus as Vicki headed for the stairs whispering "Sarah, new wife" as she passed.

"Mr. & Mrs. Otis, welcome! My name is Vincent," he said as he reached the table. "Let me offer you our selection of drinks," as he offered them both wine and cocktail menus.

Vern raised his hand, "Bring us a bottle of Merlot and a Peroni."

"Very good sir." Vincent left leaving Sarah and Vern alone.

Vern spoke. "So now you're out in public with me at a restaurant. What do you think?"

Sarah reflected on everything that had happened since they left the place in Maine. Her smile was one of wonder and joy. She took Vern's hand in both of hers, "Before we were married, my life was one of constant toil and fear of what may venture upon my cabin. Little did I know that the little boy with the bulging undergarments would come back years later and keep his promise as an older version of him and remove me of all those fears. Amos's looks and stories told me that I vanished mysteriously. Here I am, vanished from my time but living like a queen in your time. I think I am very happy you had that bulge in your undergarments. I love your world and you!" She kissed him deep. They didn't notice Vincent had returned until he cleared his throat.

They broke the lip lock and smiled as Vincent proceeded to pour the Peroni in a beer glass and put it in front of Vernon. Then he uncorked the Merlot and poured a glass for Sarah. "Will there be anything else? Sam will be up to take your order personally!"

"Yeah, Vincent? Sarah is having the beer. I was having the Merlot."

Vincent's face flushed. "So sorry …" Vincent was scrambling ready to shift the drinks.

Vern raised his hand, "I'm just bustin'm Vincent, I'm having the beer."

Vincent smiled and said "Very good sir" while thinking 'Asshole!' "Is there anything else I can get you?"

"No, we're all set. Thanks Vincent." Vincent went down to inform Sam their drinks were served.

Sarah asked, "Why did you do that to that nice young man?"

"He's the best waiter Sam's got, but he's getting cocky because he knows it. So I had to play with him. It happened to me all the time when I was playing football. I'd have a great string of runs and the older veterans would put me in my place. It helped me throughout my career and kept my head from getting so full of myself and forgetting the basics. It kept me on track to do my job better. Don't worry he'll love me when he sees the tip."

"The tip of what?"

Vern almost spit out the beer he had sipped. Luckily, Sam had appeared at their table before he had to explain tipping. Evidently the subject hadn't been covered yet on TV University.

"VERN OTIS! WHERE THE HELL HAVE YOU BEEN?" bellowed Sam.

Vern got out of his seat and embraced Sam in his kitchen attire. "Not in New York, Sam. Things have changed."

"I heard! My wife tells me this is your new bride, Sarah!" He turned to Sarah "Bellissimo!"

"Sam says you're lovely."

Sarah blushed and went to shake his hand and say thank you, but Sam had her in a bear hug of short duration and said, "Sit! Sit! He pulled up a chair from an adjoining table and joined them. "It's been a while Vern. Your brother was here a few weeks ago with your Irish friend. Your brother, he's the best, made me a lot of money. So serious though. When's he gonna settle down and get married?"

"Don't know Sam. He is serious about his work but he told me he's getting out of the business so maybe he'll be loosening up. So he was here with Colin?"

"Colin? I can't remember. I'm getting old Vern. It was the red head kid you came here with a few years ago. So what can I cook for you tonight? Young lady what do you desire? Beef, chicken, veal, shellfish?"

"Do you have lobster?" asked Sarah innocently remembering all the Red Lobster commercials she had seen.

"Consider it done. And you Vern?"

"You know, Sam, the shrimp scampi."

"For Christ sake Vern, when you going to try something else on the menu?"

"Sorry Sam, to me that dish is heaven, and I don't get back here often and this is what brings me back.

"Spoken like a poet! It shall be done! If I don't see you before you leave, give my best to your brother. And Sarah, you will have the best lobster dish you ever had," he took Sarah's hand and kissed it and added "Bellissimo!"

Vern smiled and said he would and stood and gave Sam a hug. His mind was distracted by what Sam said. Then he sipped his beer. Sarah said, "What a nice man!"

"Yea, Sam's the best," said Vern absently deep in thought.

Their dinners arrived and Sarah was in heaven. "Oh my God, Vern, this is like nothing I've tasted! It is wonderful!"

When they had finished, Vincent arrived and asked if they would like some dessert while clearing the table. "Sarah?" asked Vern.

"I am stuffed! I hate to pass up sweets but I can't," she said pushing back from the table.

"Vincent, I guess we'll just take the check unless you got any 'sweets' that can survive a five hour drive."

"As a matter of fact I do, I have these wonderful Italian cookies made by Mrs. G herself if you'd like?"

"Pack me up a dozen, and bring the check."

"Very good sir."

Vincent left and returned with the cookies nicely boxed. "Mr. G. says your dinner is on the house!" he said as he placed the box on the table.

"No no tell Sam I insist!"

"Sorry Mr. Otis, I have strict instructions. Your money is no good here."

Vern tried to protest but Vincent had left when he completed his sentence as instructed.

"Shit!" said Vern.

"Why won't Sam take your money?" asked Sarah not understanding.

"I'll explain it in the car." Vern left a hundred dollar bill on the table for Vincent as they left.

Driving through the Bronx, Sarah asked, "So why won't he take your money?

"Because I brought my brother to the restaurant and he made Sam a ton of money when he was being pressured by a local wise guy for protection money. Then my brother found out whose family the wise guy worked for and met with the head of the family and said he'd take him on as a client if he had his guy leave Sam alone. The family head heard of Amos from his connections in Boston and obliged. And Amos made him a ton of money. So everyone loves Amos and me, so our money is no good here."

Sarah tried to digest all of this and sat quiet for a while not understanding. She wanted to ask 'What's a wise guy?' but instead asked, "Can't we stay here a little longer?"

"Nope, it's time to reintroduce you to my brother."

"Really?!!!" Sarah responded excited.

"Yes Really. Something's not right. Something has changed."

146

FASMAN AND KRAT AS promised, led Hysko to the tribe in the marsh by the bay nearest the hole. It was in the area where Pomarat had killed Maushop's sons. But the land had changed and was different. He was going to return their weapons but decided to wait, fearing this could still be a trap of Maushop's. They came upon sentries guarding the camp of the Southern Itchiwan. Fasman identified himself and Krat as member of Nakim's tribe on the northern spit. Then he introduced Hysko as an Itchiwan traveler who has important news for their chief. The sentry looked at the band and particularly, Hysko.

"Why is he the only one carrying weapons?"

Fasman hesitated and looked at Hysko. Hysko jumped in with no hesitation. "I'm Hysko. I asked Fasman and Krat to bring me to your tribe for help. Nakim is dead at the hands of a madman. That madman wishes me dead also. Prior to killing Nakim, he had Nakim send Fasman and Krat to bring me to their camp. Nakim had no idea this madman would kill him. Neither did Fasman and Krat. I captured them and showed them the evil of this madman. I wanted them to bring me to the other tribes, so we can stop this madman. I believe they trust me now. But I am one man. I need your tribe's help. I need to speak to your chief."

"You must surrender your weapons!" demanded the anxious sentry after hearing this tale.

"No, no!" pleaded Fasman. "What he says is true!"

With the unintentional distraction, Hysko slew footed the anxious sentry sending him to the ground on his back and in one motion had an arrow pointed at the other sentry before he had knocked an arrow in his bow. "Drop your bow!" commanded Hysko.

"Do what he says!" pleaded Fasman. "He will not hurt you!"

The other sentry dropped his bow seeing no chance to get an arrow knocked while Hysko had him in his sights. Hysko then focused on the sentry on the ground. "Get up! I will not surrender my weapons. Nor will I require you to do so. Take your bow and cover us from the rear." He handed the sentry his bow. "If I present a danger, shoot me. My back will be to you. I will not harm you or anyone in your camp.

When I am granted a meeting with your chief, I will surrender my weapons. Agreed?"

"Agreed," said the sentry, not that he had any choice. They walked to the camp, Hysko showing no signs of aggression with his back to the rear sentry. Fasman and Krat filed in beside Hysko.

They went without incident. Hysko was thinking that every hour allowed Pomarat to gain the hearts and minds of the tribe … through sheer terror! He knew Pomarat's methodology, he would seek out individuals who were of like mind in the tribe and bring them into his inner circle. He would make examples of those who showed resistance to his commands, graphic examples. And there would be many.

When they entered the camp, a brave ran to the chief's tent. He told the chief the outlying sentries had returned with strangers. The chief had been eating with his wives. He dropped his turkey leg on the plate and exited the tent. He watched as the band was approaching his tent. He recognized two of the three strangers as Nakim's braves from the north. The one in the middle, he didn't. He was armed and Nakim's men weren't. "Give me my bow!" he commanded his brave.

Hysko followed the movement of the brave in the camp and the emergence of the chief and his call for his bow. This chief was much younger and stronger than Nakim. It was time. He stopped and turned to the rear sentry. "Is that your chief?"

The sentry drew his bow in fear of the stranger, ready to shoot if he preformed any trickery. "Yes."

"What is his name?"

"Yat."

"As I promised, I surrender my weapons to you now." Hysko put down his weapons, as well as those of Fasman and Krat that he had been carrying. He turned in the direction of the chief. "YAT! I wish to talk with you about trouble with Nakim's tribe! My name is Hysko." The rear sentry didn't relax his watch on Hysko.

Yat surveyed this. "Watch him closely!" he commanded the sentries, who had been deficient in their duties. "Hysko, wait there, I will talk to you in time. You two," he said pointing to Fasman and Krat. "Come to my tent." Krat looked at Fasman and Fasman at Hysko. "COME NOW!" yelled Yat angry at being taken away from his dinner. Fasman quickly obeyed and Krat was right behind him. Yat brought them into his tent and had them sit. Yat resumed his place and finished eating, telling his wife to give them some food. They welcomed the food.

"Is there trouble with your tribe?"

Surprised that Yat knew he was of Nakim's tribe, Fasman quickly answered, "Yes, Nakim is dead! The tribe has been taken over by a madman and his band."

"Who is this Hysko?"

Krat looked at Fasman to see how he'd answered this. "Nakim's last order to us, was to capture and bring back this man. The madman had persuaded Nakim that this man had betrayed him and was responsible for the death of our sentries. The madman wanted him killed. He was a member of his band who hadn't obeyed his orders. Nakim secretly told us not to kill him but bring him back to him. He did not trust the madman."

"How is it then, he is the only one who came into my camp with weapons?" asked Yat feasting on the turkey leg.

"That is a long story ..."

Fasman told Yat of Hysko's prowess as a warrior and how he disarmed them. He told of watching Nakim's heart being devoured. He told of Hysko's story. He told that the madman's name was Pomarat, yes, the Pomarat of legend, the tale our mothers told us. Then he hesitated and told him of the evil hole which Hysko said would validate his story, that the Pomarat who had killed their chief was the Pomarat of those legends and that they came here through the hole. He told him how he and Krat traveled to the hole itself and went inside. The hole was evil, the devil's work, like nothing they'd seen. Only evil would result from using this hole. He told Yat that this experience convinced them that Hysko's story was true and as a result they brought him to his camp.

Yat had stop eating his turkey at the part where Nakim's heart was being devoured. At the end of the tale, he asked Fasman if he could show him this hole. Fasman looked at Krat who was conflicted as he. "We can lead you to the hole, but I cannot tell you how it works. Without that knowledge, you would risk being lost in another time if you attempted to use the hole."

Yat considered this. "This Hysko has this knowledge?"

"I don't know. I think his leader, Pomarat did. Hysko seemed reluctant to try any other holes than those he knew."

"Other holes?"

"Yes when you go in the hole there are thousands, maybe more holes than the stars to choose to exit. Where and when they come out is the danger."

Yat looked to one of his wives, "Go have them bring in this Hysko!"

Hysko entered the tent flanked by two guards. Yat commanded the guards. "You take Fasman and Krat out. You stay and watch Hysko. Wives, leave." The guard assigned Hysko pulled out his steel bladed knife and had it against Hysko's ribs in the area of his heart. A simple thrust would kill Hysko immediately.

"So Hysko, now you can tell me your story," ordered Yat.

Hysko sized up the situation. "I believe Fasman told you my story or else I would be dead by now."

Yat chuckled, looked down and back up in Hysko's eyes. "Yes, Fasman did tell me what he knew. What do you know about this 'hole'?"

"Not enough. It only can result in evil as it has done to Nakim and his tribe. I do know we must stop Pomarat!"

"Why?"

"Because his actions were the reason you became hunted by the Wampanoag many hundred years ago. He regularly sacrificed Wampanoag children to the crows of Maktahdou and killed Maushop's sons. After that deed, we were returning to our home in the North Marsh. We ran into four boys, strangely dressed. They led us to the hole and vanished. We gave chase into the hole and ended up here … hundreds of years later according to Fasman. Pomarat is killing members of our tribe. My descendants! His descendants! Your brethren, fellow Itchiwan! He will not stop until all Itchiwan bow to him, including you," he pointed to Yat.

Yat considered all Hysko had said and asked, "Why had you not killed this monster hundreds of years ago in your time, if he is as bad as you say?"

Hysko looked down shame apparent on his face. "We feared him. His prowess in battle far exceeded any of us. He seemed to know what we were thinking before we did. We believe he was truly in league with Maktahdou!"

"So why now do you not fear him and seek our aid? Is he no longer in Maktahdou's favor? Or is it because you betrayed him and he wants you dead?"

Hysko sighed. "I no longer fear Pomarat. I never personally witnessed him kill a fellow Itchiwan till after we came out of that evil hole. He never had to. Everyone feared him. He does want me dead. I betrayed him when I did not kill a Wampanoag infant. He was weak from fire water from the whites and I made up a tale. He no longer trusted me and left me behind on a useless task hoping I would be killed by Nakim's men. I disobeyed him again and followed him to the camp and saw the atrocities he committed. Prior to being killed and his heart devoured by Pomarat, Nakim sent Fasman and Krat to capture me and bring me to the camp ... to Pomarat! I could have killed Fasman and Krat before they ever saw my face! I do not kill fellow Itchiwan! Pomarat took over the Northern Marsh tribe with only two men. The tribe was no longer warriors. I know Pomarat's methods. By this time, he will have converted six of Nakim's men through intimidation. The longer we wait, this number will grow and those who hesitate to convert will be dead. Their wives and children will be Pomarat's slaves or be dead also."

"So do you suggest I lead my men north to wage war with this Pomarat?"

"I know not the size of your tribe. Pomarat and two braves took over a tribe. Now he is training and making converts. The rest will fight out of fear though their hearts won't be in it. The spit is narrow and I thought it was a bad place for the tribe to defend with no escape. But Fasman told me that was not so. They had many canoes as a means to escape by the ocean and the bay. He said there are other Itchiwan tribes along the Northern shores and several here in the south. If you attack, Pomarat will take his converts and move on to infect another tribe and kill their chief. When was the last time an Itchiwan tribe waged war?"

"We are not a warring people. Since your time we have been a people in hiding, fearing retribution from the Wampanoag. Over time we have been able to establish a peaceful coexistence with them."

"If Pomarat succeeds, that will end! It has already started! Since coming out of the hole, his actions have caused the death of a white trader and a Wampanoag man and wife. It won't be long 'till their tribes realize they are dead. And if it happens in the near future they will be able to see the tracks are Itchiwan. Hopefully, there will soon be a heavy rain. But if Pomarat is allowed to continue, there will be more. He is not one to accept life as a trader. He is a taker!"

"So what do you want Hysko?" asked Yat.

"I want you to call a meeting of the southern tribes. With them we form a plan. May I move without your man's knife in my ribs?"

Yat indicate the guard should back off the knife a bit but be alert.

Hysko leaned over and started drawing on the dirt floor. He drew the spit and four X's one to the west, one to the east, one to the south at the entrance to the spit, and one across the bay to south of the tip of the spit. "Fasman told me the way the tribes communicate is with bonfires to the northern tribes and runners to the southern tribes. If you can unite the southern tribes, we can march north and divide to assume these four positions around the spit. Then we light a bonfire at the X at the west calling for a meeting at Nakim's tribe."

"But Pomarat will see this!"

"Yes but it is the only way we can warn the northern tribes. Pomarat will have to ask what the bonfire means. His converts will tell him he has called a meeting of the northern tribes. He will be furious. He won't be ready for dealing with other tribes. He will have to send converts off the spit to see who lit it thus reducing his guard. He may even send Sarkem or Massot but I doubt it because he will be weighing in his mind 'Who did this?' Was it a runner from the tribe … or me? Fasman and Krat did not return. So he probably assumes I killed them and am still out there. This uncertainty will be his downfall!"

"But the tribes will head to the spit without knowledge of all this. Tell me about these other marks."

"We must have a chief from the southern tribes at each of these marks. If there are more than four southern tribes, we have more at the west mark to defend the bonfire. At the west mark, they are to intercept the men Pomarat sends to find out who lit the fire. Also they will intercept the chiefs coming from the west and direct them to the entrance to the spit where you and I will be. The chief at the east will send the chiefs coming from east to the same. The chief by the bay in the south will recruit men from the east tribe to fortify their position. You call a meeting for the northern tribes and explain what has happened. If you get a consensus, you march up the spit to the camp. I will join the group guarding the bay, because I believe that is the escape route he will take once he realizes his situation is hopeless. The east and west groups will monitor the shoreline in case he chooses the ocean route. The objective is to minimize losses to Nakim's tribe."

"There are only three southern tribes including mine and three northern tribes including Nakim's."

Hysko, considered this and said, "One tribe covers the point to the east, one tribe the bay. Your tribe must cover the entrance to the spit and the bonfire in the west. Send three men from each of the southern tribes to meet the tribe coming from the west and have them tell that tribe to go to the entrance of the spit to you.

"If he does choose the bay route as an escape, will you be able to kill him?"

"I will try. It will be him or me."

"And if you fail?"

"We will have made known his atrocities to all the tribes of the Itchiwan nation and they will be more vigilant with their sentries!"

147

In the weeks that had passed since the spectacle of devouring Nakim's heart, Pomarat had converted ten of Nakim's braves and had brutally killed seventeen others for various seemingly irrational and random reasons. Of these seventeen, twelve of their families were brutally killed … women and children, their bodies put on display in the camp until their rotting corpses' odor became offensive to Pomarat senses. He then had them cut down and burned. The other five families became slaves, two families each for Massot and Sarkem and one for his first convert. Pomarat took no slaves. No matter how docile they seemed, they could not be trusted. In his mind he had Massot, Sarkem and his converts to serve the role of slaves. When he needed a woman, he'd take one of Massot's or Sarkem's slaves for the night and send them back the next morning. Within the next week Pomarat estimated the ratio of converts to non converts would shift dramatically in his favor.

But the week would be cut short by a bonfire to the west.

Massot was first alerted by the one of the converts. He went to Pomarat's tent. He could hear Pomarat grunting as he enjoyed one of Sarkem's slaves. The slave just looked sideways waiting for it to be over, silently praying she would not get pregnant and give birth to another demon. Massot waited for sounds indicating he was finished.

He gazed at the bonfire and looked left and right up the shore. Slowly, more fires appeared up and down the coastlines. Massot was conflicted. Something was happening! Should he disturb Pomarat, or can it wait? Should he go rouse Sarkem? No! He decided he should interrupt. He pulled back the flap of the tent as Pomarat's let out a whoop of completion.

"Chief!"

Pomarat while collapsing in bliss on Sarkem's slave was rudely interrupted by Massot's voice! "WHAT, MASSOT!"

"Sorry, something is happening! There are bonfires all along the coast! The first is to the west of our camp!"

Pomarat didn't bother to put on his codpiece. Naked he ordered Sarkem's slave to return home and send Sarkem here. "Get Pasmat!" Pasmat was the first convert. Massot obeyed.

"What does that bonfire mean, Pasmat?" yelled Pomarat as he put on his cod piece and pointed to the closest fire. Pasmat had been aroused from his sleep by Massot after having enjoyed his slave after supper. His slave was wide awake cleaning up and thinking about how her life had changed for her and her little ones. Her husband was gone and her only thoughts were to protect her babies, no matter what that meant. Pasmat was an opportunist, not married, for good reason. He was ugly. Massot had dragged him from the tent groggy making sure to show him the bonfires up and down the coastline before bringing him to Pomarat.

"It means we have summoned the northern tribes to counsel," he replied to Pomarat's interrogation.

"Who are WE??? Counsel for what!?"

"I don't know but the fire is closest to our tribe, so they will think we called the meeting."

"Who lit that fire?!!!"

"I don't know!"

"Where is Sarkem?!!!"

"I will make sure he is coming," said Massot not trusting the slave to relay the message. Yet she had for fear of death, and Sarkem arrived just as Massot was about to leave.

Pomarat brushed by them and surveyed the shoreline. His first guess was someone from the tribe. But his heart told him Hysko was behind this since Nakim's runners had not returned. Based on his experience with this tribe over the last couple of weeks, Nakim would have to had sent twenty braves to take Hysko. Sarkem, Massot and Pasmat milled around confused. "Pasmat! Go summon the nine other members of my circle."

When Pasmat left Massot asked if he should go and investigate who lit the nearest fire. Pomarat again surveyed the bonfires. "No, we have been betrayed. It could be a member of the tribe, but more than likely it was Hysko."

"Hysko?!"

"Yes Nakim's runners never returned. Either Hysko killed them or they have joined him."

Massot and Sarkem looked at each other. They knew Hysko and Pomarat had become tense with each other but had no idea why and they had no desire to ask. Pomarat was boiling inside. He knew he had not yet converted enough of the tribe to put up any defense of the spit and those he had converted had not yet gained his trust.

"When Pasmat returns with the converts, pick out the two of most recent converts and tell them to determine who lit the fire. Once they leave, tell Pasmat he is being entrusted by me to guard the tribe from the ocean and the bay and not to awaken the tribe until we tell them. The three of us will then follow the two converts to the end of the spit."

"Shouldn't one of us stay with Pasmat to organize and control the tribe?"

"No, it's time to go. The northern tribes are coming. I know not their size. Someone in the tribe will tell them what we have done and I will not have the opportunity to explain. Or Hysko has already alerted them of what we have done. But the Northern tribes won't arrive until tomorrow. We will get off this spit while we can."

Pasmat's ego was inflated by Pomarat's orders. He was rising fast in the tribe. The two converts had left on a run down the spit to investigate the fire. Pomarat, Massot and Sarkem followed after gathering the possessions they did not wish to leave behind. They were not the runners that Nakim's men were, but there was no need to be close as they were leaving and not going to the fire. Since Pasmat was not to awaken the tribe until Pomarat sent word to do so, he took the opportunity to order the remaining seven converts to go to the bay and the ocean and stand watch and ready the canoes. Pasmat decided to enjoy his slave again while awaiting orders. His slave was exhausted from her toils and just rolled over while Pasmat made passionate thrusts on her leg not realizing with his limited experience with women that she was asleep. Pasmat enjoyed the encounter nevertheless and then rolled over proud of his dominance.

When Pomarat and his band got to the beginning of the spit they saw camp fires everywhere! There was already a formidable force in place blocking their exit. They took cover and Pomarat asked Sarkem and Massot if they see the converts in the camp. Massot moved forward. The converts were sitting around a fire with members of the camp and laughing and eating. Massot relayed this information to Pomarat and asked if they should leave. "No, bring me to where we can see them and we will watch for awhile."

As Pomarat expected, soon Hysko and Fasman joined the converts and engaged them in a lengthy conversation. There was another Itchiwan standing off to the side observing Hysko's conversations. That told him he was the chief of this encampment. If what Nakim had told him was true, soon there would be many more warriors joining them tomorrow. Pomarat signaled Massot and Sarkem back. When they were out of earshot of the camp, he signaled them to stop. "Are we leaving?" asked Massot confused as to why they stopped.

"No, I did not want them to hear our voices. We are going back to where we were," whispered Pomarat. Sarkem and Massot looked confused. They were vastly outnumbered. "Remember the brave to the left, standing and listening? He is the chief of this tribe. The brave with Hysko is one of Nakim's runners that were sent after him. When we go back, we each shoot one arrow on my signal. Then we all flee back to camp. When we get to here we spilt. Sarkem you run the path along the ocean. Massot you run the crest of the dune. I'll run along the bay.

Monitor the lights while you run, tell me what you see when we get back to the camp. If you encounter anyone from our camp on the way back, kill them as Pasmat will have betrayed us. With our one arrow, I will kill the chief. Massot you will kill the brave who came with Hysko. Sarkem will kill the convert talking to Hysko. Understand?"

"I can kill both the brave and Hysko if I fire two shots! I am fast!" said Massot.

"No! Do as you're told! One arrow! Then run! I don't want Hysko dead – yet! Hysko is responsible for all the tribes coming here now! Nakim's runner is the one who convinced this chief of Hysko's story. Kill the convert talking to Hysko, I want to send a message to the other convert. I hope he flees but I can't be sure. But he will be looking over his shoulder in everything he does. I will mortally wound the chief. If he doesn't die and Hysko lives, he will doubt his decision to believe Hysko's story and wonder if this was all a trap. If he dies then Hysko will have explaining to do to the other tribes when they arrive without an advocate from Nakim's tribe. This buys us time and casts doubt on whatever Hysko has been saying."

Sarkem chewed on all this in his mind and realized he could not be chief of any tribe. He had not the calculating mind to do so. He decided then and there he would enjoy his status as Pomarat's trusted brave and accept his position no matter what he saw. He now knew there was always a reason for Pomarat's heinous actions. Poor Hysko, he shouldn't have crossed Pomarat. They went back to the spot, beyond the glow of the fire. They each fired their one arrow on Pomarat's signal and began their retreat. The chief fell, Fasman had bent over to stoke the fire and the arrow ripped through his shoulder. The convert rose with an arrow in his throat making a gurgling sound. Hysko jumped up and fired his arrows wildly in the darkness. Massot screamed as one of those arrows grazed his skull. Blood ran down his face but he kept running. The three of them ran down the spit as planned. Hysko went to Yat and saw to his wound. The arrow went right through his body probably through his lung. If it was his heart, he'd be dead.

Hysko took off his codpiece and placed it under Yat's back where the arrow exited. Hopefully it would stop the bleeding at that end. "GIVE ME SOMETHING TO COVER HIS WOUND!" screamed Hysko. "FASMAN!"

Fasman was in shock that he had an arrow in his shoulder. He sat on the ground staring at the blood flowing from the wound. Yat's men never having battled before were confused and didn't know what to do.

"I NEED YOUR CODPIECES!" hissed Hysko compressing the wound with his bare hand hoping the pressure was accomplishing the same effect on the exit wound. Two of Yat's braves removed theirs and gave them to Hysko. Two others still had their bows on Hysko, not sure what to do. He applied the codpieces not worrying about the confused braves. "FASMAN!" He looked in the direction of where Fasman was when the attack began while maintaining pressure on the wound. He saw his condition. He looked up at the brave aiming their arrows at him. He said to one of the braves who had given their codpieces, "Come here! Keep pressure on the wound."

Then to the others with arrows pointed, "My bow is on the ground over there. I need your codpieces now! Give them to me!"

Reluctantly, after looking at each other, one removed his codpiece and tossed it to Hysko while the other kept an arrow on him. Then they reversed rolls. Hysko asked the other brave who had initially gave up his codpiece to come with him. He went to Fasman who was still watching his blood flow from his wound. Hysko knelt in front of Fasman, "FASMAN! FASMAN!" Fasman removed his eyes from the wound and looked to the voice. "Fasman you will be okay!" He gave the codpieces to the brave who followed and whispered. "I am going to pull out the arrow. I need you to hold the codpieces on the wound when I do and keep them tight on the wound. He will scream. But don't stop pressing. He will probably pass out, but he won't be dead. Neither will your chief if I can get back and tend to his wounds." The brave nodded, codpieces at ready.

Hysko turned his attention back to Fasman who was getting groggy. "Fasman," Fasman met his eyes. Hysko nodded to the brave. "This is ..." he quickly pulled the arrow from his shoulder and the brave compressed the wound. Fasman screamed in pain and did not hear, "... going to hurt."

Hysko stood up and said, "Hold it on the wound and try to stop the bleeding. I am going back to the Yat."

Hysko surveyed the area, one of Pomarat's converts was dead, and the other was nowhere to be found. He either fled or was somewhere out there killed by Pomarat. He couldn't worry about that now. Pomarat, Massot and Sarkem were gone or else they'd all be dead. He wounded one of them. Based on the screams he guessed it was Massot. By now Yat's men from the other camps spanning the entrance to the spit were coming to this camp as a result of the screams. Hysko knelt by Yat. His breathing was hard. The brave had slowed the bleeding. His eyes were open. Seeing Hysko's face he struggled to ask "Why aren't you dead or wounded?"

"My guess is Pomarat wished to discredit me to you and your tribe. There are three of them. They shot and ran. Their targets were you, Fasman and the convert who was talking to us. The convert is dead. The other convert fled. Fasman is wounded, if he had not bent over at the time of the attack, he would be dead. If I had not quickly attended to your wounds, you would be dead. You still may not survive. The arrow passed close to your heart. He knows the northern tribes are coming and knows he has no chance against all the tribes together. He has no knowledge of the southern tribes that are here now except what he saw. When he gets back to his camp at the end of the spit he will bleed the knowledge of all the tribes from Nakim's people. Tonight he tried to remove all credibility to my story. If Fasman died, and you died, the Northern tribes would know not why they were summonsed. Your tribe would hold me responsible for the ambush. But if I was responsible, the four men who accompanied you to this meeting would be dead!"

The brave compressing the wound looked up at him as he was one of the four. "Why do you say that?"

"I'll show you." Hysko went and picked up his bow. The two braves covering him with bows, tensed. "See those four pines? I will hit all four before you two can hit the first. NOW!" Hysko launched four arrows in rapid fashion which all hit their targets. One of the braves shot wide and the other's arrow fell to the ground as he fumbled to get off a shot. Hysko had a knife to their throats before they could reach for another arrow. "That is why!" said Hysko as he sheathed his knife, dropped his bow and returned to Yat. Yat wanted to sleep and had not seen what had transpired.

"What happened?" he asked.

The brave who was compressing his wound told him, "If Hysko

wanted us dead, we would all be dead. He has more skills than us."

Yat grabbed the brave's arm that was compressing the wound. "Tell the tribe to listen to Hysko! Tell the other tribes to listen if I don't awake." Yat drifted into sleep. The brave looked to Hysko. Other tribe members were now arriving at the camp.

Hysko looked at Yat. He said to the brave "We must get him back to the camp but we need more skins on the wounds. Command your tribe, your chief needs you! What is your name?"

"Tam."

"Does your tribe trust you?"

Tam looked quizzically at Hysko. "I … think so."

"I hope so. While your chief rests, he has given you command of the tribe and this is no time to fail him."

148

POMARAT AND SARKEM REACHED the camp first.

"What did you see on your travel?" asked Pomarat.

"There are fires on the beach in the east across the entrance to the bay. And three converts standing guard."

"There are also fires across the bay and four converts there," responded Pomarat, "Where is Massot?" Sarkem had no answer. Pomarat looked to the dune in the middle of the spit. He scanned the slope in the light of the three quarters moon and saw a body fall and then slowly rise.

"Go Sarkem!"

Sarkem ran to Massot's aid and helped him back. "What happened?" he asked.

"Hysko! He fired wildly after we attacked. One of his arrows hit me. I am losing strength." Sarkem took his arm and wrapped it over his shoulder.

"Is he chasing you?"

"No, he's went to the man Pomarat said was the chief."

Sarkem relayed this to Pomarat.

"We leave soon before sunrise while it's still dark. Bring Massot to your tent and tend to his wound and feed him. Make him ready to travel. I will get

Pasmat and call back the converts. We're getting off this spit. It is a death trap!"

149

TAM WAS A SIMPLE man with common sense like his chief. He told the men coming from the camp to bring Yat back and have his wounds seen to. It was obvious the men respected Tam. As Tam and Hysko followed them back to the camp, Hysko quickly relayed the story that had been told to Yat by he and Fasman. Tam hardly looked up digesting all Hysko's words. When the story ended he looked at Hysko, "What do you suggest we do?"

"The plan I laid out to Yat. Pomarat has now seen the size of the tribes that await him and probably knows from the converts in Nakim's tribe that when the northern tribes arrive your numbers will be doubled. Pomarat has realized he has no chance to defend the spit. He will flee it tonight with those he thinks he can trust … to a point. There were four of us when we came to this time. I am here. I believe I wounded Massot when they attacked us. How bad he is wounded I don't know. I fired wildly into the dark. But I know his scream. That leaves Sarkem as his only true ally. Any converts he brings with him are expendable in his eyes except as bearers for Massot if he can't travel."

"I will have men guard the exit to the spit."

Hysko shook his head slowly from side to side. "He won't come back this way. Your tribe is on alert. He will leave by the ocean or the bay. He knows you couldn't have gotten words to the tribes guarding there yet. They will be the most vulnerable. I know he will take the bay. Pomarat has never ventured on the great water. None of us have in our time. I need three of your best warriors and one who will be able to convey my message and gain the trust of the chief guarding the bay."

"I don't know if our best warriors can match the skill of you and Pomarat," answered Tam honestly.

"I will take Pomarat! I need three to handle Sarkem and a wounded Massot. The others can be handled by the men guarding the bay after one of yours conveys the message and gains their trust."

"I will be that one," said Tam.

"No! You must remain here and tell the northern tribes what is happening."

"My brother can do that. He is the one trailing in the party we are following. He has been listening to all you have said. He is like me and can handle it. Based on what you have said we must leave as soon as possible." Hysko noticed Tam's brother for the first time and chastised himself that he should be more vigilant of his surroundings if he was going to take on Pomarat. When they got to the camp, Tam relayed what Yat had told him. His brother then relayed what he had heard Hysko say on the way back to the camp. With no time to lose the tribe picked three braves to accompany Tam and Hysko to the encampments by the bay.

150

POMARAT WENT TO PASMAT'S tent and aroused him from his sleep. Pasmat's slave had heard his approach but pretended she was asleep. Pasmat yelped at being awakened. Pomarat cupped his hand on his mouth and whispered, "Go back to my tent now, take your weapons." Pomarat watched the slave while Pasmat clumsily gathered his things and left. She did not stir from her apparent slumber. He knew she was awake. He bent over her, kissed her head and quickly slit her throat. Pasmat would no longer need her though he didn't know that.

At his tent, Pomarat told him to bring back the converts. Pasmat went to leave and Pomarat grabbed his quiver and pulled him back, "When you are all back I will ask you to pick two converts, pick the two I can trust the most, the bravest. Understand?"

Pasmat nodded relieved that Pomarat had not slit his throat but instead gave him an order which showed he respected his judgment … or was he testing it? Such was life in the inner circle of a madman. He ran to the ocean concentrating on who he should pick. Pick wrong and it could mean his life. Pick right it would elevate his status. Had Pomarat already picked the two he wanted and was testing his judgment? He resigned himself to picking based on seniority, but taking the second and fourth most senior of converts. This would show he put some thought into it. He didn't know Pomarat couldn't give a shit who he picked. Whoever he picked was cannon fodder in Pomarat's mind, as were those left behind.

Pomarat went to Sarkem's tent and ask about Massot. "He's asleep," said Sarkem "my slaves have tended to his wounds. They are not deep. But he was tired. Should I wake him?"

"No, let him sleep. We will come back for him. I need you when I deal with the converts. Wake your slaves. I want to talk to them."

Sarkem looked at Pomarat but did as he was told. He could tell from Pomarat's face what was to happen. He awoke the slaves who were feigning sleep and commanded them to go to Pomarat. Pomarat saw the fear in their faces in the darkness of the tent illuminated by the fading embers of their fire. This aroused him. He walked to the slaves and embraced them both at once and whispered in their ears as he held them close, "Thank you for taking care of my warrior, Sarkem. For that I grant you your freedom ..." In that second, the two slaves looked at each other hope in their eyes. Pomarat released the hug and quickly thrust his new metal knife under the rib cage into the heart of both. "... from this life." As they fell to the ground clutching their chests, he looked at the open mouth Sarkem. "I needed to ensure no harm would come to Massot while we deal with the converts. We are leaving here and can't take them with us. There will be more where we're going. Let's deal with the converts."

Sarkem was sad. He had enjoyed his slaves but Pomarat giveth and he taketh away. He had no say in the matter. He followed Pomarat out of the tent. Pasmat was waiting at his tent with the converts when he arrived. "Pasmat, I need two converts to accompany us on our mission. Who do you suggest?"

Pasmat stuck to his original plan and selected the second and fourth convert, bypassing the third. The third convert offended at being bypassed asked, "What is this mission?"

Pomarat calmly and quickly knocked an arrow and shot it into his mouth and out the back of his head. He lay on the ground in a heap paralyzed as the arrow pierced his spinal cord. "If I wanted you to know the mission, I would have told you and Pasmat would have selected you! Do any of you others have something you would like to ask?" Silence and downward stares. "Good! Here is your mission. We have killed the chief of the southern tribes tonight. They are in disarray. You will awaken the tribe, march down the spit and raze their camps as they have no leader. We will cross the bay and capture that camp with Pasmat and the warriors he selected. We will then go to the entrance of the spit and assist you from the rear ensuring your victory! Understand?" They nodded but didn't.

Pomarat pointed to the fifth convert and said, "You are in command! If you perform well, you will be legend among the Itchiwan! By tomorrow we will control all the southern tribes and will convince the northern tribes to come to a truce. Hysko has started this war and we will finish it! The southern tribes will be ours and the northern tribes will go back to their encampments."

The fifth convert was temporarily the chief of the tribe. The only reason he was a convert was because he was a coward, single and did not wish to meet the fate of those men whose bodies were displayed in the camp. Now he was to lead an attack against the southern tribes, many of whom he had come to know at tribal meetings and he was to command the men of his tribe who he knew now hated him. He would wait for Pomarat to dismiss him and his fellow converts, who he would gather away from this place and tell them to go back to their tents, eat, gather their weapons and meet him at Fet's tent. Fet was the third convert who was dead on the ground in front of them. He would then make sure Pomarat and crew had left for the camp across the bay. Then he alone would make a beeline for the ocean, grab a canoe and head to eastern camp fires that he and two of the converts had been watching. The remaining converts could then decide which of them wanted to be chief of the tribe.

151

AFTER DISMISSING THE CONVERTS, Pomarat told Pasmat to take his chosen converts and ready canoes on the bay. He and Sarkem went back to collect Massot. Pomarat's canoes headed east of the camp fires. He would land in darkness and head west. Hysko, Tam and the three warriors ran to the same camp from the west. After instruction, Pomarat's men ambushed the camp's six sentries sitting at the shoreline. The main camp was farther inland. They burst out of the darkness firing arrows as they charged. Pomarat's, Sarkem's and a revived Massot's quick fire technique killed or wounded all six. Pasmat's and the two converts' sprayed everywhere but at the targets and they stopped their charge while Pomarat and his men continued, slamming tomahawks into the heads of all six though three were already dead.

"Pasmat! You two! What are you doing?! Get over here! When you launch an attack, you do not stop! You make sure you finish the kill!" whispered Pomarat in anger, teaching his new disciples. "Take the arrows from their quivers and whatever you want and can carry without slowing you down." Pomarat and his men extracted the arrows they had shot from the bodies and put them back in their quivers. Pasmat and the converts were amazed when each one pulled an arrow from two different bodies. They had no clue where their arrows went.

One of the converts recognized a sentry but said nothing. His name was Kamt. They had met at the summer solstice gathering of the tribes. They had shared a bottle of the firewater he had bartered for from the white trader, O'Hearn. They were friends and said they would seek each other out at the next meeting. Now he considered what he was doing. These people were not enemies, they were fellow Itchiwan. He would flee this band at the first opportunity. This Pomarat was the devil Maktahdou. It seems he knew your thoughts before you did. And he did! Pomarat noticed the look on the convert's face as he stood over the body. He took note and conferred with Sarkem. They would head to the main encampment and he had devised a plan.

Hysko and his group had reached the encampment. Tam was explaining to the chief what was happening and that chief Yat was wounded but alive and said we should follow the orders of Hysko. The chief was looking at Hysko, who was not looking at him, but to the north. "What are your orders, Hy ...?"

Hysko turned and slammed him to the ground and then fired two arrows killing the two converts charging from the darkness bows drawn, their arrows firing harmlessly into the sky. He scanned the darkness ... nothing. "Yell for your tribe! We are under attack! Tam, stay low have your warriors watch the north!"

The chief screamed "Ambush! Ambush!" Those who had not retired to their tents armed themselves and came to the chief. Shortly thereafter the rest came.

Pomarat's plan had been to use the converts as cannon fodder to gauge the strength of the tribe. If Hysko and his new friends had not arrived, they would have had the element of surprise and taken the encampment as the tribe's archery skills were probably no better than his convert's. Pomarat gathered Pasmat, Sarkem and Massot. "We are leaving. We will make a wide arc around this camp and head south."

Sarkem and Massot knew this was the plan from the beginning unless they got lucky and had caught the tribe by surprise. "What about the other converts marching down the spit?" asked Pasmat innocently.

Pomarat looked at Pasmat and smiled. "They're not. They fled after we left. If I was not there, they knew they would be set upon by the other men of Nakim's tribe. You alone are the chosen one to be a member of my band. I will teach you the skills so that someday you can become the warrior that Hysko has become!" Sarkem and Massot nodded in agreement. Pasmat was flattered but scared to death of the devil before him.

Pomarat told them to leave. He hung back and selected a target. He needed them to think they were still out here for awhile. The men of the tribe were all easy targets. Hysko was crouched and alert looking directly at him but not seeing him in the darkness. There would be time for Hysko later when he had fewer friends around. The chief was back on his feet commanding his men. But one of the men who came with Hysko was staying close to the chief scanning in his direction trying to shield the chief. He was the target. Pomarat drew back his bow for maximum force and fired an arrow into Tam's eye and into the back of his skull. Pomarat ducked immediately after release. Three of Hysko's arrows whizzed by where his head had been. Pomarat left to follow his men. That should keep the tribe wondering if he was still out there.

152

VERN PULLED UP TO the cabin in Maine. Sarah was asleep. Half of Mrs. Giancarlo's cookies were gone. Sarah found out nobody can eat just one. "Sarah, we're home." Sarah slowly awoke and saw the headlights on the cabin. Vern went out and opened the door to the cabin. Sarah stumbled out of the car with the remainder of the cookies. She set them on the kitchen counter and went to the bedroom. She stripped off her clothes, climbed under the comforter and was back asleep.

Vern went to the trunk of the car and gathered their bags thinking 'Thanks for the help!' but really thinking they both were exhausted. Eventually he climbed under the comforter beside her and both slept well that night.

In the morning, Sarah awoke first as usual and started preparing breakfast after taking a hot shower. It was so much better than a dip in a cold pond, hauling in firewood and water, not to mention having to forage for something to eat. Life was grand! She turned on the TV and kept the volume low. There was the *Today Show* from New York City! She had been there! Never in her life on the pond had she imagined she would experience all the wonders she has. 'Fuck!' as Vern would say in such a state of mind.

Vern was up and entered the kitchen. "What's for breakfast?"

"Jimmy Dean Pure Pork Sausage, eggs, and toast."

"Fuck!"

Vern was happy. "Take a shower. It will be ready when you're done."

Vern obliged. As the water ran over his body his conversation with Sam came back to him. It was time to call Amos. He toweled off and returned to the kitchen. Sarah laid his plate on the table. She sat across from him and waited for him to finish his meal. When he did she asked, "Are you still going to call Amos?"

"Yep."

Vern picked up the phone and dialed Amos's office. Amos's secretary answered the phone, "Mr. Otis's office."

"Hi Samantha, this is Vern, is Amos there?"

"Good to hear from you Mr. Otis, I'll put you right through, hold on …"

"Samantha, call me Ver …" he was already on hold as music filled the receiver. Samantha was now filling in Amos who was on line one. Next thing he heard was Amos's voice,

"Where the fuck have you been?! You missed the laying of the pavilion!"

"Hi Amos, good to hear you also."

"Cut the shit, Vern! You know what I mean." Sarah was listening to one side of this conversation but could only ascertain the tone of the person on the other end but not the words.

"I eloped."

"Ya, I know."

Vern was caught off guard. "What do you mean you know?"

"Vern, you're my twin brother," said Amos amused by Vern's confusion.

"Fuck you that twin shit only goes so far. No one knows I'm married."

"You sure?"

"No I'm not sure. How do you know?"

"For sure …? You just told me. Is your bride's name Sarah? I had a feeling you went back to the hole when you didn't show up at the laying of the Pavilion."

Vern laid back in the chair and exhaled. Sarah wondered what was being said on the on the other end of the receiver. After a long pause, Vern said, "I wish you were with me man to figure out that fucking orb thing."

Amos thought on this. Alarms sounded in the recess of his mind. Time to stop the banter. "Vern, I did have the feeling you went back in the hole, and suspected I knew why. But in reality, I didn't know whether you would stay in Sarah's time or come back to our time, or for that matter … get back at all. I found out you married a girl named Sarah five hours ago from a phone call from Vicki Giancarlo."

"So much for the Mafia code," said Vern then thinking 'Shit, I left a cookie trail.' He smiled at his own joke.

"I actually called Sam the day after the Pavilion and asked him to give me a call if he saw you. He must have told Vicki. They know where their bread is buttered. You had the shrimp scampi didn't you?"

Vern laughed and said, "I did. Why don't you and Brett come to the cabin in Maine and you can see Sarah again. Maybe you can figure out what I heard on my travels."

"What about Timmy?"

"What about Timmy? He's dead."

"Timmy's not dead. What are you talking about?" asked Amos confused.

Vern paused, "He was shot from behind in Southie this summer. We went to the wake. He and Colin were connected, remember?"

"What the fuck are you talking about!? Timmy's a CPA with his own practice! He's not connected! He went to enormous lengths not to be connected so he could help generate enough money to fund the Pavilion!"

Silence.

"Vern? … Vern?"

In a soft voice, "Yeah, Amos, I'm still here … I'm thinking." Sarah saw the look on Vern's face. Things weren't going well. Vern knew something was wrong after his conversation with Sam. Now this confirmed it. Things had changed. Finally, he said, "You know how when you and Timmy came back, the life Brett and I supposedly lived was gone?"

"Yeah … I'm thinking the same thing … I"

"Maybe just you should come up. You can help me figure out what's happened. When we blocked the Pukwudgees they came out in Sarah's time but there is more."

"I'll be up there in a couple of hours."

"WAIT!!!!" screamed Vern before he could hang up.

"What?"

"I'm not thinking straight like you. Call Timmy first and ask him if he knows a guy named Danny O'Hearn."

"Yeah, why?"

"That's the guy who killed him before I went in the hole."

"Yeah and what if he asks why I'm asking?"

Vern hesitated and said, "Say he approached you to take him on as a client. He says he is a friend of his."

"Then what?"

"I need Timmy's answer when you get here. I can't believe I'm saying this, as far as I knew Timmy was dead."

"Anything else?"

"No just get up here."

When Vern hung up Sarah asked if he was coming.

"Yeah, he's coming."

Sarah was excited and asked "What should I make for dinner?"

"Anything. I'll get whatever you need in town."

"Vern, what's wrong?" she asked seeing the far off gaze in his eyes.

Vern returned from his thoughts and looked in her questioning eyes. "Something has happened. Timmy is alive."

"That is a good thing right?"

"Maybe… maybe … I don't know. Only Amos can help me figure that out." To himself he thought, 'Were all the reeds in place when he went into the hole? It was dark.' He hadn't noticed.

153

Hysko ran to Tam and pulled the arrow from his eye and pressed the socket with his palm. He looked at the chief, "GET ME SOMETHING TO PUT ON THE WOUND! GET SOMEONE TO TEND TO HIS WOUND!" He commanded the three warriors who accompanied them to watch the perimeter. He guessed Pomarat was fleeing. The chief removed his shawl and gave it to Hysko. One of his men replaced him compressing the wound.

"What about those men? They are still out there," pleaded the chief.

Hysko stood and faced the chief. "They are gone."

"Where?"

"Maybe to take over another tribe in the south like he did with Nakim's tribe," said Hysko knowing Pomarat would probably be heading for the hole but was not sure.

"What should we do?"

Hysko still had the three men from Yat's tribe. He said to one of them, "Go back to Yat or Tam's brother if Yat is dead and tell them his people in the south may be in danger! Send half his men back to his home. The danger with Nakim's tribe is over. But the northern tribes must be told what happened here." He turned to the chief, "You should also send half your men home immediately. Give me four men to join us, and we will track down Pomarat now. You must go to the chief guarding the east and tell him what has happened and to send men back to defend his camp. If Yat is dead, you must stay behind to tell the northern chief from the east what has happened and what happened to Nakim's tribe.

The chief picked four of his men to join Hysko and the two remaining braves from Yat's tribe. The seven of them headed south into the darkness. Hysko knew the way back to the hole. When he was three quarters of the way back he stopped by a kettle pond and indicated the men should drink. "From now on be alert!" he told them. "There are three with Pomarat. Two are his warriors. One is from Nakim's tribe. I will focus on Pomarat. He is the most dangerous. You six focus only on the two warriors. You will know immediately who they are. Nakim's man will be looking to the others for instruction. When he does shoot, it will be an accident if he hits anyone. The two warriors are deadly accurate. You must bring them down or they will kill you all. Pomarat is twice the warrior of both of them. I will have my hands full trying to kill him. Do you understand?" They all nodded but had no idea what they were in for. Hysko understood this, and said, "When we engage them and I tell you to attack, you find Sarkem and Massot. Take your first shots at them … but don't stop charging! Keep firing your arrows even if they have been hit. When you get closer, shoot them again even if you think they are dead. Then slit their throats to be sure. Then you can deal with Nakim's man. I am guessing he will be long gone."

154

ABOUT A MILE BEFORE reaching the hole, Pomarat stopped. He turned to Pasmat. "Where is the nearest Southern tribe?"

Pasmat was caught off guard by the question. Nervous, he tried to recover his bearing of where they were. "The closest would be Yat's tribe." He pointed southwest. "They live by the bay over that hill."

Pomarat walked up to him smiling, slapped him lightly on his cheek, grabbed the back of his neck and brought his face to his shoulder. He said to Sarkem and Massot, "Didn't I tell you this was a worthy convert?" Sarkem and Massot smiled shaking their heads in agreement trying to contain themselves from laughter. Pomarat continued, "Pasmat, it is time to get women to make our own tribe and make good my promise to you."

Pasmat was glad to be free of the hug and glad he did not wet his loin cloth. Massot and Sarkem were glad they would be getting more slaves to replace those they left behind. They traveled through the woods coming upon a bluff overlooking the bay below. The glow of dying campfires dotted the shore line. Pomarat conferred with Massot and Sarkem. "We go down that path and raid the camp. Kill any man, old or young you encounter. Kill any women who resist. We will select two women for each and kill the rest. This tribe is finished. Our tribe begins."

"What do I do," asked Pasmat.

"You keep in the back as we go tent to tent and warn us if others are coming," said Massot.

They quietly came into the camp slitting the throats of the outlying sentries who had dozed off. Then they methodically went from tent to tent slaying those left behind by Yat and his warriors. Their only resistance came from feeble old men and young boys who fired the last arrow they would fire. About half way through the tents it became more of a challenge as the yelps and last screams of women alerted camp members from their usual peaceful repasts. Even then, they came from their tents mostly unarmed and groggy. They were easy targets for Pomarat and his killing machine. Pasmat watched all of this in amazement. Most of the people were killed with knives, but when a bow was required they were immediately on the target pulling their arrows from the bodies, returning them to their quivers while slitting throats for good measure. Pomarat and his men were truly agents of the devil, Maktahdou! And they had chosen him as their apprentice. How did he get himself into this position? He wanted out, but there was no way out he could see.

As the sky started to lighten, the battle or slaughter was over, Pomarat and his men were herding the surviving women to the center of the camp. The old men, many women and children lay dead either in their tents or just outside. Pomarat, Massot and Sarkem were covered in blood from all the jugulars they had slit. Pomarat surveyed the survivors. There were twelve, four were young girls. He immediately culled the young ones from the herd. Of the remaining eight, four had to go. "Two of these are mine! The other two are Massot's and

Sarkem's," he said pointing to the young girls. "Pasmat chose your wife from these eight."

The eight older women realized what was happening. Three of them were mothers of the young girls and the rest had lost children in the slaughter. When two decided to charge the band. they all followed knowing it would be better to be dead than slaves to these animals. Pomarat and his band were caught off guard. They had women all over them trying to rip off their ears, nose, and jugulars ... whatever was in range of their mouths and claws. The young girls joined in using their teeth to cause pain where they could reach. Their bows were useless and fell to the ground. Massot slit the side of the woman on him and drove his knife into the skull of the young one biting his scrotum. Another woman jumped on his back biting deep into his ear, ripping most of it off. He screamed and fell back on her, knocking her wind out. As she tried to recover he stabbed her in the eye.

Sarkem and Pomarat suffered similar attacks, and brutally killed their attackers. Sarkem had lost flesh in his neck and stomach but not his jugular. Pomarat's nose was disfigured and bleeding and if not for a quick slicing action he would have been emasculated. Pasmat was on the ground screaming being mauled by two women and a young girl. Pasmat had never been in a fight in his life and would never be again. His eye had been pierced by a thumb. His jugular was severed and if he survived, would have not been able to continue his line. Sarkem and Pomarat recovered their bows and Massot was on his knees in pain when they heard Pasmat's agony. Pomarat got off two quick shots and Sarkem one killing Pasmat's attackers. One of Pomarat's arrows went through the heart of one of the attackers into Pasmat's stomach adding insult to his injury. They ran to Pasmat. He was barely alive, pleading help with his one functioning eye. Pomarat knelt over him and whispered "I'll bring you home. Have no fear."

Pasmat said "yauuuu?"

Pomarat put him out of his misery with a knife under his jaw up into his brain. "Get Massot," he said to Sarkem, "take the skins off the women and tend to your wounds. Start a fire and butcher one of these women and we will eat. Then we go back to the hole."

155

HYSKO PICKED UP THE trail of Pomarat's band and followed. It veered from the path to the hole. He looked at Yat's men. "They're heading to your camp. We must hurry, they could be anywhere up ahead. Be ready and watch for my signals." The skies were beginning to lighten. Faraway screams filled the air. They picked up the pace to cover the distance. Eventually, Hysko picked up the scent of burning flesh. "Stop!" he hissed. "They're up ahead. Be ready. Remember what I told you!" They approached slowly hearing voices which they did not recognize but Hysko did. He stopped and crouched. "That's them!" he whispered. Pomarat was close, the brush cover was good. They crept closer. They all saw the dead women's bodies scattered about the campsite. They could see a woman's severed legs on a spit over the fire. Hysko did not recognize quickly enough what the effect would be on Yat's men. These were their women! They ran from cover. Hysko was about to yell stop but thought better and turned to the other four, "Quick! You three flank to the right and attack when you get there! You come with me and do what I say. Now!" he whispered.

Yat's braves in their rage got off shots with their bows and missed, but kept charging. Massot and Sarkem quickly raised their bows and hit one in the chest and the other in the stomach with hurried shots. Pomarat ignored the charging braves and fired two arrows into the brush from which they emerged. Luckily, Hysko and his four remaining men had left to the flanks. Pomarat turned noticing the braves charging the camp were wounded but not stopping. Massot and Sarkem had not knocked another arrow fast enough and they were upon them with knives drawn. They deflected their initial thrusts with their bows and scrambled for their knives. Pomarat drew his knife running towards Sarkem and stabbed his attacker in the heart. The attacker managed to swing his arm with the knife into the side of Pomarat. Sarkem thrust his knife under the attacker jaw finally stopping him. Massot managed to grab the knife hand of his attacker but not before he had sliced his shoulder. As they wrestled on the ground Massot managed to thrust his knife in Yat's man's throat. Then the arrows came from opposite directions.

Two from the right whizzed by the heads of Massot and Sarkem close enough for them to hear them. Another caught Sarkem in the bicep passing through his arm. One arrow from the left, hit the leg on the spit. Hysko's arrow hit Pomarat in the shoulder. He quickly launched two more arrows hitting Massot in the thigh and hitting the body of Yat's man who Sarkem was now using as a shield. The three braves on the right flank seeing Pomarat and his men were all wounded decided to charge in and finish them. Hysko shook his head. They had them! They could maintain their position and fire arrows till they were finished. It would be like shooting fish in a barrel. But they charged in too early.

They were on Pomarat's band and though wounded Pomarat and his band engaged them in close combat. Massot swung his bow at his charging assailant smacking him on the head throwing him off balance just enough so he could drop down and slice his Achilles tendon. Hysko could not risk shooting more arrows without hitting members of his group. Sarkem threw the body of Yat's man at his charging assailant and followed tackling him to the ground with Yat's man's body between them. Pomarat threw his knife into the heart of his assailant. Hysko charged in to aid his band. He made a beeline for Pomarat who was now unarmed. His cohort ran to aid his fellow tribe members.

Hysko plowed Pomarat into the ground and straddled him raising his knife to finish the kill. Pomarat raised his forearm deflecting the blow. With other hand he grabbed powder from the satchel on his waist and rubbed it into Hysko's eyes. The effect was immediate. Hysko was blinded and his throat started closing. He swung his knife wildly nicking Pomarat several times once close to the jugular. Pomarat slammed Hysko's chest with both hands sending a sharp pain to his own wounded shoulder, but knocking Hysko off him onto his back. Hysko was still blindly swinging his knife weakly in his darkness as he struggled to breathe. Pomarat got to his feet, pain screaming from his side, shoulder and cuts everywhere. He looked for Massot and Sarkem. They were hurt badly but had managed to kill all their attackers. They were pulling arrows from their wounds and taking the loin clothes of the dead to stem the bleeding. Pomarat looked down at Hysko, still gasping for whatever air he could. He knelt down slapping the knife from his hand still slowly swinging and said softly, "You wanted to be chief! You learned well from me. You were my best warrior! But you never learned the last lesson … to be the most powerful, you must be willing to sell your soul. You never did that! So here you lie."

Hysko was fading from this world and heard none of Pomarat's words. He passed on to the world of people who had not sold their souls before Pomarat took pity on him and slit his throat. Pomarat took Hysko's cod piece and wrapped it around his wounded shoulder. Sarkem and Massot were lying among the bodies exhausted. Pomarat also decided rest was needed and slept with his head on Hysko's stomach. They rested till twilight when they were roused by distant screams of anguish from the west. Half of Yat's men had reached their campsite and had seen the carnage. Pomarat jumped up in pain and looked for Massot and Sarkem who had also heard the screams. They looked to him. "Take the cooked limb! Gather arrows and weapons. We go to the hole now! Sarkem take up the rear and cover our tracks!" But on his journey he rethought his plan.

156

AMOS CALLED TIMMY AND asked about Danny O'Hearn. "Who? No never heard of him. Why?"

Amos followed the script Vern had laid out which was a change in that Vern was the one usually following Amos's scripts. "He fucking told you he knew me?! Fuck him, tell him to screw," replied Timmy in true Timmy style. "Better yet get his info first, I'll get Colin to send one of his guys to drop by and give him a brush up."

"Timmy … you're kidding right?"

"Yeah I'm fucking kidding but I don't like strangers dropping my name. Hey when the fuck we gonna get the band back together again? You heard from Vern yet? Shame he missed the Pavilion thing."

Amos paused, "As a matter of fact I did. I got a message on my answering machine last night. He'll be back in the states next week. He had to go to Europe on a TV deal. When he gets back maybe we'll all head south and check on the progress of the Pavilion, a road trip!"

"Sounds good, let me know." 'Yeah fucking TV deal … right. He went back for Sarah. Good for him!' He opened a Bud Light and settled down to watch the Sox just as his Dad always did.

Amos hung up. Went to the garage, chose his Jimmy and drove to Maine. In two hours he was pulling up to the cabin in the darkness. As he walked up to the door it opened with Vern standing in the doorway. They embraced on the stoop. Amos whispered "What the fuck did you do now?"

"I don't know, I figure I did the same thing you did," said Vern patting him on the back and smiling. Amos smiled too. As they walked into the cabin, Sarah awaited them nervously standing by the kitchen.

"You cooking that stew again? I don't have to strip down to my skivvies do I?" Amos smiled and Sarah smiled.

"Young Amos, the knower of me future!" she said slipping into her old dialect.

"Good thing I didn't tell you what I thought I knew because neither one of us would have never dreamed that this is what happened."

"No shit!" said Sarah back in her new dialect.

Amos raised an eyebrow and looked at Vern. "You wouldn't believe the teaching power of continuous TV," answered Vern in response to the inquisitive eyebrow.

"And her manner of speech? I don't think she got 'no shit' from TV."

As they enjoyed the stew they conversed about how all this came to pass. Amos told Vern of his conversation with Timmy. "So there's no Danny O'Hearn?"

"No, according to Timmy."

Vern pushed back from the table and looked to the ceiling. "So here I am, back from the hole. Life as I know it has apparently changed. Amos, when I went in the hole, Timmy was dead. We had gone to his wake! Danny O'Hearn had supposedly killed him and disappeared thanks to Colin I imagine." He looked at Amos, "I guess I'm still famous based on Sam and Vicki's reactions. You still rich Amos?"

"Yeah. Tell me what you know."

"I'll let Sarah tell you, she saw it all." Vern looked to Sarah.

After Sarah finished Amos asked, "Itchiwan?"

"Yeah, our Pukwudgees were a tribe, not a myth. And they were peaceful people," said Vern.

"So the first group came out and ransacked your home." Amos

looked to Sarah, "You sure the second group you saw went in and came out of the hole?"

"Yes."

"And the third group was wounded but didn't go into the hole. They erased their tracks while they headed south?"

"Yes."

"So I must have fucked up by going back to Sarah?" asked Vern.

"I don't know Vern," said Amos rubbing his face in his hands. "I think we all fucked up, the four of us running into the Pukwudgees and leading them to the hole in the first place and Sarah for the markings she left when she experimented with the hole. As a result, there's a group of four, maybe now three psychopaths who know where the hole is. Hey life is grand! We're like the monkey trying to put the cork in the ass of the gassed up pig while it's farting."

"Where are mom and dad?"

"Hawaii, on vacation."

"Your place?"

"Yeah."

"Keep them there Amos."

Amos laughed. Sarah and Vern looked at him wondering what was so funny. Amos looked at them and saw their quizzical glances. "Fucking Vern, don't you get it yet?"

"What?"

Amos rubbed his face again.

"Stop fucking doing that and say what you're thinking instead of trying to figure out how to turn those thoughts into pabulum and spoon feed us idiots in small doses."

Amos stopped laughing. "I don't think you're idiots! I'm scared for the first time in my life! I'm the idiot. All the fucking calculations and plans based in logic are probably up in smoke."

Vern looked at Sarah and her at him. They did not know what to make of this meltdown. To Vern, Amos was the foundation. Now he was cracking. Amos composed himself and said, "Let's drink! What have you got for beer?"

"Bud Light. Not any of those craft brews you highbrows prefer."

"Fuck off Vern, break out the Bud's."

After he downed his first and well into his second, Amos said,

"When Timmy and I went in the hole and came back, you and Brett lost your previous lives and got a restart. When you went in the hole to get Sarah, evidently Timmy, me and Brett got restarts … more dramatic for Timmy though he has no clue. Though now I do. If those three fucks survive their wounds, come back to the hole and find the hole you used to get here, then this conversation may never have happened! God knows what happens. So let's drink before this happens." Amos smiled and raised his glass.

Then Sarah spoke, "Fuck'em!"

Vern raised his can and said, "Fuck'em".

Amos downed his beer and went to the fridge to get another and sat down. "You know what's different about this time?" Sarah and Vern looked at him. He continued, "This time no one is in the hole to come back and tell us what happened!"

"Fuck, anything happen in Mashpee since you laid the Pavilion?"

"Not that I know of, nothing that made the news anyway. But that doesn't mean something didn't or won't happen, which means anything that's happened since the day you went in the hole could be erased."

"Even the laying of the Pavilion?"

"Unlikely, but yeah, if they came out attacking and killed our construction crew."

"Soo … we really have no control over the future."

"Vern, we never did. But we tried. Drink up!"

Vern paused to mull this over. He looked at Sarah. She was looking at him as she could not comprehend what all this meant. Vern grabbed another Bud Light, took a sip and sat down. "Amos, call Timmy and Brett. Sarah and I are going back to Mashpee and see the Pavilion. It's unlikely that they'd take on a construction crew in armored, giant vehicles. There are only three of them now. If they're out, we'll deal with it."

"How are we going to know if they're out?"

"I'll get close to the local police. This time I won't be Vern the drunken D.P.W. worker. I'll be Vern, the famous son of Mashpee and the upper Cape who is returning to retire."

"Then what?"

"We'll know what happens when it happens!"

"Then what?"

"What do you mean, 'then what'? We find them and put an end to this."

"You mean me, a stockbroker, Timmy, an accountant, and Brett, a Tennis Pro? We got tennis rackets, pens, and calculators. What do you bring to the table? You gonna talked them to death." Vern smiled and sat back in his chair. For the first time in his life, he was one step ahead of Amos.

"What is that shit ass grin about?" yelled Amos.

"I got a duffel bag full of weapons."

"What?"

"Yeah, I bought a bunch of black powder weapons, prior to going to get Sarah."

"Black Powder, are you serious?

"It's an upgrade from Timmy's shit stick and Brett's slingshot. Besides we're all adult's without records, we can buy any kind of guns we want."

"So we'll buy registered guns, and end up in jail for murdering midgets in Halloween costumes."

"We'll lure them to a remote place somewhere in the woods and bury'em where they fall! Nobody will ever know."

"The chances of our orbits intersecting again and at place of our choosing is slim and none,"

Vern sighed, "Or we could get Timmy's brother to get us unregistered guns."

Before Amos could respond Vern said, "Just kidding. We'll go back to Mashpee and you round up that old gang of ours. And we'll go from there. "

"Sounds like a plan. I'm going to bed, if we wake up tomorrow and are still taking about this, than … I guess nothing happened, at least to us."

After Amos went to the guest room, Sarah asked Vern as they cleaned up, "What did all that mean?"

"It looks like we're going back to Mashpee to become investigators."

"Like Sherlock Holmes?"

"You saw that one?"

"Yes, Basil Rathbone!"

"Let's get some sleep," Vern kissed her forehead. "Thinking about the possibilities of the hole is tiring." 'Nothing will probably happen. There were only three of them, right? They probably will stay in Sarah's time. They had to be freaked by the Orb. Yet it seems they tried it again and again. Hopefully, Amos will resume the mantle of master planner tomorrow.' Vern was uncomfortable in the role of Holmes.

157

WHEN THEY ARRIVED AT the hole, Pomarat spoke to Massot and Sarkem. "We are too weak to go into the hole. It's better to stay here in this place we know than risk facing a stronger enemy in another time in this condition." He watched their faces. They both could not conceal their relief. He continued, "We'll head to the great waters in the south and use their healing powers and once we have recovered from our wounds, I will decide our next action. Sarkem, cover our trail for a while longer."

They went south to the shore as light faded and night took over.

They camped just off the shore in the dunes for weeks, bathing in the waters warmed by the gulfstream which aided their healing. They occupied their time making more arrows and finding game for food. The half of Yat's tribe that came upon the massacre followed their tracks until they came upon the second massacre – the women and girls. They walked around the site seeing that the men that left with Hysko and men from the other southern tribe were all dead. They initially thought Hysko had betrayed them but then found his body lying on the ground, throat slit, his eyes only blacken sockets, with no eyes under the lids … They searched for days for signs of the attackers' trail but found none. It's like they vanished in thin air! They discussed what they should do. The bodies of the tribe needed to be buried. But the remainder of their tribe in the north had to be warned. They expressed their doubts about having to face this Pomarat after seeing all the carnage. Even Hysko, a better warrior than them, said he would kill him. But he didn't. They decided to flee, no … warn the rest of the tribe still in the north leaving the bodies exposed.

During their time of healing, Pomarat had time to think. They were now three, and because of Hysko's soft heart, all the descendants of their people would know of their existence and their deeds. His descendants had become soft, traders not warriors. Their existence was now at the whim of the Wampanoag and white traders from over the seas. He knew that with their actions with Nakim and Yat's tribes, all the other tribes would be on alert. Now that he had seen the path the Itchiwan had followed, he decided he could not rely on his lessons to take hold. It was unlikely they would be able to take any of the other camps as easily as they had taken Nakim's and Yat's. He decided he must ensure the Itchiwan's future. Eventually he shared his thoughts with Sarkem and Massot. "Our people have become weak. Yet, we no longer have the element of surprise to take the other tribes. If we go into the evil orb I do not know if I can find the hole that brings us back home. And home may have changed as a result of Maushop's wrath. Maktahdou has told me, we and only we can ensure the future of the Itchiwan! To do this, we must find women and bring them to the hole. He will then guide us on which hole to take. This way we preserve the tribe!"

"How do we find these women? Pasmat is dead," asked Sarkem.

"What would you do Massot?" asked Pomarat.

Caught off guard Massot had never been asked anything by Pomarat. His mind stumbled and said, "Err … ask you?"

Pomarat smiled and embraced Massot's head. "Correct," he said. "Tonight we stay awake. Tomorrow we sleep while the sun is in the sky. Then at night we travel the shore. There is a tribe to the east. Itchiwan have always lived by the great waters. Their fires will betray their location." So simple, but elusive to the simple minds of Massot and Sarkem.

Within three nights they came upon camp fires. As Pomarat expected the perimeter was heavily guarded with sentries who were not sleeping due to the stories of what happened to Yat's tribe. They made a wide arc around the camp. The south faced the ocean. They observed the west and north were heavily guarded but the east was vulnerable with only two sentries. Pomarat outlined a plan and they executed it. The two sentries were dead, throats slashed from behind. Pomarat and his men took their weapons and proceeded to the camp. The fires were dying. All were asleep. They went tent to tent looking for what they sought. It was going so well Pomarat was tempted to bring an end to this tribe, but one unchecked yelp or scream could result in their downfall due to sheer numbers. Instead when he came upon a tent with three young girls and an older woman, he stopped and indicated this was the one. Their man must be one of the sentries.

Pomarat slashed the throat of the mother as she slept and dragged her body out of the tent. Then they each grabbed the girls covering their mouth and slamming their fist into their face, knocking them back to sleep. They lifted them on to their shoulders, Pomarat grimacing realizing his shoulder was not yet fully healed. Neither were the others' wounds. They left the camp the way they had came and vanished north to the woods.

Pomarat did not realize it then, but these slip in, slip out attacks would become the modus operandi of Pukwudgee incursions from then on. It had been so successful in his time. But in this time the Itchiwan were no longer his tribe. The Itchiwan would soon become extinct. The white's from the sea, the Wampanoag and disease would see to that. There would still be Itchiwan, but they would be scattered and no longer a tribe. They would flee inland and be forced to become scavengers and thieves to survive. To Maktahdou this was good. He told Pomarat it was up to him to recreate the legend of the Itchiwan. He told him how! Or in reality maybe it was Pomarat's instincts telling him how.

He began by working on their new young women. When they awoke he was nice to them. Put them on pedestals, like queens! He spent hours indoctrinating these young girls, telling them tales of his past and his plans for them in his future. They would be the mothers of their first born and thus the mothers of a new Itchiwan tribe, one that would be greater than the tribes of today. He told them that Maktahdou had told him that all the tribes of the Itchiwan they knew would be no more because of their trust of the whites and Wampanoag. They were the chosen. He told them they would camp in the woods. He would teach them how to become warriors so they could defend their children, and after they bore their first born, he would capture three other young woman to do the chores and their only duty thereafter would be to protect their children and ensure the future of the tribe.

158

THE YOUNG WOMEN BECAME warriors and bore them each children. Pomarat kept his promise and he and Sarkem went north to steal away three more Itchiwan women to serve as slaves to the mothers of their children. Not only would they would be slaves to the mothers of their first born, but also eventually be mothers to their second born, and also raised to the next level when Pomarat captured another three. By the fourth go around of this Ponzi like scheme, the world was getting smaller.

It had been thirteen years since they had captured the mothers of their first born. There were more and more white invaders from the sea roaming the land in search of trade and the Wampanoag were spreading their territory as they always had as their tribe grew. Pomarat and either Massot or Sarkem had periodically been ransacking homesteads of the Wampanoag and the camps of white traders for their possessions of value or just for the fun of it. If they encountered any resistance upon these incursions they would brutally kill those they encountered. Then they would leave a trail to the north or south ending in a body of water casting suspicion upon the Itchiwan. This focused the Wampanoag and the whites to the north or south.

The fourth go round was their last. As Massot and Pomarat were setting upon Nakim's old tribe to steal away three young women, the Wampanoag were in the process of launching a full scale assault on the camp to avenge an attack Pomarat had done months ago. In the midst of stealing the three young women after they had slit the throats of the others in the tent, they found themselves trying to escape the camp while the Wampanoag were methodically slaughtering the tribe tent by tent. They were running for the dunes when they felt arrows flying by their heads. They dropped the young women to the sand and rapidly fired a barrage of arrows at the ten Wampanoag that had spotted them. Eight were dead. The ninth had an arrow in his throat that had not pierced his jugular. He lived. The tenth was just grazed and ran screaming alert. But Pomarat and Massot scooped up two of the three young women and vanished into the dunes. The third woman escaped to an uncertain future.

They covered their tracks by traversing from the spit to the mainland benefiting from the low tide. They would do this all the way back to their camp taking advantage of any stream or river they came across on their journey. The world was getting smaller Pomarat realized. It was time to go. When they got back to camp, his tribe would go back to the hole.

Pomarat instructed Sarkem to gather everything. They were leaving. He instructed his first woman, Meta, that this was her time to be a leader. She was to convince the second women it was in their best interest to keep a close eye on the third women, their children and the two they brought in today. He told her they would be going to a place provided to them by Maktahdou, a scary place to the senses, but a pathway to a better life. "Do you understand? Do you have faith in all I have told you?"

She nodded and smiled. She had become a 'queen' for which there was no word in their language. The older woman at her former camp held no such status. She did her time doing the chores of daily existence and now had people to do those. She was determined not to lose that luxury. Her two sons, Hysko, twelve and Sakwa, ten years old were Pomarat's heirs. She followed Pomarat's instructions to the letter.

While everyone was breaking camp, Pomarat told Massot and Sarkem he did not know how any of the women and their young would react to the hole. Sarkem would go in first, the new women next. Then Pomarat would go. Massot would make sure the rest went down the hole and Pomarat would push them through the orb when they exited the tunnel. Massot would send all but the first women and their children in first. "Sarkem, once they're in the orb, make sure they don't try to leave. Massot, everyone goes in the hole no matter what they hear coming from below. There will be screams."

Pomarat went to Meta and explained what he had to Massot and Sarkem. She would be the one to go in after the children. She was not to hesitate. He described what she would see and told her when she exited the tunnel, he would be there to push her into the orb. Inside the orb, Sarkem will need her help to control the children and other women. He and Massot would be right behind her with Sarkem's and Massot's first women.

They reached the hole. Sarah's cabin had long since been abandoned. There were no recent tracks around the hole. It was getting dark. Pomarat commanded Sarkem and Massot to execute the plan. Sarkem scrambled down the hole. Pomarat grabbed the new women and pushed them in the hole. They resisted. When Pomarat got the two of them in, he followed pushing the head of the last further down the tunnel with his foot. There was screaming even though they had not yet seen the orb. Pomarat yelled to Sarkem to come back up the tunnel and drag them down. Sarkem grabbed the first's leg and dragged her to the path surrounding the orb. He yelled "Stay here!" He went back up the tunnel to get the second. The first took a long look at the orb and scampered up the tunnel crawling face first into Sarkem's ass in the darkness as he was backing back down with the second. Now he had a woman on each end, each fighting to get out. "TATH DA MUNT!" yelled Sarkem. Pomarat and the others out of the hole heard this. In the Itchiwan language it was the equivalent of "WHAT THE FUCK?!"

That's it! Pomarat reached down and grabbed the hair of the second new woman and said, "You are jeopardizing the future of the tribe! I will scalp you right here and now unless you go down this hole." She started going back down the hole.

Sarkem improvised his own plan. He kicked the women behind him in the face. She let out an "umph!" as his foot caught her in the chin. She crawled back down the hole to face the orb. The second let Sarkem drag her out realizing her future prospects were dim if she lost her scalp. She had the same reaction as the first and tried to go for the tunnel. Pomarat cold cocked her and pointed his finger at the first in warning. She gave up any thoughts of going for the tunnel. Pomarat conferred with Sarkem, "Go in. I will throw them in ..." The first made a run for it down the path surrounding the orb. "Let her go. She'll be back." Sarkem laughed remembering their first visit to the orb. "When they are inside the orb, you must make sure they don't try to get out. If one does, we may never find her. They will run once they see the orb from the inside so control them. Now go inside."

Sarkem walked through the membrane of the orb and was visible to the groggy second. While she marveled at this, Pomarat shoved her through the membrane. Sarkem grabbed her and laid her on her stomach. "Do not move or you will die!" Laying there she could see the immensity of the orb with the thousands and thousands of holes. Then came the click, and the holes shifted. She closed her eyes and cried hoping this would all go away. Pomarat waited, and the first came running from the opposite direction into his arms as she was alternately focused on the orb and wall of earth to her right. He immediately threw her through the membrane. Sarkem immediately put her face down in the dirt next to the other with the same warning he gave the second. Pomarat called up the tunnel to Massot to send down the second and third wives and then the children. Realizing that the capture of the two wives would elevate their stature and ease their burdens, the wives came down the tunnel despite their fears. As they exited Pomarat said to each, "Have no fear, mind your status, and ensure the new women do not run."

He pushed them all in the orb. Once in the orb Sarkem told them to watch the new captives. But they could not take their eyes off the immensity of the inside. As a result, the first of the new captives made a run for it out of the membrane and ended up facing a random hole. She scrambled into the hole and up the tunnel thinking it was the same hole which they had come in. It wasn't. When she reached the surface and instinctively ran she did not notice that Sarah's cabin was not there. She did not notice that the terrain was not the same as when she went in. She did not know she had exited before the time Pomarat and his group had come upon Maushop's sons. She did not realize, as a result, Pomarat and his band would stumble across her on their journey to Maushop's camp. When they did, she was in horror recognizing three of the four. They on the other hand, had no clue who she was. She screamed. They shot her dead being so close to Maushop's sons. The Massot in the hole would be out his next wife thanks to the skills he had applied in the past.

The children came down followed by Pomarat's first woman. She coaxed them into the orb. Sarkem and Massot's first women followed with Massot. Everyone was now in the orb. Pomarat told them all to sit. Sarkem told him of the escape of one of the new women. Pomarat cast an evil eye in the direction of the other women who preceded him. They broke his gaze and looked down. He then focused on the myriad of shifting holes looking for the holes with the strange scribbling, the holes which were blocked. The constant hum of the orb and the click when the holes shifted was taking its toll on those inside, even Sarkem and Massot. He searched and searched, looking up and down. He could not afford Massot and Sarkem doing the same and risk losing another member of their fledgling tribe. Then the holes revealed themselves. Down low in the orb. The scribbling! … Then the hole shifted. Pomarat cursed. Everyone looked to him. His eyes darted and located them again. There they were. Each had scribbling to the left of the hole. The first hole to the right that had no scribbling bore another mark … a vertical line at the bottom of the hole. That was it! He quickly tied a line from his satchel to an arrow and to his loin cloth and was about to shoot when the holes shifted. He swore, the rest looked and he quickly relocated the hole. Now he was use to its movement. He fired his arrow into the hole.

"I go first! Sarkem follow and hold back the rest. Massot you bring up the rear. After all the others, you follow. Sarkem listen for my commands and relay them to Massot." Pomarat untied the line from his loin cloth and tied it to Massot's.

While he was doing it Massot whispered, "What about the one that escaped?"

Pomarat smiled and grabbed Massot's shoulder, "There will be new Itchiwan where we are going. You will be first to chose which woman will be yours … before me." Pomarat smiled, marking this selfish question in his mind for later. Satisfied, Massot went about organizing the woman and children in a line to exit the hole. Pomarat and Sarkem scrambled up the hole. Pomarat's first woman stepped in and rearranged the order of Massot's line. Massot had arranged them as they had come into the hole. She essentially reversed it with minor changes. Sarkem's first woman would be first, the children next, then Massot's first woman. She would be next. She placed the remaining new captive next and the other women last and said to them "You lost one already! Don't lose her. Keep her in front of you!"

Pomarat exited the hole. The moon was full. He saw a silhouette of something large in the darkness. "Stay in the hole! Keep them back!" he whispered to Sarkem. He watched the silhouette. It did not move. Sleeping or dead? He did a three-sixty of his position. The cabin that was there when they went in was gone. There were dim lights far in the distance but not like those made by campfires, they were stationary and not moving with the wind, more magic. This had to be the hole those boys came out. It was the only hole with a tell-tale scrape of a foot. The only apparent threat was the stationary silhouette. He fired an arrow to its middle. There was a 'clank' as the arrow bounced off the metal and fell to the ground … nothing happened. What was this thing? He walked over to retrieve his arrow scanning every inch of the silhouette for signs of life. None. He touched it. It was hard and cool like the knives Nakim's men had traded for with the whites. This may be some sort of a defensive structure! But for who? The D-9 did not answer. He circled the bulldozer and found no one behind it.

He went back to the hole and called out for Sarkem. He pointed out the silhouette and the unmoving lights in the distance. "We will head south and camp for the night. We must be away from those lights and that structure when the sun rises. It seems to be a defensive structure. I don't know who it belongs to and I want to be away from here when they arrive."

"What do I tell the women when they see that?" pointing at the silhouette.

"Tell them I killed it, and to shut up and follow me or I will kill them."

Sarkem smiled and called up the women and children, "Follow Pomarat!" To those that saw the silhouette and froze he gave them Pomarat's script and they went to Pomarat. They all marched south in the darkness until Pomarat deemed it was the place to camp. No lights were visible.

That night Pomarat sat on high ground gazing at the lights in the distance. Things were different again as evidenced by the iron beast that was dead and the unmoving lights in the distance. The last time was many years in the future from his time. How far in the future was this. Much had changed. Was his tribe gone? He did not know if Yat's and Nakim's tribe even existed anymore. He could go back in the hole and try to find his time, but to what end, to battle Maushop? He now knew the past and he was scorned in future generations as a result. He strongly believed that this was the hole the four boys had come out as evidenced by the scrape below the hole. Was this a futile quest? Were they leading him here? These were questions to be pondered in future days. His immediate task was to rebuild his tribe. With the women he captured and the children already born them, some grown with the ability to hunt, he had a start.

Tomorrow they would go to Yat's old camp. He expected it to be abandoned since they had slaughtered all the women which they had not taken. But who knew in these strange times. If the tribe had revived itself, they would deal with it and slaughter the men. If not, they would set out on exploratory raids from the camp, with two as one would stay to watch the women. Soon their male children would be skilled enough to go out on raids. He had a plan. He would begin anew and re-create the legend of Pomarat. Soon he could go back and take Nakim's camp, his camp. Satisfied, he lay down and slept.

159

VERN HAD BEEN ACCLIMATING Sarah to the 20th century. Unbeknownst to Vern, Timmy was alive, handling the accounting for the sub-culture of South Boston. Amos, Timmy and Brett had been celebrating the laying of the foundation of the Pavilion and worried about what happened to Vern. Pomarat had set up camp on the site of Yat's old one as no Itchiwan were there and it was in a vast undeveloped woodland by a bay. When Vern and Sarah were in New York, Pomarat and Massot were paying a visit to Mrs. Finch. She was looking for her cat but became distracted by her garden. Mrs. Finch's body would not be discovered for weeks. And then it would be deemed a murder/robbery probably related to druggies. Pomarat and Massot acquired a fine collection of knives of the metal they coveted. Mrs. Finch's organs remained intact this time but she was nevertheless dead. Tabby returned home and wondered why her provider was lying in the yard and not tending to her dinner. She poked her a couple of times with no result. She ran off into the woods deciding it was up to her to find dinner.

Without Hysko and the responsibilities of creating a new tribe, their raiding parties of two didn't come across the reception center for weeks later. It was Colleen's day off. But Saul Kaufmann played golf most every day and today his incontinence brought on by age would not allow him to make the clubhouse due to work on the Sagamore Bridge. He pulled into the Reception Center parking lot and parked in the employee lot in the back. It was Monday, things were quiet. He could quickly stroll back into the woods surrounding the facility and take an on and off squirt. As he was looking to the sky waiting to finish, he noticed two midget Indians watching him, smiling. He quickly pulled his junk in his pants leaving a wet stain down his leg. He cursed, and yelled "What the fuck are you two looking at?"

Pomarat looked at Sarkem amused by his anger not knowing what he said. He raised his bow and drew it back.

"WAIT! WAIT!" screamed Saul. "I'M A PROMINENT LAWYER!"

Pomarat hesitated for a second and then launched his arrow into his crotch. Saul screamed and fell to the ground. Pomarat pulled his arrow out which caused another scream so he slit his throat. He saw no weapons on his body and said "Let's go."

James Taylor was playing softly on the sound system in the Reception center. The front desk clerk asked the reservationist if she heard yelling. The reservationist said no. "There! Did you hear that?" another scream.

"Yeah, I think so."

The front desk clerk called Larry, the Manager on Duty. "I think somebody's screaming outside."

"Did you look outside?"

"NO! I AIN'T GOING OUT THERE! Diane heard it too."

"I'll be right up." Larry hung up and went upstairs and went outside and listened … nothing. The employee lot was in the back on the other side of the building. Pomarat and Sarkem were long gone. He went inside and said, "I didn't see anything, it was probably a raccoon in heat," and winked at the front desk clerk. 'Fucking pig' thought the clerk. Saul's body was discovered the next day, a lawyer who represented druggies … probably a dissatisfied client.

Now that Pomarat knew the orb was portal to the past and the future based on his experiences in the 1700's, he decided his conquest of the northern tribes could wait until their sons were fully trained. He did not know that the northern tribes had mostly migrated off the Cape into the vast woods in southeastern Massachusetts due to animosities with the Wampanoag and their alliance with the invaders from over the seas. He also did not know that the legend of Pomarat was reinvigorated by his brief visit in the 1700's. Young members of the Itchiwan tribe would hear the stories of how he could wipe out whole tribes with only two braves. To some he was some sort of super villain to be emulated. To others, he was a legend who was able to transcend time and lurked in the dark, someone to be feared, a boogeyman, which came quietly in the night and wiped out your family ... one by one.

The Wampanoag scoffed at the Itchiwan stories of the resurrection of Pomarat in the 1700's. The Itchiwan were no more than a nuisance which they had chased from their lands. To them, Pomarat was a coward who in ancient times had killed the sons of Maushop and then fled leaving his tribe to face retribution. They labeled him and his kind Pukwudgees, a term of derision meaning mythical thieving creatures which lurked in the woods. They used these stories to keep their children close to home. "Don't go wandering off or the Pukwudgees may get you!"

Pomarat soon also realized that while he was establishing his camp and conducting raids those sedentary beasts they had first encountered when they last exited the hole had somehow managed to close it forever with a strange hard substance and had left. The hole was no longer an option. This was their time, their only time now.

160

THERE WERE MANY UNSOLVED cases on the upper Cape. Sgt. Sikes and Captain Miller would have their hands full but nothing like the cluster fuck of another 1992 of which they had no knowledge. A number of individual cases of unexplained deaths. Accidents? Midget Indians? Drug related, probably hallucinogenic? Sikes felt otherwise. Yeah maybe once, but not over and over again in an area as small as the Cape.

The Beginning!

2018 THE HALFWAY HOUSE AT SANDY NECK BEACH

161

IT HAD BEEN A glorious Cape night roughing it out among the dunes at the artist's cottage halfway down the spit. Rick and Karen jumped on short notice at the unexpected vacancy in the otherwise fully booked rental. It couldn't have been more perfect thought Rick as he faded off into a blissful slumber only to be brought back by Karen gently shaking his shoulder. "Rick, did you hear something ...."

"What?"

"MMPHHhhhhhh....."

"NOOOAAaaa......"

Rick was frozen in suspended animation as a shadow in the dark proceeded to emasculate him and tie his member to a thong attached to a codpiece bearing several others in varying states of decomposition. Karen was dead. He was on his way.

"Kirsten mat fa quin!" Hysko chuckled and wiped both sides of his knife blade on a remaining patch of white on the now mostly crimson sheets. He looked around the hovel, went to the table, grabbed a half-eaten bag of Cheetos and tossed them to Sakwa. "Yum."

Acknowledgments

In 1986, I was asked to write the copy for a piece celebrating the upcoming 25th anniversary of a development known as New Seabury. In doing research about the history of the area, I came across a wonderful book entitled "The Narrow Land: Folk Chronicles of Old Cape Cod" by Elizabeth Reynard first published in 1934. It was a treasure trove of local myths and legends! It caused me to ask "hey, what if ...?" And thus I brought some of those legends forward in time and gave them personalities of their own. Thank you Ms. Reynard.

Special thanks goes out to those having a hand in this story's coming to life ... Kaylyn, my dear daughter, first reader, critic and marketing advisor. Amazingly, she was able to wade through the second draft of this story with all its mistakes and make heads or tails of it. The advice she gave me way back makes me wonder if she is prescient. Thanks to my brother, Charlie, the Lt. Colonel (Ret.) who at the outset told me he never reads fiction and ended up being my biggest drill sergeant in continually urging me to get this story to market. His enthusiasm for the story was infectious. The same can be said of Kerry Corbett who also suffered through an early draft and helped with publication chores.

Then there is my nephew, Peter Cunis, the professional artist and art teacher. He read the story and blew me away with the cover he created which was so far from what I had in mind (with the exception of the translucent orb). He gave a face to Pomarat that captures the essence of his evil and soul! Throughout he taught me more about the process of creating a cover than I ever imagined existed.

Thanks to the middle draft readers, Debbie Clark, Tom Anderson and Michael Varkas. Their reactions convinced me that hey, this is a good story! Thanks to Jeff Juliard, Nancy DeMarco and Monique Huenergardt, three strangers who agreed to read all or part of the manuscript and provided valuable critical analysis. And to Susan Uttendorfsky and her group Fiction Writers and Editors on Facebook which continually provides a wealth of information.

Special thanks to the Sandwich Arts Alliance for holding a presentation on publishing. It was there I met Michael Grossman of EBookBakery Books. Prior to meeting Michael, the idea of self-publishing presented a maze which I was not willing to confront – too many facets to deal with. Michael's one stop 'bakery' turned out to be my Rosetta Stone in overcoming my apprehensions concerning the whole process. Damn! He made it easy.

And to Nancy, I hope you like it. You endured all my vices throughout its creation and were there 24/7 when it came time for me to pay the piper for those vices.

About the Author

Joe and his wife Nancy have lived year round on the Cape since 1984. However, according to local customs, only their daughter Kaylyn can be considered a native Cape Codder.

Joe has engaged in numerous occupations and activities from paperboy, to bag boy, to laborer, to metal fabricator, to bank examiner, to CFO, to COO, to ghost youth sports writer, to entrepreneur, to movie extra, while writing along the way.

His roots were in Marlboro, MA and he's been replanted in Boston, Washington DC, New York, San Juan, Houston and finally Cape Cod where he expects to remain firmly planted barring any climatic catastrophes … "knock on wood."

Learn more about J.J. Cunis and the origins of Itchiwan at www.jjcunis.com and @jjcunis on Facebook and Instagram

Made in the USA
Middletown, DE
10 June 2019